ROCKED BY A KISS

He put his fingertips under Tanzy's chin and lifted her head until he could look into her eyes. "No one's ever said anything that nice to me. Thank you."

"You don't have to thank me for telling the truth."

"I don't know that you have. I'm thanking you for believing in me."

He leaned down to kiss her. He'd intended to kiss her cheek, her forehead, even the end of her nose, but somehow found himself kissing her lips. The shock was so great he couldn't move. Then once he could, he didn't want to.

He'd never known something as simple as a kiss could reach out and yank him off his feet so quickly. He'd never realized a woman's belief in him could make him want to cling to her, to put his arms around her and pull her to him so she could never get away.

He suddenly realized his arms *had* encircled Tanzy's waist, that he *had* pulled her to him. She hadn't broken the kiss, she hadn't tried to pull away. He couldn't tell whether time stood still or his brain stopped functioning, but the kiss seemed to go on forever.

CRITICS ARE RAVING ABOUT LEIGH GREENWOOD!

"Leigh Greenwood continues to be a shining star of the genre!"
—*The Literary Times*

"Leigh Greenwood NEVER disappoints. The characters are finely drawn...always, always, a guaranteed good read!"
—*Heartland Critiques*

"Leigh Greenwood remains one of the forces to be reckoned with in the Americana romance sub-genre."
—*Affaire de Coeur*

"Greenwood's books are bound to become classics."
—*Rendezvous*

THE INDEPENDENT BRIDE
"Leigh Greenwood unfolds his Westerns like an artist.... Like his other books, *The Independent Bride* should be placed among the Western classics."
—*Rendezvous*

BORN TO LOVE
"The characters are complex and add a rich element to this western romance."
—*Romantic Times*

TEXAS HOMECOMING
"Leigh Greenwood raises the heat and tension with *Texas Homecoming*. Few authors provide a vivid descriptive Americana romance filled with realistic angst-laden protagonists as this author can."
—*The Midwest Book Review*

TEXAS BRIDE
"Exciting characters fill this continuing story of the Night Riders. I can't wait for the next installment from this wonderful author."
—*Romantic Times*

The Reluctant Bride

LEIGH GREENWOOD

LEISURE BOOKS NEW YORK CITY

To my readers, who keep me doing what I love most.

A LEISURE BOOK ®

January 2005

Published by

Dorchester Publishing Co., Inc.
200 Madison Avenue
New York, NY 10016

ISBN 0-8439-5236-9

Visit us on the web at www.dorchesterpub.com.

The
Reluctant
Bride

Chapter One

Colorado Territory, 1872

Tanzy Gallant watched with relief and awe as the towering mountains drew nearer. They meant the end of what seemed like an endless journey. It had taken her weeks to travel from St. Louis to Boulder Gap, a small town hugging the base of the Rocky Mountains. She'd traveled by train, stagecoach, and wagon, all of it as uncomfortable as it was exciting to a young woman who less than a year earlier had never been ten miles from her home in the Kentucky mountains.

Everything was new to her. In the beginning it had been the cities with their high buildings, traffic-choked roads, and men and women in clothes fancy beyond her imagination. Then, to a girl used only to tumbling mountain streams, the Mississippi, a river two miles wide. Next was the endlessness of the prairie. It seemed to go on forever with nothing to fill it except miles and miles of waving grass.

The Rocky Mountains were nothing like the tree-covered mountains and stream-filled, moss-and-fern-carpeted hollows of home. There was no slow progression from hills to mountains. These mountains thrust up out of the earth like a wall, towering thousands of feet into the sky. Their slate-gray flanks rose majestically to snow-covered caps that glistened brilliantly in the Colorado sun.

"It takes your breath away," said her fellow passenger, Dorrie Spaugh.

"Yes, it does," Tanzy replied. She had enjoyed talking with this pretty stranger. She'd grown up in a quiet hollow knowing fewer than a hundred people, all of them inter-related.

She'd fled her mountain home to escape being married to a cousin she disliked. She had hoped to find a better life in St. Louis, one in which she could find respect and the independence to make her own choices. Instead she'd discovered it was impossible to find work except in dance halls, on river boats, or in even less respectable gambling establishments. After six months of fighting to protect her virtue, she'd taken the advice of her friend Angela and become a mail-order bride.

"Do you have family in Boulder Gap?" Dorrie asked.

"No."

She hadn't told anyone she was traveling to meet her potential husband, a man she'd corresponded with only by mail. She was a member of a once-proud family that traced its roots back to Cavalier stock from the English Civil War, but a generation-long feud had claimed the lives of everyone she held dear.

"You have a friend to meet you?"

"Yes." That wasn't stretching the truth too much. Russ Tibbolt would be her husband once they'd had a short period of time to become acquainted. "Do you live in Boulder Gap?" Tanzy asked.

"No. I live at Fort Lookout. My husband is a junior officer there. I don't get into Boulder Gap very often. Colonel McGregor, the commander of the fort, considers it too rough for ladies."

"What's it like?" Russ hadn't said anything about the town in his letters, had given her only a description of his ranch.

"My husband says the town is populated mostly by rough men, miners and cowhands. Some settlers. There aren't many nice women around, if you know what I mean."

Tanzy knew exactly what she meant. She'd come to St. Louis believing honest men and women would treat her with respect unless she proved unworthy. She'd quickly learned that the barriers separating *respectable* ladies from other women were high, virtually impenetrable, and directly connected to social position. A woman who worked had questionable status. A woman who worked in a gambling hall had no status at all.

The sound of a pistol shot broke the calm. "What's that?" Tanzy asked. "Why is the stagecoach slowing down?"

"Probably bandits," Dorrie said.

"What do they want?"

"Our money and jewelry. Sometimes they rummage through luggage to see what they can find."

"Is that all?"

Dorrie laughed. "I expect you've heard bandits murder and rape their victims. If they harmed a woman, every man in the Territory would be on their trail within the hour. Men out here have great respect for a good woman."

That would certainly be different from the men she knew. Her father and brothers had had more respect for their hunting dogs than for her and her mother. The men she met in St. Louis had no respect for any woman outside their own social class.

Tanzy's curiosity increased as the stagecoach slowed and she got a look at the man riding alongside. A mask covered his face, his clothes were rough and dirty, he hadn't shaved recently, and he swore viciously at the driver, threatening to put a bullet through his head if he didn't slow the stagecoach more quickly.

"There's only one," Tanzy said. "Why doesn't the driver shoot back?" She thought western men were supposed to be full of spunk, even reckless.

"There's always at least two," Dorrie said, "one to do the stealing, one to hold a gun on the driver."

Tanzy's appearance should be proof she wasn't hiding any valuable jewelry. She wore a modest, unadorned brown dress of coarse cotton that buttoned under her chin and at her wrists. A plain, dark bonnet covered most of her black curls. Her small cloth purse contained little beyond a few coins and Russ's letters. The rest of her worldly belongings were packed in two small trunks and a valise. When the stagecoach came to a halt, the bandit leaned from the saddle and yanked the door open.

"Everybody out!" he shouted. "Come on, come on," he said impatiently when Dorrie showed no inclination to leave the coach.

"You have to let the steps down," she told him. "You can't expect me to jump."

Tanzy doubted he cared how she got down as long as

he got what he wanted, but he dismounted and lowered the steps. He even helped Dorrie down.

"You, too," he said when Tanzy couldn't make her feet move.

She knew immediately he could tell the difference between Dorrie and her. He didn't bother to help her down the steps. So much for respect for *all* women.

"Don't want to hurt nobody," the bandit said. "I just want your money and your valuables."

"I don't wear any jewelry when I travel by stagecoach," Dorrie said.

"A fancy lady like you don't go about without her rings," the bandit said.

Dorrie took off her gloves to show the man her bare fingers. "You won't find anything of value in my luggage, either."

"I'll take your purse and check for myself," he said. He waited for Dorrie to hand it to him, then turned to Tanzy. "You don't look like you got two pennies to rub together," he sneered. He was obviously angry he'd found so little. He snatched her purse out of her grasp without waiting for her to hand it to him.

"Hurry up," the other bandit called. "We can't be standing out here in the open forever."

The bandit dug around in Dorrie's purse, taking out first one thing then another, pocketing the money and tossing each rejected item on the ground despite Dorrie's protests. "I never knowed a fancy-dressed lady to be so poor," he said, handing back Dorrie's purse. He dumped the contents of Tanzy's purse on the ground, then cursed violently when he found neither valuables nor money.

"Get a move on," his companion said. "What's holding you up?"

"I'm gonna have a look through their trunks."

"Well, hurry up. We ain't got no cover."

The first bandit crossed to the back of the stage and started to unfasten the cover over the boot. The crack of a rifle followed swiftly by a cry of pain from the other bandit caused him to jump back, a frightened look on his face. His companion slumped in the saddle and, clutching his shoulder, spurred his horse and raced away from the stage. The first bandit ran, cursing, to his horse, mounted up, and swiftly followed his cohort. A second rifle shot failed to find its mark. Moments later a horseman galloped up to the stage.

"Is anybody hurt?"

Dorrie started to explain that the bandits wanted only their valuables, but the rider, apparently sensing everyone was all right, was already galloping after the bandits.

"Who is he?" Tanzy asked.

"I don't know."

"That's Russ Tibbolt," the stagecoach driver said.

Tanzy's heart lurched in her breast. Russ Tibbolt was the man she had come to marry! He'd said nothing in his letters about being a lawman. She'd had enough of men with guns.

"I've heard he doesn't have a good reputation," Dorrie said after the driver had retrieved the contents of their purses and they had resumed their journey.

"What do you mean?" Tanzy asked. "Isn't he a lawman?"

"He's a rancher who sells beef to the Indians on occasion, but my husband says he's a dangerous character."

"Why?"

"I don't know. I never asked."

If Russ Tibbolt wasn't a lawman, what was he doing chasing the bandits?

Whatever he was, her brief meeting had told Tansy he

was more handsome than she'd ever expected. A strong nose and generous mouth gave his face a definite sensuality. A prominent chin and jaw spoke of a man with a strong will accustomed to sweeping aside opposition. His cobalt blue eyes looked out at her from under heavy brows shaded by the wide brim of his hat. Tanzy had always believed a man's face was a map of his character, his eyes the window to his soul, but Russ Tibbolt hadn't given her time to peer inside.

As they approached Boulder Gap, Dorrie lost interest in anything but the impending reunion with her husband. Only half listening, Tanzy's thoughts centered on Russ Tibbolt. Until now she'd known him only as the author of captivating letters so down to earth and at the same time so charming, she'd overcome her reluctance to promise herself to a man she'd never met. How could she reconcile that man to one of dangerous reputation who chased bandits? If she hadn't been at the end of her journey, she might have turned around right then.

But there was nothing to go back to. Her only hope was to go forward. And that meant Boulder Gap and Russ Tibbolt.

The town didn't impress Tanzy. After St. Louis, it looked more like a collection of false-fronted shanties, most of which looked like they'd blow over during the first winter blizzard. The paint, if the buildings had ever been painted, had chipped off, leaving everything a weathered gray. The jail, the only non-wooden structure, appeared to have been built out of mismatched stone. The street was a churned-up mass of mud and manure. Tanzy had no idea how a lady was supposed to cross the street from one boardwalk to the other. At the very least, a pair of very serviceable boots would be required. Fortunately everything she had was serviceable.

A young man in uniform appeared the moment the stagecoach came to a stop

"That's my husband," Dorrie said, smiling happily and introducing them. "Do you see your friend?"

"No, but he said I was to wait if he wasn't here." Russ had been riding away from town. She had no idea how long it would take him to return, but being alone in Boulder Gap couldn't be any worse than being alone in St. Louis. She was glad to be relieved of the torture of a stagecoach that rattled every bone in her body and made her almost too sore to sleep.

"You can come with us if you like," Dorrie said.

"Thank you, but I'll stay here."

"There's no stage station," the officer said. "You'll have to wait on the boardwalk."

"I don't mind. It will be easier for him to see me."

"And everybody else as well."

Tanzy thanked the couple, then turned her attention to making sure all her luggage was taken off the stagecoach. It wasn't much, but it was everything she owned.

"You want me to take it to the hotel?" the driver asked Tanzy.

"No. Just leave it here."

The man looked relieved but said, "You can't just sit here on the boardwalk. It ain't safe."

"Who would harm me in broad daylight?" She looked around. Several men who looked in need of a bath, clean clothes, and a shave were showing an interest in her, but nobody looked dangerous. Except for their boots and hats, they looked a lot like the men back in Kentucky.

"If you sit out here by yourself, a body might think you was trying to invite a certain kind of interest," the driver said.

"I'm quite capable of correcting any such misapprehension," Tanzy said. Her six months in St. Louis had given her plenty of experience.

"Are you sure you don't want me to take you over to the hotel?"

"Thank you, but I'm being met."

To her relief, the driver gave up and climbed back into his box. He slapped the reins, yelled at the horses. The stage drove off and soon disappeared.

It wasn't too hot in the sun, but she still hadn't gotten used to sun coming at her from all angles. Back home, no matter how hot the day, she could always find a deeply shaded glade or a cold stream to make the heat bearable. Out here men sweated until it soaked through their clothes, but nobody seemed to mind. She already knew they smelled bad. She'd had to sit next to too many people—male and female—during the last thousand miles.

Several women stopped to speak, to ask if she was staying, and to welcome her to Boulder Gap. She talked to so many people she was beginning to feel conspicuous. She decided she wouldn't feel so self-conscious sitting on the boardwalk if she had something to do, so she started to take a mental walk through the town. Boulder Gap had only one business street, and most of the buildings seemed to be saloons and restaurants. She noted a bank, a hotel, a lawyer's office, a surveyor, an assayer, a dentist, a doctor, a general emporium, a blacksmith's shop and livery stable, several banks, a bath house, a dance hall, a boot and saddle shop, a hardware, a dry goods, a newspaper called *The Weekly Echo*, and a Wells Fargo office. There was even a shop that made ladies' dresses and hats!

"You lost?"

Tanzy looked up to see three roughly dressed men watching her from close range.

"I'm waiting for my friend to pick me up. *He* should be here any minute."

"If I was your friend, I wouldn't leave you sitting out here without no one to make sure you weren't bothered," a large and heavily bearded man said. "Somebody's liable to think you was looking for some likely man who's interested."

"That somebody would be very wrong," Tanzy said.

"It's hot," another said. "Why don't you let us buy you something to drink at Stocker's Saloon?"

Tanzy wasn't about to trust her luggage to the goodness of the citizens of Boulder Gap. Or her reputation to these men.

"Thank you, but my friend wouldn't know where to find me."

"We could keep a look out for him."

"I prefer to stay here."

"You're blocking the street," said another.

"I'm sure the good citizens of Boulder Gap won't mind stepping around me for a few more minutes."

"Are these men bothering you?"

Tanzy didn't know the stranger who spoke to her, but she knew he was important by the way he was dressed. She knew he was powerful by the way the three rough men backed away.

"They were just trying to make sure I wasn't lost."

"More likely they were trying to take advantage of you. Get out of town, or I'll have the sheriff lock you up."

"We got a right to be here," said the first man who'd spoken.

"Sorry they should be your introduction to our fair town," the man said as the three ruffians reluctantly moved away.

"My introduction was a very nice army officer's wife."

"Delighted to hear it. My name is Stocker Pullett. I own the biggest ranch in Colorado. I also own the Stocker Hotel and Restaurant. Let me invite you to join me for a cool drink."

"Thank you, but I'd better stay where my friends can find me. They told me not to worry if they weren't here when I arrived, just to wait and they'd be here soon."

"It's hard to predict traveling time, but if I'd been the one meeting you, I'd have come into town last night and stayed at the hotel to make sure I was here when you got off the stage."

"I expect they would have if circumstances hadn't prevented it."

She didn't know why she should have taken an instant dislike to this man. He seemed a prefect example of a successful businessman—well-dressed, impeccably groomed, well-spoken, courteous, well-mannered. He looked to be fifty years old, probably married with a houseful of grown children and thus unlikely to have designs on her virtue.

"Howdy, Stocker," a well-dressed woman said as she approached. "My husband's been looking for you."

"What about, Daisy?"

"We lost more cows last night."

"How many?"

"Bill doesn't know, but it's the second time since spring. There's a meeting in the church now. You gotta come. Everybody's waiting for you."

He looked back to Tanzy, hesitating.

"I'll be fine," she assured him. "Go to your meeting."

He still looked undecided, but when the woman pulled at his sleeve and said, "Stop wasting time," he gave in and left.

Tanzy was relieved. She didn't know what it was about

Stocker that was so overpowering—his abundant self-confidence or his determination to bend others to his will—but she'd had more than enough of men who had no respect for the wishes of others. She intended to make it plain to Russ that she would not be his chattel, that he must respect her as a woman and an individual. She felt confident the man in the letters would do that. She wasn't at all sure about the man chasing the bandits.

The minutes continued to collect until another hour had passed. It would soon be dark. She couldn't stay here. She gazed at the sun. It would set in an hour, maybe less. She stopped a boy who was kicking clods and picking his teeth with a straw. "Young man," she said, "would you mind watching my luggage for a moment?"

"How much will you pay me?"

She had expected he would do it out of courtesy. "How much would you expect?"

"A dollar."

"I can get a hotel room for that price. How about a nickel?"

"Don't be gone long. I'm expected home for supper."

The mention of food reminded Tanzy she hadn't eaten since morning. She hoped she had enough money to pay for a room and her dinner.

"What's your name?" Tanzy asked.

"Richard Benton, but everybody calls me Tardy."

"Let me guess: because you're never where you're supposed to be on time."

His smile was brazen and innocent at the same time. "Something like that."

"Which hotel do you recommend?"

"A lady like you probably ought to stay in the Stocker Hotel, but if it was my money, I'd stay at the boarding-house. They got the best food."

The building he indicated didn't look inviting. Neither did the men going in and out. "I think I'll try the Stocker Hotel."

"Thought you would. A lady wouldn't want to be rubbing elbows at a trestle table with miners and whatnot."

"I have no objection to miners, but I'm not so sure about the whatnots."

Tardy grinned. "I'll help you carry your luggage in for another nickel."

"Thanks. I'll be right back."

The Stocker Hotel appeared to be clean and neat, but that was about the best that could be said of it. The decorations were ordinary, the smell all too familiar.

"I'd like a room," she said when the clerk appeared through a door behind the counter.

"It'll be a dollar," he said. She started to get her money. "You pay when you leave."

"I'll be here only one night. I'd rather pay now."

"You have to sign the book," he said. He took her money and turned the ledger toward her. She signed her name and turned it back.

"Tanzy Gallant. But we already have a room reserved for you."

"Where?"

"It's right here in the book. It's reserved for a whole week."

Tanzy had said she wanted a week to get to know Russ before agreeing to marry him. It was only logical that he would have arranged for her to have a place to stay.

"I should have thought to check first," Tanzy said.

"Where's your luggage?" he asked, a crease appearing between his eyes.

"Tardy Benton is watching it for me."

"I'll get someone to help you. He's probably wandered off by now."

"He's already agreed to help. I'll be back shortly."

She'd nearly reached her luggage when a rider appeared down the street coming toward her at a gallop. Russ Tibbolt. His arm was wrapped with a bloody handkerchief. He was wounded. He slowed his horse as he approached her, came to a stop in front of her luggage.

Tanzy had been prepared to find he was handsome. She was prepared to find he was big and strong. She wasn't prepared for the immediate tug of attraction. It wasn't possible for this to happen so quickly, was it?

She should be worried about his wound. Instead she couldn't take her eyes off his mouth. She should be thinking about his integrity, the quality of his mind. Instead she noticed the width of his shoulders, the muscled power in his forearms. By the time she reached her luggage, she'd given up the struggle. Whatever magic this man practiced, it was too powerful for her to resist.

"Are you Tanzy Gallant?" Russ asked.

"Yes. What happened to your arm?"

"Somebody probably tried to kill him," Tardy observed laconically. "One of these days they're going to succeed."

"One of the bandits got off a lucky shot before I could catch up with him," Russ said.

"What were you doing chasing bandits?" Tardy asked, excitement shining in his eyes.

"Trying to make the world safe for useless boys like you. Now go about your business."

Tardy drew himself up, the perfect picture of an outraged teenager. "I'm not a boy, I'm not useless, and I *am* about my business. This lady has hired me to take her luggage to the hotel."

"Well, get going. It won't walk over by itself."

Tardy grabbed up a box tied with ropes and a port-manteau and stalked off.

Up close, Russ was even more handsome. Tanzy felt her pulses jump. This was the man who would be her husband. Mountain people were very frank about their bodies, about what went on between men and women. What she hadn't learned from her brothers, she'd learned from countless female cousins. The thought of being held in his arms, of him making love to her, gave her goose bumps.

He was tall, with shoulders wide enough to fill a doorway. And muscled. No skinny arms and chest showing ribs like her brothers. He looked powerful enough to pick two of them up and toss them into a wagon without taking a deep breath. It was hard to see much of his hair under that hat, but it was impossible not to be drawn to his gaze. His eyes were as dark blue as the sky before a storm. They glowed with an intensity that made her think of a panther stalking the forest by night. Whatever this man held to be his, he would keep safe with a passion whose heat she felt several feet distant from him.

She was jumping into the unknown again. She had such a strong sense of Russ Tibbolt from his letters that this jump didn't seem as scary as it might otherwise be. She felt a pang of guilt, wondering if the letters he had received could possibly have communicated so much about her. In any case, whether Angela proved right or not about the benefits of being a mail-order bride, there was no turning back. She had to keep going.

"Sorry you had to wait so long," he said as he dis-mounted. "It took me a while to catch those bandits."

"That's all right. I feel better knowing those men are in jail."

"Why didn't you go straight to the hotel?" he asked.

"I didn't know you'd booked me a room."

He frowned. "Archie didn't tell you?"

"I don't know who Archie is, but nobody told me."

"He's the old codger behind the desk."

"There's a younger man there now. Have you seen a doctor about your arm?"

"I haven't had time."

Tardy had come back. "Here's your money," Tanzy said, handing him two nickels.

"Thanks, ma'am," he said, giving Russ a dirty look. He picked up the last piece of luggage, a small trunk, and headed to the hotel.

"You go on over to the hotel," Russ said. "I have to stable my horse."

"How long will that take?"

"Why?"

"I want a doctor to look at your arm."

"I've already been, and he closed the door in my face."

It took Tanzy a moment to understand the significance of what Russ had said. "Do you mean he *refused* to treat you?"

"What did you think I meant?"

She could hardly believe her ears. Even feuding families didn't deny medical help to one another. It angered Tanzy that a western doctor wouldn't show equal honor. "Come on. We're going to the doctor's house."

"I told you what he said. I'm not going back."

"Do you want ours to be a successful marriage?" Tanzy asked.

Russ looked too startled to answer.

"If you do, now is a good time to learn there will be times when you don't ask why. You just do as I say."

Chapter Two

Tanzy's indignation hadn't died down by the time she reached the doctor's house. After Russ knocked three times without getting a response, it flared higher. The door was unlocked, so she opened it and walked in.

A woman came into the hallway. "Who are you?"

"Where's the doctor? This man has been shot."

"He's about to sit down to dinner."

"We won't keep him long."

"You won't keep me at all."

Tanzy turned to see a man of medium height, more than adequate girth, and a bald head come from what must be the dining room. He had a napkin tucked into his collar. "I've already told him not to come here again."

"You are a doctor, aren't you," Tanzy asked, "not some quack who stuck up a shingle and calls himself a doctor?"

The man drew himself up. "My qualifications are beyond question."

"Then get out your medical bag and see what you can do for this man."

"No."

Tanzy had expected him to refuse, but she hadn't spent most of her life dealing with some of the most obstinate, pigheaded men God ever created to give up easily. On one side of the hallway she saw a parlor. Without hesitation she walked in. "This is a nice room," she said. "You've put a lot of effort into decorating it."

"This is my wife's room," the doctor said. "She's responsible for everything you see."

"Then I imagine she wouldn't want to see anything broken."

"Of course not," the doctor's wife said.

"This is very pretty," Tanzy said, picking up a piece of porcelain.

"It's very expensive," the doctor's wife said proudly.

"Ask your husband to take care of Mr. Tibbolt's arm."

"I can't do that. He's not the kind of man—"

The porcelain figurine slipped from Tanzy's fingers to the floor and shattered into tiny pieces. The doctor's wife screamed.

Tanzy picked up another figurine. "Treat Russ's arm."

"I've already told you—"

The second figurine hit the floor. The doctor's wife collapsed into a chair.

"She's crazy," the doctor said to Russ. "She's destroying my wife's figurines."

"I'm sure the rest will be safe if you look at my arm."

Tanzy picked up a third figurine, tossed it carelessly from one hand to the other. The doctor's wife moaned in distress. "Do what they want, Arthur. Anything to get them out of this house."

"You know I can't, Endora. If I do—"

His wife sat bolt upright, her eyes wide with anger. "If she breaks one more piece of my china, I'll make your life twice as miserable as Stocker Pullet ever could."

Tanzy picked up a fourth figurine, looked from one to the other to decide which to sacrifice first.

"Arthur!" his wife screamed.

"Come with me," the doctor said, "but you're not to tell anyone you were here."

"I'm coming, too," Tanzy said. "I know a lot about gunshot wounds, so don't think you're going to do anything funny without my knowing."

Russ had been in something of a daze from the moment he'd set eyes on Tanzy. He had been dead set against ordering a bride through the mail even though, after a lifetime of being ostracized by nearly everyone in Boulder Gap, he knew it was the only way he could find a respectable woman to marry him. He could hardly believe such a pretty woman would need to be a mail-order bride. What was wrong with the fools in St. Louis? Of course, there could be all kinds of things wrong with her that he couldn't tell without getting to know her better, but his body didn't seem to feel it needed to consider the matter further. Not even the pain in his arm had kept him from getting uncomfortably stiff.

Some men liked strong-willed women. He didn't. Still, he admired Tanzy's tactics. He'd have sworn nothing short of physical violence could have induced Dr. Arthur Lindstrom to treat his wound. Tanzy had managed it by breaking two small pieces of china.

"Let me see what you did to yourself," the doctor said.

"He didn't do it to himself," Tanzy said.

The doctor didn't reply. He removed the bloody bandanna. "This is hardly more than a flesh wound."

"Don't you treat flesh wounds?" Tanzy asked. "Or do you wait until someone gets a bullet in the chest before you bother? Where did you go to school?"

"In Scotland, but I doubt you know where that is."

"It's part of England," Tanzy said. "Make sure you put some basilicum powder on that wound. I don't want it to get infected."

"Would you rather do this yourself?" the doctor demanded, irate.

"I just want to be sure you do it right. If he gets gangrene in that arm, there won't be a piece of china left in this house."

The doctor's wife groaned. "Please, Arthur, get these people out of my home."

"I'm doing my best, Endora."

"If you just hadn't turned him away this afternoon—"

"That's water over the dam."

Russ had never been able to force anyone in Boulder Gap to treat him with even common courtesy, yet Tanzy had the doctor doing his best to make sure his arm would heal quickly. He grinned. Tanzy Gallant was quite a woman.

"What are you grinning about?" the doctor growled.

"It's a grimace, not a grin," Russ said.

The doctor harrumphed. "I doubt you know the meaning of pain."

"I know it, all right," Russ said. "It's just I usually don't have time to pay attention to it."

"Well, pay attention to this arm. I don't want this madwoman in my house again."

"You have a lovely house," Tanzy said. "I might want to consult your wife when it comes time to decorate my own."

"Who'd marry *you?*" the doctor's wife asked.

"Don't be a fool," the doctor said. "All she'd have to do is stand in the street and they'd line up to propose."

Until today Russ had only known Tanzy through her letters, but now she struck him as a woman full of principles she was aching to hold on to, and he wasn't sure he wanted that kind of woman for a wife. What did he want in a wife? Someone to offer female companionship, bear his children, take care of his house. He didn't need a woman of courage and strong ideals. He had more than enough for both of them. He certainly hadn't asked for beauty. If his mother and sister were anything to go by, that was a recipe for disaster.

"There," the doctor said, stepping back. "I've done all I can for you. Keep it elevated and keep it clean."

"How much do I owe you?" Russ asked. "I'm not paying for the china," he said when the doctor turned to his wife.

"Nothing, if you promise never to let that woman set foot in my house again."

"I can't promise that, so how much do I owe you?"

"Two dollars."

Russ paid and they left quickly. He couldn't repress a smile when he heard the deadbolt click behind him. "Do you always go a little crazy when you don't get your way?"

Tanzy looked up, surprise and humor showing in the set of her mouth and her shining eyes. "I was just put out he closed the door on you. What's he got against you?"

"Why don't you go back to your room? You've got time to rest up before dinner."

Tanzy stopped in the street and squared up to him. "I won't be kept in the dark about things that concern me. My father and brothers tried to do that. They soon discovered I didn't take it kindly."

"I don't take kindly to being given orders," Russ said, firing up. He'd let her have her way about the doctor, but now was a good time to make it clear he was going to be the one making the decisions in his household. "I won't keep you in the dark about matters I think concern you, but don't think you're going to pry things out of me just because you're curious."

"I have no doubt you'll talk to me about what *you think* concerns me, but that's where I expect we'll have a problem. It never occurs to men that what you do for a living, who you fight, whether we have any money, affects women and children. We're just supposed to be content to let the men make all the decisions. I've seen the results of that, and you might as well know from the start, I'll not have it. If you can't respect me enough to tell me what's going on, you don't respect me enough for me to be your wife."

Oh, hell! He was in for it now. How did you tell a prickly woman you weren't trying to keep things from her but you weren't going to let her run roughshod over you? Was it even worth the trouble? Damn Welt. If it hadn't been for his interference, things wouldn't be so complicated.

Tanzy considered her situation while she waited to go downstairs to meet Russ for dinner. He seemed more like a despot than she would have liked, but he compensated to some degree by being exceptionally attractive. She kept telling herself she shouldn't be so impressed with his looks.

His parting words made her feel uneasy. She'd spent most of her life surrounded by men—stubborn, bull-headed, opinionated—who believed women were useful only for having babies and taking care of a man's house and his physical needs. She hoped Russ wasn't like that. She pulled out his five letters and read them through again. They spoke of a man's need for companionship, of a woman's need for security. He promised to provide her with all the creature comforts within his means in exchange for a well-managed household. He said he hoped they'd come to respect and value each other as the years went by, to find solace in their children and contentment with each other. Did he want a wife he could love, who could love him? It didn't seem important to him. For herself, she'd be content as long as they could respect each other.

Her father had treated his wife and daughter as chattel, with no rights or need for consideration. The only time Tanzy's mother had shown any spunk was when she insisted Tanzy be allowed to go to school. Then one day it seemed her mother grew tired of life, and she just died. Her father buried her, told Tanzy to make sure supper was ready on time, and went on as if nothing had happened.

One of the girls at school talked about wanting to fall in love, but the other girls laughed at her, said all falling in love ever did was to swell a girl's belly with no husband in sight. Besides, by the time you eliminated everybody related to you, those with some physical defect, or those you simply disliked too much to marry under any circumstances, there weren't many men in the Kentucky hills to choose from. Strangers weren't welcome. Men were more likely to leave than come to settle.

Nearly all marriages were arranged. After her father and brothers died—all killed in a feud more important to them than life—her uncle had intended to marry her to his son. Aside from looking enough like an opossum to be one, the man had different colored eyes, a blue one that stared straight ahead and a brown one that sometimes wandered off to the side. Tanzy had fled during the night.

St. Louis, where she'd been able to find work only in a gambling hall, had been just as bad. One night a respected banker nearly raped her. She realized it would happen again, and no one would care. One friend, Angela, had tried to talk her into being a mail-order bride as she was planning to do. When Tanzy balked,

Angela wrote the letters for her. After Tanzy had been in St. Louis four months, her friend left to marry her husband. It was the letters she wrote back, saying she was blissfully happy, that the West was full of honest men longing for wives, that convinced Tanzy to write the final letter saying she was willing to travel to Boulder Gap.

Considering what lay behind her, she didn't understand why she wasn't anxious to marry Russ as soon as she could get him in front of a preacher. The man had his own ranch, was as handsome as any she'd ever seen, had promised to keep her safe and secure, and looked strong enough to do it.

She got up from the small bureau where she'd spent thirty frustrating minutes trying to arrange her hair. A Kentucy woman rolled her hair into a bun and pinned it tight so it wouldn't come down. In St. Louis, women arranged their hair so it was attractive. She had tried to do the same, but no number of pins had ever been able to contain her rioting curls.

It wasn't that she thought she was unattractive, but Dorrie Spaugh's stylish dress had made Tanzy acutely aware of her shabby clothes. She told herself no rancher would expect his wife to be a fashion plate. Besides, she knew all about cows. Except for pigs, they were just about the dirtiest animals on any farm.

She stood, impatient to leave the room. She whisked herself down the stairs and into the hotel lobby. She would wait there for Russ.

A man she didn't recognize was behind the hotel desk. "Are you Miss Gallant?" he asked.

"Yes." She wondered if Russ had been delayed or wasn't coming.

"Sorry I wasn't here when you came in this afternoon. Sick as a dog," he said, pointing to his stomach.

"That's okay," Tanzy said, hoping to forestall a graphic description.

The man beckoned her closer. "I promised Russ I'd see to you if he wasn't here," he said in a whisper.

"Why are you whispering?" Tanzy asked.

"Mr. Pullet don't like Russ. If he knew I'd as much as talked to him, I wouldn't have a job."

"Then why not stay away from him?"

"Russ has helped me out a time or two. That's more than anybody else has done."

Archie had a bulbous nose, a florid complexion with discolored splotches, and no hair atop his head but plenty coming out of his ears and in his shaggy eyebrows.

"I told him not to come here," the man whispered.

"Why shouldn't he come here?" Tanzy asked. She was curious to know why Stocker disliked Russ and why it mattered so much to the rest of the town.

"He shouldn't be in town at all." He turned away when a man entered the hotel and went directly to the restaurant. "You can sit over in that corner," he said, pointing to a sofa behind a potted plant. "People won't be able to see you, but you'll be able to see when Russ comes in."

"Why should I hide behind a plant?"

"You'll find out." That's all he said before disappearing again.

Tanzy was confused and irritated. She didn't know what people had against Russ, but she hadn't done anything wrong and she had no intention of hiding. She sat down on a sofa where she could easily be seen by anyone entering the lobby. Russ arrived before anyone else came in.

If he had been handsome before, he was breathtaking now. He wore a plain black suit with a white shirt and a string tie. He'd shaved and combed his dark brown hair straight back. With his strong nose, full lips, and prominent jaw, he looked like a proud warrior. When he smiled, his teeth seemed especially white against his tanned face. His eyes didn't smile, but they generated a disturbing intensity he focused entirely on her. She felt heat stir within her.

"Are you feeling more rested?" he asked.

"Much better," she said as she stood. "I even had time for a short nap."

An unsmiling waiter led them to a table at the back of the restaurant. Tanzy got the feeling he was hiding them.

"Let's order," Russ said. "You must be starving."

Once they had ordered their food, Russ asked her about her trip.

"It's lucky you were out riding," Tanzy said when she'd reached the point of the attempted robbery.

"There have been some robberies lately. I thought it might be a good idea to meet you."

"That was very thoughtful. I don't know anybody who'd go so far out of his way on the chance there might be trouble."

Tanzy thought Russ looked slightly uncomfortable, but she figured he felt awkward at being thanked. Most men did. He seemed relieved when their food arrived. While they ate, Russ told her about his ranch and his plans for the future. By the time the waiter removed the dishes and left them to enjoy their coffee, they had pretty much caught up on each other.

"Why did you decide to be a mail-order bride?" Russ asked.

She hadn't expected that question. "When I was in St. Louis, it was made very clear to me that having taken a job in a gambling hall, I was no longer respectable. I'm telling you this because I don't want to keep any secrets from you, but I don't want it to be the first thing people in Boulder Gap learn about me. I don't want to be pigeon-holed as I was in St. Louis."

"Why did you go to St. Louis?"

"I had to leave home if I wanted to find a husband."

"You're a pretty woman. I'm sure you could have had your pick of the men in Kentucky."

"That's where you're wrong. My uncle was going to force me to marry his son. Otis looks like an opossum and has a wandering eye."

"I promise I'll be faithful to you."

"I mean his eyes don't look in the same direction. They aren't the same color, either. And lest you think I'm totally vain, I almost hated him."

"Surely there were other men who'd fight for the chance to marry you."

"My family was feuding, which meant we lived in a closely knit clan, the women allowed to marry only when and whom the men permitted. That was the way to cement alliances. Now it's your turn to explain why you're not married. You own a ranch and are very attractive. Surely you could find someone to marry you."

"There are very few women in the Territory, and none of them around here are going to marry me. At least, not any that are respectable."

"That's important; that she be respectable, I mean."

His eyes turned hard. "I don't want anything to do with a loose woman. I'm not the easiest man to live with, but I'll take care of my wife and make sure she comes to no harm. In return I demand complete fidelity."

Tanzy had no problem with fidelity, but she wondered what was behind the angry words.

"You've got no business being here, Tibbolt," interrupted a man who came up to the table.

"Last time I checked it was a free country, Henry."

"Then feel free to go someplace else. We don't want you here."

"If you're so unhappy with having me about, why don't you *feel free* to go someplace else?"

Henry turned to Tanzy. "You look like a respectable young woman. If you value that reputation, you'll have nothing to do with this man." He turned back to Russ. "Don't hang around town after dinner."

"I thought I'd treat myself to a few days at the boardinghouse," Russ said with a smile that didn't reach his eyes.

Henry's expression grew apoplectic. "We don't want your kind around. You've got no business here. Get back to your mountains and stealing cows."

Russ's eyes seemed to grow dark and hard. "You'll regret those words one of these days."

"Are you threatening me?"

"You're a fool to let Stocker tell you what to do and how to think. My old man wasn't worth much, but he used to think you were one of the few men in Boulder Gap with some backbone. Now catch up with your wife before she starts thinking you're hanging around me so you can ogle Miss Gallant."

Henry swelled up like a blow toad, turned on his heel, and stalked off.

Tanzy noticed several other people in the restaurant had been listening intently to this exchange. "I hope you're going to explain why everybody hates you so much. I'm not a woman who hankers after company all the time, but I'll have to think twice about marrying a man who seems to inspire virtually universal dislike."

"It's Stocker Pullet's doing. I can't blame him for hating me for killing his brother, even though it was a fair fight, but it was ten years ago. It's time to forget it. But he feels I've dragged the Pullet pride through the dirt—it's the only time anybody ever stood up to his family and made them pay for what they'd done—and he won't be able to forget it until he runs me out of Colorado."

Tanzy felt some of her bright hopes begin to fade. Russ had killed a man. It didn't matter that it was a fair fight. The only thing that allowed her to continue to hope was that the killing had happened ten years ago. That was plenty of time for a man to change, plenty of time for feelings to cool.

"Will you leave?" she asked.

"No. This is my home as much as it is his. But it's not something you have to worry about. I haven't caused any trouble since then." He smiled reassuringly. "I've become a model citizen."

Tanzy had an uneasy feeling despite his assurances. Maybe Russ had put the past behind him, but it didn't sound like Stocker had. Back home no one forgot a killing. Ever. It carried over from father to son, spilled over to include uncles and cousins. Anyone who married into the family was expected to take up the feud. It could last for generations and destroy dozens of lives. It was just about the worst thing she could think of.

But it took two people to feud. As long as Russ refused to fight, she didn't see what Stocker could do. "I'm glad to know you're such an upstanding citizen," Tanzy said, "but I have a condition to make."

"You should have told me about any condition before I paid for you to come out here. What is it?"

"I don't want to have any children."

Chapter Three

Russ had never heard of a woman who didn't want children. He considered having children a part of having a wife. In his mind a family came as a unit, the parts inseparable from one another. "Why don't you want children?" he asked.

"Do you?"

"Of course. What man doesn't?"

"Some men don't. Why do you want them?"

"I have to have somebody to leave the ranch to."

"You can leave it to your wife, your hands, your local school district, even your church."

"Why would I work so hard to build a ranch, then leave it to strangers?"

"So you could make a good living for yourself and provide your wife with a few luxuries. It's also a way to prove to people you're a success, a way to prove you're just as important as Stocker Pullet."

None of that appealed to him. It wasn't that what she said was wrong, but somehow not having children left a hole in the middle of everything. He didn't need children to run the household or do the work on the ranch. It would be easier to hire someone to do those jobs. So why did he want them? Certainly not to wake him up in the middle of the night crying, or to waste his money on gambling or extravagant weddings.

"Don't you have any family you can leave it to?" Tanzy asked.

"No. My mother lost touch with her family after she

and her first husband came West. When he was killed in a freighting accident, she needed someone to support her, her young daughter, and the baby she was carrying. Her second husband didn't like me. He resented that I ate so much food, was so big, so restless, and was always getting into trouble."

He hadn't meant to tell Tanzy so much about himself, hadn't even realized how much he still resented the way his mother sided with any man against him. Russ had always felt alone even when he hadn't done anything wrong.

"Why are you so set against children?" Russ asked.

"I'm not set against children, just what they can do to a woman. Children may be important to men, but they're an integral part of a woman's life. We carry them, nurse them, take care of their hurts of body and soul. My mother had four sons and one daughter, and she loved us as much as any woman could. Yet she had to watch those four sons die because of a stupid feud that has been going on for more than a generation. I watched her die a little bit every time, until finally she just didn't want to live anymore."

"So you aren't the one who felt the loss."

She reacted almost as if he'd slapped her. "They were my brothers. Of course I felt the loss. No families are closer than mountain families, and no women work harder to take care of their men than mountain women. Seeing my brothers die was practically like losing my own children. I couldn't feel the loss as much as my mother, but I felt it. I feel it now."

When she paused he thought she might be about to cry. But though she seemed emotional, she remained dry-eyed.

"I won't bring children into the middle of a feud where

I'll have to watch them be killed or emotionally devastated. Understand that I do want a family, but I will agree to have one only when I'm convinced they can grow up in safety."

"Any woman who becomes a wife must expect to have children. It's just the way things are."

"Not all women have children."

"Are you telling me that you don't intend to have any physical relationship with your husband?"

"I'd never do that."

"Then how do you expect to avoid having children?"

"There are ways . . . there are times . . ." She flushed and looked uncomfortable. "I can't explain it here. I feel like everybody's listening."

Russ was sure people were straining to pick up any fragment of their conversation, but this was too important to put off. "Let's say we try these ways, observe these times, and you still end up having children. What would you do?" He didn't know anything about the ways and times she talked about. No woman had ever explained it to him. He just assumed that every woman who slept with a man would have babies. "Would you hate the baby, turn your back on it, or give it away?"

"What kind of person do you think I am? No decent woman could hate her own child."

"I don't yet know what kind of woman you are," Russ said, "but I believe you're honest and willing to keep your promises. But any woman who fulfills her wifely duties to her husband knows there's the possibility of having children, no matter how careful they might be. Life never goes exactly as we plan. I wanted to know what you'd do if your plans got all messed up."

"The best I could," Tanzy said. "That's all I can promise."

"That's all anyone can expect." Russ looked around, realized the staff was waiting to close up the restaurant. "We'd better go."

"Where are you staying?"

"At the boardinghouse."

"Has Stocker forced the folks there to hate you, too?"

"They don't care who sleeps in their beds as long as they get paid ahead of time." They had reached the lobby. "I have to go back to the ranch tomorrow, but I'll be back. If something should happen to keep me there past dinner, don't worry. It's a long ride and all kinds of things can hold me up."

"Like what?"

"This is basically wild country. There wasn't much of anybody out here until gold was discovered just before the war. The cattle we run are wild, the horses we ride were born mustangs, and the mountains are filled with bears, wolves, and cougars."

Tanzy shivered. "I didn't realize."

"The land itself is mountainous, not suited for people. If a man falls off his horse, he faces a long walk home, sometimes more than one day."

"Are you trying to tell me I could easily become a widow?"

"I'm trying to say we get where we're supposed to be, but sometimes we're a bit late." He took some coins from his pocket. "You'll need to buy some clothes. You'll freeze to death in that thin dress come the first snow."

"We have snow in Kentucky."

"Do you get drifts over twenty feet high and temperatures twenty degrees below zero?"

"Okay, I'll look for something warm," she said, taking the money. There was an awkward moment; neither was quite sure how to end the evening. Finally Russ thrust his hand forward. "It was nice to meet you. I'm looking forward to getting to know more about you."

Tanzy returned his handshake.

"Now I'd better be going. I don't want some miner to steal my bed."

But Russ didn't leave because he was worried about his bed. He ran away because he was confused about his reaction to Tanzy.

He wasn't too worried about her not wanting children. It would take some careful persuading, but he could make her understand he wasn't feuding with Stocker. What bothered him was the fact that he was considering using careful persuasion to talk his wife into anything. He believed a good woman should be guided in everything by her husband. As long as he wasn't weak, cruel, or abusive, she should never question his judgment. So why was he even considering *carefully persuading* Tanzy?

He'd just met her today. How could he be attracted to her so soon? He didn't believe in love and didn't want it. It had made his mother, his sister, even his stepfather weak, vulnerable, unable to withstand the temptations that ultimately destroyed them. He wanted a wife he liked, whom he could respect, with whom he could set up a smooth working relationship. She would know her duties and responsibilities and would fulfill them. He would do the same, and they would live together comfortably into old age.

But there was something about Tanzy that didn't fit in that picture. At first he thought it was her looks. She was a damned fine-looking woman, and he was enough of a man to be strongly attracted to her. He wasn't a saint, but he didn't believe in sleeping with any woman just because she was available. It had been so long since he'd been with a woman, he'd practically forgotten what it was like.

Well, no, it was remembering what it was like that got him so interested in Tanzy.

She wasn't a biddable female. She'd dragged him off to the doctor like a naughty boy, then threatened to destroy the doctor's house. It had been funny in a way, but there was no reason to think she wouldn't turn that crazy, wild temper against him. That was something he definitely didn't want in a wife.

Then there was this business of making conditions that she had plunked down right in front of him without a word of apology. She expected him to agree to them or the deal was off. He'd seen his mother lead her husband around by the nose too many times to want that in a wife.

So what was it about Tanzy that had grabbed hold of him and wouldn't let go?

Damned if he knew, but he'd better find out before he did something stupid.

Tanzy went to her room with an uneasy mind. Too many things about Russ Tibbolt made her uncomfortable.

First, he was too good-looking. Lots of women probably thought they wanted a handsome husband, but that was only because they were too foolish to realize how much trouble good looks could cause. If he was all that handsome, he'd be able to talk her into doing just about anything he wanted, even things she really didn't want to do.

Tanzy didn't want a husband or anybody else who could talk her out of what she knew was sensible and right. It was clear he didn't agree with her worry about having children. He was probably already thinking of ways to get her to change her mind, and she was honest enough to admit that Russ Tibbolt just might be able to do it.

If he was all that irresistible to his wife, he would be just as irresistible to other women. He would be faced with constant temptations to stray. The only man who wouldn't stray was a man who didn't get any offers. So there she'd be, foolishly in love with her husband and jealous of every female. Better a homely man who was thankful for what he had than a handsome one always sampling to see if he could find something better.

Then there was this problem with people not liking Russ. She knew it wasn't the same as a feud, but it was too close to suit her. She had left home to get away from killing, regardless of the reasons for it.

But there was something else, a kind of stiff-necked stubbornness that reminded her of her father and brothers. They would never accept any opinion that wasn't their own. She got the feeling Russ expected to be the only one to make decisions. She, on the other hand, expected each of them to have separate spheres of influence and responsibility, with clear rules to keep things from getting mixed up. As his wife, she would have certain rights and privileges and her husband would have to respect them.

Her mother had never had any of those rights and privileges. What made her think Russ would be interested in giving her any?

"Did you have a nice dinner?"

Archie's voice startled her. "Yes."

"I wondered if people would cause trouble."

"A man called Henry tried to throw Russ out of the restaurant, but Russ hardly paid him any attention. Good night."

But as she got ready for bed, Archie's words came back to her. Obviously he had expected people to be rude to Russ. Was that why she felt this strange attraction to him, this need to do something about what she felt was unfair treatment? She certainly couldn't be foolish enough to think Russ needed her to defend him, yet at the same time that was exactly what she wanted to do. It was what she *had done* when the doctor wouldn't treat his wound.

She had to do some hard thinking. She had come west to escape trouble, not run into more of it. It began to look as though there might be some very good reasons to reconsider her decision to marry this man. But what she really needed to know was why, in the face of these reasons, she felt that Russ Tibbolt was the man who could make her dreams come true.

Russ gave his distinctive whistle, the one all his men used to signal that they were coming inside the ring of protection. He was pleased to hear it echo back to him from two directions, one plain and simple, one with a little flourish at the end. Oren and Tim. Tim never could do things the simple way. He always added something of his own.

"Have any trouble coming in?" Welt Allard asked Russ when he reach the corral behind the ranch house. It was still several hours before dawn, but a man riding in the open could be seen at a distance of several hundred yards.

"Not tonight." He dismounted and started to unsaddle his tired horse.

"How did it go? What's she like?"

Russ was surprised to find he was reluctant to discuss Tanzy, even with his best friend. "It's early days yet. I get the feeling both of us have more expectations of the other than we thought."

"Is she that ugly?"

Russ laughed. "She's very pretty. No, I think we're finding we didn't know our minds as well as we thought. It's real easy to think about marrying somebody you've never seen, but it's not so simple when you're sitting across the table from each other."

"I don't see what's so hard. Either she wants to marry you or she doesn't." Welt had been the one to convince Russ to consider a mail-order bride. He had actually written the letters for Russ.

"Right now I'd say she's not sure," Russ said. He put the saddle on the corral pole and started to rub down his horse.

"Then why not send her back where she came from?"

A good question, for which Russ didn't yet have a good answer. "I don't like jumping to conclusions."

"I'd know right off."

Welt probably would, but the only woman he'd ever loved was Russ's sister, and she'd left him for Toley Pullet. Since her death, Welt had been bitter about women and depressed about his life.

"I thought I would, too, but I'm glad she said we ought to take a week to see if we'll fit."

"People used to meet in the morning, get married in the afternoon, and start making babies that night."

Russ was glad his back was to Welt. He didn't trust his face not to show he'd thought a lot about the making babies part. Well, not about babies, exactly, but about the rest of it. Tanzy wasn't a flirty kind of woman, nor was she provocative, but she sure was sensual. She was just nineteen, but she had the body of a woman, round and filled out in all the right places. Russ wasn't the kind of man to dwell on things like that, but all during dinner his gaze had been drawn to her mouth. Just watching her eat was an erotic experience. Welt would probably think he was crazy if he tried to explain. Hell, he'd have thought he was crazy before he met Tanzy.

He couldn't figure out what it was about her that kept him thinking about what it would be like to be able to touch her anywhere he wanted. It would be a good thing if they ended up married, but it wasn't so good if thinking about it kept him from having a clear head. He wasn't considering marriage just to have a convenient way to satisfy his physical needs.

What did he want from marriage? He'd only thought of someone to take care of the house, have kids, cook, do all the things a wife was expected to do. But meeting Tanzy had confused him.

"I don't think I'd like getting married to any woman that quick," Russ said.

"Then why did you agree to a mail-order bride?"

"Because you wouldn't get off my back."

"You weren't doing anything about getting yourself a wife."

"I didn't feel desperate to have one until you started telling me if I didn't get one soon I'd be too old for anybody to want me." Russ straightened up from cleaning his horse's hooves. He pulled back a pole and let the animal into the corral. "It's too late at night, and I've been up too long, been in the saddle too much, to think about it anymore. Besides, my arm is hurting."

"What's wrong with it?"

"I surprised two bandits holding up the stage. They're sitting in the sheriff's jail, but one of them got a bullet into me before I could get to him."

"I'll see to it."

"Doc Lindstrom already looked at it."

"What did you do, hold a gun to his head?"

"No. When he refused, Tanzy broke a couple of pieces of his wife's best china. Threatened to smash all the rest if he didn't look after my arm. Stood over him to make sure he did it right." Russ chuckled at the memory. "With Endora screaming and begging him save what was left of her china, he couldn't wait to get us out of the house. You should have been there. It would have made even you smile."

"I hate the old bastard," Welt growled.

"I'm going to bed," Russ said. "Tell Tim if he wants to do something useful, he can check on the cows in the highest valley."

It didn't take Tanzy's first full day in Boulder Gap long to get off to a bad start. She met Stocker Pullett in the lobby when she came down for breakfast.

"I heard you had dinner last night with Russ Tibbolt," he said without preamble. It was clear the news hadn't gone down well. "What were you doing with that man?"

Tanzy hesitated to announce that she was a mail-order bride, but she doubted she'd be able to keep the news confidential for long, certainly not after she was seen having dinner with Russ again tonight. "I'm considering marrying him."

"You can't marry Tibbolt!" Stocker exploded. "He's nothing but a murdering ex-con."

"Russ told me he accidentally killed your brother in a fight." She couldn't recall if he'd said it was accidental, but surely it hadn't been intentional.

"There was nothing accidental about it," Stocker shouted. "He hunted Toley down and killed him in cold blood."

Tanzy had been upset when Russ told her what happened. Stocker's version shocked her, but she'd spent her whole life living through a feud. She knew how people reacted when a member of their family was killed. It didn't make any difference what he'd done or the circumstances of his death, it was the other man's fault and he had to pay. Reason didn't enter into it. "I'm sorry for your loss. I'm sure you miss him terribly," she said.

"It's been more than ten years, yet it seems like yesterday. He was a young, fun-loving kid. He was from my father's second marriage, a lot younger than I was, but I loved him like he was my full brother."

Tanzy didn't know what to say or how to express her sympathy, so she said nothing.

"You must have nothing to do with Tibbolt," Stocker said. "He's a villain, a wild man, a killer."

That's what the Viljoen clan had said about her family her whole life, and she knew it wasn't true. People found it hard to stick to the truth when emotions ran so high. She'd been really impressed by Russ's letters. The fact that he'd told her about killing Stocker's brother made her tend to believe Stocker was exaggerating because of his own loss, but she was becoming uneasy. Had she been foolish enough to let a handsome man cause her to forget common sense and caution? Was she throwing herself into the path of greater danger than she'd left behind?

"Come with me," Stocker said. "I'll see that you're protected."

Instinct caused Tanzy to pull back when Stocker reached out and took her arm. "Thank you for your concern, but I have to stay here. I promised Mr. Tibbolt I would meet him for dinner."

"Haven't you heard anything I said?"

"I appreciate your warning, but I can't change my plans."

Stocker drew back. Gradually the look he gave her changed from one of concern to anger. "If you ignore my advice and take up with that man, no decent person will speak to you. Your only company will be crude men and the bunch of thieves and killers who work for Tibbolt. You will have no reputation. The doors to our homes will be closed to you."

Tanzy was shocked by the force of Stocker's anger. He was acting as if Russ was a crazed killer whose mere existence endangered the whole community.

"I've been told that Westerners judge people by their actions," Tanzy said, drawing herself up, "not by gossip."

"Nothing I've said is gossip. You wait and see if what I tell you isn't the truth." With that, he stormed off.

Tanzy was so upset by Stocker's accusations, she wasn't hungry. After returning to her room for a half an hour to calm herself, she decided to go for a walk. She felt better once she was outside in the sunshine. Stocker's words didn't seem so oppressive. He would naturally be angry at the man who'd caused his brother's death, but Russ couldn't be the villain Stocker depicted. Her memory of his strong, open face assured her that Stocker's reading of Russ's character was wrong. The true soul of a person was mirrored in his face and eyes. The man who'd had dinner with her last night couldn't be evil.

Tanzy had been so caught up in her thoughts, she hadn't realized no one had spoken to her. At first she took that to mean everybody was minding his own business or was too busy to be curious about a stranger. It didn't take long for her to realize people were avoiding her. If she'd had any doubts, they vanished when a woman passing by brushed against the storefront to prevent her skirts from touching Tanzy. It was as though she'd suddenly contracted the plague.

The expressions she encountered were different from those the day before, too. The women looked at her in an openly speculative manner. She couldn't categorize the men because their expressions were too varied. One thing she knew for certain: Stocker Pullet was a very powerful man. In under an hour he'd turned the town of Boulder Gap against her.

That infuriated her. *No one* had the right to judge her merely on the say-so of another person, particularly when nobody in the town knew anything about her. And if she ever got a chance to speak to Stocker Pullet again, she'd tell him that she had no respect for a man who spread gossip or impugned the reputation of others.

Especially *her* reputation.

It came as something of a surprise when Tanzy realized she'd been walking up and down the boardwalk for nearly an hour without paying any attention to the storefronts she passed. Russ's money rested uncomfortably in her pocket. She stopped in front of Davis & Greaves Dry Goods to look at a made-up dress in the window. It was a solferino pink-and-white-striped lawn with looped overskirt. It must have taken over a dozen yards of material to make the overskirt and ruffles used for trim. It was probably much too expensive, but Tanzy thought it was the most elegant dress she'd ever seen.

"No point in looking at that," a voice said. "You won't have any use for it."

Tanzy turned to find herself facing a woman she'd never seen before. The woman was shorter than Tanzy, broader, and definitely older. She had blond hair that she wore atop her head under a clever little hat. She was dressed stylishly but in what Tanzy privately considered bad taste. It was clear she'd chosen her wardrobe to draw attention to her physical attributes.

"I was looking at it because it's pretty," Tanzy said.

"You can't afford it, either."

Tanzy was aware that her appearance would lead people to believe she was some poor farmer's wife, but the money in her purse bolstered her spirits. "I'm trying to decide whether to purchase the dress or buy some material and have a dressmaker run it up for me. Do you have a really good dressmaker in town?"

The woman looked her up and down with scorn. "Plenty good enough for you."

Tanzy ignored the remark and the curled lip. "I'm about to be married. Do you think my husband would like me in that dress?"

"Honey, if you don't know the dress a man likes best is the one he just got you out of, you'll never be enough woman for Russ. That fool Welt has talked him into thinking he wants a proper little mealy-mouthed bride from back East, but he'll soon realize you're nothing more than plain bread, white and pasty-looking. Russ belongs to me! You can't have him."

"I don't know who you are or what claim you think you have on Mr. Tibbolt, but I've yet to meet a man who feels he *belongs* to any woman."

"I'm warning you: Russ is my man. Leave him alone."

"What have you been saying to this young woman, Betty?"

A plain-featured woman past the first blush of youth had approached them. "Good morning. My name is Ethel Peters."

"I'm Tanzy Gallant," Tanzy said, accepting the hand that was extended. "I'm—"

"You're the young woman who's come to town to marry Russ Tibbolt. I must urge you most earnestly to reconsider."

Chapter Four

"That's what I've been trying to tell her," Betty said.

"I expect you've been trying to convince her Russ will never marry her because he loves you," Ethel said. "Russ didn't marry you years ago when you still had the shreds of your reputation, and he won't now. Leave this young woman alone. I need to talk to her."

"Make her leave," Betty said. "Nobody wants her here."

Ethel looked Tanzy over carefully. "I expect you're wrong there."

Tanzy felt herself blush. It was one thing to be looked over critically by a jealous woman; it was quite another to be carefully evaluated by a person she was certain was a good woman. It made her feel that her *true* value had been seen and was being weighed. Tanzy was afraid this woman would find her lacking.

"That's a pretty dress," Ethel said, indicating the pink dress. "I think it would look lovely on you with your dark coloring, but you'd be better advised to purchase something more suitable for traveling than what you're wearing."

Tanzy was wearing a yellow calico with a loose waist that allowed freedom of movement, not the kind of dress she wanted to be seen in by the man who might become her husband. She was vain enough to admit she wanted to appear attractive, somewhere between Ethel's black crow look and Betty's red cardinal.

"I know about Russ's fight with Toley Pullet."

"Do you know he was sent to prison for that killing? Do

you know he's accused of being behind the rustling going on? Do you know he hired a bunch of hardened criminals as ranch hands? Do you know there's not a respectable woman in Boulder Gap who will speak to him, much less be seen in his company?"

Tanzy wouldn't have believed any of this if it had come from Stocker Pullet, but she knew of no reason why this woman would lie. "I'm aware that Russ is not well liked in Boulder Gap."

"Then you don't need any more reason to know he wouldn't make you a good husband."

"I don't know enough about Russ to be able to answer that for myself, but I have a week before I have to make a decision."

"Leave now. Russ is a very handsome man with a reputation for danger that makes him attractive to women, foolish creatures that we are. Betty isn't the only woman to lose her head over him."

"I don't plan to lose my head over any man."

"Very wise, my dear, but we women are weak when it comes to men. The bigger and better looking they are, the more foolishly we behave. I wouldn't be truthful if I didn't say that looking at Russ Tibbolt causes my heart to beat a little faster, but I'm not sure whether it's from excitement or fear."

"With a man like Russ, they can stand for the same thing."

"Then you understand."

"I know people don't want me to marry him, but I have yet to figure out why they think what I do is any of their business."

"It must seem presumptuous of me to interfere in your life, but believe me when I say you'll have nothing but misery if you marry Russ Tibbolt. Now I won't bother you anymore. That pink dress really is tempting. I wish I had the coloring for it. Or the figure. Enjoy it while you have it, dear. A woman's body is a treacherous thing. Just when you think everything has come together at last, it starts to fall apart."

Ethel smiled warmly, shook Tanzy's hand, then turned and left Tanzy wondering who would be the next person to warn her against marrying Russ. A small shriek followed by a sputter of annoyance caused Tanzy to turn back. She saw Ethel using her purse to beat Tardy about the head and shoulders.

"I've told you a hundred times, you stupid boy, to look before you burst out from between buildings. You could have knocked me into the street."

"Stop it, Aunt Ethel," Tardy said, guarding his face and head with his forearms. "You're going to hit me in the head if you're not careful."

"Maybe I can knock some sense into it," Ethel said, making one last try before Tardy slithered to one side and escaped.

Tardy dashed through the street without looking either way and disappeared between a saloon and a lawyer's office.

"Mark my words," Ethel said in disgust, "that boy will get himself killed one of these days."

"Are you all right?" Tanzy asked.

"I am if you don't count a badly frayed temper." She readjusted her hat. "Tell me if my hair is coming down in my face."

"You look fine. Shouldn't a boy your nephew's age be in school?"

"He would be if we could find a schoolteacher. All the

men want to go off looking for gold and silver. The only women who've tried haven't been able to handle the bigger boys."

"Boys don't think they should have to pay attention to women," Tanzy said. "I had four brothers who thought Mother and I should be their slaves."

"It must be a real comfort to know you've got so many men you can turn to."

"It would be if they weren't all dead."

"My dear child, forgive me. I'm so sorry to bring up something which must be extremely painful."

Tanzy knew she should explain, but she couldn't. "If you're sure you're all right, I'd better be going. I want to buy that dress before someone beats me to it."

Ethel laughed. "You'll break Martha Greaves's heart. She's used that dress to draw people into the store all summer. Now she'll have to order another one."

"It's like they've got orders to keep us holed up in these mountains," Welt said to Russ.

"I don't think it's that simple," Russ said. "They've got some scheme up their sleeves. I just wish I knew what it was."

"They want to steal all your cows," Tim said.

"I don't think so," Russ said. "They haven't bothered us yet."

"Maybe that's because they can't get through the pass," Tim said.

They were perched on one of the rocky ridges that surrounded Russ's valley. Thousands of years ago water had created a break in the rock wall, forming a natural pass, the only way in without coming over nearly impassable mountains.

"I think they're trying to pin the rustling on me," Russ said.

"Why should they care who gets blamed?" Welt asked.

"That doesn't make sense," Tim said. "If you're arrested and the rustling keeps up, the sheriff will know it's not you and have to let you go."

Russ had his doubts about whether he'd get out of prison if Stocker ever got him there again, but that didn't concern him right now. He wanted to know why the pass was watched by a man with a rifle.

"We can keep guessing for a week without figuring out anything," Russ said. "Are you sure you and the boys can hold the ranch if I go into Boulder Gap?"

Russ wouldn't have been surprised to learn Stocker had hired a professional gunman to get rid of him. What did surprise him was this attempt to keep him locked up in the valley. He could hold out up here for years if he had to.

"There's too much here I don't understand," Russ said. "The rustlers are hitting everybody, including Stocker Pullet, but they're acting like they've got some special grudge against me."

"Like what?" Tim asked.

"I have no idea," Russ said.

"They know more about these mountains than I like," Welt said.

"Russ knows more," Tim said. He showed an alarming tendency to think Russ could do anything. Just as he showed an equally alarming tendency to think he couldn't die. Russ didn't know how to convince the boy that being nineteen was no guarantee of immortality.

"Never count out dumb luck," Russ said. "It'll kill you every time."

He had two reasons for needing to get out of his valley. Somebody had some plan he didn't know anything about. The most obvious choice was Stocker Pullet, but his herds were being plundered as much as anybody else's. He kept pointing the finger at Russ, but surely nobody believed Russ was stupid enough to rustle from his neighbors when everybody was just waiting to catch him.

The other reason was Tanzy. He'd told her that he might not come back right away, but women never understood things like that. You could tell a woman you had killers on your heels, that the sheriff was hammering at the door, and your neighbors were trying to run off your entire herd, but if you didn't show up on time, she would be certain she had said something to upset you. Or you didn't like her dress. Or her hair was wrong. Or you were with another woman. There was no such thing as external pressures that could force you to do something you didn't want to. With a woman, *everything* was personal.

Too, he wanted to see Tanzy again. She was an attractive woman who grabbed him on a physical level as no other woman ever had; besides that, she fascinated him. He couldn't decide why just yet, but he knew there was something about her that was important to him. His experience with women consisted of several unsatisfactory, superficial physical relationships, all of which had reinforced his belief that it was dangerous to become emotionally involved with any woman. He could walk away from all the others, but he had to come home to a wife.

So why wasn't he running in the opposite direction from Tanzy? Maybe the attraction wasn't emotional, but it wasn't something practical, something he could articulate, like listing the qualities that made a good cowhand. Outside of the feeling that she had something he needed, there was the feeling she had something he wanted. Still more dangerous territory. If he had any sense, he wouldn't stir out of his valley until he knew exactly what he was feeling and why.

Three days had passed and Russ still hadn't come back. Even though he'd told her he might not be able to be back the next day, Tanzy was worried. They had given each other a week to decide if they wanted to marry. Nearly half of that time was gone, and they'd met only once. She didn't believe Russ was the kind of man to rush into something without carefully considering it from all angles. Neither did she believe he was the kind to run away.

The last three days had made her aware of a deep schism in public opinion about Russ. The powerful and socially prominent all agreed he was the worst thing next to the devil himself. Then there were the little people, the ones like Archie and Tardy, who either liked Russ, sympathized with him, or thought people ought to forget the past and move on. According to Archie, most of the folks in Boulder Gap had something in their past they didn't want to reach the light of day.

It was nearly time to go down for dinner. She was wearing her pink dress tonight. It hadn't fitted quite as well as Tanzy hoped, and it had taken a couple of days before she was able to complete the alternations. After spending hours studying the women she saw on the streets, especially the wives of the officers from Fort Lookout, Tanzy had taken a couple of hours to arrange her hair in the style of a young lieutenant's wife, an adorable, petite blonde who was obviously from the East and probably at a loss to understand why her husband should want a military career in the wild and savage Colorado Territory. Tanzy was pleased with the results of her efforts, but she wondered if anybody would appreciate it.

Except Stocker Pullet.

After stalking off in anger that first morning, he'd made a complete turnaround. He'd come to the hotel each night for dinner, always alone, and made a point of stopping to talk to her. He seemed to think Russ's absence indicated Tanzy had taken his advice. She didn't like him, so she saw no reason to set him straight. He took for granted that no one could fail to enjoy his company. It had taken Tanzy's best efforts to refuse his invitations to join his table.

Tanzy looked at herself critically in the mirror. Not one to suffer from false modesty, she knew she'd never looked better in her life. Not that she wanted to snare Russ by her looks. Still, a woman liked to look her best. It made her feel good.

"You're looking mighty pretty," Archie said when she appeared in the lobby. "Will Russ be here tonight?"

"I don't know," Tanzy said. She'd taken to confiding in Archie. "I haven't heard from him since he left that first night."

"There's a lot of trouble out on the range," Archie said. "Rustlers have hit nearly every ranch within a hundred miles."

"I was certain he would have sent me a message."

"If he could have sent a message, he'd have come himself."

That didn't make Tanzy feel any better. Neither did seeing Stocker enter the lobby. She had no choice but to respond to his enthusiastic greeting.

"You're looking stunning tonight," Stocker said. "Are you going in to dinner?"

"I'm waiting for Russ."

"You've said that for the last three nights."

"He told me he might not be able to come back right away."

"Let's face it, Russ is not coming."

"He said he'd return when he could."

Stocker's smile was so patronizing, she wanted to slap it off his face. "I think it's wonderful you should be so innocent and trusting, but you must learn to be more discerning about whom you trust. I warned you that Russ Tibbolt was a criminal, a man you couldn't rely on. I know others have told you the same."

How could she explain that even though she was new to Boulder Gap, she couldn't accept public opinion without seeing some proof herself? She'd been the victim of assumptions in St. Louis. Despite her rising doubts about the wisdom of marrying Russ, she wasn't going to do the same thing to him.

"I've given myself a week to make up my mind about Mr. Tibbolt. He has the same amount of time to make up his mind about me. In the meantime, he has a ranch to run. I'm told that rustlers are running rampant over the whole territory. I expect he's busy protecting his herd."

"Russ Tibbolt is doing the rustling. I'm surprised he even sent for you. Rustlers aren't the kind to settle down. When things get too hot, they leave the country."

"If that's the case, maybe you've made a mistake in assuming Russ is behind the rustling."

"The only mistake was not realizing he was a thief five years ago. How else did he get the cows to fill those valleys of his?"

Tanzy knew nothing about Russ's past, so she said nothing. Stocker, feeling he'd won the argument, broke into a broad smile.

"Since both of us are alone for the evening, why don't you join me for dinner? Russ isn't coming."

"Maybe not, but until his week is up, I feel obligated to wait for him."

"And what will you do then?"

She didn't know. She'd been thinking about that more and more as she sat in her hotel room or wandered through the town. If Russ never showed up again, she'd have to somehow find a way to support herself that didn't require her to work in a dance hall, gambling place, or saloon. "I still have three days to make my plans."

"Well, until you do, you can have dinner with me," Stocker said, taking her elbow in his grasp and attempting to lead her toward the dining room. Tanzy held her ground.

"What if Russ came in after we sat down? Or worse, when we were halfway through our dinner?"

"He'd be out of luck."

"I think it's better I wait." She looked around for support, but no one else was in the lobby.

"I insist you join me. It's not proper for a young woman to eat alone. It's probably not even safe."

Tanzy was determined not to sit down at the table with him, but she didn't know how to avoid a physical tussle. Stocker had a firm grip on her elbow and showed no signs of letting go.

"You never can tell what kind of ruffian will come down out of those mountains. No woman can protect herself against—"

"Russ can," Tanzy said, wrenching her elbow from Stocker's grasp. "And since he's just come in, you are freed of any obligation to feel responsible for my safety."

If Tanzy had been in a better mood, she might have found the change in Stocker's demeanor comical. She knew Stocker hated Russ, but she hadn't guessed until now that he was also afraid of him.

"It's nice to know you're a man of your word."

Russ's brow creased. "How so?"

"You told me not to worry if you were late. I just didn't expect *later* to be three days."

Russ's inquiring gaze swung from Tanzy to Stocker and back. "I had some unwelcome visitors. That's a hazard of having something other people want." He appeared finally to focus on her and her new dress. "You look pretty."

"She looks damned beautiful," Stocker said, "too beautiful to be wasting her time on the likes of you."

"Are you ready to go in to dinner?" she asked Russ. She was anxious to get away from Stocker.

"More than ready." Russ stepped back to allow her to pass in front of him.

Stocker looked thunderous, but he said nothing. The waiter seated them in the back, as before.

"Are you sure you don't mind sitting back here?" Russ asked.

"I prefer it," Tanzy said. "Since everybody in this town seems to be angry at you, it's probably the only place where we can have a reasonably quiet dinner."

"I expect half the people wouldn't know I existed if it weren't for Stocker. He wants to run me out of the Territory, so he's convinced everybody I'm dangerous."

"Doesn't that bother you?"

"Not much. I can go a whole year without coming into town."

"You shouldn't have to stay away if you don't want to."

"There's nothing here I want. Now, what would you like to eat?"

"I don't care. Order two of whatever you're having. I want to know where you've been for the last three days."

By the time Russ finished telling her about the gunman guarding the pass, she was angry. "Do you think Stocker is behind it?"

"I don't know. Most of the ranchers have been hit by the rustlers, even Stocker. The only reason they haven't hit me is that there's only one way into my ranch and it's through that pass."

"So you think the rustlers are just mad and trying to keep you locked up for revenge?"

"I believe they've got something else in mind, but I don't know what it is."

"What will you do?"

"It depends on what they do, but let's forget about them for a while. Do you need more money?"

"I'm not taking another penny from you."

"You can't stay here with no money."

"I could if I hadn't been weak enough to buy this dress."

"It looks very nice on you."

"You look very nice, too."

"You think I'm good-looking?"

"Don't pretend ignorance with me, Russ Tibbolt. You know half the women in Boulder Gap get heart palpitations every time they see you."

"I know they dislike me so much they can hardly stand the sight of me."

"I don't know what they feel about you as a person, but they sure do like the way you look."

Tanzy thought Russ might have blushed. His deep tan made it difficult to judge, but she'd never met a man who was modest. Even her opossum-faced cousin thought he was a matrimonial prize.

"What was Stocker talking to you about?" Russ asked. His tan did nothing to hide the tension in his expression.

"He wanted me to have dinner with him. I told him I had to wait for you."

"Even though I hadn't come back for three days?"

"I don't know anything about your ranch or any difficulties you might be having, but I figured you expected something to hold you up or you wouldn't have warned me."

"How long were you going to wait?"

"Until the end of the week."

"What would you have done then?"

"I hadn't decided, but I was sure you'd be back before then. You strike me as a man who doesn't let much get in his way."

His expression sobered to the point of being almost angry. "A great number of things have gotten in my way over the years. I was too young to have any sense."

"Is that why you got into the gunfight with Stocker's brother?"

"No."

"I think it's time you told me what happened between you and Stocker."

"I told you."

"I mean everything."

Chapter Five

"It's an old story," Russ said, "but the tragic ending isn't enough to keep it from happening over and over again."

Tanzy had learned that lesson with her own family. Each time a member of her family had been killed, it only made the rest of them more determined to carry on the feud.

"Adele was my half sister," Russ began. "Her father was my mother's first husband. She grew up to be a beautiful girl who liked pretty things. We didn't have any money for nice things after our parents died, but Toley Pullet had more than enough. Stocker gave him pretty much everything he wanted, and he wanted Adele. I tried to tell her he was no good, but she was sure she was the woman to make him settle down and stop wasting his life. There was a real nice fella, Welt Allard, who was crazy about her, but he wasn't rich enough for Adele.

"I went all the way to Texas looking for work. I needed money and cows to start my own ranch. When I got back after two years, Welt told me Toley had taken Adele to San Francisco and left her to die alone. I went looking for Toley, determined to beat his brains out, but Stocker had surrounded his brother with a bunch of tough cowhands. I challenged him to any kind of fight he wanted. Before I knew what was happening, one of the cowhands had strapped a gunbelt to my waist and we were pacing off the distance. I didn't know much about guns, but I knew it was more important to be accurate than to be quick. Toley's first shot missed. Mine didn't."

"That doesn't make you a killer," Tanzy said.

"It did in Stocker's eyes. He had me arrested and tried for murder. He couldn't force the jury to hang me, but they sent me to prison for five years."

Tanzy's misgivings about Russ had resurfaced, but she had to give him credit for having served his time in jail, however unfair the sentence, and devoting his energy since to building his ranch.

"You've paid your debt. Why won't people leave you alone?"

"Stocker won't let them. When I came back, he tried to run me out, but I'd hired three guys I'd met in jail, and we held him off. Nobody has ever stopped Stocker from taking anything he's wanted. I've injured his pride, and he can't accept that. His father carved an empire out of Indian land and became the richest, most powerful, most feared man around. Stocker has been trying to live up to his father's reputation ever since."

The more Tanzy heard, the more uneasy she became. She'd heard practically the same words out of her father's and brothers' mouths. *Their pride had been hurt and they couldn't accept that.*

"What are you going to do about it?" Tanzy asked.

"Nothing. If they bother me too much, I'll start buying my supplies at Fort Lookout and never set foot in town again."

Tanzy didn't believe any woman looking to marry Russ would appreciate being confined to a mountain ranch for the rest of her life, but it did allay some of her misgivings. His sister was dead, but he knew nothing could bring her back. He was looking to the future rather than poisoning his life by constantly stoking his anger at past injustices, and perhaps the most significant proof that he was looking toward the future was his wanting to marry her.

The more she thought about marrying Russ, the more she liked the idea. He was a man of action, a man who held strong convictions and backed them up. His time in prison had resulted from trying to avenge his sister's honor. She was certain he'd be equally ready to defend his wife, which would be a change from her own family. She was also impressed that he'd been able to establish a ranch in the teeth of such fierce opposition.

Then there was the not inconsiderable fact that he was so handsome she felt keyed up whenever she was with him. Though she was unused to the feeling, it wasn't unpleasant. There was an element of anticipation about it that intrigued her. She felt something was always on the verge of happening, something very personal. That led to the one area about which she was completely in the dark.

What should her feelings toward him be?

"I would like to see your ranch," Tanzy said to Russ.

He seemed surprised. "Why?"

"Wouldn't you expect your prospective wife to want to see where she was going to live?"

"It's a long, difficult ride, impossible unless you go by horseback."

"I used to ride our mules when I was a little girl."

"I don't have a sidesaddle."

"I wouldn't know how to use it."

"Riding astride out here is the only sensible way to get around in the mountains, but I didn't expect an Eastern lady to agree."

She relaxed with a smile. "I'm a Kentucky mountain girl. You'll soon learn that people don't consider me a lady. They wouldn't be surprised by anything I did."

It appeared to take him a moment to digest that

thought. "I see no reason to fault a female for where her parents chose to live. It's not your birthplace that counts. It's—"

"God dammit, Russ. I swore if you touched another head of my cattle, I'd shoot you where you stood."

Rudely jolted out of her concentration, Tanzy looked up to see Stocker marching toward them, his face twisted by fury, diners ducking to get out of the way of the gun he was waving in the air.

"Don't be a bigger fool than you already are," Russ snapped. "My men couldn't get out of my valley if they wanted to. Gunmen have blocked the pass for the last three days."

"Then how did you get out?" Stocker demanded.

"I know more about the mountains than they do. Now put away that gun before you hurt somebody."

"I'm going to shoot you between your lying eyes," Stocker shouted. "The only gunmen guarding the pass to *my* valley are your men making sure nobody gets in to see what brands your cattle are carrying."

"I wouldn't want your scrawny longhorns. I've upgraded my herds."

"You've bought bulls with money you got from selling my scrawny cows. I'm going to put an end to this right here and now."

Stocker lunged unsteadily at Russ. Tanzy was sure he was too drunk to know what he was doing, but Russ was out of his seat and trying to wrench the gun from Stocker's grip.

"I should have killed you when you murdered my brother," Stocker groaned. "I'll never rest until you're dead."

"I'll never forget what your family did to my mother and sister," Russ said.

"They'd have gone with anybody who had money," Stocker said. "They were nothing but sluts."

Tanzy couldn't believe what she was seeing. Stocker Pullet, the richest and most respected man in town, wrestling on the floor and shouting that he was going to kill Russ for rustling his cattle. Russ Tibbolt, the man she'd promised to marry, was no different. Both of them were pummeling each other without regard for the wide-eyed interest of at least fifty diners. If she hadn't been so angry, she'd have been embarrassed.

"Stop it, both of you," Tanzy shouted. "You're making fools of yourselves." They ignored her, tumbling around the floor like boys in a wrestling match.

"They've hated each other for at least ten years," the town banker said. "It won't end until one of them is dead."

It won't end until one of them is dead.

Her mother's words echoed in her head like an ominous warning. She'd traveled more than a thousand miles only to find herself right back where she started. Anger sizzled through her with the speed of a lightning bolt.

"This is going to end right now," she said. She snatched a pistol from the holster of a man watching the fight, waded into the fracas, and struck Russ a stunning blow when she got her chance. The moment Russ slumped to the floor, she pointed the gun directly at a very startled Stocker.

"Why are you pointing that gun at me?" he asked. He wiped his hand across his mouth. It came away bloody. "He's the rustler."

"If you think he's guilty, produce some proof, then let the sheriff arrest him. It's not for you to take the law into your own hands, especially not when you're drunk and waving a gun about in a restaurant full of people. If you'd shot Russ, you'd be a cold-blooded murderer, a worse criminal than you accuse him of being."

Stocker gaped at Tanzy, clearly more dazed by the force of her words than the impact of Russ's fists.

"She's right, Stocker," the banker said. "You can't go taking the law into your own hands."

"How am I supposed to get proof with murderers guarding my valley, ready to shoot any honest citizen who approaches?"

"I expect Russ would be willing for a responsible delegation to go to this valley and inspect his herd," Tanzy said. "That way you could settle the dispute once and for all."

"Sounds like a good idea," the banker said.

"He won't let anybody in," Stocker said.

"You can ask him when his head clears," Tanzy said. "Do you think you can walk?"

"Of course I can walk. I'm not incapacitated by a few drinks."

Tanzy had no idea how much whiskey it took to make Stocker drunk, but she was certain he'd drunk more than enough.

"You need to go home. You'll feel better after a good night's rest."

"I won't feel better until he's dead in his grave," he said, looking at Russ, who was sitting up, groaning and gently touching the lump on his head.

"Try to put the past behind you and think about the future," Tanzy said.

"I *am* thinking about the future," Stocker said, "when I can get back what this murdering thief stole from me."

Russ cradled his head in two hands. "You'll never prove I've stolen so much as one cow from anybody, so why don't you quit trying?"

"This young lady has said you'd be willing to have a group of ranchers inspect your herd," the banker said. "To prove you're not rustling," he added when Russ directed a menacing look at him.

"Nobody is setting a foot in my valley," Russ said.

"See," Stocker said, "that's proof he's a thief."

"I'd be a fool to let any committee of your choosing on my land," Russ said. "You got a jury to convict me of murder when everybody knows your brother drew first. What reason do I have to expect fair treatment from anybody in this town?"

Tanzy noticed an uncomfortable shuffling of feet, several averted faces. Apparently some people believed there was truth to what Russ had said.

"Why don't each of you choose people you trust?" Tanzy suggested.

"I can't trust anybody in Boulder Gap," Russ said. "Stocker's got everybody in his pocket."

"You could choose some officers from the fort," Tanzy said. "I see no reason to suspect their honesty, and I doubt anybody in Boulder Gap would be able to intimidate them."

"The colonel has a reputation for integrity," the banker said. "He caught the agent who was cheating the Indians, and his partner who was rustling their cattle."

"There," Tanzy said, taking both Russ and Stocker in her glance, "what more could you want than a man who's known for his integrity and is familiar with rustling as well?"

"As long as Colonel McGregor is in charge of the committee, they can inspect my herd," Russ said. "Now go away. I can barely think, my head is pounding so hard."

A man tried to steady Stocker on his feet, but Stocker angrily shook him off and stalked out of the restaurant, stumbling into two tables before he managed to reach the door. The other diners returned to their tables, but Tanzy could feel surreptitious glances still being directed toward her.

"Maybe you ought to go to your room," Tanzy said. They had finished their meal so she didn't see any reason to stay in the restaurant. She followed Russ back into the hotel lobby.

"In a minute," Russ said, massaging the knot on his skull. "Why did you hit me? Stocker is the crazy one."

"I couldn't reach him. It didn't matter anyway. As long as I made one of you stop, the other would, too."

"You had no reason to stop me. Stocker was too drunk and too old to be a danger to me."

"He had a gun. He could have shot you. Or anybody in that restaurant."

"I wrenched it out of his hands just before you clobbered me."

Maybe she should have let them fight it out, but she'd been too angry.

"Maybe you ought to see the doctor."

"As Culley said, I have a hard head. I don't need the doctor."

"I hope you're staying at the boardinghouse tonight," Tanzy said. "You shouldn't be riding until your head feels better."

He winced as he touched the knot on his head. "Seems to me you'd clobber Stocker before attacking your future husband."

"Let's sit down." She indicated a settee in the corner. "We need to talk."

"I'm not sure I want to talk about getting married. I don't want a wife who'll bang me on the head without a moment's hesitation."

"I don't want a husband who's carrying on a feud with half the town."

"I'm not carrying on a feud with anybody."

"I'll never forget what your family did to my mother and sister. Do you remember saying those words?"

"What of it?"

"I've lived through a feud. I know what happens when men say things like that."

"I was trying to keep Stocker from killing me. I wasn't thinking about every word that came out of my mouth."

"That's exactly when people say what they really mean."

"It's also when we say foolish things we don't mean," Russ shot back.

Tanzy wished she could believe Russ. Even if he didn't want to carry on a feud, Stocker did. And Russ wasn't the kind of man to back down from a fight.

She was also certain Russ wouldn't respect her wishes if she became his wife. She would be part of his crew, expected to follow his orders. She'd be in the same position her mother had been in, tied to a man and forced to endure the life he chose to make for them.

She wouldn't do that. She'd already survived half a year on her own. She didn't want to do it again, but she could.

"I've decided we won't suit," Tanzy told Russ. "I'm sorry to have put you to the expense of bringing me out here, but I can't marry you."

She had expected anger, even a refusal to allow her to

change her mind, but Russ didn't answer. From his expression, it was difficult to tell whether he didn't know how to respond to her decision or his thoughts were entirely of the pain in his head.

"Did you hear what I said?" she asked when she couldn't wait any longer for a response.

"My head hurts like the devil, but there's nothing wrong with my hearing."

"Do you agree with me?"

"No. You're strong, intelligent, and able to make decisions on your own. That's exactly the kind of woman a rancher needs for a wife."

She was disappointed he didn't say a word about liking her or finding her attractive. If she'd come straight to Colorado from Kentucky, she'd never have thought about being attractive. In Kentucky a wife was valued by how much work she could do and how many sons she could produce. It wasn't until she worked in the gambling hall that she discovered men were strongly affected by a woman's physical appearance.

"That may be," she said, "but *you're* not the kind of husband *I* want."

"What's wrong? I own my own ranch. I'm not exactly ugly, and I'll take good care of you."

"You can't do any of that if you're dead or in prison."

"I'm not going to get killed, and I'm certainly not going back to prison."

"You will if you keep up this feud with Stocker."

"I'm not feuding with Stocker."

"He's feuding with you."

"That's his problem."

"Will you fight back if he tries to take your cattle or run you out of your valley?"

"Of course."

"If he burns your house or barns, will you burn his?"

"Probably."

"If his men kill some of your men, will you retaliate?"

"Without hesitation."

"Then you'll end up dead or in prison. And what's more, if we have sons, future generations will be drawn into the fight."

"Not if I kill Stocker. He doesn't have any future generations."

"I'm sure he has uncles, cousins, other relatives who'd want to avenge his death."

"This is all nonsense."

"It's not nonsense. I grew up in the middle of a feud that killed my whole family. I know how feuds start and what keeps them going."

His look was penetrating. "Are you sure you're not making this up to keep from telling me you don't like me and don't want to marry me?"

"It's not that at all," Tanzy hastened to assure him. "I find you very attractive and nice. I was especially impressed you would come to meet the stage to make sure I arrived safely. Your pursuit of the thieves shows you have courage and a high sense of moral responsibility. I know you work hard because you couldn't have built up your ranch if you didn't. I also know you take good care of your men, or they wouldn't have remained faithful to you. Everybody knows you're unafraid of danger and willing to stand up for yourself against any odds. You've exactly the kind of man every woman dreams of having for a husband."

"If I'm so perfect, why won't you marry me?"

"Because of the feud."

"There is no feud."

"I disagree."

"I live here. I *know* what's going on."

"You're so bound up in your anger at Stocker, you don't see what both of you are doing."

"And you don't understand that a man has to defend his property. If he doesn't, he won't have it long."

"You haven't forgotten your sister's death, and Stocker hasn't forgotten his brother's. That's more than enough to keep the two of you at each other's throats."

"Good Lord, woman, I can't believe you're foolish enough to build an argument into a war."

His words were like a slap in the face. "That's something else I find unacceptable."

"What?" Russ asked. "I didn't say anything."

"The fact that you don't realize what you said makes it even worse."

"I don't like guessing games. Tell me what you're talking about."

"You clearly don't respect my opinions."

"That's because they're wrong."

"It's also clear you don't expect your wife to have any say in how you run the ranch."

"I'm not going to tell her what to cook. I don't care—"

"That's not what I mean."

"Then say what you mean. Say something a man can understand instead of all this nonsense."

"You did it again."

"Did what again?" He was getting increasingly impatient.

"You dismissed my opinion as nonsense."

"Because it is."

"It's not nonsense to me."

"That's because you don't understand what you're talking about."

"You expect me to accept your opinions without question, without your taking the time to explain to me why they aren't nonsense, without your taking the time to listen to my concerns and give them the same amount of consideration as your own."

"No self-respecting rancher is going to let his wife make all the decisions, any more than he would expect to run the household."

"Of course you'd tell me how to run the household," Tanzy replied. "You'd tell me what you wanted to eat and when, you'd decide how much money I had to spend, and you'd tell me when I could go into town. And if my doing the wash on any given day got in the way of your plans, you'd tell me that, too."

"You didn't put any of this in your letters," Russ said.

"You didn't say anything about the feud."

"There is no feud!"

"You don't need to shout," Tanzy said. "I've tried my best to make you understand why I made my decision, but you aren't listening. There's nothing more to say except that I'm not going to marry you."

Russ's look turned hard. "What are you going to do about the money you owe me?"

Chapter Six

Russ was angry. He hadn't liked this mail-order bride business from the beginning, but Welt had kept saying it was the only way Russ was going to find a wife as long as everybody within a hundred miles thought he was a cold-blooded killer. Russ hadn't wanted a wife. His mother and sister had given him no reason to want another woman in his life. He had his work, and his cowhands provided plenty of companionship. There was no reason to complicate his life.

Welt hadn't let up. He had dwelt on the advantages to the ranch, had said Russ needed a wife so he could have children to inherit his land. Russ hadn't paid attention to half of what Welt said until Welt told him he'd sent the money for Tanzy to come to Boulder Gap. Despite being furious that Welt would practically ask a woman to marry Russ without Russ even knowing about it, he had gone to meet the stagecoach to tell her he'd changed his mind because bandits had already attacked it twice. Much to his surprise, a strong physical attraction had sprung up between them from the very beginning. Tanzy was a very pretty woman. She was also very nice. He liked her and enjoyed her company. He still hadn't believed getting married was a good idea, but he was willing to give it serious thought. No man could look at Tanzy and not think of what it would be like to cuddle up with her on a cold Colorado winter night.

It was probably best that she didn't want to marry him, but he was still angry. She had made her decision for all the wrong reasons.

"If I had lied to you," Russ said, "you'd have every right to walk away without any debts, but I'm an honest rancher, reliable, willing and able to support a wife and family, everything you said in your letters you wanted. Since you're turning me down for no good reason, you owe me the cost of bringing you out here, putting you up in a hotel, and for that dress you're wearing."

"I didn't want the money. You practically forced me to take it."

"You didn't have to spend it."

"What was I supposed to do, hold it until we decided if we wanted to marry?"

"That would have been the logical thing to do."

Russ was aware he was being unfair. He was also aware he was being anything but a gentleman, but he was too mad to care. She hadn't based her refusal on anything important, just this stupid argument with Stocker. What did she expect him to do, sit there and let that drunk brandish the gun about until he shot someone?

He'd made a fool of himself to protect her, and now she thought he was feuding with Stocker and would get himself and any future sons killed. How could a sensible woman turn a simple fight into something like that? Not only that, she'd hit him on the head instead of Stocker! She looked good on the outside, but she must be a little crazy. It was a good thing they'd decided to give themselves a week before making a commitment to this marriage.

"I don't have any money," Tanzy said.

"I'll wait until you find a job before I expect you to pay me back."

"What kind of job can I find in this town?"

"What are you qualified to do?"

She opened her mouth to speak, then closed it again. He was certain she had almost said she was qualified to be a wife. He expected she would be efficient, would manage things well, but she'd also made it clear she wanted to make a lot of the decisions. She'd soon learn western men wouldn't put up with that.

He certainly wouldn't. His mother and sister had cured him of any belief that a woman could sufficiently separate her intelligence from her emotions. Their behavior had been the cause of all the trouble he'd had in Boulder Gap.

"You agreed to give me a full week to decide whether to marry you," Tanzy said. "Will you give me the rest of the week to find a way to repay you?"

"How will you do that?"

"I don't know. I'll have to find out what jobs are available."

"You might ask at Fort Lookout. I hear the woman who runs the store there prefers to hire women. You could always be a laundress."

"How far away is the fort? Where would I live?"

Russ thought better of the idea as soon as it came out of his mouth. A pretty, single woman would have the soldiers beating down her door to ask her to marry them.

"I'm not sure the fort is such a good idea. Talk to Ethel Peters. She knows everything about Boulder Gap." He stood. "Now I'm going to bed and hope my head stops feeling like I got kicked by a mule. If you have a message for me, give it to Archie. He'll see that I get it."

Russ didn't go straight to the boardinghouse. He was angry and frustrated. Irritated, annoyed, and just plain mad at being rejected yet again for something he hadn't done. Also, he hadn't realized how much he'd come to like the idea of getting married.

He didn't like the idea of never seeing Tanzy again. He didn't know what it was about her that had gotten to him, but he liked being around her. It wasn't just that she was pretty and spirited. There was something about her that made him feel different, that enabled him to put aside his worries about Stocker and the rustling, helped him forget that everyone in Boulder Gap seemed to hate him. It was almost as though hers was the only opinion that mattered.

That was stupid, of course. No woman's attention

could make up for all the inequities of his life. He guessed he was more susceptible to feminine wiles than he realized. It was good she didn't want to marry him. He could have found himself stuck with a bossy, opinionated woman who'd make the rest of his life miserable. It was definitely better to end it now.

Then why did he feel as if he was losing something important, something he'd never find again?

Tanzy couldn't decide whether she was more relieved or upset that she'd decided not to marry Russ. She liked him and admired many things about him. He was handsome and she enjoyed being with him, but none of that could compensate for the fact that he was involved in a feud. Neither did she want to tie herself to a man who clearly had no respect for women, their opinions, or their rights to share in decisions that affected them. She had no doubt that he would be fair *as he saw things*, but he would discount any opinions that diverged from his own. No, she was well out of that situation.

But that left her with more problems than when she'd started.

Where could she find a job that would enable her to earn enough money to pay Russ back? Should she stay in Boulder Gap or move to another town? Would she ever find a husband who would give her the respect she demanded?

She wandered over to the window, looked at her reflection in the windowpane. Her calm expression gave no hint of the conflicting emotions swirling within her, any more than the quiet streets reflected the rough and sometimes brutal nature of the town. How could she look so normal when absolutely nothing was normal? Every decision she had made since she'd left home had made her situation worse. It would have been easier to marry her disgusting cousin.

Easier, but not better.

She turned away from the window and began to undress. There was nothing she could do to solve her problems tonight. Her first priority tomorrow would be to find a respectable job. The respectable part was important. She would clean houses, cook, do laundry, almost anything before she worked in a gambling hall ever again.

She didn't know what she would do or where she would go if she couldn't find work in Boulder Gap. She had no way of knowing if things would be better in the next town. Or the town after that. She shrugged off a flash of anger at Russ. She didn't think it was fair of him to require her to pay him back, but she had been the one to turn him down. And if it came to a choice of paying him back or marrying him, she'd find a way to pay him.

Which brought her to the question of what she was going to do with her life. She'd always assumed she would get married. Would she be willing to forego marriage if she couldn't find a man who'd give her the respect she wanted? Odd that she'd never considered that option before. She'd always been certain that once she escaped the feud, everything would be all right, but things hadn't worked out that way. St. Louis had been a disaster. Now she'd turned down an opportunity to get married. Where did that leave her?

Tanzy laid her dress out carefully. She doubted she'd be able to afford another for a long time. She climbed into bed but was too keyed up to sleep just yet. She had too many questions that still needed answers.

She wasn't willing to compromise about the feud or

about respect, so she had to accept that her requirements greatly reduced the number of men who were available as potential husbands. In order to attract the kind of husband she wanted, she had to protect her reputation. That meant not taking a job that automatically compromised her. No saloons or gambling establishments. That didn't leave much besides housework. From what she'd seen, she doubted there were more than half a dozen women in Boulder Gap who could afford to pay someone to clean their houses and cook their meals. So where did that leave her?

She'd have to talk to Ethel Peters. Maybe she would help her now that she wasn't going to marry Russ.

Tanzy felt a tinge of regret at turning her back on Russ. Aside from the fact that she liked him and found him very attractive, she sympathized with his dilemma. Maybe she should be more critical of a man who'd killed another man in a gunfight, but she was convinced he was basically a good person. There was no nonsense about him. He didn't shower her with flowery compliments or try to seduce her with extravagant praise. Nor did he pretend to any emotions he didn't feel. He was a man of courage and integrity, exactly the kind of man a sensible woman would want for a husband.

But he couldn't be her husband. It was pointless to remind herself of all the points in his favor. He had two flaws she couldn't accept. No point in feeling a pang of disappointment. So it was time for her to put all thoughts of Russ out of her mind and go to sleep. Tomorrow held plenty of challenges of its own.

Tanzy slid down into the bed and settled under the covers. She just hoped she didn't dream of him.

* * *

"I don't want you to kill him," Stocker said to Chick Hoffman. "I want to be able to pin the rustling on him. I intend to watch him hang."

"It's not easy to get inside that valley," Chick said. "He's got the pass guarded day and night."

The two men met regularly after midnight in Stocker's office in the back of his saloon. The noise of music and laughter, as well as the smell of whiskey and cigars, had penetrated the very walls of the building.

"That's what you're supposed to do, but he's been in town twice this week."

"He can go in and out because he knows the mountains better than we do."

"You've got nothing to do all day but sit around," Stocker said. "Learn them better."

Chick would have liked to tell Stocker to go to hell, but it would be foolish to turn on a man who was paying him to rustle cows and protecting him at the same time. This sweet deal couldn't last long, but he intended to milk it as long as he could.

"Where are you keeping the rustled cows?"

"You don't have to worry about anybody finding them," Chick said. "They're perfectly safe."

"You putting Russ's brand on them?"

"Just like you said."

"How long will it take you to put together a herd of about two hundred cows?"

"Maybe another month if we keep going slow."

"Then that's how long I'll wait."

When the time was right, Stocker intended to lead all the angry ranchers to the rustled cows.

"When I'm able to return all those stolen cows to their rightful owners, everybody will be so thankful, they'll do anything I want. Hold back all the cows you steal from Russ. We can sell them later and split the profit."

"I don't need nobody to help in the store," Mrs. Overby said. "I certainly don't need no single woman pretty as you drawing in all kinds of drunks and gamblers more interested in your virtue than in my merchandise."

Overby's Mercantile was the biggest store in town. It carried virtually everything a person could want, from harnesses to female undergarments.

"I assure you, I have every intention of preserving my virtue," Tanzy said.

"I should hope so," Mrs. Overby declared, "but I don't aim to have the struggle take place in my store. You'll have to wage your war against sin and temptation someplace else. Besides, I got my own daughters' virtue to think about."

Tanzy knew it was uncharitable of her to think such thoughts, but Mother Nature had seen to it that Mrs. Overby's daughters were well protected.

"Do you know of any other suitable positions available?" Tanzy asked.

"Respectable ladies are married, with husbands to protect them," Mrs. Overby said. "Until then they live under the protection of their fathers."

"My parents and all my brothers are dead," Tanzy said. "I don't have any family to take me in."

Mrs. Overby's stiff-necked disapproval eased. "There's not much work in Boulder Gap for respectable women. You might go out to the fort. I hear tell there's plenty of soldiers begging to marry the first woman they see."

"I'd rather marry after consideration than in desperation," Tanzy said.

"Wouldn't we all, but in the end we take what we can."

"If you hear of anything, please let me know. I'll be staying at the Pullet Hotel for the next three days."

"What will you do after that?"

"I haven't decided yet."

How could she expect to find a job in another town when she couldn't get one in Boulder Gap? She stepped outside onto the boardwalk. So far she didn't have even one option. It looked like she'd be forced to go back on her promise to herself not to work in a saloon. Fighting to defend her virtue was better than starvation.

"You don't look very happy," Ethel Peters said.

Tanzy was so lost in thought, she hadn't heard her approach.

"Sorry if I seemed rude, but I was thinking," Tanzy said.

"You look about ready to cry. Does that mean you've discovered Russ Tibbolt's true character?"

"I'm not going to marry him, if that's what you mean," Tanzy said.

"I'm so relieved," Ethel said to Tanzy. "May I ask what caused you to change your mind?"

"I can't marry a man who's feuding with his neighbor," she said. "My father did that. It killed him and my brothers."

"Russ isn't feuding with Stocker," Ethel said. "They just don't like each other. They'll probably keep fighting until one of them is dead, but it's not a feud."

Tanzy didn't see any difference.

"What are you going to do with yourself now?" Ethel asked.

"I don't know."

"I'm on my way home," Ethel said. "Why don't you come with me and we can talk about it."

"Thank you. I'd appreciate that." Tanzy occupied the few minutes it took to reach Ethel's house recounting her unsuccessful search for employment.

Tanzy was surprised Ethel's parlor looked so comfortable, even elegant. From the roughness of the town and its inhabitants, she'd assumed Ethel's home would be similar to the stark simplicity of her family's cabin. Instead she found a parlor as substantial and well-furnished as any she'd seen in St. Louis. It made her feel slightly uneasy, as if she were somehow intruding on her betters. She chided herself for that feeling; though she insisted she was an honorable woman deserving of respect from anyone she met, she'd spent too many years being made painfully aware that others didn't see her in the same light.

"I can't expect Russ to cover my expenses now that I've decided not to marry him," Tanzy said.

She didn't think Ethel needed to know that Russ had demanded that she repay him the money he'd spent on her. That would only give people another excuse to dislike him.

"Russ said you'd know of a job if anybody would," Tanzy said.

"There aren't many jobs for a respectable woman in Boulder Gap," Ethel replied.

"I can cook and clean."

"Nobody here can afford to pay anybody to cook and clean for them."

"Mrs. Overby suggested the fort."

"You can't live there, and it's too far to travel each day. Not to mention the danger. A woman alone wouldn't be safe."

"That doesn't appear to leave anything but the saloons."

"You can't work there!"

"I have a little money left," Tanzy said, "maybe enough to get me to another town. Do you know where I might go?"

"There's no place better than Boulder Gap unless you go to Denver."

Tanzy prepared to rise. "I shouldn't trespass on your hospitality any longer. I need to talk to Russ. Maybe he will advance me the money to travel to Denver."

"My dear, on no account should you do anything to make you more beholden to that man."

Ethel sounded so alarmed, Tanzy almost wanted to ask if she thought Russ had designs on her virtue.

"I know people here don't think kindly of him, but he's been very nice to me."

"Well, of course he would. He was trying to get you out to that ranch, where you would've been defenseless."

"Have you forgotten that he captured those bandits in my defense?"

"He does things like that from time to time in an attempt to make people think better of him, but he's truly a dishonorable man."

She couldn't imagine what Russ had done—surely it had to be more than killing a man in a fair fight—to make everybody hate him. There had to be something she didn't know. Ethel Peters didn't strike her as a woman who would believe the worst of someone without a good reason.

"Given the choice of depending on Russ or working in a saloon, I prefer Russ."

"Are you sure you have no family who would take you in?"

"Quite sure. I appreciate your help," Tanzy said, getting to her feet, "but—"

"What a fool I am!" Ethel exclaimed. "I don't know why I didn't think of it in the first place."

"Think of what?"

"You can be our schoolteacher."

"I've never taught school."

"It doesn't matter. As long as you're able to read and do the times tables, you know enough to teach our kids."

Chapter Seven

It hadn't taken Ethel Peters long to get approval for Tanzy to teach until the town could find a fully qualified person for the job. Tanzy had gone to the schoolhouse the previous afternoon to familiarize herself with the building as well as the materials she had to work with. She had been prepared to spend several hours. It took only a few minutes. There were several copies of one book and a stack of slates for writing. She didn't know if she even had enough desks for all the children. She didn't have one for herself, only a small table and a chair.

She hoped it wouldn't matter. She would have to teach only for a couple of months to repay Russ. Anything she earned after that would be her own.

Tanzy anxiously checked her appearance in the mirror before leaving for her first day in the classroom. She wanted to appear moderately attractive yet respectable, the kind of woman boys honor and girls admire. She was proud of her slim body, rounded hips, and full breasts, but she was well aware that her attractiveness could present a problem in dealing with young boys. She was pleased to see her dress fitted just as she wanted, loose enough not to emphasize her figure but form-fitting enough not to hide it. Her hair was a different matter. It was long, black, and wanted to curl riotously. It required vigorous brushing to keep from looking like she'd been caught in a high wind.

There wasn't much she could do to alter her face. Dark blue eyes stared back at her out of a face she was certain was only a few years older than some of her students. She hoped there were no male students older than twelve. She knew what young boys thought about when they saw an attractive woman. Pretty much the same thing as grown men.

Tanzy was determined to make sure every student knew what was expected of him or her from the very first. In order to do that, she had to appear confident, capable, and in charge.

She couldn't let anybody guess her knees were knocking.

"You headed to the schoolhouse?" Archie asked when she reached the hotel lobby.

"Yes. Do you think I look like a schoolteacher?"

Archie appeared to give the question serious thought. "Barring the fact that you aren't a man and that you aren't homely as a longhorn calf, I'd say you'll pass muster." He grinned suddenly. "Bet you'll have more boys showing up than the last teacher."

"I don't want them showing up to gape at me. I want them coming to learn."

"You can't pound any sense into their heads until you get them inside the schoolhouse," Archie said. "Getting to look at you ought to do the trick. Be firm with them. Boys respect a good woman."

Tanzy found Tardy waiting for her when she emerged from the hotel. "What are you doing here?" she asked. "School doesn't start for another half hour."

"Aunt Ethel said I was to go to school with you today and stick by your side until it was time for you to come home."

"Surely I don't need protection from the students."

"Aunt Ethel says you're too pretty. She says I'm to tell her if any miners or cowhands try to sneak in the back or hang around during recess."

Tanzy laughed and felt some of her tension ease. "Tell your aunt I'm flattered, but I'm not nearly pretty enough to make a grown man enter a schoolhouse."

"Maybe not, but there's some mighty big boys who'll be showing up. Aunt Ethel says they can be trouble."

"You're a big boy, but you don't seem to be having any trouble being around me."

Tardy dropped his gaze to his booted feet. "Aunt Ethel says I'm so lazy I can't find the energy to be attracted to a pretty girl. She says no normal boy would be as worthless as me."

Tanzy didn't know Tardy well enough to know whether he deserved his nickname, but she did know no child deserved to be told he was worthless. She'd been forced to swallow that lesson from as far back as she could remember, and she hadn't liked it one bit. Women expected to be told they were no good for anything except keeping house and making babies, but a boy was expected to grow into a man. If he didn't measure up to the standards, his failure would be thrown in his face his whole life.

"Your aunt can't think you're useless if she believes you can protect me from rough cowhands and big miners," Tanzy said. "That would be a big job for a man. It's an extra big job for a boy."

They walked side by side past the last buildings along the dusty path leading to the schoolhouse.

"She doesn't believe I can do it," Tardy said, his gaze still on his feet. "She didn't have nobody else to ask."

"Well, I believe you can do it," Tanzy said. "I also believe you can help me make sure the first day goes well. I need you to tell me what the last teacher taught you. After that you can tell me about the students, especially the ones you think might cause trouble."

Tanzy was pleased to learn the last teacher had emphasized reading, history, and math. She wasn't pleased to learn he'd been driven away by the bullying of the bigger students.

Sunlight streaming through the widows made the schoolhouse less gloomy than it had been the previous afternoon. The ribs of the building were exposed, as were the doves that had built nests among the rafters.

The first students to arrive were the youngest. They came in twos and threes, brothers and sisters, neighbors and friends, all eying her circumspectly as they chose a desk and took a seat. The older girls came next. On the surface they were just as quiet and respectful, but Tanzy could see them weighing her, trying to decide what kind of teacher she'd be, what she'd expect from them.

Then the older boys arrived.

There were only three, but Tanzy could tell from the nervous looks of the young students and the expectant looks of the older girls, they all thought something would happen.

"Those are the boys I was telling you about," Tardy whispered.

"I guessed as much," Tanzy replied. "You'd better take your seat."

"But my aunt said—"

"I can deal with them," Tanzy said.

The boys slowly ambled toward the front, the biggest ogling Tanzy in an open manner. Tanzy held his gaze. Tardy said he was seventeen and considered himself a man. His buddies attempted to ape his movements, but Tanzy could tell they weren't comfortable with such an open display of disrespect.

"So you're the new teacher," the boy said.

"So you're Jem Bridger," Tanzy replied.

Jem showed surprise that she knew his name before breaking into a self-satisfied smile. "So you've heard of me," he said with a slight swagger.

"Yes. I've heard of Jody and Cub, too. And Allison, Emma, Sally, and Marvin," Tanzy added before he could attach any significance to her knowing his name.

Looking a bit sheepish, Jem's friends sought the safety of their seats, but he made a valiant recovery. "I've heard about you. You're a mail-order bride. You were supposed to marry Russ Tibbolt."

"We decided we wouldn't suit, so I took the position of schoolteacher," Tanzy replied, deciding it was best if all the children learned what had happened from her rather than from gossip.

"Are you in the market for a replacement?"

Tanzy found it ludicrous Jem could believe she would think of him in the same breath as Russ.

"No, I'm not."

"You'll be mighty lonely on a long, summer evening. Could be you'd be grateful for some company."

One of the girls giggled, then clamped her hand to her mouth, her guilty gaze fixed on Tanzy.

"Are you offering yourself?" Tanzy asked Jem.

He preened. "I'm a busy man, but I might be able to spare a little time now and then."

"Let me see how you stack up compared to Mr. Tibbolt," Tanzy said.

She put her hand to her chin as though she were giving the question serious thought. She looked Jem up and down even more throughly than he had inspected her. She frowned, shook her head, then walked a circle around him. Her frown deepened and her tongue clicked in her mouth. As the silence lengthened, Jem's confidence began to ebb.

"I need another look," Tanzy said and slowly circled him a second time, her *tut, tuts* of disapproval falling with deafening weight into the silence. Jem grew increasingly uncomfortable. A snicker from one of the girls did nothing to bolster his confidence.

"What do you think, Miss Gallant?" one of the girls asked, a pretty blonde she'd been told was the object of Jem's attention. The girl's expression was mischief all over.

"I appreciate your offering to help relieve my boredom," Tanzy said to Jem, "but you don't measure up to my standards."

Jem looked stunned. "I'm better looking than any of these dummies."

"Possibly, but I turned down Mr. Tibbolt, not one of these *dummies.*"

"He's nothing but a thieving killer," Jem said.

"A woman looking for company on a soft summer night might not care too much about that."

"Why not?"

"Well, he wouldn't be stealing from me, would he? And he certainly would not want to kill me."

"But I'm—"

"Mr. Tibbolt is the most handsome man around. He's

also taller than you." She stepped close to Jem to emphasize the fact that he was barely taller than she was. "Women like to look up to a man. And I do believe he's got broader shoulders and more heavily muscled arms."

Jem blanched.

"I guess it's not surprising that he's bigger, stronger, and *older*," Tanzy added, "since he owns his own ranch and does the same work as his cowhands. Then there's the matter of courage."

"You saying I'm a coward?" Jem sputtered, completely shaken by the turn his little joke had taken.

"I don't know anything about you, but Mr. Tibbolt captured two bandits by himself. Thanks for the offer of your company, Jem, but I'll have to decline. Please take your seat."

Tanzy turned her back on Jem, hoping he would go quietly to his seat so she could start her lessons.

"Are you saying you prefer an ex-con to me?"

"I haven't stated any preference, but were I to do so, I'd prefer a man to a boy. Now please take your seat."

He might have done what she asked if someone hadn't snickered. "I don't need to be locked up with children and little girls," he said angrily. "I'm already a man."

He turned on his heel and walked out. Tanzy expected his friends to follow him, but they remained in their seats, heads down.

"Good morning," Tanzy said, addressing the students for the first time. "My name is Miss Gallant. I will be your teacher. Since I don't know where you are in your work, I'll need to test you. Please take out your slates and do the times tables through twelve. Don't worry if you don't know all of them," she said when the younger children started to look panicked. "I just want to know where to start. While you're doing that, I'm going to ask each of you to read for me. Tardy Benton, why don't you come first?"

Some of the girls giggled.

"Sorry, I should have used your proper name," Tanzy said.

"No point," Tardy said, as he got up and shuffled to the front. "Everybody but Aunt Ethel calls me Tardy."

Barely fifteen minutes had passed when the school-house door opened with a bang and Jem entered, followed by a woman Tanzy assumed must be his mother.

"He's to be in school every day," the lady said, shoving him toward an empty desk and pushing him down into it. "You let me know if he's not. Did he give you any sass this morning?" It was obvious Jem expected Tanzy to tell on him.

"None of the students have been a problem," Tanzy said.

Mrs. Bridger appeared skeptical. "Well, you let me know if he does. I don't tolerate his showing disrespect."

"I'm sure he wouldn't do that," Tanzy said.

Mrs. Bridger harrumphed in a manner that said she didn't believe Tanzy was up to the job and took her leave.

"It's your turn to read," Tanzy said to Jem. He came to the front, his attitude still defiant.

"Why didn't you tell on me?"

"I expect you were just testing me," Tanzy said. "I hope I passed the test."

"We'll see," Jem muttered.

A sigh of relief escaped Tanzy as the last students left the schoolhouse. "You don't have to wait today," she said to Tardy. "I can get back to the hotel safely by myself."

"But Aunt Ethel said—"

"It's been a whole week and everything has gone smoothly. You don't need to watch out for me anymore."

"Aunt Ethel will break my head if I don't stay."

"I'll tell her I wouldn't let you stay. Now go. If you hurry, you can catch up with your friends."

Tanzy pretended not to notice when Tardy blushed.

"I don't have any friends. The kids think I'm a half-wit. Hell, who am I kidding? *Everybody* thinks I'm a half-wit."

"I don't," Tanzy said, "and I'll quite happily speak to anyone who does. You read as well as anybody in school, you know as much math as I do, and you can remember history better than anybody I ever met."

"People in Boulder Gap don't care about book learning," Tardy said. "If I had my own ranch like Mr. Tibbolt, they wouldn't care if I was as dumb as Jem."

"Mr. Tibbolt's ranch hasn't made people like him, so maybe you're better off just as you are."

"They may not like him, but they respect him."

Tardy's statement surprised Tanzy. "Why do you say that? All the people I've met have done their best to convince me not to marry him."

"They respect him because he stands up for himself against Mr. Pullet, against the whole town if need be. Nobody but Mr. Tibbolt ever has. They hate him for it, but they respect him, too."

Tanzy understood that. Nobody likes the man who shows up the weaknesses of others, particularly when he compounds the injury by *not* throwing it in anyone's face.

"Everybody likes you," Tardy said. "If you was to marry Mr. Tibbolt, they'd be hard pressed to turn their backs on him. Besides, everybody knows Mr. Pullet doesn't want you to marry Mr. Tibbolt. If you stood up to him—you being a woman and all—the women would have to stick with you. That would make Mr. Pullet mad, and nobody wants that."

"Apparently it's a good thing for the people of Boulder Gap I've decided not to marry Mr. Tibbolt," Tanzy said with some asperity. "I'd sure hate to force them to start behaving like decent human beings."

Tardy laughed. "I'd sure like to see them choking on their words."

"Go home, Tardy. I don't want to speak disrespectfully of the people who've entrusted me with their children's education, but if we continue this conversation, I just might."

After he left, Tanzy sat puzzling over why a town would hate a man who seemed to be the embodiment of the western ideal. She realized she didn't know the *real* history of Russ's relationship with the town any more than she knew what caused Tardy to be perpetually late. She knew it was intentional because he had never been late for her.

A sound outside the schoolhouse startled her. She looked at her watch, amazed to see she'd been sitting at her desk for nearly an hour without doing any of the work she'd stayed behind to do. Well, she'd have to do it tomorrow. It would be dark soon. She had no desire to be walking about town after dusk.

The sound of the schoolhouse door opening caused a frisson of apprehension to race down her spine. Rather than fade when she saw Russ framed in the doorway, it transformed itself into a quiver of excitement. She didn't like to think that the mere sight of Russ Tibbolt could instantly charge her body with surplus nervous energy, but she couldn't find another reason for the sudden tautness that aroused her body to full alert.

She needed him to leave. She could empathize with his plight, be angry that the townspeople appeared to be treating him unfairly because of their fear of Pullet's retaliation, but none of that was her concern.

"There's nobody here," she said. "Whoever you're looking for has been gone for over an hour."

"What would I be doing looking for a student?" he asked as he came inside and closed the door behind him.

"Since I know nothing of your affairs, I couldn't possibly answer that question." She wanted him to leave, not walk toward her. "What are you doing here?"

"I've come to see you."

"Why?" She couldn't see his expression. The sunlight coming through the window blinded her to everything beyond its reach. "Have you come to make sure I have a job so I can pay you back the money you spent on me?"

"No."

She didn't believe him. She was surprised he hadn't checked on her before now. "I have this job until the town finds a new teacher. Since the parents seem satisfied with my work so far, they aren't looking very hard. I should be able to repay you in a couple of months."

It annoyed her that he didn't go away, that he remained in the shadows. More important, it disconcerted her that she didn't need to see his face to feel the effect of his presence. Merely hearing his voice was enough to call forth a clear memory of the man who'd sat across the table from her that first evening, dust and blood staining his clothes without detracting from the animal magnetism that had aroused in her a sensual response unlike anything she'd ever experienced. She wanted it to stop. She didn't want to experience it again. Nothing good could come of it.

"How do you like teaching school?" he asked.

"I can't say yet."

"You've been doing it for a week."

"I'm still too busy trying to figure out what to do. Every student is in a different place, and I don't have enough teaching materials to work with."

"Tell Ethel Peters. She'll see you get something."

"Why do you speak so highly of Miss Peters? You've got to know she warned me not to marry you."

"Ethel's feelings toward me are based on her sense of what is right and wrong. She doesn't know the information they're based on is all a lie."

"It's a shame you can't be as forgiving with Stocker. If you could, that might put an end to the feud."

"We're not having a feud. And even if Stocker could forgive me, I could never forgive him."

"What did he do that's so terrible?"

"That's my business."

She hadn't expected him to be so blunt, but her refusal to marry him had broken the only link between them. He had no reason to share confidences with her.

"Forgive me for being so inquisitive. I've always wondered why people do the things they do. I call it curiosity. Others probably call it nosiness."

"If you don't want to marry me, why should you be curious about me?"

"Nothing I've heard about you has led me to believe you're given to asking stupid questions."

"Why is it stupid?"

"Come out of the shadows. I don't like talking to a man I can't see."

"Do I make you nervous?"

"No." It wasn't exactly a lie because he didn't *exactly* make her nervous. Her feeling was more like apprehension mixed with anticipation. Physical attraction she could understand, but this feeling that there was a connection between them was ridiculous as well as hard on her peace of mind. She tried to tell herself to stop being fanciful, but talking to herself didn't do any good. She had to face the simple fact that something about this man affected her as no other had.

"I just don't like people hiding in the dark," she said. "It was men hiding in the trees at night who killed my father and brothers."

"How many brothers did you have?"

"Four."

"How many died?"

"All of them."

He didn't answer for a moment. "What about your mother?"

"She's dead."

"Any sisters?"

"No."

"Why didn't you stay in St. Louis?"

"I discovered men there were too much like the men in Kentucky."

"Surely there was at least one man in St. Louis who would have offered you a respectable marriage."

"No man—at least not the ones I met in St. Louis—believes a woman who works in a gambling hall is respectable."

"So you came west thinking we were different?"

"Only to discover that men are the same everywhere."

"That must have been a disappointment."

"I'll get over it. I've got to be going before it gets dark, so tell me what you're doing here."

Russ stepped forward out of the shadows. "I want you to teach me how to read."

Chapter Eight

Tanzy was tired, cranky, and feeling the stress of trying to control her reaction to Russ. "I don't know whether you're angry that I won't marry you or whether you think it's fun to bait the schoolteacher, but I'm in no mood for jokes. If your presence has a purpose, state it."

"I just did. I want you to teach me to read."

If losing her temper would have done any good, Tanzy would gladly have done so. "You had to be able to read my letters to write yours to me."

"I didn't write those letters. I didn't read them either. Welt Aldred, one of my cowhands, wrote all of them."

"He wrote them for you?"

Russ looked a little uneasy. "Not exactly."

Tanzy was losing patience. "Then what exactly did happen?"

"Welt read the letters and wrote the answers."

"You mean he wrote what you told him to write?"

"No."

"If this is the clearest you can express yourself, no wonder people in Boulder Gap don't understand you. What are you talking about?"

"I'd better start at the beginning."

Tanzy sank into her chair. "Maybe you'd better."

"I wasn't looking for a wife. No young woman here would have married me if I asked."

Tanzy had a strong feeling that more than one young woman would have gladly braved parental anger, as well as the wrath of Stocker Pullet, to have a husband like Russ. No woman could think straight when he was around. The physical attraction alone was enough to cloud a girl's thinking. When he looked into her eyes like she was the only person in the world, nothing else mattered. When he smiled . . . well, there was no way to describe his smile except to say most any woman would sell her soul to have its warmth for the rest of her life.

"Welt kept telling me I needed a wife. I didn't pay any attention to him until he told me you were on your way to Boulder City, that he'd already sent you the money. I was mad as hell at him, but there was nothing I could do to stop you."

Tanzy was in shock. He hadn't wanted her to come to Boulder City. He hadn't wanted to marry her. All the heat that had been building inside her turned to anger. "Why did you let me come all the way out here knowing you weren't going to marry me?"

"There was nothing I could do. Breaking Welt's head—which I nearly did in any case—wouldn't stop you. I went to meet the stage to tell you to turn around and go back to St. Louis."

"Then you got more interested in playing the hero and capturing the bandits than saving my feelings."

"By the time I found you at the hotel, everybody knew why you were here. I figured at that point it would be best to let you decide you didn't want to marry me. With everybody telling you I was a lying, thieving murderer, I figured you'd head back east on the first stage."

Tanzy suddenly realized what he'd said. "You *are* a liar! You didn't send me the money to come out here. I don't owe you anything."

"I'm afraid you do. I repaid Welt."

Tanzy was so furious, she itched to throw anything she

could get her hands on. Responsibility for this whole debacle rested with Welt, but she couldn't work up a real temper against this unknown cowhand. If Russ hadn't been such an outcast, somebody in Boulder Gap would have married him and his cowhands wouldn't have had to go looking for a mail-order bride. If he'd been paying attention to what his cowhands were doing, he'd have known Welt was up to no good. And if he hadn't been so brave and handsome, she wouldn't have liked him from the start. She was humiliated, and it was all his fault. She opened her mouth to blister him with both sides of her tongue, then abruptly closed it again.

"Why aren't you yelling at me?" Russ asked. "I expected you'd be calling me every name you could think of."

"I have a confession to make," Tanzy said. "I didn't write my letters, either."

She expected Russ would be angry with her, but his look of surprise was quickly replaced by a grin. No sooner did that happen than his eyes began to twinkle and he started to laugh. She couldn't see anything funny. The whole thing was a horrible mistake. And all he could do—this brave, handsome man who was so sexy sensible women would want to marry him even knowing they courted disaster—all he could do was laugh. She had to be crazy *not* to throw something at him.

"Who wrote your letters?" Russ asked when he stopped laughing.

"A girl I worked with in the gambling hall."

"Why?"

"Both of us were too naive to realize what looked like a good job was in fact a permanent bar to respectability. When it became clear that every man who saw us figured he could have us for a price, she offered herself as a mail-order bride and encouraged me to do the same. I still wouldn't have considered it if the owner of the gambling hall hadn't threatened to fire me if I wasn't more *friendly* toward the customers. Then I got a letter from my friend saying she was deliriously happy with her marriage and I decided to meet you at least."

"Two people who didn't want to get married," Russ said, "and look what a mess we got ourselves into."

"I wasn't set against marriage," Tanzy said.

"Until you met me."

Tanzy couldn't characterize the look on his face. At first glance he seemed unaffected. After all, he had no reason to care what a stranger thought of him.

Yet there was something in his expression that defied her ability to characterize it. It couldn't have been vulnerability. The man was as impregnable as the mountains around him. She'd never seen him express a soft emotion. If he'd ever had any, they'd probably been beaten out of him by five years in prison. He hadn't put it into words, but she believed he might be trying to apologize for his part in what had happened to her.

"Not all our plans are meant to work out," she said, pulling herself back from the brink of wanting to explain that she didn't share the town's feeling toward him. There was no possibility of any relationship between them. It was simpler to leave things as they were. "I'm sure you'll find some woman who'll make you a perfect wife."

"Not unless I do what everyone in Boulder Gap prays for daily—go somewhere else. But I didn't come here to talk about me. I came to ask you to teach me to read."

"I find it hard to believe a man as intelligent and successful as you can't read."

"I can read the names of things I need, like flour and coffee, boots or saddles, and names of places, like the bank and the saloon. I know how to sign my name and recognize signatures. But if I wanted to buy some land, I couldn't read the contract. I can't read the breeding of a bull advertised for sale or the directions to the ranch where I could get a look at him."

"What do you do?"

"I get into a discussion with people, ask their opinions, pose questions that give me the information I need."

"Wouldn't it have been easier to learn to read?"

"Probably, but I wasn't wise enough to see that."

"So why do you see the necessity now?"

"Those letters. If I'd been able to write, they'd never have been written. If I had read your replies, I'd have known you weren't suited to be a rancher's wife."

"So you want to avoid anything like this again?"

"I'll never do anything like this again, but it has shown me I can get into real trouble by not being able to read things for myself."

Tanzy didn't want to teach Russ to read. It was impossible to be around him for more than five minutes without wondering what it would be like to be married to him. Despite what the people of Boulder Gap said about him, there was a strength in Russ that was very appealing, very reassuring. If the hatred of the community was a barometer of his success, his accomplishments had been remarkable. She also had to admire a man who could inspire so much loyalty in his friends that one of them would do his best to find him a wife. Why didn't the people of Boulder Gap realize there was something very important about Russ they'd missed?

She tried to imagine what it was like to live in a community that didn't want you, to face hostility and open condemnation from nearly everyone you met. It had to take a tremendous amount of courage, a bedrock conviction you were right, and the stubbornness to hold your course regardless of what people said or did. It took courage to stand up to the slander, not to let it beat you down, to keep believing you were doing the right thing.

She had left her home rather than face her nemesis. Russ had come back home to face his every day.

"If you're trying to figure out a way to say you won't do it, just spit it out," Russ said.

"It's not that. It's—"

"Are you afraid you'll lose your job?"

She hadn't even thought of that. "Would they fire me for teaching you?"

"They might."

"They don't have anybody else to teach their children."

"They may hate me so much they won't care."

Tanzy's hesitation vanished without a trace. "I'll do what I can to help, but I can't do it while the children are here. You would be too much of a distraction."

"Their parents would run us both out of town before they'd let me have that much contact with their daughters."

She hadn't thought of that. If other women felt as she did, and she was certain they did, it was probably wise for parents to keep their daughters well away from Russ Tibbolt. She didn't believe he would take advantage of a young girl's innocence, but there was no assurance the young girl would be equally restrained.

"Why didn't you ask Welt to teach you?" She couldn't imagine why she hadn't thought of that in the first place. It just went to show she couldn't think clearly when she was near him. "He's right there on your ranch. He could work with you every day without your having to ride so far."

Russ's face stiffened, the light in his eyes became hard

as stone. Even the muscles in his jaw seemed to tense and bulge. "Welt doesn't know I can't read," he said. "Nobody knows."

Only then did Tanzy begin to understand how much courage it had required for a proud man like Russ to admit he couldn't read. "What made you decide you couldn't keep your secret any longer?"

"You."

"Me! How?"

"It took a lot of courage to come out here to meet a man you didn't know, to subject yourself to his approval, to know you'd be on your own if things didn't work out."

"Not half as much as it must take to face this town every day."

"I'd like to keep this secret. Admitting I can't read will give folks a real reason to look down on me."

"I imagine there are others who can't read either."

"It doesn't matter, because they're solid citizens. I'm an ex-con. Any fault they can find in me will just prove they were right to despise me."

"You're too smart for it to take long to learn to read. No one will have to know."

"How will you explain my coming to the schoolhouse?"

"We can meet at the hotel."

"Where? In your room? That would be even worse."

She racked her brain, but she couldn't think of a solution off hand. "We can think of something."

"Don't worry about it. Secrets always manage to leak out. This one will, too, especially if we have a chaperone."

"Why would we need one?"

"Your reputation would never survive being alone with me."

He moved for the first time since stepping out of the shadows and came closer. Tanzy could practically feel the heat generated by his presence. She had to make a conscious effort not to get up so she could put more space between them.

"I don't care about that."

"You will. When is the best time for me to come?"

After school would have been the logical time, but that would assure that everyone would know what he was doing. "I think coming before school starts would be best."

"Get me out of sight before the students show up?"

"I was thinking of your comfort rather than mine."

He seemed to feel admonished. Maybe he wasn't as impregnable as he appeared.

"I'd hate for you to have to get up so early."

"I prefer it." She laughed suddenly. "I wonder if Tardy will, though."

"What's he got to do with it?"

"He'll be our chaperone unless you prefer someone else."

"When can I start?"

"Why not now?"

"What about a chaperone?"

"A single visit isn't likely to cause comment." She handed him a reader used by the younger children. "Show me which words you recognize."

"Where's Tardy?" Tanzy asked when Russ entered the schoolhouse alone the next morning.

"Archie said he took sick last night," Russ said. He walked briskly to the front where Tanzy sat waiting at her table. He put down a piece of paper with some writing on it. "He had his head hung over the back fence throwing up his dinner, but Ethel expects he'll be okay by tomorrow."

"Why did you come?"

"I was already here. Besides," he said pointing to the paper, "I wrote something."

It had taken just one lesson for Tanzy to realize Russ knew a great deal more than he thought. He could puzzle out many sentences with only minimal help. He had an excellent memory, and in only two lessons had learned enough to read simple sentences. She hoped he wasn't memorizing the words rather than sounding them out.

"When do you find time to study?" she asked, knowing he didn't want his cowhands to know he couldn't read.

"I assign myself lookout duty twice a week. That means I'm stuck in the mountain pass with nothing to do but watch for rustlers." He grinned. "For the past three weeks my horse has been doing more watching than I have."

She was no more immune to his smile now than she had been in the beginning. The fact that Tardy commented last week that it was the first time he'd ever see Russ smile made it even more significant.

He smiled because of her.

She was probably the only woman in Boulder Gap who didn't screw up her face into a frown when she met him. He could relax and be more like himself with her. And that was part of the problem. She liked the man she'd seen in her classroom the last three Wednesday mornings. He got angry when he couldn't master everything the first time, but he also laughed at his mistakes. He even relaxed enough to let Tardy work with him. When Russ finally allowed Tardy to help him, the boy's chest swelled with pride. The look in his eyes was almost hero worship. Tanzy knew Ethel wouldn't approve, but she was glad for Tardy.

She was less glad for herself. She was a little jealous, a little peeved, and quite disgusted she should feel either of these emotions. She shouldn't be jealous of the time Russ spent with Tardy. The excuse she'd made up for coming to school so early was that she needed to prepare for her students. If Tardy helped Russ, that would give her time to do exactly that. Now she had Russ all to herself and she was wishing Tardy hadn't been so foolish as to fall sick. She wasn't going to be happy either way, apparently

"Here," he said, pointing to the paper he laid on her desk. "Read what I wrote."

Correcting it would give her something to take her mind off the fact that she was alone with Russ and that her reaction was alarming.

> *Roses are red, violets are blue,*
> *Wherever I go, I'll take you, too.*

She looked up at Russ. "Why did you write this?" He couldn't have meant it for her. He'd said he didn't want to marry her. Though he'd been extremely nice to her, he'd done nothing to indicate he'd changed his mind.

"It was something my mother used to say all the time." His expression was grim. "She didn't mean it. I don't know why I thought of it. I guess it made me think of you."

Her stomach lurched. "Why?"

"If you had a son, you'd never turn your back on him, would you?"

The meaning of his words was obvious. His dark

expression eliminated any doubt he might be referring to somebody other than himself. She didn't know what to say. Her father had never valued her except as a work-horse, but he'd have defended her to the death.

"No," she said, feeling the weight of his sadness. "I can't see how any woman could."

"It depends on what you value most."

"I value people I love above everything else," she said.

"That's why you refused to marry me, so your husband and sons wouldn't die in a feud. Or go to jail for killing Stocker Pullet."

"It was one reason."

"What was the other?"

"Why does it matter?"

"Call it pride. You're a sensible, intelligent woman. I figure you had a good reason. I expect it's something I ought to know, maybe something I need to change."

"So you can marry somebody else?"

"Maybe. Or maybe you'll figure out I'm not having a feud and you'll change your mind about marrying me."

Tanzy wished she'd insisted they cancel the lesson when Tardy didn't show up. This was exactly the kind of conversation she had hoped to avoid.

"I won't change my mind about the feud."

"Nobody's shooting at anybody."

"You and Stocker can't meet without getting into a fight. That's how hatred feeds on itself until it consumes everyone around it."

"It hasn't consumed me."

"It has Stocker."

"That's Stocker's problem."

"Would it be your problem if he killed some of your hands?"

"We've got laws and courts to take care of things like that."

"Like they took care of you when you killed Toley Pullet?"

"If you're not careful, you can end up wasting your life being afraid of things that'll never happen."

"Maybe, but there are some things I'm not willing to take a chance on, and feuding is one of them. You can't know what that's like until you've lived through it."

"So what's your other reason?" Russ asked.

Chapter Nine

"You don't have any respect for women."

Her answer surprised Russ. He'd shown her more respect than any woman he'd ever met. Hell, he'd put her up in a hotel for a week even though he'd never wanted her to come to Boulder Gap. He hadn't told her she was crazy when she decided she couldn't marry him because he was having a feud. He hadn't told her no sensible man would marry her because she hadn't the foggiest notion how to be a rancher's wife. Most of all, he'd told her he couldn't read. She could have spread the information all over town, turned him into a laughing stock.

"Of course, I do. You know I think Ethel Peters is the most remarkable person in Boulder Gap."

"Would you marry her?"

"Hell, no!"

"Why not?"

"Inside of a week she'd be running my ranch as well as

my house and my life. I'd probably have to shoot her to get my own life back." Much to Russ's surprise, Tanzy laughed.

"I gather you don't like competent women."

"I don't care what any woman does as long as she's not my wife."

"What kind of wife do you want?"

"I've already told you I don't want a wife. The boys and I are getting along just fine as it is."

"Is that the reason you didn't want to marry me?"

Russ didn't know why women couldn't just accept things as they were, why they were forever asking questions. They wanted to know what you liked, what you didn't like . . . and why. They wanted to know how you felt about things . . . and why. They wanted to know if you were happy or unhappy . . . and why. And once they pried all the whys and wherefores out of a fella, they would set about trying to fix things. Hell, wasn't a fella allowed to wake up grouchy, not want to visit with his neighbor, or be just plain mad at the world in general without them setting up an inquisition? He didn't want to know all the garbage that filled people's heads. He couldn't see why women wanted to, either. Even the best of them were always planning and plotting. It was like living in the middle of a conspiracy.

"Are you going to answer me?" Tanzy asked.

"No."

"Why not?"

"You're asking for personal information."

Tanzy looked a bit surprised, then embarrassed. That was something else about women. They wanted to know everything about you, for your own good, of course. As far as he was concerned, people knew too much about everybody.

"I wasn't asking for personal information," Tanzy said. "I assumed your reasons were general."

"Like saying I don't respect women?"

"Something like that."

"But I'd have to have some personal experience to base that on, wouldn't I? I mean, it's stupid to go around not respecting one half of the population without a reason."

"I wasn't asking for your personal experience, just your reason."

"I don't trust women."

She looked surprised. "You mean that's your reason for not marrying me?"

"For not marrying any woman."

He knew she wanted to ask for his reason. He could see it in her eyes. He watched her lips form the beginning of one word after another without speaking any of them. He watched as she gathered herself and prepared to go on as though nothing had happened.

"Thank you for telling me. It's a relief to know your decision wasn't based upon some deficiency in me."

Apparently she didn't think she was like other women. He supposed nobody liked to think they were like other people, especially when the similarity implied they had faults.

"Let's hear what you've done this week."

Russ pulled out the book and turned to the pages he'd practiced. He read everything without a mistake.

"Do you really know the words, or have you just memorized all six pages?" Tanzy asked.

"I make myself write words all the time to make sure I remember what they look like. That's why I wrote those lines."

"Good. I want you to write something else for next week. Something a lot longer."

"What?"

"Whatever you want, anything that comes to mind."

"It's easy to write a word I've had in a reading. But when I try to write what I'm thinking, I find I haven't learned all the words I need."

"Just leave out the ones you can't remember. Now are you ready to read?"

This was the part of his lesson Russ liked best. Tanzy would open a book just like his and read a story while he followed along. When she finished, he would ask her about any words he didn't know, and then she'd read it again. Sometimes he'd ask her to read the passage a third time. Then he was supposed to go home and learn all the words. He didn't need her to read anything three times. He could memorize pages and pages if he was really paying attention. He asked her to read things over because he liked the sound of her voice.

It sounded stupid to get out of bed in the middle of the night and ride two hours in the dark just to listen to a woman read. His liking for Tanzy's voice was a weakness, but he *did* want to learn to read. Ranching wasn't always going to be about who could hire more gunfighters. Soon it would be about the quality of the beef and efficient management, and Russ knew he had to be able to read if he was going to succeed.

However, Russ was too honest to talk himself into believing he was here just because reading would make him a better rancher. He was here because of Tanzy. And he would keep coming until he figured out what kind of hold she had on him.

Any fool could see she was pretty. There was something about her that would attract any man's attention. It was hard to describe it, but a man could see it the moment he clapped eyes on her. It was femininity, whatever that was. The very essence of what it meant to be a woman had been distilled in her. She wasn't the most beautiful woman in the world and she wasn't the sexiest, at least what was usually considered sexy. No, it was a quiet kind of sexiness, the subtle kind.

Like her voice.

It was quiet and soft, yet it had strength and clarity. There was a fullness to it that caressed the words, rounded out the sounds, caused them to fall gently on the ear. It was sensual in a way that made him aware of his senses, the temperature of the air around him, the fragrances in it, even the muted sounds from the outside. It softened colors and intensified sensations. It made him more in touch with his world and more detached at the same time.

"Any questions?" Tanzy asked when she finished.

"A few, but I think I can figure them out if you read it again."

The way she looked at him made him wonder if she knew what he was doing.

He liked to watch her read. There was a quietness about her, a kind of peace that enveloped him as well. Nothing in his life had ever been quiet or peaceful, and he found the sensation too intoxicating to resist. For these few moments he could forget that he was the bastard son his mother never loved. He could just be—

The schoolhouse door banged open. With a reflex action that was so instinctive it happened before he had time to think, Russ threw himself out of the chair, rolled six feet to the left and came to his feet behind a bookcase, his gun drawn and pointed at the figure entering the door.

"I'm sorry I'm late," Tardy said as he hurried toward Tanzy, "but Aunt Ethel said I had to stay in bed today. She locked me in, so I had to crawl out the window."

Russ turned to Tanzy, who was staring at him. His reaction had reinforced all her suspicions about the feud. Tardy broke into a wide grin when he turned to Russ.

"I never saw anybody move so fast. Did you think I was Stocker?"

"One of the rustlers," Russ said, holstering his gun and moving back to the center of the room.

"Maybe they don't know you've got the best gun hands in the territory working for you," Tardy said.

"I've got *cowhands*," Russ said.

"Mr. Pullet thinks they're gun hands," Tardy said. "I heard him telling the sheriff he ought to arrest them as a public hazard."

"He can't arrest them as long as they don't leave my ranch," Russ said.

"That's what the sheriff told him. Mr. Pullet said he might see about finding a different sheriff."

"What did the sheriff say?" Tanzy asked.

"He said that was all right with him, that he was tired of being told how to do his job. He suggested that Mr. Pullet talk to Colonel McGregor at Fort Lookout, but Colonel McGregor has already told him he's here to deal with the Indians, not meddle with feuding neighbors. Mr. Pullet got so mad the colonel had him escorted off the fort and told him not to come back. Mr. Pullet said he'd write the government and get him posted to the backside of nowhere. The colonel said Boulder Gap *was* the backside of nowhere."

Russ wondered if knowing this would help convince Tanzy that any continuation of the hostilities was Stocker's doing.

"You done with your lesson?" Tardy asked.

"Guess so," Russ said. He wasn't in the mood to continue, and he doubted Tanzy was, either.

"He did well," Tanzy said to Tardy. "You helped him a lot last week."

"I didn't do nothing," Tardy said, yet still looked pleased at the compliment. "He learns stuff as fast as I can tell him."

Learning words was easy. It was learning how to get along in life that was the problem. It seemed everything he did either turned out wrong or landed him in a heap of trouble. He'd come back from prison with three promises to himself.

First, he was going back to Boulder Gap to prove he was a model citizen, not the thieving ex-con everybody thought. That had come to nothing when Stocker made it his business to see that nobody would give him a chance.

Second, he'd made up his mind to build a ranch on land nobody else wanted with cows nobody claimed. That had been fine until Stocker realized he had the best grass in the area.

The third promise was that he'd steer clear of women. That all went to hell when Welt brought Tanzy to Boulder Gap. How did a guy with so many good intentions go so far wrong?

Now he'd decided to do something sensible—learn to read—only to find he liked being around Tanzy. He was an intelligent, determined, practical, logical man. So if he could just figure out what kind of hold Tanzy had on him, he could get rid of it, explain it away, or just outright ignore it.

"You'd better go," Tanzy said. "The children will start coming soon."

"Yeah. If Jem sees you here, he'll tell everybody in town."

"Why?" Russ asked.

"He's sweet on Miss Gallant," Tardy said, grinning.

Russ turned to Tanzy, who flushed uncomfortably. Could she possibly be interested in Jem? They were close in age, but he'd never thought of Tanzy as a girl.

"That's ridiculous," Tanzy said, turning to Russ, then back to Tardy. "I've never done anything that could possibly make him think I was interested in him that way."

"He says you're the best-looking single female around, and he's the best-looking boy. He says it's only natural for the two of you to hook up. He says that's the only reason he's still coming to school."

"He's here because his mother makes him come," Tanzy said.

"I wouldn't worry about it too much," Russ said. "It's only natural for boys to think they're in love with a young, pretty schoolteacher."

"Were you ever in love with your teacher?" Tardy asked.

"I didn't go to school."

"I guess that's why you didn't learn to read."

Russ was annoyed that Jem was mooning over her. Had she made it really clear she wasn't interested in schoolboys? Jem's father owned a successful business transporting supplies between Denver and Boulder Gap. He made a still greater profit transporting supplies to Fort Lookout. Any woman who married Jem would be assured of a comfortable future. Russ wanted to believe such a thought had never crossed Tanzy's mind, but he couldn't be sure.

It made him furious he even cared. When he got back to the ranch, he was going to break Welt's head all over again. If Welt had minded his own business, Russ wouldn't be bothering himself with anything as foolish as whether or not Tanzy was making eyes at a boy who was still wet behind the ears.

"The children are coming," Tanzy said.

Russ knew he'd agreed to be gone before the children arrived, but it irritated him that she sounded so anxious to get rid of him.

"You can go out the back way," Tardy said. "They'll never see you if you duck behind the bushes along the creek."

It was clear from Tanzy's expression that she expected him to slink out of the schoolhouse like a guilty fox with his tail between his legs. It infuriated him, but it was his own fault for hanging around so long. Damn, you'd think a man could try to learn to read without it turning him into a kind of fugitive. He should have known better. Nothing good ever came of being involved with a woman.

"See you next week," Tardy said as Russ prepared to make a hasty escape. "I promise I won't be sick again."

The boy could save himself the trouble of getting up early. Russ wasn't coming back for any more lessons.

The two men tumbled around the cabin floor, their punches more angry than dangerous, displacing rugs and overturning chairs in their struggle.

"I knew you couldn't read," Welt said to Russ. "That's why I wrote those letters."

"What do you mean I can't read, you lying son-of-a-bitch?" Russ fired back. "I can read as good as you can."

"Maybe you can after a few more lessons—you're a lot smarter than I am—but you're not that good yet."

By the time Russ finished working out some more of

his frustrations, Welt had a second bloody lip and a cut over his eye.

"Feel better now?" Welt asked, breathing hard.

"I won't feel better until I've broken your head for real."

It had all started because Russ came back to the ranch in a foul mood. Since Welt was in a worse mood, their tempers clashed immediately. Questions turned to accusations, and accusations turned to anger. Russ blamed Welt for ever thinking Russ ought to be married. Welt countered that it was stupid for Russ to let what his mother and sister had done ruin his life. Russ shot back that Welt wasn't doing any better forgetting his sister, and Welt responded by saying Russ was wasting a perfectly good opportunity to get himself a perfect wife.

At that point Russ demanded to know what Welt was talking about. Welt, thoroughly angry now, replied that he'd followed Russ when he left the ranch in the middle of the night. He had listened at the schoolhouse door long enough to know Tanzy was teaching Russ to read. At that point the tempers of both men boiled over.

"Why didn't you say something before?" Russ asked, between gasps for breath.

"Are you kidding?" Welt asked as he pushed Russ off him and rolled away without getting up off the floor. "You'd have beaten the hell out of me."

"I still might."

"No, you won't. You've managed to tell two people you can't read. Me knowing isn't going to make any difference."

"Breaking your head will make me feel better."

"You just about did," Welt said, touching his bleeding lip. "Tim's going to know we've been fighting again. He'll want to know why."

"You tell him I can't read and I *will* bust your head."

"He'll think it's about Tanzy."

Russ punched the air with his fist. "Why should he think that?"

"Because you've been in a lousy mood ever since she got here. Besides, he knows you've been sneaking into town."

"Is there anybody who doesn't know everything I've been doing?"

"Not anybody on this ranch. You taught all of us how to find out everything that's going on around us. You can't blame us if we use those skills on you."

Yeah, he could. He could blame them a hell of a lot, but it wouldn't do any good. They'd keep right on doing it because they were the best bunch of guys he could ever have work for him. Money couldn't buy the friendship and loyalty they gave him of their own free will. Except for Welt, he'd met these guys in prison. They'd helped each other endure their time. Now Russ was giving them the opportunity to make something of their lives, and they meant to see that nothing went wrong.

Russ got to his feet. "Go dunk your head in the trough. You've got blood all over yourself."

"You put it there."

"Well, go clean up before I spill some more of it."

"What are you really so angry about?" Welt asked.

"I'm just in a bad mood."

"Russ, I've known you since we were boys. You couldn't lie to me then and you can't now."

That was what came of being best friends with a guy for more than twenty years. You practically had to move across the country to keep him from knowing everything about you. Even best friends deserved some privacy.

"If you're so smart, you tell me why I'm in a bad mood," Russ said.

"It's because of that woman."

"If you're right—and I'm not saying you are—then you know why I want to break your head."

"I don't see what's to be upset about. You don't want to marry her."

Russ ran his fingers though his hair and straightened his clothes. "Fix yourself up. You look a mess." He started righting chairs and putting rugs back in place.

"It'll heal up in a couple of days. What's eating you is going to fester until it busts like a boil."

"Then I'll be over it, won't I, so there won't be anything more to worry about."

"I don't think you'll be over it any more than I'm over Adele."

Russ rounded on him in a fury. "Don't you dare compare my irritation with that female to your obsession with my sister. Hell, man, Adele has been dead for more than ten years. When are you going to get over her? She was no good. You can't let her ruin your life."

"It's already ruined. There's nothing I can do about it."

"Sure there is. You can forget her and move back to town."

"I'm not going back to Boulder Gap until that town apologizes for what they did to you."

"Stop talking like a fool."

"You deserve better. That's why I wrote those letters. That's why I sent the money for her to come out here."

"I'm not the marrying kind."

"Sure you are. You just don't know it yet."

"And what makes you think you know me better than I know myself?"

"I've been watching you for more than twenty years. I hear what you say and see what you do, but I also know what you don't say and what you don't do. You're mad as hell about what your mother and sister did, but that doesn't stop you from wanting what they wanted. You want a family so bad you're trying to make do with four lousy cowhands."

"You're nuts. I only put up with you because nobody else is crazy enough to work for me."

"You might fool the others, but you won't fool me. You're trying to take care of us like you would your own family, but sooner or later we'll all get other jobs, get married, drift away, do something. In the end you'll be left alone. You don't want that, and I don't want it for you. There's something about Tanzy you like," Welt insisted. "You used to joke all the time with the boys," he said when Russ opened his mouth to deny it. "I haven't heard you laugh once since she got here."

"Which ought to be proof I want nothing to do with her."

"I might have thought so except for two things."

"And what were they?"

"You were interested in her once you got over being mad at me. I know she's pretty and all that, but there was something else about her that attracted you. I saw a change in you until the day she said she wouldn't marry you."

"No guy likes to be told he's not good enough to be some female's husband."

"You've been in a crappy mood ever since, but that's not what really convinced me she's the woman for you."

"What's that?"

"You told her you couldn't read. Hell, Russ, I've seen you exercise near genius getting people to tell you things you can't read. You never even told me, your best friend, the guy who's known you the longest, but you told her in less than two weeks."

"She's a teacher."

"She's only doing it because she needs a job. I would have helped you, but you never asked."

"Because I was ashamed!" Russ exploded. "There, are you satisfied?"

"No. I won't be until you go back."

"I told you I'm never going back."

Welt stiffened. "I never thought I'd see the day you turned into a coward."

"I could break your neck for calling me that."

"It wouldn't change the fact that you're afraid to face that woman."

"I'm not afraid of her."

"You're right," Welt said, and Russ didn't like the look on his face. "You aren't afraid of her. You're afraid of yourself."

Chapter Ten

"You've written a whole page," Tanzy said.

"Three," Russ said, pulling two more pages from his shirt pocket.

"Damn!" Tardy exclaimed. "I never wrote that much. Can I see it?"

"It's rather personal," Russ said.

"Then why did you write it?"

"Writing things down made them clearer in my mind."

Tanzy's hand paused as she reached for the other two pages. "Are you sure you want me to read it?"

"No, but it would be foolish not to let you."

"It'll take me a little while to read and correct it."

"That's okay. Tardy can read for me."

"Can I pick the story?" Tardy asked.

"Sure," Russ replied.

When Russ missed last week, she hadn't expected to see him again. She certainly wouldn't have guessed he'd show up with three neatly printed pages. It was a good thing the rustlers had disappeared. They could have infiltrated the whole valley in the time it took him to write those pages. She waited until she heard the light baritone of Tardy's voice before beginning to read Russ's composition.

They say going to prison is good for you, that it gives you time to think about what you've done and learn how to live right. But "they" never went to prison, or they'd know it's just about the worst thing that can happen. If you're there because somebody lied, it's even worse. You've got nothing but time to think about what happened and plan how to get even.

There's no good in prison to push away the bad. People are filled with anger, hate, or just pure evil. Even when you try to drive it away, it hides in the corners, seeps in through the cracks, floats in with the stinking air, invades your dreams, and hounds your waking hours. It makes the food you put in your mouth taste sour and bitter.

If you're lucky enough to find someone you can trust, you guard each other's back with your life. You tell yourself you're different from the others, and make plans for when you get out. But you share one thing with every man in that prison. Once you get out, you know you'll do anything to keep from coming back, even face death. Because coming back would be worse than death.

Tanzy was in a state of shock by the time she finished. She felt she'd been given a window into Russ's soul and had seen the anguish of a lonely, impulsive young man sent to prison because of the wrath of a powerful enemy. She didn't know what had caused him to write any of this. She understood even less why he should have allowed her to read it, but it showed he was caught in a dilemma between the person he wanted to be and the one circumstances had forced him to become.

She pulled herself out of the daze long enough to realize the composition was perfect. There was nothing to correct.

She looked up, turned her gaze on him as he worked with Tardy. The scene before her was so peaceful, so wonderful, she was tempted to forget about the feud or his lack of respect for women. What did any of that matter when there was a chance to have such a man for a husband?

There was clearly a gentle, thoughtful side to Russ. He had taken a risk in turning to Tardy for help. The boy could have enjoyed spreading a bit of sensational gossip, but he was turning into a different person right before their eyes. People still made fun of him, but he had started to feel confident enough to make a joke of it.

It wasn't just his kindness to Tardy that was changing Tanzy's opinion of Russ. Though he seemed to be easygoing and soft-spoken when he was with her, there was a tension about him, an alertness that said he never relaxed his vigilance, never let down his guard. It was as though a shadow person stalked the room, ready to respond instantaneously to any threat. It was like living on the edge of a mountain knowing a rock slide that could destroy everything might start at any moment.

Maybe that tension came from having been in prison. It must be awful to have to live that way. She wished there were something she could do to make things better. It was hard to look at a man who was so nearly ideal and not feel she ought to do anything she could to make his life better.

She thought of Tardy's statement that people would have to treat him better if she were his wife. She was startled by the immediate rush of excitement within her. She would gladly do anything she could to help people see Russ in a better light, but surely she couldn't consider that a sufficient reason to marry the man.

Still, she couldn't stop wishing things were different. She wasn't fool enough to think Russ could be changed overnight by the love of a good woman, but she was certain that if he married a woman who loved him and was good to him, especially if it would make the people of Boulder Gap treat him differently, she would bring out parts of him that had been repressed, and he'd gradually become more fully the man he most deeply and truly was. The man who worked hard to make Tardy feel better about himself was a far cry from the lying, thieving killer people believed Russ to be. Tanzy didn't believe two people that different could live inside the same man. One had to be false.

Which one was it?

Tardy looked up from his book. "He can read almost as well as I can," he said to Tanzy.

"I don't know a lot of words," Russ said.

"You never forget anything. I wish I could do that. Maybe then Aunt Ethel wouldn't think I'm an idiot."

"You're not an idiot," Tanzy said. "You're just lazy."

Tardy grinned. "It's easier than being smart. That way people aren't expecting stuff of you all the time."

"I'm expecting a lot of you," Tanzy said. "Get your work ready while I talk to Russ."

He must be wondering how she was going to react to what he had written, but his expression was blank when he approached her.

"There were no mistakes," she said. "That's remarkable."

"Not as much as you think," he said, his expression still neutral. "I had Welt go over it. I wasn't as clever as I thought," he said when she didn't respond. "He's known for years I couldn't read."

She knew she probably shouldn't ask, but she had to know. "Why did you write something so personal for me?"

"I didn't. I wrote it for myself."

"I don't understand."

"Prison was the worst thing that ever happened to me. It also did me a lot of good. Writing that was a way of separating the two. It helps to be able to know that. It keeps you from being bitter."

Tanzy decided she didn't know this man at all. Neither did the people in Boulder Gap. The tragedies of his life had pushed something very fine and wonderful about him into the background. She hoped it wasn't too late to retrieve it.

But who was she to attempt the task? She wasn't going to marry him. Any woman who attempted to tear down the walls he'd built against the censure of the town would have to stay to make sure he survived.

"I'd better be going," Russ said. "The children will be here before long."

She didn't want him to go. She didn't know what to say about what he'd written. It seemed so personal, so beyond her experience, that it would be impertinent to pretend she could understand.

"Will you be here next week?" She wanted to know if he intended to stop coming now that Welt could help him.

"Yes."

"Will you write something else?"

"We'll see. Thank you."

"For what?"

"For not saying anything about what I wrote."

"If you didn't want me to say anything about it, why did you show it to me?"

"So you'd know."

With those words, he seemed to turn into a different person. He was once more the confident, successful, unreachable rancher everybody knew.

He held up the book and waved it at her. "I'm going to finish it this week." He grinned broadly before turning to Tardy. "Don't expect people to act different. People are slow to accept change, even when they like it."

Then he went out the front door, almost defying anyone to see him and ask what he was doing there.

"I always liked Mr. Tibbolt," Tardy said to Tanzy, "but I never realized he could be so nice."

"Neither did I." She wondered what he would have been like if he hadn't killed Toley Pullet, if he'd never gone to prison, if people had liked him.

Asking such a question was as pointless as wondering what she would have been like if she'd been surrounded by sisters-in-law and dozens of happy, noisy, naughty nieces and nephews instead of burying her family one by one. Or how she would have felt about men if her father had treated her and her mother with love and respect. The accidents of their lives had shaped their personalities, and there was nothing they could do about that.

Or was there?

*   *   *

"What was Russ doing at the schoolhouse this morning?" Betty Hicks asked Tanzy. The woman was waiting outside for Tanzy to come out.

"You can go on home," Tanzy said to Tardy. "I'm sure Miss Hicks will be glad to make sure I get to the hotel safely."

"You will tell my aunt you told me to go if she asks, won't you?" Tardy asked.

"Sure."

"See you tomorrow," he said and hurried away.

"I don't know why you waste your time on that stupid boy," Betty said.

"Tardy has a great deal of ability, and one of these days people are going to realize it."

"You don't know anything about people out here," Betty scoffed.

"I don't think people are very different wherever they happen to be."

"Which just goes to prove you don't know what you're talking about. Now what was Russ doing at the school-house? And you needn't deny it, because I saw him coming out."

"I'm not going to deny it. Anybody could have seen him if they happened to be down by the schoolhouse at that time."

The schoolhouse was set in a grove of trees by the small creek that flowed around Boulder Gap. Anybody wanting to know who was coming and going at the schoolhouse would have to go well out of their way to find out. Apparently Betty had done just that.

"That's Russ's business. If you want to know, you'll have to ask him."

Betty looked more suspicious than ever. "What did you tell him to make him come here?"

"I doubt anybody can force Russ to do anything he doesn't want to do."

"You're trying to get him to marry you."

They had cleared the trees and were in view of the town. Tanzy stopped and turned to face Betty. "Everybody knows I decided not to marry Russ. In fairness to him, everybody needs to know he decided he didn't want to marry me either. The only reason I'm still here is to earn the money to repay him for bringing me from St. Louis."

"I think you've changed your mind," Betty said.

Tanzy started walking again. "Why should I do that?"

"Once you realized what it was like to be a single woman out here, you decided he was too rich and good-looking to turn down."

"I doubt you'll believe this, but it was worse in St. Louis."

Betty stopped suddenly, put a hand out to stop Tanzy. "I had a feeling that first day you looked familiar. Now I'm sure I've seen you. Maybe we worked at the same place once."

"I'm sure we didn't," Tanzy said. "We may have passed each other on the street, but it's more probable I look like somebody you used to know."

"Where did you live? Where did you work?"

"Look, you've obviously confused me with somebody else. Now I need to go."

"You won't get Russ to marry you."

"Since I don't want to marry him, that ought to be a relief to both of us."

"Russ loves me. He's going to marry me."

Tanzy knew she should have just kept going, but a demon of jealousy made her stand her ground. "This is really none of my business, but since you're doing your best to *make* it my business, what makes you think Russ wants to marry you? I understand that he rarely comes to town and that he is never seen in any woman's company. That doesn't sound like a lover's behavior to me."

"Russ and I have been in love ever since we were kids. It near broke my heart when they sent him to prison. Everybody knows Toley Pullet thought he was a real slick gun hand. He'd already killed one man."

"Why didn't he marry you when he got out of prison?"

"He said it was unfair to condemn any woman to the hell he had to live in. He doesn't come to town often, but when he does, he always comes to the saloon to see me."

"Why did you go to St. Louis?"

"I thought maybe I'd meet some nice man, get married and have a family, but I didn't meet anybody who could measure up to him."

Tanzy hadn't met anyone who could measure up to Russ either.

"So you came back hoping he'd marry you?"

"He would have if you hadn't come along."

"Betty, I don't know what more I can say to convince you I'm not going to marry Russ and that he doesn't want to marry me."

"Then what was he doing at the schoolhouse this morning?"

"Not asking me to marry him, if that's what you're worried about," Tanzy said, beginning to lose patience. "Now I really have to be going." They had come to a stop before the hotel.

"I know I've seen you before," Betty said. "I never forget a face. I'll find out what you're doing and put a stop to it. Russ is going to marry me."

"Are you still deluding yourself that Russ Tibbolt will ever make you his wife?"

Tanzy turned around to find Ethel Peters had approached them. Betty looked angry as well as slightly intimidated.

"I love Russ and he loves me. He's just having a hard time getting over being in prison and everybody hating him for killing a man who deserved killing."

"Nobody deserves killing," Ethel said severely, "not even one as shameful as Toley Pullet. There were plenty of witnesses to what happened."

"All paid hands of Stocker Pullet," Betty said.

"Russ had a history of trouble before the fight with Toley," Ethel said. "I'm sorry he had to go to prison, but more sorry he came back."

"Why?" Tanzy asked.

"He's rustling. How else do you think he got all those cows?" Ethel asked when she saw Tanzy's surprise. "He used to spend every penny he got on liquor; then he'd get drunk and get in fights. I'm sorry he had to go to prison, but the quiet after he left sure was a relief."

Tanzy found it difficult to believe the absence of one man, no matter how noisy, could have made a noticeable difference in the nighttime atmosphere of Boulder Gap. Even more of a problem was how to reconcile the man Ethel was describing with the one who wrote that short composition. Russ had changed, something apparently neither Ethel nor Betty could understand.

"I got to go," Betty said. "Good day," she said to Ethel before turning to Tanzy and saying, "I'm warning you: Stay away from Russ."

"She's like that with any woman she sees talking to Russ," Ethel said. "Now tell me what my nephew is doing when he should have been protecting you from Betty."

"I told him to go when I saw Betty wanted to talk to me. I figured it might be something he shouldn't hear."

"He's watching out for you?"

"He's always on time, is unfailingly polite, helps me with the younger children, and never leaves me alone with Jem."

Ethel's snort was not elegant. "That *boy* needs a good talking to, and I'm of a mind to give it to him."

"He doesn't bother me. Besides, protecting me has given Tardy a whole new way of seeing himself."

Ethel seemed to relax. "I have noticed a change in his general behavior. He's doing his work and he's not nearly so absentminded. I'm thankful for the beneficial effect you've had on him."

"He's a nice boy who's a little slow growing up. I think you'll find he'll turn into a very fine young man."

"If so, it'll be to your credit. Is everything going well with the school? I haven't heard any complaints from the parents."

"I need more teaching materials."

"I'll do what I can, but getting money for education out of the town council is like finding hen's teeth."

"Maybe you could approach some of the parents about making personal contributions," Tanzy said.

"That's a good idea. Well, I must be going. Let me know if there's anything I can do."

The thought that she'd like to know more about what Russ was like when he was younger flashed through her mind, but she pushed it aside. It would only make her want to know still more.

Have you ever spent a summer night lying on your back staring at the stars in the sky? Did you ever try to count them? Did you ever wonder how far away they were? How they got up there? If they ever moved or just hung there twinkling like they had a secret and were dying to tell you what it was? Did you ever

*wonder why people try so hard to make themselves
feel important when the whole world around us is
proof we're insignificant?*

*I enjoy taking the night watch at the pass. I like the
quiet and the solitude. You don't have to try to be anything. You don't have to fulfill any expectations.
Nobody is depending on you for anything. It's just you
and the night sky, some sleepy cows, and a forest full
of animals that couldn't give a damn about you. Even
the squirrels don't pay you any attention because
they know you can't harm them.*

*It doesn't make me feel powerless the same way
picking up a rifle does. It doesn't make me feel rejected
like riding into town. It doesn't make me feel lonely
like being in a crowd. The night and the emptiness
welcome me, hold me close, take me for what I am.*

The schoolhouse door opened, and Tanzy looked up
to see Jem enter. She had finally convinced Tardy he
didn't need to walk her home every afternoon, so she
was alone. "I didn't see you in school today," she said.

"I don't need any more schooling," Jem said, advanc-
ing slowly toward her.

"That's not what your mother thinks."

"Ma thinks I ought to go to college, but I'm not going to
be a preacher like her pa."

Tanzy couldn't imagine Jem as a preacher. As far as
she could tell, the only thing he believed in was his
impressive good looks. Jem believed he was irresistible
to women. From what she'd seen, the young women of
Boulder Gap had given him no reason to doubt himself.

"I wasn't thinking about a college education," Tanzy
said, "though with enough application you might find
that very beneficial."

"The only reason I'm not working for my pa right now is Ma's insisting I go to school, but I'm tired of sitting around all day in a room full of children."

"You're still young. There's so much you can—"

"I'm a man!" Jem declared. "Look at me. Do I look like a boy?"

He was handsome enough in face and body to have women who ought to know better give him a second and third look, but he was immature.

"A man's maturity isn't measured only by his physical growth," she said. "The internal is more important, the mental and emotional, the spiritual and—"

"All that stuff can wait," Jem argued. He'd come so close to Tanzy that she had to stop herself from stepping back. "I'm a man in body, and I want what a man is supposed to have. I want a wife. I want to get married."

Trying to see Jem as a husband was difficult. Visualizing him as a parent was absurd. He acted liked a child himself.

"I don't know why you're telling me this, but if you're hoping I'll intervene with your parents—"

Jem stepped forward and grabbed her arms with both hands. His action so surprised her, she stopped in mid-sentence.

"I'm telling you because I want to marry you," he said.

"You can't possibly be in love with me," Tanzy said, too surprised to watch her words carefully.

"I've loved you from the first time I saw you. Annie told me what a fool I was to act the way I did that first day, but I wanted you to see I wasn't a boy like that stupid Tardy."

"Tardy's not stupid. He's—"

Jem's grip tightened, pulled her closer. "You've got to know I love you. I haven't taken my eyes off you."

Actually, he'd spent a lot of his time flirting with any

girl who'd pay him attention. "Look, Jem, I don't know why you've decided you love me, but I assure you—"

"You're the most beautiful woman in Boulder Gap," Jem said.

"There's a lot more to marriage than looks."

"I know. I can't wait for our wedding night either. I've dreamed about it for weeks. I know what to do. I'm not inexperienced," he said proudly.

The thought of being the object of an adolescent boy's sexual fantasies made Tanzy's blood run cold. "I'm sorry if I've done anything to mislead you, but I don't love you."

"That's okay. You'll come to love me. Everybody does."

This boy was living in a fantasy world. What had his parents been doing all this time?

"I'm two years older than you. Besides, you still live at home and have to answer to your parents."

"I'll buy a house. You'll have money to buy beautiful dresses. I'll give you jewels and—"

"Listen to me!" Tanzy said, desperate to inject some reality into Jem's thinking. "I don't love you and I won't marry you. There are lots of young girls who'll—"

"I don't want a girl. I want a woman."

"A woman wants a man, not a boy."

Jem's face twisted in anger. "Maybe this will convince you I'm a man."

Chapter Eleven

Russ didn't see any students around, but that wasn't the reason he paused outside the schoolhouse. He was breaking his own rule by appearing in the afternoon. But knowing he was doing something stupid hadn't been enough to make him turn back. Neither did the possibility that she didn't want to see him. She had a hold on him he couldn't break, one she didn't appear to want any more than he did. The thought of being a helpless slave like the man who'd pretended to be his father made his blood run cold.

Now that Welt was helping him, he didn't need to see her at all. Besides, she was bringing out parts of him that he didn't want disturbed. What on earth made him write the things he did to her? It was as if she was his conscience or something. That was more dangerous than the physical attraction. Once a woman got hold of your body *and* your mind, you were a goner. He'd better turn around and pretend he'd never heard of Tanzy Gallant.

But he heard a sound from inside the schoolhouse that had nothing to do with learning. Russ bounded up the steps and flung open the door. Shock immobilized him when he saw Tanzy in the arms of a man. How could he have been tormenting himself over a woman who was flinging herself into the arms of another man?

"Stop!"

The single word clarified everything for Russ. Less than a half-dozen strides carried him to the front of the schoolhouse. He reached for the back of the man's shirt and virtually lifted him off the floor as he pulled him away from Tanzy.

His right arm was pulled back, ready to smash into the face of the bastard, when he realized the man was Jem. "What the hell do you think you're doing, boy?" Russ demanded.

"I'm not a boy!" Jem shouted. "I'm just as much a man as you."

Russ swallowed the words that rose to his tongue. He remembered how he'd felt at the same age, how injured feelings had caused him to nearly ruin his life.

"Then act like it," Russ said. "No man worthy of the name forces himself on a woman."

Russ released his hold on Jem and stepped back. Jem looked for a moment like he would attack Russ. Instead, he straightened his clothes.

"I'm not forcing myself on her. I want to marry her."

Russ turned his shocked gaze on Tanzy. He hadn't thought she was the kind of woman to be interested in a boy just so she could have a rich husband.

"I tried to tell him I'm too old for him," Tanzy said.

"I told her it didn't make any difference," Jem said.

Jem's embarrassment had had time to turn to anger. Now he was as mad as a wolf ready to fight a grizzly. Russ had never been in love, never fancied himself in love, but he could empathize with the boy wanting people to treat him like a man.

"If you want to marry a woman, there are several things you ought to do first."

"What, kill somebody, spend time in prison, and steal cows?"

Russ didn't rise to the bait. He'd heard worse before.

"You need a job."

"I have money."

"Your own money, not your father's," Russ said, "enough to support a wife and the children who will follow. You need a house of your own, not a bedroom in your father's house. And you need to find your place among the men in the community."

"Ma won't let me go to work. She says I'm too young."

"You know the work and you're strong enough to handle your father's teams. I think you ought to talk to your father right away."

Jem looked caught between anger and the picture Russ had painted for him.

"Ma won't let me."

"If you're the man I think you can be, you'll convince your father and *he'll* convince your mother."

Jem looked undecided. "What are you doing here?" he asked Russ.

"Miss Gallant still owes me the money I advanced her for traveling expenses. I'm just checking to make sure she still has a job."

"If she married me, I'd pay you and be rid of you."

"I'd be happy to disappear. Now you'd better go talk to your father. There's no time like the present."

Jem apparently wanted to leave, but he didn't want to feel like he'd been run off.

"I'd speak for you," Russ offered, "but I doubt your father would listen to me."

"Nobody needs to speak for me," Jem said, firing up. "I'm man enough to speak for myself. And the next time I'm talking to a woman, you'd better not get in my way."

He turned and stalked out without waiting for an answer.

"What did you do to make the boy think you were in love with him?" Russ asked Tanzy.

"I can't believe you would ask me something like that," Tanzy said.

"You can act shocked and angry if it makes you feel better, but I know about boys that age. They sometimes get crushes on older women, but not unless the woman makes him think she's available."

"I can't believe I was about to congratulate you on your sensitivity. Instead of humiliating him, you actually managed to make him feel better about himself."

"I can sympathize with him. You might win over his father, but his mother won't let him marry you."

Tanzy looked like she was ready to hit him. She clenched her hands to her sides, turned, and walked away a few steps, appeared to get herself in hand, then turned to face him. Her shoulders sagged and her expression shifted from anger to something perilously close to defeat.

"I don't know what I did," she said. "Tardy told me Jem was telling everybody he liked me, but I figured that was just the posturing of a boy who thought he was too big to be in school. I tried to encourage him to work hard, but no more than I encouraged anybody else."

"I've seen a conniving woman bring strong men to their knees, ruin others, make men do things they never dreamed of doing. You've got that kind of power."

"I can't. I don't want it."

He'd never had any reason to believe she was deceitful, but maybe she'd refused to marry him because she thought she could make a better bargain. Not only were young fellas like Jem susceptible to her charms, older men like Stocker had shown they were equally attracted to her. Could she be just like his mother, always angling for a better deal?

"I don't think you can keep people from being attracted to you, but you can make certain you don't tempt young boys."

"You've just added another item to the list of reasons not to marry you," Tanzy said, angry again.

"What, being honest?"

"No, thinking I would attempt to take advantage of any man, but especially a boy, just so I could make a rich marriage."

"Women do it all the time."

"I don't, or I'd have put aside all my scruples and married you. What are you doing here? And don't pretend you came only to rescue me."

"I came by to give you what I wrote."

"You've already written something for this week."

"I've been doing a lot of night duty in the pass. The boys don't like staying awake all night so they're not complaining."

"Doesn't it bother you?"

"Since prison, I don't sleep too well."

"That must leave you feeling sleepy a lot of the time."

"My ma always said I was too fidgety to sleep much. It's just as well. Cows need a lot of looking after."

"You're always talking about what the cows need. Don't the people who take care of the cows ever want anything, *need* anything, for themselves?"

"Sure, we do. We're no different from anybody else."

"Yet I never see any of your men in town, and you only come because I'm teaching you to read."

"Some of us know what we can't have. There's no use fighting against what can't be helped, so we just put our minds to other things."

"Like taking care of cows?"

"It's as good as anything."

"What would you have if you could be treated like everybody else?"

Russ wondered if Tanzy really wanted an answer to her question, or if she was just asking to have something to say. Even idle curiosity would be better than that.

"It's better not to think about the things I can't have. I'm much happier that way."

"I don't agree. If you don't think about what you want, you can't be sure what it is. If you don't know what it is, you might not notice if you come upon it by surprise."

"You act like it's the same as finding something that's fallen off a wagon. You can't have it if it doesn't exist."

"I don't believe people want what doesn't exist."

Russ was becoming impatient with the conversation. Tanzy obviously didn't understand what it meant to have been unwanted all his life, to have everybody turn their backs on him, to automatically blame him for anything that went wrong, refuse to give him credit for anything he did that was right. Otherwise, she wouldn't stir up feelings that were better left undisturbed.

But they'd already been disturbed. He hadn't wanted her to come to Boulder Gap, but he'd had a reaction to her unlike anything that had ever happened to him. It had been so unexpected, so immediate, so genuine, that doors to the inner recesses of his heart had burst open and hope escaped before he could corral it and lock it up again. For three days he was able to believe someone would take him just as he was—no baggage from the past—and give him a chance to allay some of the loneliness that had been his companion all his life. He hadn't hoped for much, just someone who could like him just a little bit.

He knew in his heart Tanzy liked him still. Yet his past had come between them, destroyed any chance that she would step within the circle of friendship. If she couldn't get past Stocker's accusation and Ethel's doubts, no woman could.

"I have my ranch and friends," he said.

"Is that all you want?"

"Lots of people have less."

"You can't want so little. It's not normal."

Nothing about his life had been *normal.* "Not every man is anxious to get married or have a family. Even some women aren't. They like the freedom to change partners when they get a hankering for something different . . . or they find someone else who's willing to spend more money on them."

"I'm not talking about *everybody.* I'm talking about you."

"Why should you care about me if you dislike me so much you don't want to marry me?"

"I never said I dislike you. On the contrary, I admire you. I think it takes tremendous courage to do what you've done, and it makes me angry people don't recognize it."

Russ didn't trust himself to speak for a moment. No one had ever said they admired him. Well, some of the boys had, but that was because he could fight with his fists, shoot the buds off a cactus, and ride any horse you put him on. That wasn't the kind of thing a woman admired. Tanzy was talking about *him.*

If he could trust her. After Jem, he wasn't sure.

"What have I done?" He had to get this straight. He didn't want to go around believing she was meaning one thing when she was talking about something else entirely.

"From what I've heard, you had a wild youth and an unfortunate fight that landed you in prison. Yet you haven't let it sour you on life or make you bitter. You haven't let people's dislike and distrust do it, either. You've gone about your business and built your own ranch out of nothing. You've got cowhands who trust you enough to stay with you even though things can't be easy. That's more than most people can say for themselves, but you also had the courage to admit you couldn't read and to do something about it."

"If I'd had all that much courage, I'd have done something about it a long time ago."

Her voice softened. "I don't know what your life was like before I got here, but I expect you had more pressing things on your mind."

Russ realized he'd been standing like a stone yet he couldn't move. Nobody had ever said half the things Tanzy had just said. Not even Betty. He could tell there was a huge difference between what Betty felt for him and what Tanzy said, a difference so big he could hardly take it in all at once. He felt weak in the knees, as if the iron will that had sustained him for so long had suddenly been yanked out of his spine.

"These things you've been writing," Tanzy said, pointing to the pages he still held in his hand, "have shown me there's a very different person inside from what your neighbors see. I'm certain one day, when they're tired of listening to Stocker's bitterness, they'll begin to see what I see."

Those were some of the nicest words anybody had ever spoken to him, but they had the same effect on him as being tossed in an icy stream. They brought him back to reality.

"They'll never stop listening to Stocker. He wouldn't let

them. They only admire toughness. That's what it takes to survive."

"You've got the toughness to fight for what you want, to hold on to it, to protect it. You also have the heart and sensitivity to appreciate that life's greatest moments aren't born of fighting but of giving, sharing, loving. You're one of the lucky ones."

Then why did he feel like one of the damned? He was proud of his strength. It was all that enabled him to survive, but he cursed this *sensitivity* she valued so highly. It wouldn't let him ignore the truth that something essential was missing in his life. Why couldn't he be like Stocker, loving nothing but money, being obsessed with controlling other people, being blind to everything except what he wanted? What was it about this woman that kept pulling at his insides like burrs that wouldn't let go? Her refusal to marry him hurt even though he'd already decided they'd never suit. It was to her that he'd come to confess he couldn't read. Then he'd compounded the error by putting thoughts onto the pages he wrote that he should never have revealed. She could pull things out of him despite his resistance.

"You still don't want to marry me, and everybody in Boulder Gap hates me. All this *sensitivity* does is make me realize how miserable I am."

"You'll find someone who'll love you and make you happy. Betty Hicks loves you. She—"

"Betty became infatuated with me when I was the town bad boy. In five years she'd be miserable and make me miserable, too."

"There are lots of women in the world, many who would think themselves lucky to have a husband like you."

"But you're not one of them."

She looked uncomfortable.

"You already answered that," he said. "Here's what I wrote," he said, holding it out to her. "I did this one by myself, so I expect there'll be lots of mistakes."

She reached for it, but he didn't let go.

"You've done remarkably well," she said. "If all my students did as well, I'd think myself a magician."

"In a way I guess you are."

"How?"

He couldn't tell her. That was something even she couldn't pull out of him. "Thanks for caring," he said. "I'd forgotten how nice it feels."

Then he bent down and kissed her.

Russ couldn't say why he had done such a thing. He'd come here intending to do everything he could to break the relationship between them. Yet here he was kissing her.

And he couldn't stop.

He'd kissed a lot of women in his youth, not all while he was sober enough to remember what it was like, but he was certain it had never felt like this. There was the soft intake of breath, of surprise, but she didn't pull away. She was hesitant, unsure, but her lips were soft and sweet. It wasn't an aggressive kiss. He felt more like they were both suddenly suspended in time. No swift movement, no sudden decisions, just a flood of emotions that immobilized him.

Russ had never thought of women as soft and vulnerable, a desirable part of his life. They were necessary to the reproductive process, a way to accommodate the drives that were part of being a man. But in his experience, they were also hard or threatening, to be avoided whenever possible.

She didn't pretend helplessness, but there was a vulnerability that reached out to his instinctive need to protect those weaker than himself. Her kiss was tentative without being weak, cautious without being fearful, adventuresome without being aggressive. It invited him to come along while giving him the freedom to back away. It promised nothing but held out the possibility of everything.

They broke the kiss but somehow seemed to remain in its thrall.

Russ wondered if his expression was as full of surprise as Tanzy's. He wondered if her feelings for him were as confused as his for her. He felt incapable of speech. Too many thoughts whirled about in his head, all part of a pattern of thought that was changing so rapidly that the words were wrong the moment he thought of them.

He wondered how it was possible for Tanzy to look one way for a moment, then completely different seconds later. He wondered if he was going crazy. Things weren't like they were supposed to be, yet he couldn't figure out exactly how they were, what had changed. He felt a little off balance, at a loss to do anything about it.

He had to say something. Surely the sound of his own voice would start his brain functioning again, make some order of the chaos of his mind.

"Get your hands off my man, you hussy."

Chapter Twelve

Russ spun around to see Betty marching down the aisle toward them looking as mad as a scalded cat.

"I warned you to stay away from Russ!" she hollered at Tanzy. "He's my man."

"I don't want—" Tanzy began.

"I'm no woman's man," Russ said, furious Betty would think he belonged to her.

"I knew you weren't the sweet little thing you pretended to be," Betty said, closer now and focusing her attention on Tanzy.

"What are you doing here?" Russ asked Betty.

"I saw you headed in this direction and I followed," Betty said. "I knew she was up to no good from the first day she set foot in town."

"If I'd been after Russ," Tanzy said, "I'd have married him when he offered instead of turning him down."

"I don't know what your game is," Betty said, "but I know you're up to something."

Russ was angry that Betty had caught him kissing Tanzy. He didn't know what to make of that kiss himself just yet. He certainly didn't want anybody else knowing about it until he figured his feelings out. Ten years ago he'd have been pleased to have two women fighting because of him. Now he grabbed Betty by her arms and turned her away from Tanzy to face him.

"I'm not your man," he said. "I never have been. I never will be."

"That's not true," Betty said, trying to put her arms around him. "You loved me before you went to prison. You said you wanted to marry me."

"If I did, I was drunk. I had more than enough reason to know I never wanted to get married."

"You can't hate all women just because of your mother," Betty said. "I love you."

"I don't love you," Russ said. "I told you that before I went to prison. I told you again when I got out."

"You can't love her," Betty said, directing a furious glance at Tanzy. "She's a lying tramp."

"I don't love anybody," Russ said, "not you, not Tanzy."

"See, you call her by her first name!"

"I call you by your first name and I don't love you."

"Yes, you do. You've always loved me."

Russ didn't know why Betty couldn't accept the fact that he didn't love her and was never going to, but he was tired of having to deal with her jealousy and possessiveness.

"I don't love anybody. Now go back to the saloon before you lose your job."

"The old man would never fire me. I'm the only reason half the men bother to come into his lousy saloon. I'm prettier than her," she said, pointing at Tanzy, "and I know what it takes to please a man." She adopted a wheedling tone. "I could please you again, Russ. Why won't you let me come out to your ranch? I could make you so happy you'd never want to leave."

"It's no place for a woman."

"You were going to take her out there."

"She'd have been my wife."

"I'll be your wife. I could be a much better wife than she'd ever be."

Russ had worried marrying Tanzy could upset the quiet and camaraderie that made it possible for him to endure his life. He knew instinctively Betty would destroy it.

"I don't want a wife."

Betty turned rigid with anger. "Then why were you kissing her?"

Why *did* he kiss Tanzy? He didn't know himself, certainly wouldn't have told Betty if he did.

"It was a friendship kiss, a kind of thank you."

"What for?" Betty asked, eyes alive with suspicion.

"I was the one kissing him," Tanzy said.

"I knew it!" Betty exclaimed.

"He had just saved me from a potentially embarrassing situation with a student."

Why would Tanzy take the blame for something she hadn't done? It would only make Betty more angry and eager to cause as much trouble as possible.

Betty made a face of disgust. "If you're talking about Jem mooning over you like the young fool he is, everybody knows that. He'll get over it."

"Young boys often have momentary attachments for older women. The fact that they're foolish doesn't make them any less real."

"That's just a bunch of nonsense," Betty said. "Jem was drooling all over me less than a month ago. I gave him a good slap across his face and told him not to bother me again. That did the trick, I can assure you."

"As long as he's a pupil in my schoolhouse, I will treat him with respect."

"Surely you aren't fool enough to believe any of this stuff she's saying?" Betty said to Russ.

"I remember what it was like to be Jem's age."

"You never loved anybody but me," Betty declared.

Apparently nothing was going to convince Betty that Russ didn't love her.

"We have to go," he said to Tanzy. Retaining his hold on Betty's arm, he turned her and marched her out of the schoolhouse. He kept moving, ignoring everything she said, until they reached the main street of Boulder Gap. Then he turned and cut her off in mid-sentence.

"Stop your hysterical yammering for one minute," he said, keeping his voice soft so he wouldn't attract attention, "and listen very carefully to what I'm going to say."

"I know you're angry with me," she began in that wheedling voice he hated so much, "but—"

"I'm not angry at you," Russ said. "I'm disgusted and fed up. I don't love you and I never told you I did. Don't argue with me," he said when she attempted to interrupt. "I don't know why you decided I belonged to you, but I never gave you any reason to think I did."

"You come to the saloon to see me."

"I go the saloon to get a drink. *You* come over to see me. Get it through your head that I'm not going to marry you."

"It's all her fault," Betty said, her anger flaring again.

"It has nothing to do with Tanzy. I wasn't going to marry you before she came here. Now forget all this and go back to the saloon. Why don't you marry one of those nice cowboys who moon over you? Any one of them would make you a good husband."

"I'm not marrying some cowhand," Betty said disdainfully. "I'm going to marry you."

Russ turned and started walking away.

"You can't run away from me, Russ Tibbolt. You belong to me. That woman can't have you. I won't let her."

Russ walked faster, anxious to get back to the ranch. It would be easier to deal with rustlers than a screaming, delusional woman. How could he have ever been such a fool as to think of bringing a female into his own house? He was lucky Tanzy hadn't wanted to marry him. For once being accused of something he hadn't done had turned out to be a good thing.

Tanzy sat immobile, trying to comprehend what had just happened, trying to put it into perspective, trying to say it didn't change anything. But it did. That one, nearly insignificant kiss had changed her mind about virtually everything. She now had to admit her attraction to Russ was more than merely the normal attraction of a woman to a big, handsome, masterful man. She liked Russ. She was attracted to *him,* not just to his body.

She was disgusted she could allow her principles to be overcome by an emotional reaction. She'd always thought she couldn't like anyone who violated one of her big taboos. Now she knew better. She liked Russ *despite* that. His writing had shown her there was a very different side to Russ, one that had little to do with the persona he let people see. She believed he had more capacity to love than she'd ever seen in a man, more capacity to be sensitive to the people around him. She was sure no one knew the *real* Russ, not even Russ.

Just as shocking was her physical reaction. The kiss had been brief, hardly more than the brushing of lips. Yet in that short time it set off sparks in parts of Tanzy's body that had never before been ignited. She'd never felt anything like the physical force that compelled her, despite her shock and surprise, to stay with the kiss so long she was drawn in even more deeply. In one instant she'd gone from complete indifference to a strong urge to bury her hands in his hair and pull his mouth hard against her own. She'd wanted to feel his body pressed against her, to feel his strength, his heat, his desire for her. She ought to get down on her knees and offer a prayer of thanks that Betty had burst into the schoolhouse. No telling what kind of fool she would have made of herself if she'd been left alone with Russ any longer.

Why had he kissed her? Was it really merely in appreciation for the things she'd said about him? If that was all it was, she could dismiss it and move on. She'd have to deal with her reaction, but it would be easier knowing he attached no importance to the kiss.

But what if it had been more? What if he really wanted to kiss her because he was so attracted to her that he had overcome his reluctance to have anything to do with women? She couldn't deny that she *wanted* it to mean more, that she didn't want the kiss to be a nearly meaningless gesture of appreciation for a few kind words. She wanted it to have happened because he wanted to kiss her and couldn't stop himself. Ironic that she'd spent so much time evading men's embraces, avoiding their kisses, being repulsed by their attempts to grope her body. Now her own feelings had been turned upside down.

She could say what she wanted, but she was so powerfully attracted to Russ she couldn't depend on her reason to hold her feelings in check. From now on she'd have to make sure Tardy stayed with her whenever she was in the schoolhouse.

"Betty Hicks tells me she surprised you kissing Russ Tibbolt in the schoolhouse yesterday," Ethel said to Tanzy after she seated herself in the only chair in Tanzy's hotel room. She had been waiting for Tanzy when she and Tardy emerged from the schoolhouse. She'd sent Tardy off with a sharp admonition to do his lessons at once.

"I wondered how long it would take Betty to go running to you," Tanzy said.

"The behavior of the schoolteacher is my responsibility. Kissing in front of the children is not acceptable behavior."

"There were no students in the schoolhouse. Russ and I were alone."

"Betty said Jem Bridger was there."

"He was when Russ arrived, but he'd already left."

"You should have nothing to do with Russ Tibbolt. I warned you about him when you first arrived."

"I remember that quite well, but I was glad he did stop

by. Jem Bridger has taken the notion in his head that he loves me and wants to marry me."

"Good Lord!"

"When I tried to explain that I didn't love him, that I was too old and his parents would never agree, he tried to kiss me. If Russ hadn't come in just then, I imagine he would have succeeded. The boy is very strong."

"I shall speak to his mother at once," Ethel said. "I won't have you subjected to assaults by the students."

"Please don't say anything. I think Russ handled the situation quite well."

"How did he do that?"

"By pointing out what Jem needed to do before he could consider marrying anyone. It put the burden on him to make something of himself. The episode may prove to be good for him."

"That is still to be seen," Ethel said, not nearly as impressed with Russ's tactics as Tanzy, "but if you didn't kiss Russ, why did he kiss you?"

"It was more a brushing of lips than a kiss. I doubt it meant anything to him."

"Russ is extremely handsome and he knows it. He's used his good looks many times in the past to get his way, but it won't work anymore. We all know him too well."

"Betty Hicks doesn't. She's convinced he would have married her if I hadn't arrived."

"Russ will never marry her. He hates women. I don't agree with his sentiment, but he's got good reason to feel that way. That's why I was so surprised when I heard he'd sent for a mail-order bride." Ethel stood. "Well, I've said what I came to say. Just steer clear of Russ Tibbolt. He's trouble. Always has been." Her stern expression changed to a smile. "I've been hearing good things about your work. The parents are very pleased with their children's progress. I must say I've been impressed with the changes you've wrought in my nephew. The boy will never amount to much, but if he continues to improve, at least he won't be an embarrassment."

"Tardy has a great deal of potential. He just needs to develop confidence in himself. It would help if people stopped treating him like an embarrassment."

Ethel clearly didn't take kindly to criticism. Both her smile and appearance of satisfaction vanished.

"It's good that a teacher should think only the best of her students, but I assure you I have ample reason to feel as I do about him. I'll be most grateful if you're able to give me reason to change my mind," she said stiffly.

"He's made so much progress, he's able to help me with some of the others," Tanzy said, determined not to be bullied.

"I expect you to do the teaching."

"With all the children at different levels, I can't possibly find the time to give them all the individual attention they need. I depend upon several of the older children to help me."

It was clear Ethel didn't like this, but she couldn't dispute the facts. "I will be evaluating your work at the end of the month. We can talk further about it then."

Tanzy didn't know what Russ had meant by that kiss, but he'd done her a great disservice. From now on everything she did would be questioned and viewed from every angle. The wisest thing to do would be to discontinue Russ's lessons, but she wasn't going to give in to the prejudice against him. She'd have to make sure Russ never came without Tardy. One more innocent kiss and she'd be out the door.

* * *

"You tired of teaching school yet?" Stocker asked Tanzy. He was in the hotel lobby when she came back after school and walked away from a group of men to join her.

"No," Tanzy replied. "I enjoy it."

"You're too pretty to be wasting your time on a bunch of kids."

"I have to have a job, Mr. Pullet. I have to repay Russ the cost of bringing me out here."

"If you'd come out to marry me, I'd never make you repay me."

"Since you don't want a wife and didn't send for me, that doesn't come into consideration."

"I never said I didn't want a wife," Stocker said with the kind of leering look Tanzy hated. "I do need someone like you to work in my saloon. Betty Hicks is luring customers over to the Silver Nugget."

"Then why don't you hire Betty?"

"Because you're prettier and higher class."

"You weren't so complimentary when you thought I was going to marry Russ."

"I was upset that any decent woman would consider marrying him."

Tanzy wasn't interested in what Stocker had thought of her. She was tired and wanted to go to her room.

"I appreciate your offer, but I much prefer teaching school."

"You're wasting your time—"

"Let's start the meeting, Stocker," one of the men said.

"You won't want me here." Tanzy was eager for a chance to leave, but something made her ask, "What's the meeting about?"

"Deciding who's going out to check on Russ Tibbolt's herd," one of the men said.

"I think we all ought to go," another man said. "We've all lost cattle."

"You're wasting your time," still another said. "He wouldn't invite us to go out there if he had stolen cows in that valley. That'd be the same as putting his head in a noose."

"This is just a ploy to make us stop suspecting him," Stocker said. "We know it's none of us doing the rustling, so it's got to be him. I say we ride in there together and hang him and every one of those crooks who work for him."

"You can't convict a man without proof," Tanzy said. "And you can't hang him without a trial."

"This is the Colorado Territory," someone shouted. "Horse thieving and cattle rustling are hanging offenses."

"I don't like Russ one bit, but he ain't stupid," one said. "We've tried to pin something on him for years and we ain't succeeded so far."

"We sent him to jail for killing Toley," Stocker said. "We pinned that on him."

The sudden quiet, the averted gazes, told Tanzy more clearly than anything she'd heard that something had not been right about that trial. Whatever happened, these men weren't proud of it.

"I say we don't waste our time poking around Russ's valley," a man said. "I say we go looking for the missing cows. We ought to search every canyon, pass, valley, and gully within a hundred miles that could hide even two head. We'll know as soon as we find the cows who's been doing the rustling, and we'll have the evidence to hang them."

"You're wasting your time searching all over for cows he's already sold," Stocker insisted. "I'm not pulling my men off my herds to send them on a wild-goose chase so

Russ can steal even more cows while they're gone. Either we go in there and hang him without all this fiddle-faddle, or I'll have nothing to do with it."

Stocker stalked from the hotel lobby. The men talked among themselves for a while, arguing loudly for one course of action or another, but ultimately left without making any decision. That didn't surprise Tanzy. She hadn't expected they'd do anything without Stocker's approval and leadership.

She couldn't forget the men's reaction to Russ's conviction. Maybe it *had* been a fair fight and Stocker had pressured the jury to convict him unfairly and send him to prison. That would be more than enough reason for Russ to bear a grudge that would never entirely go away. Then maybe she'd overstated the enmity between Russ and Stocker. Maybe Russ wasn't feuding with Stocker. If he had wanted to kill the other man, surely he could have found an opportunity in the five years since he'd been released from jail. Fear of the law never stopped feuds in Kentucky. She didn't expect it would in the Colorado Territory.

It was easier to believe Russ since she'd read some of the things he'd written. She knew it was possible he'd written them just to change her mind, but she couldn't see any reason for him to worry about the opinion of a woman he didn't want to marry. Despite the kiss, she hadn't seen any change in his attitude toward her.

It must have been a moment of weakness, even loneliness, that prompted the kiss. She smiled to herself as she climbed the steps to her room. It was nice to know she had the power to pull him free of his iron reserve for at least a moment. He'd probably cursed himself all the way back to the ranch, expecting her to start making demands, expecting special treatment, or whatever it was he thought women did that had given him such a bad opinion of them. It had something to do with his mother. That realization made her more sympathetic toward him. It was a shame he wasn't different. Being married to him could have been quite exciting.

What was she talking about? She didn't want excitement in her marriage. She wanted dependability and stability. She wanted a home of her own, children, and the knowledge that they could grow up safely. And she wanted a husband who would see her as his equal, someone whose feelings mattered, whose opinions were to be valued, whose knowledge was important to the success of the family. On that score Russ failed dismally.

Tanzy knew something was afoot when she saw Ethel Peters, Jem Bridger's mother, and another woman coming toward the schoolhouse accompanied by Betty. Their stride, aggressive and determined, and their expressions, grim and angry, warned her that it probably wouldn't be something to her liking.

"What are they all coming here for?" Tardy asked.

"I don't know," Tanzy said. Ethel had said she would be checking Tanzy's progress, but this didn't look like a progress report committee. The women looked more like vigilantes. "Time to go back inside," Tanzy called out to the students.

"We haven't been out our full time," several protested.

"I'll let you stay out longer this afternoon," Tanzy said. "Now go back inside and get to work."

The children grumbled, but one look at Ethel's committee convinced them to follow orders.

"Tardy, I want you to be responsible for the children until I'm done."

Tardy looked stunned. "Me?"

"Don't you think you can do it?"

"Nobody's ever made me responsible for anything."

"Well, you are now. And I don't want everybody with their noses stuck to the windows."

Tardy headed toward the schoolhouse, a spring in his step, but he turned back with a worried look just before he went inside. Tanzy thought he probably had reason.

"Good morning," she said when Ethel and the others came to a stop in a semicircle around her. "Is something wrong?"

"I hope not," Ethel said, "but Betty Hicks has made a very serious accusation against you. We're here in hopes you can prove she's mistaken."

"I'm not mistaken," Betty said, her lips formed in a false smile, her eyes gleaming in anticipation. "I knew I'd seen her somewhere the moment I laid eyes on her. It just took me a while to remember."

"What did you remember?" Tanzy asked.

"I remembered that we worked at the same gambling hall in St. Louis. *That's* what I remembered."

Chapter Thirteen

"I don't remember seeing you in St. Louis," Tanzy said to Betty.

"I quit about the time you started. I remember you because one of the girls said you'd be getting all the trade 'cause you was younger and prettier than the rest of us."

Tanzy had gotten far more attention than she'd wanted.

"Are you denying you worked in a gambling hall?" Ethel asked.

"Nobody's asked me where I worked or what I did before I came here."

"I'm asking now," Ethel said, her lips firmly compressed in a disapproving frown.

"I lived in my father's house until he and my brothers were killed. I went to St. Louis looking for a job. I discovered the only jobs for young women with no skills and no references were in places like gambling halls, so I took what was offered. I worked in the River Queen for six months. I left when I came as a mail-order bride to marry Russ Tibbolt."

"Why would you do that?" Ethel asked.

"A friend of mine had come west as a mail-order bride and wrote to tell me how happy she was. I had hoped that marrying Mr. Tibbolt would prove to be just as wonderful for me. As you know, I decided not to accept his offer."

"We can't have a woman who worked in a gambling hall teaching our children," Mrs. Bridger said.

"Why not?" Tanzy asked. "I didn't lose my virtue."

"We don't know that," Betty said.

"We don't know that you didn't, either," Tanzy said, turning on Betty, "but I didn't come making accusations against you. I didn't attempt to ruin your reputation."

"It wouldn't have mattered," the other woman said. "Everybody knows she's a fallen woman."

"We can't let you remain as the teacher," Ethel said. "Soon everybody in town will know about your past."

"You can't expect *that* one to keep her mouth shut," Mrs. Bridger said, giving Betty a nasty look, "when she thinks she's got a piece of juicy gossip."

"I was just doing my civic duty," Betty said.

"If you was doing that, you'd leave town," Mrs. Bridger shot back. "But Ethel is right," she said, turning back to

Tanzy. "I don't want you teaching my Jem. No telling what kind of ideas you might put in his head."

"There's nothing I can do but relieve you of your position," Ethel said. "Immediately."

"No! You can't do that! She's the best teacher we ever had."

Tanzy turned to see Tardy bound down the schoolhouse steps and run toward them. Several students had their noses to the windows.

"Richard Benton," his Aunt Ethel intoned, "you know you're not allowed to speak to your elders like that."

"You can't fire Miss Gallant," he repeated, looking from one face to another. "Nobody cares where she worked."

"I'm afraid that's not true," Ethel said.

"I bet she lied," Tardy said, pointing to Betty. "Everybody knows she'd do anything to get Mr. Tibbolt to marry her."

"She didn't lie," Tanzy said. "I did work in a gambling hall."

"That doesn't make you bad."

"No, but your aunt and probably most of the town believe that makes me an unsuitable person to be teaching young children. They're afraid it might signal their approval of such things."

"What things?"

"That's none of your business," Ethel said.

"Activities associated with gambling," Tanzy said.

"You didn't do any of those *activities,* did you?"

"No, but that doesn't seem to matter."

"It ought to."

"I agree, but I'm not the one making the decision."

"I'll talk to everybody," Tardy said defiantly to his aunt. "They'll want her to stay. You'll see."

"I don't want to be at the center of a senseless commotion," Tanzy said. "I've seen what happened to Mr. Tibbolt and I don't want it to happen to me." She turned to Ethel. "Since you've seen fit to relieve me of my position immediately, one of you will have to take over for the rest of the day."

"None of us is a teacher," Ethel said.

"You should have thought of that before you fired me with a schoolhouse full of children. Now if you'll excuse me, I'm going back to my room."

"The town will cease to pay for your board," Ethel said.

"I'll see to my own expenses."

"I hate you, Aunt Ethel," Tanzy heard Tardy said. "I hate all of you."

"Be quiet, Richard Benton, and get back into that schoolhouse," his aunt said.

"I'm never going back there and you can't make me," Tardy shouted and ran past Tanzy toward town.

Tanzy felt like running away, too, but she had nowhere to go.

"I heard about what happened at the schoolhouse today," Stocker said to Tanzy. He'd found her in the restaurant and sat down at her table without asking permission. "It's a shame some people are so prejudiced, but there's not much we can do about it."

Tanzy didn't know how he expected her to respond. No one had been more responsible in perpetuating prejudice than he.

"I've discovered people are often eager to put their own weaknesses off on others."

Stocker eyed her silently for a moment. "You're a very direct woman. I didn't see that at first."

"Why not?"

"All women have to do is lay eyes on Russ and they do anything he wants."

"I don't see how you can say that. Except for Betty, every woman in town seems to dislike him very much."

"Because I've made sure they do."

"Do you think that's fair?"

"He's a killer, a liar, and a thief. I want everybody to know it."

"They do. Did you have a reason for sitting down with me?"

"I came to offer you a job."

"Why should I take the kind of job that just got me fired?"

"Because you need a job, and I'll pay you twice what they paid you to teach school."

That was indeed a temptation. She could pay Russ back and save money to leave town in half the time. It hardly mattered now if she worked in a saloon.

"I still want a husband and family. I don't see how working in your saloon will get that for me."

"You'll meet lots of men."

"Not necessarily the kind who will make good husbands."

"Why haven't you run any of those stolen cows into Tibbolt's valley?" Stocker asked Chick.

"I can't get in there with him guarding that pass day and night."

"I don't know how much longer I can keep the ranchers from taking a look for themselves. You know what's going to happen when they don't find any stolen cows, don't you? They're going to come looking for you."

Chick chuckled inwardly with the knowledge that nobody could catch him with rustled cows. He'd already sold every one.

"I'll keep trying," Chick said, "but it looks like we'll have to try something different."

"I don't care what you do. Just get those cows in there."

First he had to steal some more cows. It amused him to know he intended to steal them from Stocker. He might even keep one or two back to sneak into Russ's valley. If he could find a way to get them in without getting killed.

Tanzy watched as Tardy stacked the last of her luggage on the boardwalk, surprised at the sadness she felt at leaving Boulder Gap. She ought to be relieved to be going. And she might have been if she had any idea where she was headed. She could no longer stay in Boulder Gap. Betty's accusation and the school committee's reaction had ruined her chances of getting respectable work, but she hadn't left St. Louis to give up so easily. Somewhere, somehow, she'd prove she was just as respectable as anyone else.

"That's the last one," Tardy said.

He was more upset than Tanzy about her leaving. She'd tried to convince him that he had the necessary talent and strength of character to succeed on his own, but he seemed to believe he would go back to being the butt of everyone's jokes. She wondered how Russ had survived much more brutal treatment with his self-confidence intact. She handed Tardy a coin, but he refused it.

"You'll need it more than I will," he said. His eyes were red. She wondered if he'd been crying. "Why can't you stay here?"

"What would I do? Work in Mr. Pullet's saloon? That would just confirm everyone's opinion of me."

"I hate Aunt Ethel," Tardy said. "She's mean and—"

"Don't blame your aunt. She did what she thinks is right. Besides, the rest of the town agrees with her."

"I hate them, too. I hate all of them. As soon as I'm big enough, I'm getting out of here."

Tanzy didn't tell him sixteen was already big enough. She'd been told that was Russ's age when he went to Texas. She'd only been two years older when she ran away to St. Louis.

"Don't let yourself hate anybody," Tanzy said. "It'll eat you up from the inside out." She reached out to put her hand on his shoulder. "Don't neglect your studies. You can become a very successful man."

"How? What can I do?"

"Why don't you ask Mr. Tibbolt? Maybe he'll have some ideas."

"I can't go out to his ranch. I don't even know where it is."

"Then find out. Don't ever let lack of knowledge stop you from doing something you want to do."

"What is all your baggage doing on the street?"

Tanzy turned to see Stocker Pullet approaching. Didn't the man ever stay on his ranch? No wonder rustlers were taking his cows.

"I'm waiting for the stage," Tanzy said.

"Why?"

"I don't have a job."

"I'll give you a job. You can start right now."

"I appreciate your offer. I don't think working in a saloon is a disreputable job, but it seems everybody else in town does."

"That's nonsense," Stocker said. "Tell me who said that

and I'll see that they change their minds right now. You're a fine, honorable woman, and I'll make sure everybody knows it."

Stocker's influence might be able to force the townspeople to show outward acceptance, but he couldn't change their hearts and minds.

"Can you make her be the schoolteacher again?" Tardy asked. "She's the best teacher we've ever had."

"I'm thankful for your belief in me," Tanzy said to Tardy, "and your willingness to attempt to force the town to accept me," she said to Stocker, "but I don't want to remain where people don't want me."

"I want you," Tardy said. "All the kids do."

"I want you, too," Stocker said.

"I've already told you I won't work in a saloon."

"I wasn't talking about the saloon. I was thinking of something more personal."

"What do you mean?" Tardy asked.

Tanzy wasn't eager to hear Stocker's response.

"You're a fine young woman," Stocker said, "very pretty and full of spirit. I like spirit in women. It keeps them from being boring."

"Miss Gallant is never boring," Tardy said. "She even made school interesting."

"Quite an achievement," Stocker said. "Which just goes to back up what I said."

"What *are* you saying?" Tardy asked. He seemed to be one step ahead of her.

"I like you," Stocker said to Tanzy. "I'd like to get to know you better."

"You mean you want to marry her?" Tardy asked.

"That's premature, but I find her a fascinating young woman."

"You're old enough to be her pa," Tardy said.

"I'm old enough to know what a woman wants and young enough to be able to deliver it," Stocker said.

Tardy's snort was more descriptive than any words Tanzy could have chosen.

"I'm flattered by your interest," Tanzy said, "but I can't afford to remain here when I have no money."

"I can give you all you need," Stocker said.

Tanzy didn't need Tardy's look of shock to know how the townspeople would react once they learned of that arrangement. "Thank you, but that would be far worse than working in any saloon."

"No one would say a disrespectful word about you," Stocker said. "I'd see to that."

Russ Tibbolt's unexpected arrival in a buckboard saved Tanzy from having to explain to Stocker that while he might be able to control what people said in public, he couldn't control what they thought or what they said in private.

Russ pulled his buckboard, which was loaded with flour, sugar, coffee, bacon, and other staples, to a stop before her. Russ looked for a moment at the luggage stacked behind Tanzy—his gaze lingered longer on Stocker—before turning to her.

"You can't leave," he said.

"That's what I've been trying to tell her all day," Tardy said.

"Just what interest do you have in Miss Gallant's actions?" Stocker asked.

"She owes me money," Russ said.

"I'll send you the rest as soon as I'm able," Tanzy said.

"I don't think much of that kind of security," Russ said.

"Speak more respectfully to Miss Gallant," Stocker said.

"I meant no disrespect to her," Russ said without taking

his eyes off Tanzy. "I just don't think she'll be able to find the kind of job that will enable her to pay me back."

"Damn the money," Stocker said. "I'll pay you. How much is it?"

"You can't pay it!" Tardy exclaimed.

"You don't think I can afford it?" Stocker asked, insulted.

"I think what the young man is trying to say is that it wouldn't reflect very well on Miss Gallant's reputation to have you pay her debts," Russ explained.

"Why not? I'm so rich I won't even miss the money."

"Now, I appreciate everyone's interest in my well-being, but I have to leave. The stagecoach will be here any minute."

"You can't leave," Russ repeated.

"What do you suggest I do," Tanzy asked him, "stay here and take a job in Stocker's saloon?"

"You could come out to the ranch and work for us until you've paid your debt."

"No decent woman would let herself be lured into that nest of criminals," Stocker declared. "I won't permit it."

"We're not neat and we're terrible cooks," Russ said to Tanzy, "so we'd appreciate it if you'd agree to take care of us."

"This is ridiculous," Stocker said to Russ. "Get out of town before I have the sheriff lock you up."

"What charges are you going to invent this time?" Russ demanded, suddenly turning on Stocker. "Not even a hand-picked jury could put me in jail for driving my buckboard down the street."

"You're assaulting an innocent young woman," Stocker said.

"He ain't!" Tardy explained. "He never would. He likes—"

"He's doing nothing of the sort," Tanzy said before Tardy's impetuous tongue could make matters worse. "He's merely offering me employment. I appreciate the offer, but I have to decline."

"Why? The townspeople can't think worse of you than they do already."

Tanzy thought he was probably right, but she couldn't like him for saying it.

"They'd think she was a whore if she went out to your place," Stocker exclaimed.

"They wouldn't," Tardy said.

"They think that already," Stocker said. "Well, don't look so surprised. You came out here planning to marry Russ, didn't you? The only woman who'll speak to him is Betty Hicks, and you know what everybody thinks of her."

"Is that what you think of me?" Tanzy asked Stocker.

"Of course not. I—"

"If Betty's only sin is working in a saloon, how could you think anything else?"

"I'm afraid Betty's got more sins on her slate," Russ said. "I'm probably the worst one, but Stocker's not blameless either."

"You can't believe a word he says," Stocker said. "He was a lying hell-raiser even before he became a killer and a thief."

"One of these days I'm going to make you eat those words," Russ said. "But right now I've got to convince Miss Gallant she should pay off her remaining debt by working for me."

"Miss Gallant isn't setting one foot on your ranch," Stocker said. "And if you try to force her, I'll stop you myself."

"You've tried that before and not succeeded," Russ said, his tone and stance becoming more threatening.

"Before you two get into another senseless fight, let me remind you that I'm the one who'll make this decision," Tanzy said.

"I think you ought to go with Russ," Tardy said.

"Your aunt always said you were stupid," Stocker said to Tardy.

Tardy flushed at Stocker's cruel words, which made Tanzy angry.

"Tardy is very intelligent, very responsible when he wants to be, and just about the nicest person in this town."

Tardy blushed. Russ looked vaguely surprised. Stocker scoffed. "I suppose trying to see the best in everybody is what made you a good teacher."

"I can also see the worst," Tanzy said, "and there's plenty of that around here. The stage is coming. If you will—"

"I'll follow it," Russ said. "I know how to stop it."

"Why would you take a risk like that?"

"It's my duty to see you're safe."

"How do you propose to do that?"

"I'll help you look for a place to go and make sure it's safe for you to go there. Then when you've paid your debt, I'll take you there and stay until I'm sure you'll be all right."

"I'll help," Tardy said.

"You can't trust him," Stocker said. "I told you, he's always been a liar."

"Mr. Tibbolt doesn't lie," Tardy said.

Stocker ignored him.

"Why would you do all that?" Tanzy asked Russ.

"Because I brought you out here. I take responsibility for everything the men who work for me do in my name."

"I believe you do," Tanzy said, barely able to get over her surprise.

"People might talk behind your back if you work in the saloon," Stocker exclaimed, "but your reputation will be destroyed if you so much as set foot on his ranch."

"I'll go with her," Tardy said. "Nothing bad will happen as long as I'm there."

"What kind of chaperone is a sixteen-year-old boy?"

The stage pulled up in front of the hotel. "You getting on?" the driver asked Tanzy.

She hesitated only a moment. "I've changed my mind."

"Thank God you've come to your senses," Stocker said.

"I'm going to work for Mr. Tibbolt as his cook and housekeeper."

"I'm coming with you," Tardy said. "Nobody here wants me anyway."

If Russ thought a kick in the behind would have done any good, he'd have let all the citizens of Boulder Gap have at it. He'd gone into town to buy supplies and was leaving with a housekeeper who was as prickly as she was pretty and a teenage bundle of enthusiasm with absolutely no concept of what was in store for him.

"I intend to work for my keep," Tardy was saying. "Lots of cowhands are no older than me. Besides, my aunt is always saying it's time I started to make something of myself."

Russ was certain Ethel Peters wouldn't want her nephew having anything to do with him.

"I don't suppose there's any harm in your staying a couple of days," Russ said.

"I'm not going back," Tardy said. "I'm going to stay with you forever."

Even on his best days Russ knew he wasn't the kind of role model a boy like Tardy needed. And ranch work was no way to break in a green kid who probably had never ridden a horse for more than an hour at a time and never more than a few miles from town.

"I'm sure there's a lot to be learned on a ranch," Tanzy said to Tardy, "but I won't let you neglect your studies."

Russ still couldn't figure out what fit of insanity could have overtaken him to make him believe bringing Tanzy back to the ranch could ever be a good idea. He still wasn't sure why she'd agreed to come. She'd have done better to take Stocker's job.

But that was part of the problem with women like Tanzy. They always wanted things to go the way *they* wanted. They weren't tolerant of people who disagreed with them, and they held their principles as close as their petticoats. Which brought him back to the question of why he'd saddled himself with a woman he knew was going to be nothing but trouble.

He did feel responsible for her. He could wring Welt's neck all over again. Hell, it was obvious she didn't know what she was doing. Only a crazy woman would get on a stage and head off to a town where she didn't know anybody and didn't have enough money to survive more than a few days without a job. Why couldn't women understand anything about the practical side of life? They knew every trick there was when it came to manipulating men to get what they wanted, but what they wanted was never anything useful like land, cows, or even a business. They always wanted pretty clothes, jewels, and a good time.

His woolgathering ended when he pulled to a stop before the ranch house and Welt stepped out on the porch.

"I'll help you down," he said to Tanzy. "It's time you met the man who wrote those letters."

Chapter Fourteen

"So you're the man who thought Russ needed a wife," Tanzy said when Russ introduced her to Welt. He looked a bit flustered but didn't appear to be the shy type.

"Yes, ma'am."

"I must compliment you on the letters. You made life at the ranch sound good and your boss even better."

"I was only telling the truth."

"You can stop trying to persuade her I'm husband material," Russ said.

"Then what's she doing here?"

"Your boss decided I couldn't leave town without paying what I owe him. Since the school committee has decided that a former hostess at a gambling hall is unfit to teach their children, I had to choose between working for Stocker Pullet in his saloon or working as cook and housekeeper for your boss. With Tardy to serve as my chaperone, I decided to take Russ's job."

Welt looked from Tardy to Russ and back to Tanzy.

"You intend to install a woman who refused to marry you in your house with a boy who should be in school as chaperone?"

"That's about the size of it. Why don't you give Tardy a

hand with her luggage while I show her where she's going to sleep?"

Welt muttered something that sounded like a curse and stalked off. Tardy threw a questioning glance at Russ.

"He's always grouchy as a bear with a sore head."

"Why don't you fire him?" Tardy asked.

"Because he's my best friend."

The house was a log cabin made up of one long open space that appeared to be used for cooking, eating, and sitting around the fire. At one end was what appeared to be a storeroom, at the other was what she hoped was a bedroom.

"I haven't had time to build a proper house."

"Where do the men sleep?"

"In the log cabin I used to live in."

"Where will I sleep?"

"In the bedroom."

"It's the only one."

"You're the only woman on the ranch."

"It doesn't seem fair."

"Maybe not, but it's logical."

Tanzy had wondered about the wisdom of her decision nearly every mile of the extremely tedious trip to the ranch. Only by comparing Russ's offer to working for Stocker or going to a strange town without money or prospects did it seem like a good decision.

"What do you expect me to do?" she asked.

"Cook two meals a day, keep the cabin clean, and wash some clothes once in a while."

"Only once in a while?"

"We only change clothes when we smell worse than our horses."

"You'll change more often if you eat at any table I set."

"Where do you want this?" Tardy asked as he entered carrying a suitcase.

"In the bedroom," Russ said

"Where am I going to sleep?" Tardy asked.

"Are you sure you want to stay?"

"I promised Miss Gallant I'd take care of her."

Welt entered and carried a box to the bedroom without comment. Tanzy could feel the tension in the air. "When do you eat supper?"

"Whenever you get it ready."

"What about breakfast?"

"I like to be in the saddle at first light."

"Who's been doing the cooking?"

"Welt."

Great. Not only did he dislike her because she'd refused to marry Russ, he was going to be angry she was putting him out of a job. This decision was looking worse by the minute. "How many people do I have to feed?"

"Seven counting yourself."

"We got all the stuff in the bedroom," Tardy announced. "Now show me my horse."

"Ask Welt to show you," Tanzy said. "Russ and I have a few business matters to discuss."

"You been on a horse before?" Welt asked Tardy. "Do you even know how to saddle one?"

"Of course," Tardy said, insulted. "I ride all the time."

"You haven't ridden until you've been on a horse that tries to buck you off every morning and spends the rest of the day trying to bite your leg off."

Tardy blanched. "I'm not afraid of no horse," he said manfully.

"You'd better be," Welt said. "That way you might leave here with all your fingers."

"Is it really that bad?" Tanzy asked as they left the cabin.

"Only if Welt puts him on the worst horses."

"He won't, will he?"

"You can't ever tell about Welt. He was thwarted in love. He's been a little crazy ever since."

Tanzy realized it was probably too late to change her mind about the job, but she'd have to figure out a way to send Tardy back to his aunt. She refused to be responsible for the boy being maimed for the rest of his life.

"How long do I have to work?" she asked.

"You only have to work a month to pay me, but you'll need cash when you leave. I'll pay you for every day past a month."

"Let's settle for one month right now. If things work out better than I expect, we'll talk about two months, but I'm definitely not staying after that."

"Fair enough. Anything you need to know that I haven't told you?"

"What do you do for entertainment?"

"We sing to the cows." Russ suddenly grinned. "They're not an appreciative audience, but we're not good singers. If we get bored, we talk. Welt has some books he'll share if you get desperate."

"I won't be desperate. I'll be teaching you how to read."

He looked surprised. "Running this ranch keeps us real busy."

"You had time to ride into town before. Think of how much time you'll save by my being here." She wondered if his reluctance stemmed from not having told the rest of his cowhands that he couldn't read.

"Would you be willing to teach two of us?"

"Two?"

"Tim can't read either."

"How about your other cowhand?"

"He reads fine. He went to some college back east for two years."

"He went to college and he's a cowhand?"

"He didn't like being closed up, so he came west."

"And neither you nor Tim asked Welt or the other man—"

"Oren."

"—to help you learn to read?"

"You have to understand about a man's pride."

"I understand. That's why my father and brothers are dead."

"I don't think Tim and I are that bad."

"I hope not. Now why don't you go rescue Tardy while I see what I can do with this kitchen?"

"What do you mean by bringing that woman here?" Welt demanded when Russ joined him at the corral.

"This was the only way she could pay me back."

"Lie to yourself, but don't lie to me," Welt snapped. "You don't give a damn about that money."

"Okay. If you know so much, why did I bring her here?"

"I don't know. That's why I'm asking. It's like you're trying to punish me for writing those letters."

"If I wanted to do that, I'd shoot you in the belly and watch you die slowly. Still might do it."

"What are the other guys going to think?"

"They'll be happy to see a face a lot prettier than yours at the table."

"They won't be happy to have that boy on their hands," Welt said, indicating Tardy, who was trying to enter into a friendship with an uninterested sorrel gelding.

"I expect he'll go home in a couple of days, but bringing him made it easier for Tanzy to come out here."

"Why should you care about that?"

"Dammit, Welt, she was about to set off for some strange town with no money, no job, and no one to keep her out of trouble. I'm the reason she's out here, so I've got to make sure she's okay until we can figure out what to do with her."

"I still don't understand this crap about a feud."

"You ought to. I just dislike Stocker. You want to see him dead."

"She says you don't respect her," Welt said. "That shouldn't have been hard to figure out when you make it clear to everybody you don't like women. You're still afraid they'll turn out to be like your mother and sister. Which brings me back to my first question. Why did you bring her here?"

"I told you."

"No, you didn't. I hope she's got hold of you somehow. It would be good for you to find out that not all women are like your mother and sister, but don't go pretending you only brought her here because you're doing a good deed."

"She did get a raw deal," Russ said. "First from me, then the school committee."

"I knew something was different when you admitted to her that you couldn't read. Seeing her, I can understand. She's a beautiful woman."

"I'm not in love with her."

"Maybe not, but you care about her. I'm just trying to figure out how deeply."

"Stop worrying about me and see if you can keep Tardy from killing himself in the next few days."

"That's something else," Welt said. "When did you start taking in orphans?"

"Maybe when I saw myself in him. We both know how I turned out. He can stay here as long as it takes to make him believe he's not worthless. Believe me, it's not a nice feeling."

Russ stepped into the corral, lassoed a horse, and began to saddle him. He didn't need Welt to tell him Tanzy had her hooks into him. He'd figured that out days ago. What he couldn't figure out was why.

He didn't care about the money, so why had he lied and said she had to stay in town so she could pay him back? He had decided he didn't want Tanzy in his life, so why had he brought her to the ranch?

Because he couldn't help himself.

Damnation! He was just as stupid and helpless as any other man. What the hell was he going to do now?

"That's an awful lot of food," Tardy said to Tanzy.

"I'm cooking for five hardworking men and a boy with a hollow leg," Tanzy said, bringing a bowl of steaming peaches to the table. "I don't expect there'll be much left when they're done."

"You want me to call them?"

"Where are they?"

"Outside washing up. Welt said they had to look decent now there was a female on the place."

Tanzy wondered if her presence was enough to make Russ feel he ought to clean up some. So far he'd treated her like one of the hands, which didn't set well with Tanzy. She didn't believe she should be accorded special treatment, but neither did she feel she ought to be ignored. Russ hadn't returned to the house, so she'd had to brave Welt's sour temper to glean the information she needed to cook her first meal.

"Everything smells better than when Aunt Ethel does it," Tardy said.

"You'd better call the men in before supper gets cold."

Tanzy didn't want to hear Tardy tell her again that he thought Russ was in love with her. She was irritated Tardy could be so blind, but she was also irritated Russ was ignoring her. She'd agreed to take the job as Russ's housekeeper because the evil she knew looked safer than the evil she didn't, but she was beginning to wonder if there hadn't been a bit of female pique mixed up in there somewhere.

Russ's reaction to her had been a strange combination of indifference and determined interest. She didn't understand either. He didn't want to marry her, but he had taken responsibility for her safety until she could support herself. He didn't show her any special attention, but she'd been the first person to whom he'd confided that he couldn't read. Even though he was now her boss, he'd agreed to let her continue to teach him. That involved her reading short writings that were very personal and unusually revealing, that in essence established an intimacy between them he didn't share with anyone else. She had assumed that intimacy moved their relationship to a personal level. Apparently she'd been wrong.

She needed more time to determine the real nature of her disappointment, but right now it felt very personal, and that worried her. She liked feeling she had a special relationship with Russ through his writing, but she didn't want it to be a relationship she needed for her happiness. That would make her vulnerable, defenseless, the pawn of a man who would treat her as property rather than as a partner. She'd seen what came of that and had no intention of letting it happen to her.

"Something smells mighty good," an attractive young man said as he burst in the door with unruly enthusiasm and a smile that split his face from ear to ear. "I hope you got biscuits. I love biscuits, but Welt can't make them worth a damn."

"This is Tim." Russ had entered on the boy's heels. "He's real shy, doesn't say much. You practically have to wring opinions out of him. He's afraid of hurting somebody's feelings."

"He doesn't have any feelings," Welt said. "No brains either."

"Tim keeps the rest of us young," an older man said, the one Tanzy assumed must be Oren. "He reminds us of what we used to be like."

"I was never that crazy," Welt said.

"You were worse," Russ said.

"I was never in jail."

"You were never in *prison*. You spent many a night in jail."

"Prison wasn't so bad," Tim said. "I'd probably be dead if I hadn't been locked up."

"You'd have gotten killed anyway if Russ hadn't decided to save your useless hide," Welt said.

"Never could figure out why you did that," Oren said.

"I figured he'd make a good cowhand," Russ said. "Tim's not afraid of anything, man or beast."

"Not smart enough to be afraid," Welt said.

"Stop yammering and let's eat," Tim said.

He'd plopped down in his seat, but Welt jerked him up by his collar. Tim looked confused until Welt made it clear he couldn't sit down until Tanzy was seated. Tanzy hurried to take the biscuits out of the oven, put them in a bowl, and place it on the table.

"Hot damn!" Tim exclaimed. "I hope you got a second batch a' baking, 'cause I intend to eat every one of these."

"Try it and you'll lose a hand," Oren said. "I'm just as fond of biscuits as you are."

Tanzy took her seat. The men seated themselves quickly. She was amused to see Tardy had managed to get a chair next to Russ.

"Who's going to say blessing?" Tanzy asked.

"Is it bad enough it needs a blessing?" Tim asked, a disappointed look on his face.

"No, you heathen," Welt said. "She's talking about asking God to bless the food before we eat."

"We never did that before."

"And some of it definitely needed blessing," Oren said.

"I think Mr. Tibbolt ought to say the blessing," Tardy said. "He's the boss of this outfit."

Welt looked disgusted; Russ looked amused.

"If you're going to stay here, you'll have to call me Russ. I'm not sure these *heathens* know who Mr. Tibbolt is."

"Nobody I want to know," Tim said.

"Shut up and bow your head," Welt said.

Tanzy was used to eating at a table filled with men, but she'd never sat though a meal like this one. To start with, the men raved about everything they put in their mouths. She'd have to make two plates of biscuits from now on. Tim and Oren nearly got into a fight over the last one. Even Welt said it was a pleasure to eat food prepared by someone who knew how to cook. Russ complained that his food bill was going to double. Buck, the fifth man, was guarding the pass. Tanzy wouldn't meet him until tomorrow.

It struck her as remarkable that she should feel more

comfortable sitting down at the table with three men who'd served time in prison than she did having dinner in Stocker Pullet's hotel. There had to be something wrong with her. Maybe all this Colorado sunshine was drying out her brain. Maybe her situation had gotten so far beyond her experience she couldn't think rationally. Maybe she'd grown up so used to danger that something like this didn't bother her. Imagining what Ethel would say made her smile.

"You got a secret?" Tim asked.

"No."

"I know that look," Tim said. "My girl used to get it all the time."

"She was probably imagining how happy she'd be as soon as she could figure out how to get rid of you," Welt said.

"At least she didn't run off with another guy until *after* I went to prison," Tim said, uncaring about the pall he'd thrown over the conversation. "I'm volunteering for ranch duty," he said. "I'll take it for a whole week."

"What's ranch duty?" Tardy asked.

"It's boring," Tim said. "You just have to make sure nobody steals the horses or burns down the house."

"The kid can do that," Oren said.

"Nah," Tim said. "What's he going to do if a great big bunch of bad guys comes riding up and threatens to carry off Miss Gallant? Why, the poor kid wouldn't know who to shoot first. And while he was making up his mind, they'd make off with her and the horses. We can't afford to lose a woman who can cook this good."

"That's mighty considerate of you," Russ said, "but I wouldn't trust you to watch a pretty sorrel filly, not to mention a pretty woman."

"You think I can't protect her?"

"He's afraid you'd pester her so much making coyote eyes at her," Welt said, "begging for more biscuits, and generally making a nuisance of yourself that she'll throw herself into the arms of the first bad guy who shows up."

"I'll fight you for it," Tim said.

"Before anybody gets in a brawl," Russ said, with a grin that eased the tension in the room, "I'm giving myself the duty."

"You're too old for her," Tim cried.

"And you're too young for a nine-year-old," Welt said.

"Lest you think I'm going to spend all my time making coyote eyes at her and begging for extra biscuits," Russ said, "let me explain that I'll be teaching young Mr. Benton here how to become a cowhand."

"That ought to have you begging to watch the pass," Welt said.

"I'm not that bad," Tardy protested without heat.

Tanzy listened as the men all joined in the gentle ribbing of a very embarrassed Tardy. Though they picked apart his physical size and strength with ruthless accuracy and predicted dire results in every attempt to master handling a horse or a rope, it was done in a way that quickly made Tardy feel he was part of the crew. A raw hand, surely, but one who was accepted nonetheless. She wished the people of Boulder Gap could see Russ now. She didn't know what he had been like in the past, but he had changed in a way that enabled him to take a group of ex-cons and meld them into a smooth-working crew that liked and respected each other.

"Would anybody like more coffee?" Tanzy asked, getting up.

"Don't get up," Tim said. "I can get it."

"Don't let him touch the pot," Welt said. "He can't pour without spilling half over you, the floor, and himself."

"I'll get it," Tanzy said, grinning at Tim's pretense of being affronted. "I don't want to be treating any burns."

"I supposed that means I don't have to help clean up," Tim said. "Me being so clumsy and all, I'm bound to drop something."

"There's nothing to drop," Tardy pointed out, somewhat awed. "You ate everything."

"A cook likes to be appreciated," Tanzy said. "Now you men take your coffee over to the fireplace and I'll clean up."

She was amused to see Tardy again found a way to settle himself next to Russ.

"I think we have a clear case of hero worship," Welt said to her in an undertone.

"Russ is the first person to try to make him feel good about himself."

"Russ is good at that. Look at Tim. That useless piece of rawhide thinks he's wonderful."

"And you give Russ all the credit?"

"Sure. I'm soured on life and hate to see anybody happy. Do you need help putting anything away?"

"No. I think I remember."

"You'll probably rearrange everything anyway."

"Probably."

Welt turned away, leaving Tanzy to clean up while she listened to Russ assign the next day's duties. She finished in the kitchen, filled her coffee cup, and headed toward the men. Russ got to his feet to meet her.

"Let's go for a walk," he said.

Chapter Fifteen

Russ didn't have much to say, but he felt uncomfortable talking to Tanzy in front of the other men. He was sure everything he said would sound different from the way he intended it. He had to make sure Tanzy didn't misinterpret his reason for inviting her outside. This was no romantic tryst, though it might be a thawing in the relationship between them.

"That was a wonderful meal," he said. "The boys have decided hiring you was my best decision since choosing to make my ranch in this valley."

"They're nice men. I find it hard to believe you met them in prison."

"A lot of men in prison shouldn't be there. I'm trying to put that time behind me."

"By surrounding yourself with ex-cons?"

"By concentrating on rebuilding my life and giving these men an opportunity to do the same."

"I think what you're doing is wonderful."

"It's selfish. I couldn't have held this valley without them. Stocker has done everything he could to drive me out."

"He says it was his land."

"Stocker only wants it because it's the best grazing land around and because he hopes to drive me out. More than ninety percent of each rancher's range is open land. Until the government sells it to someone, it belongs to the man who's strong enough to claim it and hold it."

"Why did you come back after you got out of prison?"

How could he explain his decision to her when he didn't really understand it himself? "This is my home. I don't know why it's so important, but I never considered going anywhere else. Why did you leave your home?" He'd always wondered what could have happened to make a young woman who wasn't looking for glamor and excitement leave the protection of her home.

"My family has been involved in a feud for more than a hundred years. I was tired of the fighting. I was tired of seeing the people I loved buried in cold graves. And I was dead tired of talking and never being heard, so I ran away to St. Louis."

"Only to find working in a gambling hall wasn't too good either, and you thought being a mail-order bride might be better."

"Something like that."

"What are you going to do when you leave here?"

"I don't know."

"You need a plan."

"I know."

"Want me to help?"

"You already told Stocker you would."

Clever way of accepting his help without asking for it. Odd that he should have thought he needed to help her. Even more unusual that he wanted to. It all went back to that mysterious hold she had on him.

"Do you ever get lonely out here?" she asked.

"No."

"Don't you feel cut off?"

"No."

Returning to the valley had been an important part of his rehabilitation. It had given him something of his own, something to build, something to defend. It had given

NAME: _____

ADDRESS: _____

_____

_____

TELEPHONE: _____

E-MAIL: _____

_____ I want to pay by credit card.

__ Visa   __ MasterCard   __ Discover

Account Number: _____

Expiration date: _____

SIGNATURE: _____

*Send this form, along with $2.00 shipping
and handling for your FREE books, to:*

Historical Romance Book Club
20 Academy Street
Norwalk, CT 06850-4032

*Or fax (must include credit card
information!) to: 610.995.9274.
You can also sign up on the Web
at www.dorchesterpub.com.*

Offer open to residents of the U.S. and
Canada only. Canadian residents, please
call 1.800.481.9191 for pricing information.

If under 18, a parent or guardian must sign. Terms, prices and conditions
subject to change. Subscription subject to acceptance. Dorchester
Publishing reserves the right to reject any order or cancel any subscription.

him a reason for staying alive when he thought there wasn't any. "There's something about being out here that gets down to the essentials, to what really matters."

"What really matters to you?"

"Being free. I don't mean just being out of prison. I mean being completely free to be what I am, to believe as I do, to live the way I want. You see Boulder Gap's rejection of me as a handicap. I see it as a blessing. Those people want nothing from me, so they don't care what I do."

Why didn't he feel as confident of those words tonight as he had in the past?

"I grew up in a tightly knit family," Tanzy said. "I guess that bred in me the need to be around people."

"I *am* with people. I'm with my friends."

"Friends aren't the same as family."

"They're better. Friends stay with you because they want to, not because they feel it's their duty."

"You don't have a very high opinion of people, do you?"

"Except for the men here, I have little reason to."

"Has it ever occurred to you that everybody considers your best friends criminals?"

"Frequently. Does that worry you?"

"It might have before tonight, but it doesn't seem so important now that I've met them."

"That's your answer. It's the people who are important, not their reputations."

"You have a lot of interesting points, but I've had a very busy day. I'm too tired for a serious philosophical discussion." She sighed. "It's peaceful here," she said, looking around. "I never realized how beautiful the night sky could be."

"Didn't you have sky in Kentucky?"

"You can't see much of it through the trees. Here the sky seems endless."

"It is."

He had situated the ranch buildings on a slight rise up against a nearly vertical stone wall to provide protection from the bitter winter winds and storms. It would also provide protection if he should ever be attacked. They walked a short distance to some trees that served as a screen. From there they could look down on the valley as it spread out for nearly twenty miles before them.

Once a person's eyes got used to the diminished light, the moonlight made the valley appear nearly as light as day. It illuminated the gray flanks of the mountains that ringed his valley and glistened off the snow that capped some of the highest peaks. The trees that clung to the flanks of the mountains looked like dark, ominous bands. Russ knew them to be cool in summer, protective in winter, and a screen against unwelcome eyes peering into his valley. Water from a dozen different rivulets cascaded noisily down the mountainsides, coming together to form a stream that wound its way lazily down the length of the valley and out the narrow entrance at the other end. He could see the dark shapes of cows, some grazing, others lying down.

"I feel like I could stay here forever," Tanzy said.

Those words should have hit him like cold water in the face, but they had nearly the opposite effect. He *wanted* her to stay. That didn't make sense. What the hell was the hold she had on him, and how was he going to break it?

"You just said you couldn't stay in a place like this, that you had to have people around you."

"I'd like to go to town occasionally to see other women, but I could be very happy here if I had a husband who respected me and children to love."

"Don't you want a husband who loves you?"

"Every woman dreams of that, but I'd settle for one who respects me."

He almost said he could respect a woman if he found one who deserved it, but he wasn't sure he'd be telling the truth. It seemed incredible to him that any man would let himself be advised by a woman, much less act on her advice when it went counter to his own opinion. "I think many men love women, their mothers, wives, daughters, but they love them as helpless creatures who need a man's strength and guidance."

"I wouldn't want to marry a man who thought I was so weak, stupid, and helpless I couldn't survive without him."

"A man doesn't want a wife who'll argue with him over everything."

"I wouldn't argue with my husband over everything, but I would expect him to respect my opinion enough to listen and give it fair and honest consideration."

Russ couldn't restrain a small chuckle. "Where do you think you're going to find a man like that?"

"The same place you'll find a woman who'll marry you."

"Then we'll both be single. I'm a lying, thieving ex-con."

"You're smart, ambitious, hardworking, kind, and thoughtful."

She sounded like she really meant it.

"Some people might give you the ambitious and hardworking, but not the rest."

"Everybody treats Tardy like some kind of idiot, but you've gone out of your way to make him feel better about himself."

"In a way he reminds me of myself years ago."

"You must have done something to have earned your men's loyalty."

"I pay them."

"There's more than that. You said yourself they'd stick with you no matter what. Men don't do that without a good reason. I wish the people in Boulder Gap could see what I've seen tonight. I think some of them would change their minds."

"Not Stocker or Ethel."

"Maybe not, but not everyone feels about you as they do."

"They'd never let on."

"I know. They're cowards. At least nobody can say that about you."

Russ was having a difficult time believing anyone other than Welt could think so well of him. It sounded as if she liked him. He had a feeling he was about to start liking her, but maybe this new feeling was all right. She didn't want to marry him and he didn't want to marry anyone, so liking her was safe.

Deciding that seemed to release a ball of tension inside him.

"What are you sighing about?" Tanzy asked.

He hadn't realized he'd made any sound. "Just thinking how nice it is to be standing outside on a beautiful summer night talking with a woman who doesn't think I'm the devil's son. It'll take a while, but I think I could get used to it."

"I'll get Tardy to help."

He didn't want Tardy's and Tanzy's feelings about him combined. He wanted them separate so he could tell exactly what she felt.

"Boys like Tardy can't help admiring somebody who

stands up against the same forces that have belittled them," Russ said.

"You might be the one person who can save his life."

"You've done that."

"I only started. He needs a man to take him the rest of the way."

"And you think I can be that man?"

"I think you're the *only* man who can do it."

Russ wasn't certain what he was feeling just then, but he was certain it could be very dangerous if it got out of control. This experiment in liking a woman wasn't going very well. It hadn't been five minutes and already he was starting to feel unlike himself. He'd better bring this attempt to a close in a hurry.

He put his fingertips under Tanzy's chin and lifted her head until he could look into her eyes. "No one's ever said anything that nice to me. Thank you."

"You don't have to thank me for telling the truth."

"I don't know that you have. I'm thanking you for believing in me."

He leaned down to kiss her. He'd intended to kiss her cheek, her forehead, even the end of her nose, but he somehow found himself kissing her lips. The shock was so great he couldn't move. Then, once he could, he didn't want to.

He'd never known something as simple as a kiss could reach out and yank him off his feet so quickly. He'd never realized a woman's belief in him could make him want to cling to her, to put his arms around her and pull her to him so she could never get away.

He suddenly realized his arms *had* encircled Tanzy's waist, that he *had* pulled her to him. She hadn't broken the kiss, she hadn't tried to pull away. He couldn't tell whether time stood still or his brain stopped functioning, but the kiss seemed to go on forever.

"Russ, where are you? Welt says I can't sleep in the bunkhouse."

Tardy's voice cut through the night with the sharpness of a thunderclap. Russ came to his senses to find Tanzy wrapped in his arms in a passionate embrace. He released her and nearly jumped back. He didn't know what the hell had gotten into him.

"Russ, where are you?"

"Sorry," Russ said to Tanzy. "I just wanted to thank you, but things sorta got out of hand."

"For a man who doesn't want to get married, you sure have a dangerous way of saying thanks."

"I never thanked anybody like that before."

"I'm sure your cowhands are grateful."

"Dammit, Russ, where are you? Why can't I sleep in the bunkhouse?"

"We're over here by the fence," Russ called out. "I'm sorry. I won't do it again. The boys will never forgive me if I drive you away the very first night."

"That was unexpected, but it's a very nice way of saying thank you. Maybe you ought to try it more often."

"You saying you wouldn't get mad if I did it again?"

"I'm saying it might make a few ladies think differently about you."

"More likely it would get me shot."

"Welt says I have to sleep in the house to protect Tanzy," Tardy said, coming close. "What are you standing out here for? It's dark."

"Somebody needs to protect my reputation," Tanzy said, "and you're the only one who can do that."

"Is that true?" Tardy asked.

"Nobody in town would believe Tanzy was innocent if any one of us slept in the ranch house."

"No, but—"

"You said you were coming to protect her reputation," Russ said. "I'm afraid you're going to have to do what you promised."

"Why wouldn't they doubt her reputation if *I* slept in the ranch house?" Tardy demanded. "I'm a man."

Russ remembered all too clearly feeling much the same way. "Because they trust you, people will believe you if you say Tanzy's virtue is safe."

"Is that true?" Tardy asked Tanzy.

"Your aunt would never have asked you to look after me if she hadn't trusted you."

It was apparent Tardy had previously looked on that task as a chore rather than an honor, but he appeared willing to reconsider. "Okay, but as soon as she leaves, I'm moving into the bunkhouse."

"Agreed. Now we'd all better go to bed. We get started early in the morning."

It was much later before Russ felt any desire to sleep. The kiss in the schoolhouse had been impulsive, something he hadn't anticipated and therefore wasn't prepared for. He didn't have a similar excuse this time. He knew how dangerous kissing Tanzy could be and he'd done it anyway. He could tell himself it was in appreciation for her believing in him, but that wasn't the whole truth. He *wanted* to kiss her, had been thinking about it nearly the whole time since he'd decided to bring her to the ranch. He hadn't been consciously planning to kiss her, but ever since Tanzy arrived, he'd wanted to do all kinds of unexpected things.

Why the hell had Welt written those letters? If it would

do any good, he'd break his head all over again. Only
Tanzy would still be there, believing that he was good,
that he was kind, that he was thoughtful. Now, God help
him, he wanted to be all those things. Maybe he ought to
watch the pass for the next few days. He needed time to
think, and helping Tardy turn into enough of a cowhand
so he didn't kill himself was hardly going to leave him
extra time to pee.

Tanzy undressed slowly, mechanically, her mind elsewhere. Russ's kiss worried her. It upset her that a man as
strong, determined, and successful as Russ would be so
grateful that someone could believe in him. Something
truly awful must have happened to make him so thankful
for a little bit of praise. She wasn't saying he was a hero or
anything. Yet he'd kissed her like a man desperately eager
to find a reason to believe in himself.

Then there was the kiss itself. Never mind his reasons
for it; what about her reasons for letting him kiss her, for
kissing him back? Was she just grateful he'd rescued her
from an uncertain future, or was it more than that?

She'd already admitted she was attracted to him, but
now she *liked* him. She empathized with him. She also
admired him and was grateful to him. With all those feelings mixed up together, it was hard to separate out the
pieces and decipher just what each meant.

Still, it wasn't the common practice to go around kissing people you admired, at least not like Russ had kissed
her. And even if western men did do that, she shouldn't
have been so willing to melt into his embrace. She
couldn't deny that was exactly what had happened. If the
kiss had lasted much longer, she might have dissolved
entirely. She wasn't sure whether she was grateful or
angry about Tardy's interruption.

That in itself was another sign that something was wrong. She always knew her own mind, never had any problem articulating how she felt, never vacillated or changed.

Things were different out here. Maybe a person had to be ready to change her mind, look at things in a different way. But flexibility could be dangerous, too. A person who swapped her principles every few weeks would soon have no principles at all. Maybe she needed to learn to interpret her principles a little differently, apply them with more latitude, not break anything but bend a little.

She wasn't going to decide anything tonight. She was too tired. Too much had happened. She understood too little. She needed to sleep, to clear her mind. Tomorrow she'd figure out what to do.

"That was a mighty fine breakfast, ma'am," Tim said. "I want you to know if it ever comes to a vote, I'll vote we send Welt off and keep you."

"You're not fooling anybody," Oren said. "You'd vote to keep her if she burned the biscuits."

"Not if she burned the biscuits," Tim said, reaching for another before he finished the one on his plate in case someone else got it first. "A man's got to draw the line somewhere."

"I'm sure she's drawn the line at listening to the foolery of a stripling," Welt said.

"I'm young, but I'm pretty," Tim said.

"Not as pretty as your horse," Oren said.

"Ma'am, I ask you if it's right to be so cruel to a man before he's finished his breakfast."

"The only way to make you finish your breakfast is to take your plate from you," Welt said.

"I'm going to ask her to marry me and make me biscuits for every meal."

"Miss Gallant wouldn't marry any cowhand," Tardy said. "She knows enough to be a schoolteacher."

"I know enough not to insult a man who puts in an honest day's work," Tanzy said. "You ought to apologize to Tim."

"But he was making fun of you," Tardy protested.

"He was just joking," Russ said. "No one at this table would ever think of making fun of Tanzy."

"Sorry," Tardy said.

"Don't worry," Tim said. "I'll never fault a man for defending the honor of a lady."

"Whew!" Orem said, getting to his feet. "I'd better relieve Buck before things get too rich for my blood."

"You don't have any blood," Tim said. "It was drained out of you at birth."

There was a good deal more ribbing before the men finished breakfast and headed to the corral to saddle their horses for the day.

"Why don't I have a job?"

"You don't know the ranch yet," Russ explained. "You need a few days to get familiar with things before I let you go off on your own."

"How can I get lost in a valley?"

"Come on. I'll show you."

"What time do you want supper?" Tanzy asked.

"We'll be back about dusk. We'll have supper whenever you get it ready."

"It'll be ready half an hour after you get back."

Tanzy could hardly keep from grinning at the way Tardy danced around Russ like a frisky puppy.

"I wouldn't be surprised if Russ strangles that kid before noon," Welt said.

"I expect he's a lot like Tim."

"I hope not. Some of the things Tim has done would turn your hair gray."

"Then why did Russ bring him here?"

"I can't tell you. You'll have to figure that out for yourself."

"It looks like there are a lot of things people expect me to figure out for myself."

"Like what?"

"Why you're staying at the house instead of Russ."

"Russ always leaves somebody here. He can't watch the house and work with Tardy. There's only one road into the valley to bring in cows and supplies, but there's dozens of ways over the ridges. Somebody's got to guard the house and the livestock."

"So he doesn't believe I'm going to run away once his back is turned?"

"Would you?"

"I'm not sure. You see, I've heard a lot about Russ from everybody I've met, but not much about Russ from himself. He said you have been his best friend his whole life, so you'll know why he's like he is. We've got the whole day together, so by the time they get home for supper, I want to know everything you can tell me about Russ Tibbolt. Most importantly, I want to know why you wrote those letters."

Chapter Sixteen

As soon as Russ and Tardy rode out, Tanzy picked up the coffeepot and two cups and went in search of Welt. She found him at the corrals that had been constructed in a grove of lodgepole and ponderosa pine. Spikes of purple

lupine and the lacy white flowers of Solomon's Seal
sprang from the forest floor in scattered clumps. Beyond
the pines, clumps of white mountain phlox and pink-
and-white pussytoes grew in the marshy ground alongside the stream. It seemed nearly impossible that sadness
could exist in such an idyllic setting. She poured coffee
and handed a cup to Welt. "Start talking and don't leave
anything out."

"Russ's mother's first husband, his sister's father, died
shortly after his sister was born," Welt told Tanzy after he
took a sip of his coffee. He leaned against the corral, one
foot resting on a pole. Tanzy settled on the trunk of a
fallen pine. "His mother took up with a handsome miner
who said he'd marry her. Instead, he went back east after
he made his big strike, leaving her pregnant with Russ."

"Did the man know she was pregnant?"

"Yes."

"Didn't he want to know about his own child?"

"I guess not. Russ doesn't have any idea where he
came from or where he went. His mother married Bob
Tibbolt to give Russ a name."

"That doesn't seem like such a dark past," Tanzy said.

"Bob Tibbolt adored his wife and daughter, but he
didn't like Russ because he wouldn't knuckle under.
Russ grew up knowing he was unwanted by the man
who fathered him, an embarrassment to his mother, disliked by his stepfather."

"That must have been hard."

"Things got worse. Bob Tibbolt loved his wife, but June
was a beautiful woman who wanted beautiful things.
When she met Stocker Pullet, she found a way to have
them."

Tanzy had a sinking feeling in the pit of her stomach.

"Stocker was just as attracted to June, and she became his mistress. People out here don't have much room for gray when it comes to women. Either you're good or you're bad."

"I discovered that for myself," Tanzy said.

"Russ loved his mother despite what she was doing. If I was to tell you about the number of fights he got into because of what people said about her, we'd be here all day. I don't know what happened, whether June got too greedy or Stocker just got tired of her, but he threw her out. June was so overwrought, she killed herself. To make things worse, Bob Tibbolt killed himself, too. In a needless bit of cruelty, he left a note disclosing that Russ was a bastard."

"What could make a man do such a cruel thing to a boy?" Tanzy asked.

"I don't know. He was distraught over his wife's death."

"What did Russ do?"

"What any grieving, humiliated, and desperate teenager would do. He rode to Stocker's ranch and confronted him. Stocker laughed at him, told him his mother was nothing but a common whore, and had his men throw him off the place."

"My God! How could he do something so cruel?"

"Stocker has always been so rich he could do anything he pleased."

"What did Russ do then?"

"There wasn't much he *could* do. People around here had never liked him, so after the episode at Stocker's ranch, they turned their backs on him. He couldn't get any work, so he went to Texas."

Now Tanzy understood a lot better why Russ didn't respect women, why he didn't want to get married, why he hated Stocker. She'd never forget the pain of losing her brothers and father, but it must have been worse for Russ to lose his mother in such humiliating circumstances.

"That doesn't explain why you wrote those letters," she said to Welt.

"There's more," Welt said. "And I have to take the blame for some of it."

He had looked somber before, but now his expression turned bleak.

"I had been in love with Russ's sister from the time I realized girls were different from boys. My father had a decent business, so I was probably the most eligible bachelor in town. I had big plans for getting married as soon as I was eighteen. Then Toley Pullet turned up."

"You mean he didn't live here already?"

"No. After her husband died, Stocker's stepmother moved away and married again. Toley only came back when his mother died. He was a handsome young man, full of laughter and a love of good times with money to spend. He and Adele took a liking to each other from the start. When he left, she went with him. I was such a lovesick fool, I wrote Russ, telling him his sister had gone off with Stocker's brother. The letter was nearly a year finding him. I wish it never had. By the time he got it, Toley had left Adele. Apparently she was so drunk one winter night she couldn't find her way back home. She died from exposure."

Tanzy would never have thought she'd say anything good about a feud. But at least it hadn't left her feeling rejected by the people who should have loved her.

"Russ got home about the time Toley was paying his brother a visit. I didn't want to tell him about Adele's death because I knew he'd do something stupid, but people in town just had to point out that Adele was no better than her mama. Russ had grown a lot bigger and stronger during his two years in Texas. When I tried to stop him going after Toley, he knocked me down."

"So that's why he shot Toley," Tanzy said.

"I rode with him, using every argument I could think of to change his mind, but he was kinda crazy that day. I think he felt like he had nothing else to lose, that his life didn't mean much anymore. He called Toley out and challenged him to a fistfight. He wanted the satisfaction of beating the man senseless, but Toley fancied himself a gun slick. He told Russ he wouldn't dirty his hands with him, that if he wanted to avenge the honor of his whoring sister, he'd have to use a gun."

"He said that?"

"I was afraid he'd make Russ so mad he'd draw first. Then no matter what happened, one of Stocker's men would kill him. But it was a fair fight. Both of them drew at the same time. Toley missed. Russ didn't. They might have killed him anyway if I hadn't pulled a gun on Stocker. I told them I'd kill him right there if they didn't take Russ to the sheriff. I was sure he'd be safe. I could testify it was a fair fight.

"I was a fool. Stocker's men all swore Russ pulled a gun on Toley and killed him before he could get his gun out of his holster. I testified to what happened at the trial, but Stocker had threatened or paid off the jury—I don't know which—so they said Russ was guilty. I think the judge gave him only five years because he knew they were lying, but there was nothing he could do about it."

Tanzy had been used to thinking that nobody had a more tragic life than she, but it was a miracle Russ wasn't a misogynist who hated the world. That he could turn his life around, devote his energies to building his ranch and helping his friends rebuild their lives spoke of a depth of character she'd underestimated.

"Why did you write me?" she asked Welt. "I can't imagine a man less likely to want to marry than Russ."

"I knew Russ had always wanted a family. He suffered so much because he loved his mother and sister. He'd probably have loved Bob Tibbolt if the bastard had given him half a chance. People said he was a troublemaker, always looking for a fight, that he had an uncontrollable temper, that he was vicious. What they didn't see was that the things they said about his family were like knife thrusts. Russ was just defending his family's honor."

"Did he tell you that he wanted to get married?"

"He said he *didn't* want to get married, but I knew it wasn't true. I expect a couple of local girls would have braved their families' disapproval to marry Russ, but he could only see that everybody hated him. I figured he might not be prejudiced against a woman from back east. I hoped once she was here, he'd give himself a chance to get to know her before he made up his mind."

"It was a big gamble."

"Russ is the best friend I've ever had, and I was responsible for ruining his life. I wrote to more than a dozen women before I settled on you."

"You didn't settle on me. You settled on what my friend said about me."

"That's what Russ told me, but you're exactly what she said you were."

"Only she didn't tell you that I hate feuds and refuse to marry a man who won't respect me."

"Russ isn't feuding, and he does respect you."

"It doesn't matter. He doesn't want to marry me. He's said so."

"Russ doesn't know what he wants because he

wouldn't let himself ask those questions. His whole life was a series of losing battles until he and those guys he met in prison came back here and started a ranch."

"I can tell you're about to ask me to do something, but don't ask me to marry Russ. I've already told you why I can't."

"He respects and likes you. Since he doesn't want to marry you, you're perfect for the job."

"What job?"

"Make Russ believe in women again so he'll marry and have the family he has to have if he's ever to be happy."

"What makes you think I can do that?"

"Russ asked you to teach him to read. That's the first time he's ever trusted a woman enough to ask anything of her. I don't know what you did to break through that wall he built around himself, but help me demolish the rest of it."

"I'm going to be here two months at most. I can't—"

"It might not take that long. He wouldn't have brought you here if he didn't like and trust you. You've got to help me."

"I don't have to help you," Tanzy said, irritated at being put on the spot. "You lied to me when you wrote those letters for Russ."

But her arguments weren't carrying any more weight with her than they were with Welt. She liked Russ. She was going to be here anyway. If she could do anything to help restore his faith in women, why shouldn't she?

"Okay," she said, "but you've got to understand I'm doing it only because he's been nice to me about this whole mess."

"Fine. I don't care why you're doing it as long as you do it."

"I'll make sure he understands from the beginning that

I'm leaving as soon as I have enough money to go somewhere else, so don't you say anything that might lead him to think otherwise."

"I won't."

"I don't trust you. You've lied to us both."

"I just want you to make him believe he's the kind of man a nice, respectable woman would be proud to marry."

"I can't believe the women around here are so stupid they haven't figured that out for themselves. Maybe it's a good thing he hasn't married anybody from Boulder Gap. It would be a shame for Russ's kids to be morons."

Tanzy spent the rest of the morning reorganizing the pantry and making a list of things she needed. That afternoon she started cleaning the kitchen. Welt might be a decent cook, but she'd never met a man who understood what it meant to have a clean kitchen. Tomorrow she'd start on the house. After that she'd tackle the men's clothes. At some point she'd have to clean up the men themselves, but that was down the road. One step at a time.

How did you restore a man's faith in women in a few months when its destruction had been going on all his life? It wasn't as if she could perform some heroic act or demonstrate sterling character in the kitchen. She guessed she could begin being the best cook and housekeeper she could possibly be. And she'd make sure Russ could read by the time she left.

While she was thinking about his future, she'd better spare a few thoughts for her own. She had to figure out what she was going to do when she left Boulder Gap. Twice she'd run off without a good plan. She didn't intend to do it a third time.

* * *

Welt stuck his head in the doorway. "You'd better come out. You've got visitors."

"Who?" Tanzy asked. She had grease smeared over her arms and her clothes. She expected she probably had some on her face, too, and the cloth she'd tied around her hair. She was in no condition to receive visitors, not even dusty cowboys.

"Come see for yourself," Welt replied unhelpfully before disappearing.

Tanzy got up from her knees, where she'd been struggling with a badly encrusted oven. Whoever it was, her visitors had come uninvited, so they would have to take her as they found her. She stepped outside and saw Welt lounging in a chair under the porch roof.

"Where are they?" she asked.

He pointed in the direction of the trees under which she and Russ had stood talking the night before and was horrified to see Stocker approaching in a buggy with Ethel Peters seated next to him.

"Oh my God! What are they doing here?"

"Come to save your virtue, I expect," Welt offered.

It irritated Tanzy that they could be so officious as to think they could tell her what to do, but she was touched they thought enough of her to be concerned for her welfare and safety.

"They can't think I'm going to drive any man crazy with lust looking like this." Her own words surprised her. She was startled she could speak so openly about lust to any man, especially one she'd met only the day before.

"They think we're determined to ravish any woman unfortunate enough to fall into our clutches."

"I wonder what argument they'll present to convince me to go back with them."

Stocker hadn't pulled the buggy to a halt before Ethel, her face a mask of horror, exclaimed, "What have they done to you?"

"I've been trying to clean the stove," Tanzy said, smiling when she realized Ethel took her appearance as proof her worst fears had been realized. "Men have no idea of cleanliness when it comes to a kitchen."

"You shouldn't be doing work like that," Stocker said.

"Of course I should. I'm the cook. I'll be the house-keeper, too, once I get the kitchen clean and the provisions properly organized."

"You can't stay here," Ethel said. "It's not safe."

Tanzy approached the buggy. "If you mean my reputation isn't safe, you're wrong. It's already ruined. Betty Hicks saw to that."

"I'm quite prepared to believe she lied," Ethel said.

"She didn't. I did work in that gambling hall, but my virtue was intact when I left, just as it will be when I leave here."

"You can't trust Russ Tibbolt or any man who'd work for him," Stocker said. "They're all liars, thieves, and ex-convicts."

"I don't have to trust them. I sleep in the cabin, they sleep in the bunkhouse, and Tardy sleeps on the couch outside my door."

"Who's to say you can trust that boy?" Stocker asked.

"My nephew is very unsatisfactory in many ways," Ethel said, her voice steely, "but he would not violate a respectable woman. Nor would he allow anyone else to do so."

"He couldn't stop Russ."

"He wouldn't have to," Welt said. "The rest of us would do it for him."

"I'm sorely disappointed in you, Welt Allard," Ethel said. "You know your being out here is breaking your parents' hearts."

"I won't have anything to do with folks who lie so they can put a man they don't like in prison. My parents bought into the lie just like the rest of the sycophants who are so afraid of Stocker they'll do anything he says."

"You calling me a liar, son?" Stocker said.

"You're damned right. I did ten years ago. Nothing's changed since."

Stocker reached for the rifle lying across his lap, but Tanzy moved between him and Welt.

"If you're thinking of challenging him to a gunfight," Tanzy said, "I'd advise against it. If Welt doesn't kill you, one of the others will."

"You can't approve of such violence," Ethel said.

"I don't approve of any violence, but neither do I approve of Stocker reaching for his gun because somebody said something he didn't like."

"He called me a liar."

"I would think a man of your wealth and reputation could afford to ignore anything people said about you."

"A man's got to protect his reputation."

"Killing Welt won't prove you're not a liar. It'll just lead to more killing."

"Help me down, Stocker," Ethel said. "I must talk to Tanzy. I can't allow her to remain in such a dangerous situation."

"You'd better come in, too," Tanzy said to Stocker. "I don't want to leave you alone with Welt. Things are somewhat disorganized in here," Tanzy said when they were inside. "I'm still working on the kitchen."

"Is that where you sleep?" Ethel asked, pointing to the door beside the fireplace.

"Yes. You can see for yourself there are no windows and this is the only way in."

"No one will believe that you could live alone with five men without compromising yourself," Stocker said.

"It's possible I could talk the committee into reinstating you as the teacher," Ethel volunteered.

"You can work for me," Stocker said.

"And have everybody whispering behind my back? If they believe I can't remain virtuous for two months, they won't believe I managed it for one week either, or even one night. And as for your offer," she said, turning to Stocker, "the men would assume I'd been compromised, or tell themselves I had been, so they wouldn't feel guilty for trying to do it themselves. So you see, I really have nowhere to go if I leave."

Ethel and Stocker used every argument they could think of to persuade Tanzy to return to Boulder Gap with them. She listened politely, then explained why none of their solutions was an improvement on her present situation. In the end, she thanked them for their concern but said she had committed herself to this job and felt compelled to honor her word.

"A commitment to a lying thief doesn't count," Stocker said.

"I'm not convinced Russ is nearly as bad as you believe," she said. "He's been nothing but kind to me and Tardy."

"Where is my nephew?" Ethel demanded, as though she'd only now remembered him. "He must return with me immediately."

"Russ is teaching him how to become a cowhand."

"How to rustle cows, you mean," Stocker said.

"No, I mean how to ride a horse and handle a rope. But I expect at some point he'll teach him how to protect his cows *from* rustlers."

"You can't believe Russ isn't stealing cows from everybody within a hundred miles," Stocker asserted.

"I've seen no proof he is. And as far as I know, neither have you."

"I don't need proof. I *know*."

"I could say I don't need proof, that I know he's *not* rustling cattle. Which one of us would be right?"

"You're a very stubborn young woman."

"And you're a hate-filled old man."

"That's because Russ Tibbolt killed my brother."

"Welt says it was a fair fight."

"He's a liar."

"He believes it enough to have turned his back on his family and the easy life they could offer him. I saw the way the men in town acted that day when you mentioned sending Russ to prison. They wouldn't look each other in the eye. Something is wrong with what happened back then, and people in Boulder Gap know it." She turned from Stocker to Ethel. "I appreciate your concern for me, but I'm staying here. I'll tell Tardy you were here and that you want him to come home, but I won't have any hand in influencing his decision. Now, I don't want to be rude, but I have to start supper so it will be ready when the men return."

She stood. Ethel, accepting defeat, stood reluctantly.

"I should take you back by force," Stocker said, still seated.

"You can console yourself with the knowledge that you did your best to help me."

Stocker stood and stalked out of the cabin.

"I hope you're not making a fatal mistake," Ethel said.

"Don't worry about me. I'll be fine. These men are much better than people believe."

"You've only been here one day."

"It doesn't take that long to sense evil. There's none here."

"For your sake, I hope you're right."

There was no more to be said, though Tanzy believed Ethel would have tried. She followed her guests outside to find Russ and Stocker facing each other like tomcats, spoiling for a fight.

"By rights it's my land," Stocker was saying.

"You didn't even know it was here until I put cows on it," Russ said.

"You're a liar and a thief," Stocker shouted.

"I could say the same thing about you," Russ replied.

"That's the second time today I've been called a liar," Stocker shouted. "I won't stand for it again."

He went for his gun.

Chapter Seventeen

Tanzy and Ethel screamed as one, and Tardy jumped in front of Russ. Stocker's gun was pointing directly at the boy. Almost in the same breath Russ grabbed Tardy and threw them both to the ground.

"Put the gun away, Stocker," Welt said. "I've got a rifle pointed right at your heart."

For a moment the scene froze in Tanzy's mind: Stocker standing with his gun in hand, Russ and Tardy on the ground, Tardy with an expression of shock and Russ with one of unbridled fury, Welt standing beside the cabin, his rifle to his shoulder. Russ had somehow managed to pull Tardy aside with his left hand while drawing his gun with his right. Everyone was within point-blank range. If a gunfight started, at least two people would be dead.

Tanzy didn't realize she'd moved until she heard herself speaking. She snatched the gun from Stocker's hands. "I can't believe you'd pull a gun on a boy who's never done anything to harm you."

"I wasn't going to shoot him," Stocker said, suddenly recovering from his shock. "I was going to shoot that lying thief," he said, indicting Russ.

"It would have been murder, and I would have testified to that fact," Tanzy said.

"So would I," Ethel said. She hurried to where Tardy was scrambling to his feet, embarrassment and anger battling for supremacy in his eyes. "Are you hurt?" she asked.

"No thanks to that crazy fool," Tardy said, impatient with his aunt's concern.

"Don't call me a fool," Stocker thundered. Reflexively he reached for his gun.

"Don't you have any other reaction to hearing things you don't like?" Tanzy asked, fury and scorn mixed in her voice.

"It's his fault," Stocker said, pointing to Russ, who had holstered his gun, gotten to his feet, and was brushing the dirt off his clothes. "Seeing him free to keep on lying and stealing makes me want to do something crazy."

"If you really believe that, find the evidence to prove what you say."

"He's too clever."

"That's a poor excuse for doing nothing."

"He's not rustling," Tardy said. "I rode all over this valley today and there's not a single cow that isn't Russ's."

"You don't know what you're talking about," Stocker said. "You're a stupid little boy."

"He's neither," Russ said, putting his hand on Tardy's shoulder and giving it a squeeze. "He's a quick study. I never had to show him anything more than once."

"I lassoed a calf, Aunt Ethel," Tardy said, pride making him stand a couple of inches taller. "Russ said I shouldn't try to wrestle it to the ground until I got more muscle, but I'm already doing that. Every muscle in my body aches. Russ says that means they're growing."

"I can't say I'm pleased with your accomplishments," Ethel said, "but I am glad you've survived your foolish decision unhurt. Now it's time to come home and stop playing cowboy."

"I'm not *playing* cowboy," Tardy said, incensed. "I'm going to be one. Russ says I'm a natural."

"I don't care what *that man* says," Ethel replied. "This is not a suitable place for a boy of your age. Nor is he a man whose company I want you to share. You will come home immediately."

"Why? You don't like me. You're always saying my mom and dad probably got themselves killed just so they could get away from me."

Ethel looked mortified. "I only say those things when I'm angry. You are my Christian responsibility."

"Well, you're not responsible for me anymore."

"Maybe you should consider going home," Russ said quietly. "When you're a little older—"

"Getting older isn't going to make any difference," Tardy said. "If you don't want me, I'll find somebody who does."

"It's not a question of me wanting you," Russ said. "It's a question of what's right for you."

"This is," Tardy said, excitement shining in his eyes. "I've never had more fun than I had today. I know you didn't let me do anything hard or dangerous, and I know being a good cowhand is hard work, but it's what I want to do."

They were quickly approaching an impasse. Tanzy felt both Tardy and Ethel had good arguments, but both couldn't win.

"Why don't you let him stay a few more days?" she said to Ethel. "He'll be going into town with me for supplies soon. That will give him time to consider whether he really wants to stay."

"I won't change my mind," Tardy said.

"Quiet," Tanzy heard Russ whisper in Tardy's ear. "She's trying to help."

Ethel was clearly unhappy with the compromise.

"You ought to bring the sheriff out here," Stocker said. "He can force Russ to let the boy go home."

"If Tardy changes his mind," Tanzy said, "I'll be the first one to encourage him to return home."

"You'll never get the boy away from him," Stocker said, pointing at Russ. "He'll turn him into a thief and a rustler."

"Have you ever thought," Russ said to Stocker, "that if I pulled my gun every time you called me a liar, thief, and rustler, I'd have killed you a hundred times?"

"You'd never kill me."

"I wasn't faster than Toley that day, but you're old and slow. The only way you'd beat me would be to cheat, and I don't think you'd get another jury to lie for you."

"He wouldn't get the chance," Welt said, his rifle lowered but still in his right hand. "I'd kill him first."

"That would be murder," Ethel said.

"It would remove a great evil from Boulder Gap," Welt

said. "Then maybe people could look themselves in the mirror in the morning."

"*I* have no trouble facing myself in my mirror," Ethel said.

"I'm sorry to hear that," Welt said. "I had some hope for you."

Welt's words unsettled Ethel.

"You'd better get started for town if you want to get there before dark," Russ said. "I'll ride with you to the pass."

"I don't want you anywhere near me," Stocker said.

"I'll go," Welt said. "I'm not so high-minded as Russ. I'll kill him if he tries to draw on me."

"I don't want either one of you," Stocker said. "Come on, Ethel. Let's get out of here."

"Be sure you come see me when you come to town," Ethel said to Tardy.

Now there really was no more to say. Everyone stood silently while Stocker helped Ethel into the buggy, turned it around, and started home.

"Well," said Tanzy, breaking the silence, "I have to get supper started."

"I have to teach Tardy how to take care of his horse," Russ said.

"I was right about you," Welt said after Russ and Tardy took their horses and headed to the corral.

"Russ was right about you, too."

"I never knew being a cowhand was such hard work," Tardy said. "I can't walk straight."

"You did very well for your first day," Russ said.

They had finished unsaddling their horses and were rubbing them down before turning them into the corral.

"It's important to take good care of your horse and equipment," Russ said. "Equipment in good condition will keep you from getting hurt. Sooner or later your horse will be the difference between surviving and ending up dinner for some wild animal."

"You got animals out here that'll eat people?" Tardy clearly didn't like hearing that.

"Wolves, cougars, and some bears."

"Is that why you keep the horses in a corral?"

"I keep them here because they're easier to catch. They don't like being ridden. They'd be halfway down the valley before dark if I'd let them."

They finished with the horses and started cleaning their equipment, Tardy chattering away like a magpie. Russ couldn't get over how open, trusting, and impressionable the boy was. He took everything Russ said as gospel and looked at him with undisguised admiration. Russ hadn't been that trusting and open as a kid, but he wished he had been. People might think Tardy was useless, but they also thought he was harmless. He was free to go where he wanted, do what he wanted, with the goodwill of all.

Russ envied him that.

"I hope Tanzy is cooking something good," Tardy said as they walked toward the cabin. "I could eat a cow."

"If you're going to start eating my cows, you'll have to leave," Russ said.

Tardy laughed. "I didn't know you were such a kidder. You haven't missed a chance to nail my hide all day."

"I figured if your skinny hide wasn't nailed on tight, you might lose it."

"You wait until I build my muscles," Tardy said, flexing his biceps. "Then we'll see who's skinny."

"You can flex your muscles on that saddle soap later. Soft, flexible leather is less likely to burn your hands or chafe your bottom and inner thighs."

"We should have worked on the saddles first thing," Tardy said. "Then I wouldn't be walking like the saddle is still between my legs."

Much to his surprise, Russ liked being around Tardy. He hoped he wasn't trying to relive his own youth through Tardy, but there had to be some reason why he was so drawn to the boy. Maybe it was the undisguised pleasure in Tardy's eyes every time he managed to do something right. Maybe it was the fact that Tardy was probably the only person in Boulder Gap besides Betty to show openly his liking for Russ. He could tell himself he didn't care what people thought of him, but Tardy's naked admiration had shown him otherwise.

He could understand and be sympathetic with Tardy's rebellion against his aunt's opinion of him, but being a cowhand was a dead-end job. The boy had ability. He just needed confidence in himself. Maybe being here for a while was the best thing for Tardy, but at some point Russ had to convince him to go home. He didn't want the boy to become an outcast, too.

"Stay out of the kitchen," Welt said when Russ and Tardy entered the cabin. "The cook says she'll clobber the first man who gets in her way."

"Supper will be ready in ten minutes," Tanzy said. "I hope everybody's hungry."

The sound of a cheerful female voice welcoming him home had an unexpected effect on Russ. An alien feeling of warmth began to spiral through him; tension began to ease. He actually felt like he'd come home. Even the air, laden with the odors of cooking, smelled fresh with a feeling of the outdoors.

Flowers. Tanzy had gathered some wildflowers and put them in a jar on the table. It wasn't something a man would do or something Russ had expected would appeal to him, but it gave the cabin a feeling of welcome that neither he nor Welt had ever been able to create. It reminded him of his own home before his mother's vanity destroyed it. It called to mind some of the daydreams he'd had in prison when only thinking of the implausible made it possible to get through the day.

"The rest of the guys are right behind us," Tardy said. "Is there anything I can do to help?"

Tardy's question reminded Russ that neither he nor the men were in the habit of offering to help Welt. It wouldn't hurt if they offered to help Tanzy.

"Anything the rest of us can do?" he asked.

"Just stay out of the way," Tanzy said, coming to the table with a bowl of steaming potatoes. "The first person who causes me to spill anything will have to eat on the porch."

"About the only thing Aunt Ethel doesn't complain about is me helping her put the food on the table," Tardy said.

"Then see if you can get the gravy there without spilling it," Tanzy said. She came in with a bowl of stewed peaches.

"This place smells delicious," Tim said the minute he walked in.

"I vote we give Tim permanent pass duty during supper," Buck said. "That way the rest of us will get something to eat."

"There's plenty for everybody," Tanzy said, setting the

sliced pork roast in the middle of the table. "There's another pan of biscuits in the oven now."

"I worship you," Tim said. "Will you marry me?"

"That's your stomach talking, not your head," Tanzy said.

"He doesn't have anything in his head," Welt said.

"Nothing in my stomach, either," Tim replied.

"Sit down before you starve. No one touches anything until somebody says the blessing."

"We're the ones blessed because you're here to cook for us," Buck said.

"No poaching," Tim said. "I saw her first."

"Russ saw me first," Tanzy said as she sat down, "so no poaching, any of you."

"You don't want Russ," Tim said. "He's old and tough."

"She won't want you, either," Welt said. "You're young and stringy."

A feeling almost akin to contentment began to spread through Russ. His crew liked and trusted each other, but the feeling of camaraderie, the jokes, the laughter, the good-natured kidding had never been this spontaneous. Even Welt managed to smile four times during the meal, usually a month's allotment. Some of it had to do with the fact that there was a woman in the cabin. Men liked to show off when there was a woman around, especially when she was young and pretty, especially when she seemed to enjoy them as much as they enjoyed her.

But it wasn't that simple. Tanzy wasn't *just* a woman, and she was a great deal more than a good cook. She brought a storehouse of energy, a sense of fun. It was as though the axis of their lives had shifted to allow the sun to break through the clouds. He'd forgotten what it was like to laugh so hard his stomach hurt. He'd forgotten

Welt used to be a cheerful man before the brooding hurt left by Adele's betrayal. He couldn't forget Stocker Pullet was determined to ruin his life, but right now that didn't seem as important as it had a couple of days ago.

And all this because of Tanzy. If it was like this for two months, he didn't know how he would be able to stand it after she left.

"Anybody ready for pie and coffee?" Tanzy asked when the men pushed back from the table.

"I'm so full I could bust," Buck said.

"It's apple pie baked fresh this afternoon," Tanzy said.

"I hope you made several," Tim said. "I can eat a whole one myself."

"Maybe you can, but you won't. You're not a pig."

"Yes, I am," Tim said. "Just ask anybody."

"Then it's time you changed. I don't allow pigs at my table."

"It's Russ's table," Tim pointed out, "and he's been allowing me to eat at it for years."

"Then it's time for things to change."

"How?" Buck asked, somewhat uneasy.

"You'll begin by eating a slice no bigger than a quarter of a pie."

Buck relaxed. "Hell, I thought you meant no cussing and we had to wash up and change our shirts before we came inside."

"I didn't, but that's a good idea."

"Shut up," Tim said to Buck. "Don't go giving her ideas."

"It wouldn't do any of us any harm to learn to live like humans," Russ said.

"See what you've gone and done," Tim complained to Buck. "All this talk of behaving is making me lose my appetite."

"We'll have to do it more often," Russ said.

Even after Tim left to relieve Oren at the pass, the boys continued to joke with one another. Tanzy kept refilling their coffee cups and handed round sugar cookies just before bedtime. Best of all, she joined them. It wasn't that she said or did anything Russ could point to, but the whole evening had an unreal quality to it. He didn't want it to end, but when Tardy's yawns got so frequent and so loud they couldn't be ignored, it was time to bring the evening to an end. Besides, they were sitting on Tardy's bed.

"Time to put the halfling to bed," Welt said. "He's so sleepy he can't keep his eyes open."

"That's not true," Tardy said without conviction.

"It's all that fresh air," Tanzy said.

"I bet it was all that effort it took to stay in the saddle," Welt said.

"He did very well," Russ said.

"Yeah," Tardy said and yawned again.

"I ought to be going to bed, too," Tanzy said. "I have to get up early in the morning."

"Thanks for the wonderful supper," Russ said.

"What are we going to do when she leaves?" Buck asked. "She's spoiling me so bad, I'll starve before I'll eat Welt's cooking again."

Russ didn't want to think of when she'd leave any more than Buck. He found it hard to believe he could have gotten comfortable with her being here so quickly. She'd even enabled them to make a space for Tardy, something he would never have expected. He wondered if he'd ever figure out how she did it.

"Enjoy what you've got while you have it," Russ said. "You'll be miserable if you keep thinking about what it'll be like when she's gone."

He meant to say *when they had to go back to eating Welt's cooking*.

"Do you suppose you could teach Welt to cook?" Buck asked.

"She can teach anybody anything," Tardy said, with a yawn so big it couldn't be ignored.

"Go before Tardy falls asleep where he's sitting." Tanzy started taking the coffee cups from their hands.

"If there's nothing more to eat or drink, I guess I'll go to bed," Buck said.

"Me, too," Welt said. "I've had an exhausting day watching her cook and clean."

"Why can't I stay tomorrow?" Buck asked Russ.

"Because I'm staying. Tardy can go with Welt."

Tardy was too sleepy to care, but Welt didn't look happy with the arrangement.

Welt and Buck left and Tardy settled down on the couch without taking off his clothes. Russ followed Tanzy to the kitchen. Even his inexperienced eye could see everything was cleaner, more neatly arranged. He found that comforting. Odd how things were affecting him.

"Thanks for making the men so comfortable," Russ said.

"I grew up in a house full of men."

"Still, it can't have been easy."

"I enjoyed it. My family never appreciated anything I did."

"Maybe if you teach Welt to cook like you, they won't desert me after you leave."

"With all this teaching you want done, I ought to ask for double pay."

"Then you'd be able to leave sooner." She looked a little disconcerted by his response.

"I was just making a joke," she said.

"Sorry. I'm not used to evenings like this."

"Have you always been this serious?" she asked.

"No place can be entirely dull with Tim around."

"Is he always this way?"

"No. He's showing off for you."

She turned away. He wondered if she was blushing, if she felt uncomfortable with compliments, if she felt uncomfortable with him.

"I just want the men to relax and be themselves."

"They are."

She had no idea what a difference her presence made. She brought ease and harmony rather than strain and rivalry, had enabled them to enjoy the pleasure within and concentrate less on the danger without. That was something no one had ever been able to do for him before.

"I like your men," Tanzy said.

"They like you."

"They'd like anybody who fed them, didn't argue with them, and generally stayed out of their way."

"That's a nearly perfect description of what all men want."

"I know. Pathetic, isn't it? Now I have to get to bed if I'm to have breakfast ready before you ride out in the morning."

Russ didn't want to leave even though he could hear Tardy snoring softly on the couch, didn't want to break the spell that had settled over the evening. Tanzy picked up the small lamp and turned toward the other end of the house.

"Will you have time to help me with my reading tomorrow?" he asked.

"Yes. Now go before the men start wondering what you're doing here. They all know Tardy was so tired a herd of cattle could run through here and he'd never wake up."

"They know you're safe with me."

He wondered if she was just a little bit disappointed she was so safe. He was beginning to feel a bit disappointed himself. He bent, kissed her lightly on the lips.

"Good night."

He turned and left before he could see her reaction.

Chapter Eighteen

All day long Tanzy had been unable to stop thinking about what Welt had told her of Russ's past. Everything he said, everything he did, even things he failed to do, took on a new meaning. How could Welt have thought a man so disillusioned with women would have married a stranger? Russ wasn't rejecting Tanzy. He was rejecting all women. The two most important women in his life had brought disgrace and tragedy. With the women of Boulder Gap treating him as if he was some kind of criminal, how could he possibly want a woman in his life?

He would never get married—or, if he married just to have children, be able to have anything but the most superficial relationship with his wife—until he could believe women could be genuine, honest, trustworthy, capable of measuring up to his own high standards. More than that, he had to believe someone could love him, that he was worthy of love.

There was a great deal of love inside him. No man could feel as passionately as Russ felt about things and not be capable of great love. He also had a tremendous ability to draw men to him, to inspire loyalty. And he had great kindness. She'd never expected him to be so understanding of Tardy or to accept the challenge of turning him into a cowhand. There was simply too much that was wonderful about the man to allow him to waste himself. But she had to be very careful. It wouldn't be easy to encourage Russ to let himself fall in love while making sure he didn't fall in love with her.

She also had to make sure she didn't get so soft on him that she forgot her own reasons for not marrying him. It wouldn't be hard. He was just too good-looking, too *manly* to ignore. He could charge the atmosphere of a room just by entering it.

But the thing that had eaten away at the foundation of her determination to keep her distance from him, that had most likely been responsible for her decision to be his cook and housekeeper, was his writings. As few and short as they were, they showed a very different man from the one he allowed others to see. It was that man who fascinated her, intrigued her, caught her interest, aroused her curiosity, invited her sympathy, deserved her help. It was that man who was the *real* Russ Tibbolt, and he would never be happy until he could reveal that part of him.

He wouldn't verbalize his thoughts, but he seemed comfortable committing them to paper. The man inside was struggling to get out, probably had been for some time. The more Russ explored himself in writing, the more he would continue to open up to others, the sooner he would become the man his creator had meant him to be.

Then maybe he would tell her why he kept kissing a woman he had no intention of marrying.

* * *

Tanzy put down the latest writing Russ had done. "You've been inside long enough today."

"It sounds like you want to get rid of me so you can have the cabin to yourself," Russ said.

"You're wrong. I need your help."

"I didn't think you needed a man for anything," Russ said, a faint twinkling in his eyes.

"Okay, I don't really *need* you in the strictest sense."

"I knew it."

"But your help will make my task a lot easier."

"A significant admission. What is this important task?"

"I want you to help me pick some berries for a pie." Tanzy laughed at his dismayed expression. "You don't have to pick any if it offends your masculine pride. Welt told me there are currants in the valley, but he didn't tell me how to find them."

"They aren't close. You'd have to ride."

"That's fine, but I still don't know the way."

"You really want to do this?"

"Are you going to help me?"

"I guess I don't have any choice."

"Don't be so gloomy. I'm looking forward to seeing this valley I've been hearing so much about."

"It's a long ride."

"I'll take a picnic so we don't have to come back for lunch. I don't want you eating all the berries."

"Would I do that?"

"I don't know. Actually, I don't know much about you at all." That took the edge off his pleasure.

"I'm sure people would be glad to tell you anything you want to know."

"Opinion is widely divided."

"Not if you discount Tardy."

"What about Welt, the others? How about Archie?"

"A rebel, three ex-cons, and a clerk. Don't you know their opinions don't count?"

"They do to me. Now stop being argumentative and saddle me a nice, gentle horse."

Russ's laugh provided no comfort.

"You do have a gentle horse, don't you?"

"I have half-wild mustangs that run free much of the year. They like to start an argument every time a man gets on their back."

"Then you ride it first and give it a good talking to."

Tanzy hummed as she made her preparations. She was determined that today she'd force Russ to open up about himself. He had to get over the fear that everybody he met was going to disapprove of him. If she emptied her mind of everything she'd been told, there would have been very little about Russ to take exception to. There was the feud with Stocker, of course, but she kept remembering that he'd backed off, thought of protecting Tardy before shooting Stocker, when he had a perfectly good excuse to do so. She was sure that if a feud was thrust on him, he wouldn't back down, but she was beginning to see that feuding wasn't a black and white issue. She realized, much to her embarrassment, that she'd been as black and white about feuds as the town had been about Russ.

She was beginning to think his lack of respect for women stemmed from the fact that he'd never met any woman who was kind enough to him to earn his respect or affection. She realized her father's treatment of her and her mother had caused her to feel the same about men. Maybe both of them needed to have a more open mind.

"That horse doesn't look very gentle to me," Tanzy said when Russ introduced her to the ugly brute she was to ride.

"He was a little frisky so I took the edge off him."

Tanzy had an idea that Russ's notion of *frisky* wouldn't be the same as hers. "Lead him over to the fence," she said.

"Why?"

"So I can climb the fence and get on him from there."

"It'll be a lot easier if I lift you into the saddle."

"And see my skirts flying in the wind? It would give you something to laugh about all day."

"I wouldn't laugh at you."

"Maybe not, but you'd get a great deal of pleasure out of remembering it."

"I promise not to see a thing and wipe it out of my mind if I do."

"I begin to wonder if your reputation for untruths is entirely unwarranted." The smile left his eyes, and she regretted her words immediately. "Not that I believe you would lie about anything important, just fudging the corners a bit to put a greenhorn like myself in her place. You can lift me if you promise to close your eyes."

The sparkle was back in his gaze. "How am I supposed to know where to set you down? I might put you on the fence instead of the horse."

"Stop trying to frighten me and let's get this over with."

"You aren't looking forward to being in my arms?"

"I learned long ago to take the bad with the good."

"What's good?"

"If you manage to put me in the saddle without mortifying me, maybe I'll tell you."

Russ put his hands around her waist. "Take hold of

your skirts. When I lift you, make sure they don't get doubled up under you. They'll give you a chafed bottom otherwise."

"How do you know what chafes a woman's bottom?"

Russ flashed a wicked grin. "If you tell me something you like about being here, maybe I'll tell you."

"If you keep talking, it'll be noon before we get started. And people say women do all the chattering."

Russ looked a bit startled, but his grin won out. "They say men either become tongue-tied around beautiful women or talk too much. I guess we know where I fall."

"They say a woman can't trust even a good man to be good all the time. I think I'll keep that in mind. Now put me on that horse before he decides our proposed trip is just an elaborate hoax to disturb his peaceful morning doze."

Russ lifted her so high her breath caught in her throat. She barely had time to get control of her skirts before he settled her in the saddle. The material was spread smoothly over her bottom.

"Are you comfortable?" Russ asked.

"I'm fine. This horse isn't nearly as big as Papa's mules."

"He's a grass-fed mustang. They're never as big as grain-fed animals, but he's tough and can run all day."

"I'd prefer a gentle canter."

Russ chuckled as he settled astride his mount. "We'll see what we can do."

It turned out to be a magical day. Tanzy hadn't gotten over her amazement at the sheer size of the Rocky Mountains. They looked magnificent in the sunlight, their bare peaks etched in minute detail against the clear blue sky, their flanks clothed in rich greens of ponderosa and lodgepole pines, firs, and aspen.

The valley itself stretched out nearly flat before her as though some primeval force had leveled any hills with a giant hand and smoothed the earth's surface so the stream that flowed through it moved with a languid pace along its meandering path.

Birds fluttered among the branches of the cottonwoods and willows that clung to the edge of the creek, cooling its waters and providing shade for man and beast. Overhead a bald eagle circled lazily in the air, its huge black wings supporting it effortlessly on the thermals that rose from the valley floor. The cattle, scattered over the valley, seemed almost static as they cropped the thick grass nourished by rich volcanic soil and subterranean moisture. It was truly a mountain paradise. She could understand why Russ was determined to take any risk to defend it.

"This place is almost too good to be true," she said. "How did you find it?"

"I was running away. I did a lot of that when I was a boy. That time I was so angry I decided I was never going back. I followed a stream and discovered this valley. After that, it was my refuge when things got too bad."

She could imagine a boy, angry and humiliated, would need some place where he felt protected from the scorn and pity of his neighbors.

"Thinking about coming back here is just about all that kept me sane in prison. I talked about it so much, the boys decided to come with me."

"How did you get started?"

"There was a small herd of wild cows here already. The boys and I combed the hills for mavericks, anything unbranded. We sold the old stuff and bought calves. I've put every cent I've made back into the herd. I'll be poor for years to come. Now let's stop talking business and sample that lunch you brought."

"I thought cowboys only ate two meals a day."

"Only when it's too far to ride back to the cabin. Now stop teasing me. I'm hungry."

They found a grassy knoll shaded by a grove of cottonwoods. Feeling stiff and a little sore, Tanzy was relieved to be off the horse.

While Russ hobbled the horses, she spread a quilt over the ground. She had made sandwiches of sliced pork and thick pieces of fresh bread and brought some dried apple slices for dessert. They drank from the clear waters of one of several streams that tumbled down the mountainside. They ate in silence. Then, much to her surprise, Russ lay back, put his hat over his face, and went to sleep.

At first she was inclined to take umbrage. She didn't claim to be a great beauty or a scintillating conversationalist, but no man had ever gone to sleep on her before. Surely she wasn't that boring. But even as she contemplated throwing a cup of water over him, her feelings reversed themselves. She wondered how long it had been since he'd felt comfortable enough to go to sleep in a woman's presence. Okay, it wasn't the greatest compliment in the world, but then they weren't lovers. She wanted them to be friends, and she supposed this was as much a demonstration of friendship as anything.

She wished he hadn't covered his face. That forced her to look at his body, which gave rise to a host of thoughts that had the power to destroy her comfort. Having grown up among men who were lean and sinewy, she couldn't look at Russ without being continually reminded of the breadth of his shoulders, the power of his arms, the imposing size of his chest. But now that they were alone and she wasn't required to return his gaze, she had leisure to explore the rest of his body.

That was when the afternoon grew considerably warmer.

She liked that he had a flat stomach without having a skinny waist. She liked that he had narrow hips without a flat bottom. But it was his muscled thighs, and the ample evidence of his masculinity nestled between them, that caught and held her attention. She'd never thought of herself as a carnal being so she didn't understand why looking at Russ should make her uncomfortably hot, too edgy to be able to relax.

But even as she tried to identify the reasons for the feelings that had come over her, they continued to grow and change. Heat coursed slowly through her body, but its effect on her was anything but languid. She felt more restive by the minute. Though she'd never done anything like this before, she found herself trying to imagine what Russ would look like without his clothes.

The image in her mind nearly caused her to lose control. Much to her surprise, her breasts had become very sensitive. She felt as though her nipples were trying to push their way out of her dress. She looked down and was shocked to see they had hardened so much she could see their outlines. Even more shocking, the heat that had settled in her belly had caused the release of moisture between her legs. For the first time in her life her body was in the grip of sexual heat and she didn't know what to do about it. She sat there paralyzed, unable to take her eyes off Russ, unable to erase the visions from her mind, unable to control her body's reaction.

She might have sat there until Russ woke and discovered her blatant examination of him if two kingfishers hadn't started an argument over a tiny fish. Their raucous squawks brought her out of her trance. Tanzy surged to her feet, determined to put some distance between herself and the source of this disquieting reaction.

She forced herself to identify the plants along the steam, bulrushes, cattails, willows, and box elder, in addition to the ever-present cottonwood. She searched for frogs, salamanders, even snakes to drive thoughts of Russ out of her mind. She searched the trees for birds and their nests, the sandy shore for the footprints of muskrats or deer. But it wasn't until she nearly stepped on a skunk that she shook off the mood that had held her in its grip.

"I never thought I'd be glad to meet a skunk," she said with a shaky laugh. "You've done your duty, now go home to your children."

She returned to her picnic. She tore up some blades of grass and sprinkled them on Russ. He didn't move. Next she resorted to tiny clods of dirt. Still no reaction, so she searched for some small stones.

"If you want me to get up, all you have to do is ask."

She jumped at the sound of his voice. Then blushed furiously. She wondered if he'd been awake the whole time! She told herself to relax. He couldn't possibly know what she'd been thinking.

"That's not half as much fun," she said, trying to sound as normal as possible.

"Just like a woman. You never choose the easiest or most direct method. You always have to complicate things."

"Sometimes the easiest and most direct methods are also the most boring," she said, relieved to feel irritation rather than lust.

"Life is interesting enough without trying to make it more difficult."

"That's not a very adventurous attitude."

He removed his hat and sat up. "I've had more than enough adventure for a lifetime. Boredom sounds good."

"Well, I haven't. Now get up and show me where to find the currants. I'll never get enough for my pie if you sleep the afternoon away."

"Everything is always some man's fault, isn't it?"

His bad mood surprised her. "What do you mean?"

"Feuds. Women would never do anything like that."

"They don't."

"But they can cause more damage with their tongues than a man can with a rifle. And their victims are left alive to suffer for a lifetime."

"Not all women are like that."

"It's all our fault that we don't show women proper respect even though the woman makes a whore of herself, uses her beauty to destroy men, uses her physical weakness to tyrannize her family."

"I don't know what kind of dream you had, but if this is an example of your mood after one of them, I would strongly suggest you avoid naps."

He appeared to struggle with himself for a moment. "It was a bad one," he said finally. "Sorry I took it out on you."

She started to say it didn't matter, but it did. She didn't like knowing that his past could still exercise such a hold over him. Neither did she like admitting there was a kernel of truth in what he said. Men weren't perfect. Women weren't perfect, either.

"Let's get those berries," he said. "If the boys find we went looking and didn't bring any back, they'll never let me hear the end of it."

He collected the horses, helped her into the saddle.

"The berries grow mostly under the trees," he said. "Bears like to eat them for storing up winter fat."

"Will they get mad if we steal their food?"

"I think they can be persuaded to share. You're awfully quiet," Russ said after they'd ridden in silence for a while.

"I was thinking."

"About what you're going to do when you leave here?"

"I was wondering what kind of woman you'd ask to marry you. I'm not upset that you don't want to marry me. I was just curious. Even with the isolation, I could imagine many women being eager to build a home here."

"It's not the isolation that bothers them. It's me. *If* I was to get married, I'd want a woman who could look at me with her own eyes, see what I do, learn what I think and feel, make up her own mind about me."

"I can do that."

"You don't want to marry me."

"That's not the point. If I can do it, so can other women. You've got to give them a chance to get to know you, to see the person I see."

"I have."

"I doubt it. You don't go into town more often than necessary. You stay only as long as you must and speak to as few people as you can. You frown at everybody you meet and fight with Stocker. None of your men come to town, so silly stories about them can go unchecked."

"I talk to just about everybody sooner of later."

"I mean *really* talk. I wouldn't know half of what I do about you if I hadn't read the things you write."

"It would just make them think I was weak-minded."

"If they met your men, knew their stories, knew what you'd done for them and they for you, folks would change their minds."

Russ jerked his horse to a stop and turned to face

Tanzy. "That's not how things work out here. You show any kind of weakness and people will be standing in line to take advantage of it. You back away from a fight just once and you're forever branded a coward. You let somebody take one of your cows and your herd will be plundered before the month's up. Nobody out here cares about what's inside me.

"I'm not feuding with Stocker, just defending what I've got. There are no laws out here to protect you, no police to call when you need help. We fight when our property is threatened. We fight for our women, too. I'd consider it an honor to fight for a woman like you. So would the boys, but I can't marry you because you don't understand any of what I just said. Living out here would break your heart and your spirit. I could never let that happen to you. I like you too much."

Tanzy was so surprised by his outburst—for Russ, that many words at once could only be called an outburst—she didn't know what to say. She wanted to protest that people here weren't very different from people everywhere else in the world, but she wasn't sure she was right. She wanted to protest that people did care about character. She wanted to say she understood the need to fight to defend property and family. There hadn't been any police in Kentucky either, but all that seemed unimportant just now.

Instead, she asked, "Why did you kiss me?"

Chapter Nineteen

"Because I wanted to."

"Is that all?"

"Do I need any other reason?"

"You can't go around kissing a woman without a reason unless you're falling down drunk."

"I wasn't."

"I know. So you've got to have other reasons."

"Like what?"

"Like you like her a lot."

"I do like you a lot."

"That's not enough. She has to be special to you. You'd have to spend a lot of time thinking about her, wanting to be with her."

"I do."

This conversation wasn't going the way Tanzy had expected. She was supposed to make Russ believe he could trust women in general, not her specifically. "If you're not careful, a woman will think the kiss means more than you're offering."

"How do you mean?"

"She'll think she's someone special, the *only* one who's special to you."

"It's clear you're not a man."

Tanzy laughed. "I'm glad you noticed."

It was Russ's turn to laugh. "I mean you don't understand how men think, why they do things."

"Please explain, since I've never been around men and have no notion of the strange ideas that go through their heads," she said, her exaggerated tone saying just the opposite.

"Men can kiss women just for fun," Russ explained, ignoring her sarcasm.

"I'm talking about respectable women."

"Me, too. They can kiss just because it's a pleasant experience, because they had a nice time, because the moon was up or the supper was good."

"Good Lord, you *are* a man."

"I'm glad *you* noticed."

"I mean you act just like the rest of them."

"How did you think I was going to act?"

"I thought you were serious and responsible."

"I am."

"Not if you go around kissing me whenever the moon is up or supper is good."

"I wouldn't kiss any other woman like that."

"Why not?"

"They might start getting those expectations you mentioned just a minute ago."

"But I won't."

"You've already said you wouldn't marry me no matter what. You practically swore it on a stack of Bibles."

"So it's safe to entertain yourself with me?"

"I wouldn't put it like that."

"How would you put it?"

"I'd say you're a beautiful woman I like. I enjoy your company. I appreciate the fact that you haven't believed everything people say about me. You've been kind enough to help me learn to read and write without making me feel stupid."

They had reached the trees that grew on the flanks of the mountains. Tanzy was glad for the shadows that veiled her confusion. It was hard enough to control her attraction to Russ when she was irritated. Right now she wanted to kiss him. She held fast in her resolve not to marry into a feud, but it was hard when Russ said things like that.

"You've been through some pretty rough times," she said. "It's natural you would be slow to trust people, but your friends are proof you can trust others. Get out of this valley more often and you'll find there are lots of nice, pretty, respectable women longing to meet a man like you."

"That's going to be harder than it would have been a month ago."

"Why?"

"I didn't know you then."

She was losing ground. She needed to say something mean or remarkably stupid to make him realize she wasn't all that wonderful. She hadn't done anything dozens of women wouldn't have done. She could name that many from among the women she'd worked with in St. Louis. They wouldn't have cared about respect or the feud either. They'd have hauled him before a preacher so fast his head would still be swimming.

But she didn't want Russ to end up with a woman who would take him just because he was available. He deserved someone who understood the hurt that still lived fresh and painfully inside him, someone who would see the man he could be and love him for that.

"I appreciate all the nice things you said, but don't say them anymore."

"Why not?"

"I'll be leaving in a month or two. I'd hate to think I'd made it more difficult for you to find a wife."

"It's too late for that."

"Why are you doing this to me?" she cried out in frustration. "You know you don't want to marry me."

"Here are some currants," Russ said, pointing to some low bushes covered with small red berries. "It looks like we've found them before the bears. Do you want to stop here?"

She wanted to smack him upside his head so he'd pay attention to her. He acted like she hadn't said anything of importance.

"Help me down, please. If you don't, my skirt will get caught and I'll fall on my head." Which might not be such a bad idea if it could rid her of two notions. First, that she had any business embarking on the risky job of helping Russ learn to trust women. He was a grown man, intelligent and thoughtful. He could do that on his own if he wanted.

The other notion she'd like to shed was that Russ was so nice she couldn't stand for him to go to waste. Again, that was his business.

Russ dismounted, tied his horse, and relieved her of her baskets. "You ready?"

She nodded. He put his hands around her waist, lifted her effortlessly from the saddle, and set her on the ground. It was really unkind of him to do that so easily. It made it hard not to want to melt into his arms. Lord, why did he have to be so big and strong?

"You can let me go," she said when Russ just stood there, his hands still holding her waist.

"Not until I make you believe you have done something special," he said. "Maybe women in other places would do as much, but no one ever has. So until someone does, what you've done will remain very special."

"Okay, if that's all—"

"It's not."

"For a man who claims to be a recluse, you sure have a lot to say."

"I just want to say thank you."

"You have, so—"

He cut her words off by kissing her hard on the mouth. There was nothing of the gentle or friendly kisses they'd shared before. It didn't seem very thankful either. It felt demanding, forceful, overwhelming, laced with enough heat to melt her resistance. She relaxed in his embrace and returned his kiss with a passion she didn't know until that day she could feel for any man.

Until Russ, Tanzy had never liked being kissed. She'd never felt anything except indifference, annoyance, or anger. But it was impossible to be indifferent to Russ. When she was in his arms, feeling his strength, his desire, being pulled inexorably into the heat of his passion, it was like stepping into a new dimension. Long-secret parts of her opened up and came instantly to glorious life. She felt newly created, reshaped, rising from the ashes of her old being, the one she must cast off because it no longer fit.

They both seemed to realize simultaneously the danger of what they were doing. They drew back, each staring at the other.

"Was that the kind of kiss you said promised more than I wanted to give?" he asked.

Feeling utterly shattered, she could only nod.

"I'm sorry."

She was, too, but not the way he meant. She was sorry he wasn't a man she could marry. In that brief moment she realized emotional and physical love could join to make a bond too powerful for a woman to break, no matter what dangers she might face. She had to keep her distance from him before she ruined her life.

"Look, Russ, I don't care how ready men are to kiss women for the multiple reasons you seem to think qualify as an excuse, but I'm not like that. A kiss like we just shared touches me in places I can't reach by myself. It can unleash emotions I can't control, maybe even make me do things I don't want to do. We both understand the situation between us, so this isn't something we can do. If you can't promise you won't kiss me again, I'll have to leave."

"You can't. You don't have anywhere to go."

"I'll have to find a place."

"How do I know you'll be safe?"

"I'll be safer than I will be here."

"Would it be that bad to want to marry me?"

It was hard to tell what was going on in Russ's mind. He hid his real self so far out of sight, he could act as if they hadn't just undergone a gut-wrenching experience, that she'd asked him nothing more important than if he thought there were enough berries here for two pies.

"Of course I'll promise not to kiss you. I wouldn't want to do anything to hurt you or make you unhappy. I'll give someone else cabin duty."

"How are you going to continue your lessons?" That wasn't what she wanted to say, but it was all she'd let herself say.

"I can work with Welt."

"You two are never in the same place at the same time."

"I'll work something out. We'd better get started picking those berries. They look real small. It'll take a lot to make enough pies to satisfy the boys."

Apparently the subject was closed before they'd had a chance to discuss it. She wanted to grab him, sit him down on a fallen tree, and force him to thrash out all the issues between them, but she knew enough about men to know when they were done talking. Russ was done sooner than most.

"These sweet enough?" Russ asked. He held a berry up to her lips for her to taste.

If they'd talked things over, he'd have known this was exactly the kind of thing he shouldn't do. She was just as bad. She didn't take it with her hands and put it in her mouth. She took it with her lips, weak, foolish female that she was. He didn't pull his fingers away from her lips, nor did he avert his eyes. She felt locked into his gaze, feeding and being fed through it. It was almost a physical struggle to break away.

"They're a little tart," she said when she managed to collect her wits and crush the berry between her teeth, "but they're the kind that make the best pies."

"Then let's pick a lot."

They picked in silence. Tanzy's mind was too busy to need conversation. She argued her way around the questions and back again without coming to any conclusions. She examined her behavior from the day she'd arrived until this minute and couldn't find anything she'd done wrong. She'd had no way of knowing things would turn out as they had.

Exactly how *had* things turned out?

For one thing, she liked Russ far too much for her own comfort. For another, every minute she spent in his presence seemed to increase this dangerous attachment. In addition, his feelings for her didn't match his words. If she was any judge, Russ was fooling himself about these kisses. He might have lots of logical reasons for saying he wouldn't marry her, but his brain wasn't the only part of him to have a say in this decision. If he didn't watch his step, his brain was going to find itself on the losing side.

Her brain wasn't faring much better. She had good arguments for not marrying him, but she was finding them harder and harder to remember. She couldn't remember them at all when he kissed her. She'd wanted him to go on kissing her forever, to hold her tightly every night, to make love to her—

Oh my God! When did she start thinking about Russ making love to her? She couldn't, she *wouldn't!* If she knew what was good for her, she'd leave this very minute, but she didn't have anywhere to go. That meant no more kisses and no more going off alone with Russ. He didn't try hard enough to resist temptation and she wasn't doing any better. The best thing would be to have Tardy spend the day with her, but the problem didn't lie with Tardy or Russ. It lay with her.

It was up to her to act like the responsible adult she considered herself to be. If she wanted her husband to respect her opinions and consider her wishes, she would have to show more strength of character than she'd shown so far. Why should Russ care for her opinion if she would let one little kiss overset her arguments?

Well, it wasn't *one little kiss.* It was an earth-shattering moment she'd remember for the rest of her life, but she couldn't allow it to cause her to ignore what she knew was possible and what was impossible. And life with a man involved in a feud was impossible.

"I wish you hadn't made me come with you," Tardy said to Tanzy as they left Boulder Gap behind, their buggy loaded with supplies for the ranch. "I knew Aunt Ethel was going to do everything she could to get me to go back home. I'm surprised she didn't get the sheriff to arrest me."

"Russ says you're doing really well, but you are still awfully young. I think you ought to consider going back home, at least for a while."

"I might if she didn't treat me like I was six. Why is it strangers treat me better than my relatives?"

Tardy had quickly become a favorite of all the men, even Welt. He worked hard to master the skills to do his job, believed everything they said like it was gospel, and took their kidding and criticism with a cheerfulness that defied anyone to stay annoyed. He offered to help with any job and was so unfailingly cheerful and optimistic, he almost singlehandedly improved the spirits of the whole group. The men had started to treat him like a younger brother, one they kidded unmercifully but for whom they had a growing affection. It thrilled Tanzy to see Tardy blossom into a happy young man quickly developing confidence in himself. If he spent the rest of the summer here, he would go back to Boulder Gap a very different person.

"Are you really leaving after two months?" Tardy asked.

"Yes."

"I wish you wouldn't."

"I will have repaid my debt and I'll have enough money to get settled elsewhere."

"Why do you have to go somewhere else?"

Tanzy had asked herself that same question. It didn't worry her so much that she didn't have a good answer as it did that she had asked the question in the first place.

"One day I would like a husband and a family, but a woman has to have a blameless reputation if she wants a respectable marriage. I don't have such a reputation in Boulder Gap."

"Do you want to marry anybody in Boulder Gap?"

"No."

"Then why do you care what they think of you?"

Another good question, one she couldn't explain to a boy on the edge of manhood. She couldn't make him understand that men could actually gain stature by disreputable behavior, but that a woman's chances of a good marriage could be destroyed by even a whisper of scandal.

"I wouldn't want my children to suffer because of my damaged reputation."

"Russ doesn't think you're damaged. He thinks you're wonderful."

That was the kind of thing Tanzy didn't want to know. She didn't really believe Tardy knew what Russ thought. She tried to tell herself it didn't matter if he thought she was the most wonderful woman in the world. Unfortunately, she was rapidly coming to the conclusion that her foolish heart was determined to make her fall in love with the one man she couldn't possibly marry. If she'd had any sense, she'd have stayed in town, begged Ethel for her old job back, and sent Tardy back with the supplies.

But she didn't have any sense. She *wanted* to go back to the ranch. She had been happier these last days than she had ever been before. No one had complained when she rearranged the furniture or objected when she said she intended to buy material to make curtains for the windows. She had only to express a wish and someone rushed to fulfill it. They all told her repeatedly how much they liked having her there, that they wanted her to stay forever. All except Russ.

"Russ is happy the men seem happy, but he doesn't like me."

"He does. I know because I asked him," Tardy said when Tanzy looked doubtful.

"You what?" It was good Tardy was driving. The shock would have caused Tanzy to jerk back on the reins, probably causing the horse to rear and get tangled in the harness.

"I asked him if he liked you."

"Tardy, you had no right to ask that."

"He didn't mind. He even said you could stay longer than two months if you wanted."

"What else did you ask him?"

"I asked him if he wanted to marry you. He said it didn't matter what he wanted. You wouldn't marry him."

"Richard Benton! If you ever ask Russ a question like that again, I'll personally tie you up and take you back to your aunt."

"Was that really bad enough for you to call me *Richard?*"

"It was terrible. It was even worse of you to tell me."

"Why? I thought you'd want to know he liked you."

Why did God make young people so innocent? They could cause enough trouble to destroy civilizations and not have the faintest idea what they'd done.

"I'm glad he likes me, but don't ask him any more questions."

"Why? He wasn't upset."

Tardy didn't think to ask if *she* was upset. Men figured if something was flattering, a woman had to like it. *When will they ever learn to look at things from a woman's point of view? Never*, she thought to herself and chuckled aloud. *Then they'd be just like women, and we—foolish creatures that we are—wouldn't like them anymore.*

"What are you laughing at?" Tardy asked.

"A joke on me that I don't intend to share with you."

"Why not?"

"Because you'd blab it to Russ first chance you got."

"Is it about him?"

"Not directly."

"That's the kind of answer Aunt Ethel gives when I ask questions."

"I'm sorry, Tardy, but very few questions in life have simple answers."

"Is it a simple question to know if you like somebody?"

"No."

"It is for me. I like you. I like the other men, too, but I like Russ best."

"He's a very good man."

"So why don't you like him?"

"I do."

"Then why isn't it simple to—"

They had been so engrossed in their discussion that they were unprepared when a man rode out from a juniper thicket and blocked their path. He was masked and led a horse wearing a sidesaddle. Once she got over her surprise, Tanzy wasn't alarmed. There was something familiar about the rider.

"I don't want to harm anybody," the man said in a gruff voice clearly meant to disguise his identity. "I just want Miss Gallant to return with me to Boulder Gap."

"She's not going anywhere with you," Tardy hollered at him.

Tardy turned his horse off the road, cracked the whip, and headed off at a gallop over terrain so rough Tanzy expected to be thrown from the buggy at any moment. The rider abandoned the saddled horse and rode after the buggy. He gripped the horse's bridle and forced it to come to a stop even though Tardy was using the whip.

"Don't abuse the horse," Tanzy said. "It's not his fault."

"He can't make you go back with him now," Tardy said. "He doesn't have a horse."

"You will get the horse for me and bring it here," the rider said.

"Make me," Tardy replied.

The rider pulled a gun. "I would hate to injure you, but I will if I have to. Either you get that horse or I'll put a bullet in your leg."

"Get the horse," Tanzy told Tardy. "There's no point in getting hurt."

Tardy didn't want to go, but Tanzy convinced him it was pointless to resist.

"Why are you doing this, Stocker?" Tanzy asked when Tardy was out of earshot.

"I'm not Mr. Pullet," the man said, "but I'm working for him."

Tanzy was willing to play along. "Why did he send you to kidnap me?"

"Because you're too stubborn to know what's good for you," Stocker said, his voice less gruff, more like himself.

"What makes you think Stocker knows what's best for me?"

"He's a man."

Ah, the only reason men needed to justify their actions.

"That may be, but he has no reason to try to control what I do."

"He's only thinking of your welfare."

"I'm capable of doing that."

"No woman can understand the dangers that surround her. It's up to a man to protect her from her own folly."

If she'd ever had any intention of going with him, that comment would have ended it. Next time she was going to bring a rifle.

"What's keeping that boy?" Stocker asked.

Tanzy turned around to see Tardy uncinch the saddle and throw it on the ground. Grabbing a handful of mane, he vaulted onto the horse's back and kicked it into a gallop down the trail.

"Where is he going?" Stocker asked, completely forgetting to disguise his voice.

"I think he's going after Russ," Tanzy said, grinning, yet dreading what would happen when the two men met.

"It won't matter. You'll be back in Boulder Gap long before Russ can get here."

He reached down, grasped her horse's bridle, and turned it toward the trail. She considered jumping from the buggy but decided she preferred to let Stocker take her back to town. Once there, she intended to make his actions public, let it be known she would bring a rifle next time, and say that if he didn't let her go, she'd have the sheriff arrest him for theft and kidnaping. The picture in her mind of what his face would look like then made her smile. He stopped where Tardy had dropped the saddle and dismounted.

"He'd better not have ruined a perfectly good saddle. It cost—"

Tanzy couldn't believe Stocker thought she would sit calmly with her hands in her lap while he checked the saddle. She grabbed the reins, cracked the whip, and headed back down the trail as fact as she could. She knew it wouldn't take Stocker long to catch her. She also knew he'd be tired, dusty, and out of temper. The knowledge made her smile.

"Dammit, Tanzy," he said when he'd brought the buggy to a stop a second time and turned it around. "You might as well get used to the fact that I'm not letting you go back to Tibbolt's ranch."

"I had to try," Tanzy said innocently.

"It's a waste of time. You know I'm smarter and stronger than you are."

She clamped her lips together to keep from telling him exactly what she thought of him.

"I'll have to send someone back for that saddle," he said. "It's too valuable to leave behind."

"No point in sending anyone back," a voice called from the same juniper thicket Stocker had used to ambush Tanzy. "You can take it back with you now."

Chapter Twenty

Tanzy nearly laughed aloud at the look of shock on Stocker's face. She felt less amused when he reached for his gun.

"I wouldn't do that," Russ said from concealment.

"Come out, you coward, and face me."

"Not until you holster your gun. I don't want to endanger Miss Gallant."

"If you really meant that, you wouldn't have dragged her out to your ranch," Stocker said as he shoved his gun back in its holster.

Russ emerged from the thicket, his rifle cocked and ready. "Even if you succeeded in taking her back to Boulder Gap, my boys would come after you. With their being ex-cons, they surely wouldn't balk at a little shooting and pillaging. I'm sure your friends would hate that. So you see, I'm doing the fine people of Boulder Gap a favor by not letting you kidnap Miss Gallant."

"By kidnaping her yourself?"

"Miss Gallant was returning to the ranch of her own free will. Do you wish to go with Stocker?" Russ asked.

"No," Tanzy said.

"Do you wish to return to the ranch?"

"Yes."

"Dammit, Tanzy," Stocker said, pulling off his mask, "you don't know what you're doing."

"I appreciate your concern for my welfare, I truly do," Tanzy said to Stocker, "but I'm going to work for Russ until I've paid what I owe him."

"A gentleman wouldn't hold you to that debt," Stocker said.

"You've always said I was a liar, a thief, and a rustler. How could I be all that and a gentleman, too?" Russ asked.

Tanzy didn't know whether Russ had a dry sense of humor or whether he was just trying to irritate Stocker. If it was the latter, he'd succeeded. Stocker was so angry his gun hand twitched.

"Don't try it," Russ warned. "I can put a bullet through your trigger finger at this distance."

"You'll pay for this," Stocker fumed. "I'll hunt you down."

"You'd better take Stocker's gun," Russ said to Tanzy. "He's such an impulsive man, he might be foolish enough to try to use it even though I've got the drop on him."

Tanzy climbed down from the buggy and approached Stocker. She had to stand on her tiptoes to reach his gun, but she was able to remove it from his holster.

"Put it in the buggy," Russ said. "I hate to have to ride back into town to return it, but I don't trust him not to use it on my back."

"I'm not a coward," Stocker shouted. "When I kill you, I'll be facing you."

"If you want to show Tanzy you're really concerned for her, you can put that saddle in the buckboard," Russ said, indicating the sidesaddle still lying where Tardy had dropped it. "I'll pay you next time I'm in town."

Stocker had a lot to say, none of it good and much of it threats, before he disappeared down the road to town.

"You want to know how Tardy found me so quickly, don't you?" Russ asked. He'd tied his horse to the buggy and was driving.

"Yes," Tanzy said.

"I wasn't sure you'd be safe, so I decided to meet you."

"Where is Tardy?"

"I sent him to the ranch to get another mount so he could return Stocker's horse. I don't want him charged with horse stealing."

They rode in silence. She couldn't help wondering if Russ had changed his mind about wanting to marry her. He had kept his distance since the day they'd picked currants, but he'd been watching her with an intensity she found unnerving. She was always expecting something to happen that never did. She wasn't sure how to describe it, but she knew something was going on between them.

She had to face the fact that her resistance to the idea of marrying Russ was weakening, but was it weakening because she was falling in love with him? It was hard to say. She'd been attracted to Russ from the moment she first saw him. She'd categorized her feelings as physical attraction, something that was natural and understandable with such a handsome man, but not something on which to build a marriage. Then she realized she liked him as a man, too. He was gentle with her, thoughtful, and courteous. It was only after the fight with Stocker that she realized he didn't respect women.

Her feelings about that changed drastically when Welt told her about his mother and sister. He had ample reason to distrust women, to suspect their motives, to believe they couldn't be faithful to their promises when something more interesting came along. The way the women in Boulder Gap acted only served to reinforce his opinion.

When she decided against marrying him, he respected her enough not to pressure her. When she lost her job, he offered her one. He rarely commented on what she did at the ranch, but he never stopped her. But most important, she was the only one to whom he exposed any of his inner self. Surely a man would never do that if he didn't believe she'd treat his revelations with consideration and respect.

She wondered what he'd do if they ever disagreed on something important. He gave the men a lot of freedom to decide how to handle their share of the work, but he made the big decisions. As the owner, it was his right. Marriage was different.

As for the feud, she was beginning to question her understanding of the situation. He said he was defending his property, that if you weren't strong enough to hold it, somebody would take it from you. She understood that. He had an abiding hatred for Stocker and responded without hesitation to each conflict, but he had never been the aggressor. Was Stocker the only one feuding? Was she trying to rationalize away her objections because she was falling in love with Russ?

It would be easy to fall in love with him. He was misunderstood and mistreated by all but a few friends. That injustice stirred up her need to see fair play, stimulated her desire to see good find recognition and evil receive punishment. With the exception of Stocker, Russ had responded to his neighbors' ostracism with a stoically calm acceptance of the situation.

Then there was his relationship with Tardy. Russ devoted valuable hours to teaching the boy skills, to giving him the companionship of an older man who liked him and had respect for his abilities. He'd made a place for Tardy, made him feel appreciated, like he was *wanted*.

She hadn't seen it at first, but Russ had done that for her, too. He'd insisted that she have the protection of his ranch rather than confront a strange town with little money and no one to protect her. Even now he'd neglected his work to make sure she returned safely from town. Would a man do all of this for a woman he didn't care about?

"Why did you follow me?" she asked.

"I told you, I wasn't sure you'd be safe."

"That's not what I'm asking. Why did you even stop to wonder if I'd be safe?"

"That's a strange question."

"Why?"

"I'd wonder if any woman would be safe."

"You told me western men are very respectful of a good woman."

"Stocker would do anything he could to get back at me."

"Why bother about me? I'm just a cook and housekeeper. You can hire another one any time you want."

"I don't want another one. The boys don't, either," he added after a pause. He kept his gaze forward, never turning to look at her.

"What's so special about me?"

He didn't answer.

"Lots of women can cook and clean. Men, too."

"I don't want another man at the ranch. Except for Welt, we're all ex-cons. An outsider might think he was better just because he'd never been in prison."

"Nobody has a problem with Tardy."

He didn't turn to her, but she could see a slow smile transform his face. It was at times like this that she found it hard not to want to see that smile for the rest of her life.

"I think all of us see the best of ourselves in Tardy. We know where we went wrong and want to make sure it doesn't happen to him." Russ's smile turned almost sentimental. "He's like a big puppy, full of energy and willing to worship anybody who'll give him five minutes of attention."

"Did anybody ever give you five minutes of attention?"

The abrupt change in him made her regret asking that question. They rode for several minutes, Russ looking straight ahead again but his face working against some strong emotion.

"My father abandoned my mother before I was born. The man everybody calls my father didn't care what I did as long as I stayed away from him. My mother didn't really love either of her children. I pretty much grew up on my own."

They'd wandered far from her question, the one to which she still wanted an answer. "Do you think I'm like Tardy, a puppy needing saving?" she asked.

He turned then, and she could have sworn she saw a twinkle of amusement in his eyes.

"I expect you've excited a good many emotions in men, but I'm sure none of them ever thought of you as a puppy."

"But maybe I needed saving."

"Protection."

"I'm a big girl. I can take care of myself."

"You don't know the West. Even most men can't take care of themselves."

"Now just why do you care?"

"Because I like you, dammit. I've told you before. Is that what you wanted to hear?"

"I'm not sure."

"Did anybody ever tell you you were an unnatural, incomprehensible, frustrating woman?"

"Several. I didn't like it."

"Then stop being that way."

"Maybe I will if you'll talk to me."

"What do you think I've been doing the last half hour?"

"Trying to pick words that tell me as little as possible."

That stopped him in his tracks for several minutes.

"What do you want to know?" he finally asked.

"I'm not really sure."

"Woman, you're stretching my patience."

"It's about time. You've stretched mine often enough. I have a name. I prefer it to being addressed as *woman*."

"You made me angry."

"At least I got some emotion out of you."

"Did you feel any emotion when I kissed you?"

He'd effectively put her in her place.

"Yes, but I'm not sure what kind it was."

"You women beat all. Now you've got *kinds* of emotion. What will you have next?"

"Of course there are kinds of emotion. The most common is naked attraction. As good-looking as you are, you ought to know about that. There's the emotion of friendship. There's also the emotion of momentary infatuation. Then there's the emotion of something quite different, deeper, more long-lasting."

"What's that?"

"That's what I'm not sure about. I think it's made up of little bits of the first ones. But it's got to have something stronger to make it last. Maybe need. Maybe finding something you want so much you never willingly go without it, something you need so much you'll sacrifice for it."

"What could be that important?"

"I'm still trying to figure that out, but maybe you already know. What was so important about Boulder Gap that you came back here even though nearly everybody wanted you to leave?"

She wondered if she'd ever get used to his long pauses in conversation.

"I found my soul when I found my valley. It's where I came when I was so angry I wanted to hurt everybody. Where I came when the pain of knowing nobody wanted me grew too great to endure. It's the only place where I could lie down and sleep soundly. It's my home. It fills me up when I start to feel empty. It comforts me when I wonder if I shouldn't give up and go away. Without it I wouldn't be whole."

"I think you've just described it better than I ever could."

"Described what?"

"The kind of emotion that lasts forever, the kind every man and woman wants to find. The kind that's called love."

"I don't ever want to feel that for a woman."

"Why?"

"My stepfather worshiped my mother. He would do anything for her, even live with the shame of knowing his wife was another man's mistress. He loved her so much he couldn't live without her."

Tanzy was beginning to wonder if there was no limit to

the pain and destruction Russ's mother had managed to cause in her short life.

"You've opened yourself to your men, and you've opened yourself to Tardy," she said.

"That's not the same."

"I know, but it's for that very reason you must open yourself to women—well, at least one woman. You'll never be complete, never be happy until you do."

Another pause. He was driving her crazy.

"Why do you care?"

"Because I like you."

"You don't want to marry me."

"That doesn't mean I can't like you. You don't want to marry me, but you like me."

"That's not true."

"You just said—"

"About not wanting to marry you."

Now it was her turn to fall silent. This wasn't what she wanted to hear.

"I don't think being married to you would be bad," Russ said. "You're pretty, you're nice, the boys like you, and you didn't lie to me."

As unsatisfactory as Russ's reasons were, they represented a big step for him. Even if they involved less emotional content than a lecture on the role of gold in the settling of the West, he *had* changed his mind. It was progress.

"I'm glad you approve of me, but that doesn't mean I'd be a good wife for you."

"Why wouldn't you?"

"Because I want to mean more to my husband than your valley means to you."

"That's impossible."

"Then you'd better start looking for someone who'll settle for less."

"I don't want to."

"Why?"

"Because the only one I'd settle for is you."

Tanzy didn't think she could stand any more revelations. Or the wild, out-of-control shifting of her emotions. She hated it when her head was in conflict with her emotions. It was even worse when her body disagreed with both. She felt like a battlefield with no victor, only the casualties of an indecisive conflict.

Why on earth should such an artless confession touch her in ways beautifully turned phrases never could? Russ was an emotional cripple caught in a fight for his life. She didn't want anybody she had to prop up. She wanted a partner—equality and mutual respect.

"Were you able to get all the supplies you wanted?" Russ asked.

The change in subject startled her but was a relief. She needed time to organize her thoughts, control her emotions, understand why her body was drawn to Russ like iron to a magnet.

"I want you to kill him," Stocker said to Chick during their midnight meeting in his office at the saloon.

"You told me *not* to kill him, that you wanted to see him hang."

"I've changed my mind. I don't care how you do it as long as he's dead."

Everything seemed to change after that ride from town. Tanzy became so aware of Russ that he seldom left her thoughts. She watched his every move, listened and remembered his every word, tried to fathom his moods.

"He's the best man you'll find anywhere." It was Welt's turn to stay at the cabin. Today Tanzy had him helping her move furniture as she cleaned and rearranged the main room.

"How can you say that?" she asked. "Your friendship with him has alienated you from your family."

"Russ was the only guy I knew who didn't care that my father was almost as rich as Stocker. If he thought I'd said or done something stupid, he didn't hesitate to let me know, but he was more ready to stand up for me than I was."

"I know he has the ability to develop strong friendships with men, but why won't he let himself do that with women?"

"Russ tried to see the best in his mother and sister. When he couldn't, he just stopped looking at women altogether. It didn't help that Ethel Peters turned on him when he wasn't interested in her."

"Ethel liked Russ?"

"She wasn't obvious about it. Didn't you know?"

She hadn't known, but it explained a lot. Welt also told her about Betty.

"She took up with some guy when Russ went to Texas. She took up with another when he was in prison. She was a fool to believe Russ wouldn't think she was doing exactly what his mother and sister had done."

It seemed Russ's life was littered with women who'd betrayed him. That made her self-imposed task of restoring his faith in women all the more difficult. How could she teach a man to have faith in women when she didn't plan to stick around? That raised a more difficult question: Was she sure she didn't want to stick around?

*   *   *

Russ had stayed at the cabin. He'd spent the morning working outside with Tardy, but the boy had gone off with Tim after lunch, and Russ had spent the last hour inside writing. He was getting faster and his writings were getting longer. Tanzy continued to be impressed with both his ability and his determination.

"Are you through?" He'd been sitting at the table, more often in thought than actually writing.

"Just about. I've only got another sentence or two."

"I thought I'd take a walk. I'm feeling the need to get outside."

"Wait a bit. I'll go with you. I don't want you wandering about by yourself."

She'd hoped he'd say that. A few minutes later he got up and left his writing on the table. "I'll saddle some horses," he said and left. She should have expected as much. Welt told her a cowboy never walked when he could ride.

She walked over to the table and picked up the paper Russ had left. She really didn't need to correct much anymore, but he needed the exercise of formulating his thoughts.

Sometimes I can't find the words to say what I want. Most of the time it's the wrong ones that come out. I don't know how to talk to women. I never did. I don't know how to tell you that you're special. All the boys think so. It's not anything you cook so much as it is the pleasure you take in our enjoyment of it. It's not that you keep the cabin neat and clean. It's that you're doing it for us. You never remind us that we're ex-cons. We all want to marry you. We hope you'll never leave.

Tanzy had to wipe the tears from her eyes. That was probably the closest thing to a love letter Russ would ever write. It must have taken a lot of courage to expose himself like that. She wondered if he'd ever be able to tell the woman he loved what was in his heart. She guessed it might not matter to the woman as long as she was secure in his love, but she knew it would matter to Russ. She grabbed a hat to keep the wind from tangling her hair and went outside to wait for him.

"You'll have to teach me how to ride in this saddle," she said. "I've never used one."

"It's easy. Just hook your leg over the horn when I lift you in the saddle."

Tanzy found the feeling of Russ's hands around her waist so distracting, she nearly fell out of the saddle on the other side. Russ grinned.

"Don't tell me I'm going to have to tie you to the saddle."

"It's easier to ride astride."

"Not if you want Ethel to approve of you."

She wondered how he could speak so lightly of a woman who'd turned on him because he didn't return her feelings. She managed to wrap her leg around the saddle horn and get her skirts smoothed under her.

"Except for myself, the only person whose approval I'll want will be my husband."

"That's a mighty independent way of thinking."

"I left my home so I could think that way. I'm not about to give in to Ethel, Stocker, or anybody else. If you can live with their disapproval, I can, too."

Russ mounted up and they walked their horses out of the ranch yard toward a band of trees that nestled against the valley wall. Though the nights could be very cool, the midday temperatures were hot. The sun was so intense she felt it burning her skin. It was cool and moist under the trees, the fragrance of pine and spruce giving the air a tangy, clean scent. Water seeped from the rocks, forming numerous pools and bogs that nourished tall, thick grasses, broad-leaved cattails, pink primroses, and blue columbine. She would have to remember to search here for flowers when those exposed to the hot sun faded.

"What do you plan to do when you leave here?" Russ asked.

She hadn't expected that question. She didn't welcome it. She didn't have an answer. "I haven't decided yet."

"Then why don't you stay?"

Chapter Twenty-one

"Are you saying I could have this job as long as I want it?"

"Yes."

"Why?"

"We like your cooking."

"I mean why me and not somebody else who cooks just as well?"

Russ kept his gaze straight ahead, as though he expected some dangerous animal might jump out into the path before them.

"The boys like you."

"They might like somebody else."

"They might, but they already like you."

Clearly subtlety was lost on Russ. "You're the owner of

the ranch, the one who makes all the decisions. Do you want me to stay?"

"Yes." He still didn't look at her.

"Why? And don't mention my cooking."

"I already told you."

"No, you wrote it on a piece of paper. It's not the same."

He didn't answer, nor did he turn his gaze to her. She wondered if he was merely uncomfortable being alone with a woman he cared for, if he was uncomfortable talking to a woman directly, or if he was still having trouble letting himself trust a woman not to hurt him.

"Welt told me why you don't trust women. I don't know what you want to say, what you feel, but if you could trust me enough to tell me that you couldn't read, you ought to be able to tell me if you have any feelings for me."

"I do." The answer came quickly, was spoken firmly. "I like you."

"I like you, too, but I'm talking about something stronger than that."

"It doesn't matter what I feel. You've already said you wouldn't marry me."

"I said that before I knew you very well. I'm starting to think I ought to reconsider my answer."

He turned toward her in surprise, but his expression was more apprehensive than expectant. "I thought your ideas were fixed."

"My values, yes, but my understanding of people and situations can change as I learn and understand more."

"What have you learned?"

"Can we get down? Trying to get used to this saddle is ruining my concentration. Send it back to Stocker. I can't let you pay for something I can't use."

"Try to get used to it," he said as he put his hands

around her waist and lifted her from the saddle. "I don't want to give anybody an excuse to say you're not a lady."

He set her down and reached for the horses' reins before she could look into his face.

"There's a fallen tree a little way from here. You can rest there."

"I don't need to rest. I just want to be able to talk to you without having to worry about the saddle."

"It's not far."

She was beginning to wonder if the reason Russ had never married could all be blamed on women. She couldn't imagine the wild youth Welt described having turned into a man who was too unsure of himself to look at a woman when he talked to her. If she'd been one of his cows, she'd bet he wouldn't have hesitated to look her straight in the eye.

Russ stopped in a small clearing made by a shallow pool several feet wide that ran off in a little rivulet to join several other similar trickles of water on its way to the stream that coursed through the valley. A thick covering of ponderosa pine shielded them from the sun. The needle-strewn floor was dotted with patches of purple lupine. Birds in the trees above argued with squirrels, while a mouselike creature scampered over the ground collecting bits of food dropped by careless squirrels. The bark had fallen off the downed tree long ago, allowing the elements to wear the trunk smooth.

"It's hard to believe such a quiet corner exists so close to the cabin," Tanzy said as she settled herself on the tree trunk. "I'll have to get outside more often."

"Don't come alone," Russ said. "I don't trust Stocker not to try to kidnap you again."

She doubted Stocker cared that much, but she didn't

want to cause any of the men to worry about her. "I'll remember. Now, explain why you think it would be a good idea for me to stay here."

"You don't know where you want to go or what you want to do when you get there. It only makes sense to stay here until you do."

"I'm not talking about that. I'm assuming you meant you wanted me to stay even if I did know where I wanted to go and what I wanted to do. Is that true?"

"I already told you in what I wrote."

"That was very nice, but it didn't tell me what I would need to know to stay here."

"What's that?"

"I want a husband and a family. I could only stay here as a married woman."

"One of the boys might marry you."

"I'm not asking about one of the boys. I'm asking about you."

"You said—"

"Suppose I changed my mind. Would you marry me then?"

"It wouldn't be a bad idea."

"We're not talking about a trip to the blacksmith to replace a loose shoe," she snapped, frustrated. "We're talking about marriage."

"Any man would want to marry you. You're beautiful, nice—"

"And I don't lie to you. I know all that, but it's not enough. I would have to love the man I marry and he would have to love me. Do you love me?"

"No."

His answer came with startling quickness.

"But I like you a lot. You're just as good as you said in your letters."

"Considering I didn't write those letters, maybe you'd better tell me what they said."

"You could read them if you like. I kept them."

Now that was a surprise, when he couldn't read. Russ was more of a sentimentalist than she'd thought.

"I'm sure my friend exaggerated my good qualities."

"She didn't."

"I could only stay here if we loved each other and got married."

"Why?"

"One, it would ruin my reputation otherwise. Two, I want children of my own. I wouldn't get them keeping house for a bunch of cowboys. Three, I want a husband I can love and who loves me."

"If you stayed, maybe I could learn to love you."

"It has to work both ways."

"Do you think you could learn to love me?"

She thought for a moment. So much had changed in her feelings for Russ, she didn't know what she felt, but she didn't want to turn her back on the possibility that she could come to love this man. She was already halfway there.

"We've got about a month and a half to find out."

"Can we start now?"

Tanzy was a little surprised. "I suppose so. How do you propose to begin?"

She didn't have long to wait to find out. Russ stepped forward, drew her to her feet, pulled her to him, and kissed her. It wasn't their first kiss, but it still had the power to surprise her—and excite her as well. The sheer power of the experience was enough to overwhelm her senses, but there was more to it now, much more, and that added greatly to its effect on her.

She was eager to kiss him back. More than eager. She

needed to kiss him. A large part of her had been reaching out to him from the moment they'd met but had been held in check. But once released from the mental control, she felt nearly swept away by the desire to burrow into his embrace, to cling to his body, to lose herself in a feeling that was so pleasurable she wondered how she'd lived this long without it.

Russ broke the kiss long before she was ready. She reached for him, held on tight for fear he would take his arms from around her. They gazed at each other wordlessly, he looking as awed as she felt.

"Do you always kiss breathless the women you're trying to fall in love with?" she asked when she was finally able to gather her senses. "It's probably a good tactic. It leaves them so intoxicated they can't think why they'd want to resist you."

"I never wanted to make any woman fall in love with me," Russ said, "but you're different. I knew that the first night I saw you. I'd have married you then if you'd wanted. It was only after regaining my senses that I knew it wouldn't work."

Russ didn't seem to have any difficulty expressing himself now. It seemed kissing loosened his tongue. She'd have to keep that in mind.

"You still believe it wouldn't work?" she asked.

"Not for you."

"Why?"

"Because you think that by defending my property I'm feuding with Stocker. I'll always hate him for what he and his brother did, but I know it was my mother's and sister's weaknesses, their lack of principles, that allowed it. Nothing I can do will bring them back or change what happened, so all I want is to be left alone."

"When did you start to think that?"

"When I was in jail. I had more than enough time to think about what I'd done with my life and what I wanted to do in the future. The four of us—Tim, Oren, Buck, and me—sort of gravitated toward each other because we wanted a second chance. This ranch is for *all* of us. Without it, they have no place to go, no way to rebuild their lives."

Tanzy couldn't believe she'd misread the situation so badly. Russ wasn't feuding. What had made her so afraid she couldn't see what Russ was doing? For one thing, she hadn't known about Tim, Buck, and Oren. For another, she hadn't had a chance to see beyond the surface of a man who wasn't eager to have anyone get to know him. Though she hadn't believed everything she'd heard, she'd been too willing to let what others said prevent her from learning the truth on her own. In a way, she was just as bad as the people of Boulder Gap.

She lowered her gaze, unable to look him in the eye. "You make me ashamed of myself," she said.

He lifted her chin until their gazes met. "Why?"

"I let my fears and prejudices keep me from looking deeply enough to see that you're not at all what I thought, that the situation isn't like it was back home. You've suffered too much from being misjudged."

His gaze intensified. "I suffered because of what my mother and sister did to themselves, because my family made me feel unwanted and unloved. There's nothing the people of Boulder Gap can do to hurt me."

"They can take away your ranch."

"I won't let them."

"They can take away your chance for happiness."

"Only you can do that."

Tanzy felt her breath desert her entirely. The very air seemed devoid of oxygen. She felt dizzy, disoriented, as though she was going to faint.

"You can't mean that. I've just confessed to being as blind and prejudiced as everyone in Boulder Gap."

"I did some stupid things when I was young. But I learned from those mistakes just as you learned. I say we forget the past and start over."

"You can do that?"

"I've already done it once. It'll be easier the second time."

He leaned forward and kissed her again. She desperately wanted to get lost in his arms, to become intoxicated by his kisses, but she had to think before she let herself be carried away on the tide of her emotions.

"You keep kissing me like that and I won't be able to think at all."

"Is that a bad thing?" he asked with a lopsided smile.

"It is for me. I'm plagued with a mind that insists upon understanding everything I do."

Russ didn't retreat. He took her hands in his. "What does your brain need to know?"

"Lots of things, like if I'm really seeing you rather than your handsome face."

"I can't imagine that my poor face could be that distracting to a strong-minded woman like you."

"Would you be distracted if the most beautiful woman you'd ever seen suddenly appeared down the trail?"

"Sure, but—"

"Well, women are no different, even though we pretend to be. You show us a handsome man and we get warm all over."

"I was about to say I'd be distracted because I'd be trying to imagine how she could get past Tim."

It took Tanzy a moment to realize Russ was kidding her. "I'm trying to be serious," she said, slightly annoyed.

"And I'm trying to make jokes."

"I didn't know you had a sense of humor."

"I don't. I promise to be quiet until you finish."

She didn't trust him. There was the look in his eye that said he wasn't telling the truth about something. It wasn't a bad look, just one that seemed slightly amused, slightly more knowledgeable than she was. That made her feel uncomfortable, like there were questions and answers he knew that she didn't.

"I have to make sure my liking for you owes nothing to my anger at people for treating you so badly."

He still looked serious, but without the gravity she was accustomed to seeing.

"I also have to make sure that liking you owes nothing to my fear of the future and my relief at finding a place where I'm happy and safe."

"I didn't know about the happy part." He sounded like that surprised him.

Without warning he'd put her on unsafe ground. "I told you I wanted my husband to respect me, to give my opinions equal consideration with his own, to consider my wishes and happiness as important as his own. I still do, but I've discovered I could have all of that without feeling accepted, wanted, valued as a person. I feel that here. It's like I've found the place where I fit."

"Somehow I feel there's a qualification coming."

"I need to make sure I'm not so comfortable I forget the rest."

"Did anyone ever tell you that you think too much?"

"My father told me no woman was worth being treated the way I wanted to be treated."

"Was that when you decided to leave home?"

"No. It was only after my father was killed and my uncle tried to force me to marry his son, a man who thought less of women than he did his hunting dogs."

Russ squeezed her hands. "I'm glad he's a fool. Otherwise you wouldn't be here now."

"Are you really glad I'm here? I've been an awful lot of trouble."

He took her in his arms and kissed her, but she broke away almost immediately.

"You'll have to find another way to convince me. When you kiss me, I could believe anything."

"What's bad about that?"

"You can't be kissing me all the time."

"I can try."

"Be serious."

"I am."

"No, you're not. You might *want* to kiss me all the time, and I might be willing to let you, but there's a lot more to life than kissing."

"I consider that bad planning on Mother Nature's part."

"We have to make sure we're compatible under more ordinary circumstances."

"If we kiss all the time, wouldn't that become our ordinary circumstances?"

Tanzy got to her feet, only pretending to be annoyed. "If you're going to talk nonsense, I'm going back to the house."

"You've blessed my poor cabin by calling it a house. See, you've made everything I own seem better just by your being here."

Tanzy's gaze narrowed. "You know, if you talked like this to the ladies in town, I'm surprised at least half a dozen didn't try to drag you before the justice of the peace."

His expression turned serious. "Just one, and she hasn't forgiven me for escaping."

"I want to make sure my feelings for you are honest. I want you to feel the same way about your feelings for me."

"I already do."

Tanzy felt uncomfortable, as though Russ was crowding her to make a decision she wasn't ready to make. Her change of heart had been so recent, so unexpected, she hardly knew what she thought. She needed time to order things in her mind, to bring her heart and mind into conjunction. Right now everything was overshadowed by her desire to be in his arms, to have him kiss her again. As nice as that was, she knew it was only part of being in love.

"We'd better go back."

Russ stood and reclaimed her hands. "I'll give you all the time you need, but I've waited a long time to find someone like you. I'd actually given up on the idea. Now I don't want to waste any more time."

"Thank you. Now I'd better become reacquainted with that sidesaddle."

He brought the horses but stopped when he'd lifted her halfway in the air to the saddle. "It's only fair to warn you I'm going to use every means at my disposal to convince you to stay."

"Is holding me suspended in the air one of them?"

"Would it work?"

"Not when the boys show up and there's no supper ready."

He lifted her into the saddle and she struggled with her skirts. "You have to promise you won't make me ride sidesaddle. I'll never get used to one of these things."

"I'll buy the prettiest buggy and the fastest horse to pull it."

"Bribery will not work."

"You can't blame a guy for trying."

"It's going to take me a while to get used to this side of your personality."

"I'm afraid I can be rather impetuous, even foolish. My mother and sister certainly were."

"I can't see you being either. Now I've got to hurry back or supper will be late."

"If you're not careful, I'll think you like the boys better than you like me."

"Why settle for one when I can flirt with five?"

"You're looking mighty pleased about something," Welt said when he rode in to find Russ at the corral, his foot on the lower rail and an expression of bemused happiness on his face. "Anything I ought to know?"

"Just that I may decide to forgive you for writing those letters to Tanzy."

"I gather you've changed your mind about her." He dismounted and began to strip the saddle from his horse.

"I never changed my mind about her. It was just about her suitability to be my wife."

"Are you telling me you wanted to marry this woman and you nearly beat me to death anyway?"

"Something like that."

"I have a good mind to knock you senseless."

"You know you can't do that. You like me too much."

Welt attacked his friend, and the two men enjoyed a brief tussle until Welt ended up on the ground.

"Don't fool yourself," Welt said as he got to his feet. "It's not because I like you too much. It's because you're stronger and a better fighter." Welt removed the saddle blanket from his horse and began to rub him down.

"Explain yourself. I thought you decided she wasn't wife material."

"I did," Russ said. He held the horse's head while Welt curried him. "But I knew the minute I set eyes on her I wanted to marry her anyway."

"Why didn't you tell me, you hardheaded cuss?"

"For once I thought it was my business and not yours."

"So you let me go around feeling miserable, cussing myself for writing her."

"Yeah. I wanted to teach you not to meddle in other people's business."

Welt finished currying the horse and turned him into the corral. "Since it's turned out right, I can keep interfering in your life," he said with a self-satisfied grin. "For your own good, of course."

"Don't try it again. You were lucky this time."

"If she wants to marry you, so were you."

Russ's expression changed.

"She does want to marry you, doesn't she?"

"I don't know. I feel like she does, but she's got a lot of questions she's trying to answer."

"God help us," Welt moaned. "Another person who thinks too much. If you two don't stop thinking all the time, you'll never have time to *do* anything."

"Tell Tanzy. I've done all the thinking I need."

Russ had finally figured out why he'd been desperate enough to ask Tanzy to teach him to read. He was looking for an excuse to be with her. That he was willing to open so much of himself to her was an indication that his feelings for her were more than momentary attraction. He'd never considered asking a woman to come to his ranch, but when he'd found she was leaving town, it was the only way he could think of to keep her close.

Now he was willing to admit he'd fallen in love with her, had probably been in love with her from the first. He'd been fighting his attraction at the same time he was fighting for ways to keep seeing her. It was almost like two halves of him were playing a game with each other, but there was no need for that any longer. He knew he wanted Tanzy to be his wife. Both parts of him agreed on that.

The last week had been almost like a dream for Tanzy. Russ had spent every other day at the cabin with her. He'd worked outside but always seemed to be around whenever she looked up from a task. When the other men were there, he retreated to his normally taciturn self. But he was gradually letting down the barriers with her and Tardy, gradually showing himself to be a man who could spend as much time enjoying the little pleasures of life as he did worrying about the problems posed by Stocker and the rustlers. He'd even suggested they go on a picnic. It had been an idyllic afternoon, one that convinced her that she was well on her way to falling in love with Russ.

Today he'd gone outside after lunch. She'd decided the inside of the cabin was too dark and the walls needed to be whitewashed. Russ had already agreed to buy whitewash the next time they went to town. She was cleaning every surface of the grease and dust that had collected over the years. It wasn't an easy task, but it was made lighter by knowing this might soon become her home, the home she intended to make for her husband and her future children.

She'd have to talk to Russ about adding on or building a house. There was no space in the cabin for children. Tanzy's home in Kentucky hadn't been big or comfortable, but it had been built with a family in mind, with places of privacy as well as places for everyone to gather. She wanted that for her family.

She hadn't said anything to him yet. He'd said he had to catch up on the men's back wages. They had given him unstinting labor and unquestioned loyalty for five years. It was only fair that he reward them first.

Living in cramped quarters seemed a small price to pay for the happiness she foresaw. As much as she wanted the men to find happiness in their own lives, she couldn't look forward to their leaving the valley. It wouldn't seem right without them.

And that included Tardy.

She didn't know what was best for him, but the boy had blossomed since he'd been living at the ranch. His cheerfulness and energy were—

A gunshot shattered her thoughts. Before she had time to wonder what could cause Russ to have fired a rifle so close to the cabin, he rushed inside.

"Stay away from the window," he said. "Some gunmen have come across the mountains. I think they're trying to kill me."

Chapter Twenty-two

"Who are they?" Tanzy asked. It seemed crazy that someone would just start shooting at Russ for no reason.

"I didn't stop to ask." Russ had rushed to a rifle rack, taken down one of the rifles, then hurried back to the doorway to fire at the approaching gunmen.

"Why should strangers want to kill you?" Tanzy asked as she picked up two boxes of ammunition and placed them next to Russ.

"Check the window and see if anybody is on the back side of the cabin," Russ said. "It could be the rustlers are trying to kill me because it'll make it easier for them to steal the herd."

Tanzy could see a man approaching the house from the corrals. She got a rifle from the rack, checked to make sure it was loaded, opened the window, took careful aim, and fired.

"What happened?" Russ asked, turning quickly at the sound of the rifle shot.

"I shot at a man trying to reach the house from the corrals. I think I hit him."

"I didn't know you could shoot."

"I spent most of my life living through a feud. We all learned to use a rifle as soon as we were big enough to lift one."

"I thought you didn't believe in feuds."

"I don't, but I don't believe in letting people just come in and shoot you either. Now pay attention to your side of the house. I can handle this one. How many are out there?"

"Three on my side. How many on yours?"

"One. They can keep us pinned down."

"The boys will have heard the gunfire. I expect they're riding hell-for-leather right now."

Tanzy fired again. Apparently she'd missed the man the first time. He sprinted from his position at the corrals to a big ponderosa pine that gave him more protection.

"They could be thieves who think living in an isolated valley makes us easy pickings," Russ said, "but thieves don't usually go to so much trouble without knowing there's something here worth the trouble."

"Is there?"

"Just the normal stuff anybody would find on a ranch."

The sound of a rifle being fired exploded inside the house.

"One down," Russ said.

Minutes passed. Tanzy managed to hit the man hiding behind the ponderosa pine, but she was certain it was only a graze. He returned her fire, breaking the panes in the window. Tiny pieces of flying glass punctured her skin like so many pinpricks. Drops of blood oozed to the surface and quickly dried.

"One of them has disappeared," Russ said. "Keep a look out on your side."

"He's not on my side," Tanzy said.

Silence reigned for a few moments.

"I think he's on the roof," Russ said. "Maybe he's hoping to force us outside. Come over here and cover me."

"What are you going to do?"

"I'm going to throw myself through the door and get a shot at him before he can take a shot at us. You've got to keep the guy in the trees ducking for cover so he won't have time to get a clean shot at me. Think you can do that?"

"If he sticks his head out, he'll lose it."

Russ chuckled. "Sounds like you've got a little bit of mountain lioness in you."

"I don't like being shot at. It makes me real mad." She took her position by the doorway. "Ready?"

"Whenever you are."

Tanzy aimed a series of rifle shots into the trees. Having exchanged his rifle for a gun, Russ dashed through the door, threw himself on the ground, rolled over, and fired rapidly in the direction of the roof. Tanzy heard a rifle fall, then the thud of a body. The man in the trees jumped from cover to take a shot at Russ, and she put a bullet through his hat. He jumped back under cover as Russ dived back through the doorway.

"Two down," he said. "Check the other window."

"He's leaving," Tanzy said when she saw the man moving through the trees away from the corrals. "He's trying to get away."

"Maybe the boys will get here in time to catch him. Stay here. I'm going after the guy in the trees."

Russ ran through the door and around the corner of the cabin.

Tanzy hurried to the doorway but couldn't see Russ or the gunman. She turned back to the window, but the man at the corrals had disappeared. For one indecisive moment she stood still, but she couldn't remain inside doing nothing while Russ faced two gunmen alone. She put extra shells in her rifle and went outside.

The eerie silence made it seem as if she'd imagined the gunfight. The body on the ground, however, was proof it was no illusion.

Where had Russ gone? She walked around the corner of the cabin toward the corrals but saw no one. She returned to the front. Still, no one. A faint sound attracted her attention and she rounded the far corner of the cabin. She thought she could make out Russ working his way through the trees in the direction of the path they'd taken several days earlier. The trees were thick along that side. She caught some slight movement out of the corner of her eye and turned in time to see a man raise his rifle and aim at Russ.

A fifth gunman! Acting so quickly she was unaware of

the individual motions, Tanzy raised the rife to her shoulder and fired immediately. She didn't kill the gunman, but she hit him in the shoulder, causing him to drop his rifle.

"Damned good shot," Oren said as he galloped past Tanzy straight into the woods. Tanzy heard a gunshot behind the cabin. Before she could round the cabin to see what was happening, Tardy rode his horse into the yard at a gallop. He threw himself off, grabbed Tanzy, and started toward the cabin.

"Welt said he'd take every piece of skin off my hide if I didn't make sure you stayed inside," he said. Tanzy tried to resist, but Tardy was insistent. "I'm not taking any chances. Welt can be real mean when he's crossed."

"So can I," Tanzy said, angry at being treated like a woman.

"Yeah, but you won't hurt me. Welt will."

"If anything happens to Russ, you'll find out how wrong you are."

Tardy pushed her inside and closed the door. "You love him?" Tardy asked, his thoughts momentarily deflected from the conflict outside.

"I like him enough not to want him shot."

"Hot damn! I told Welt you were going to marry him."

"I haven't decided what I'm going to do," Tanzy said, irritated that Tardy and Welt had been discussing her relationship with Russ. A gunshot recalled her attention to the attack. "Who's guarding the pass?"

"Tim. He can't leave his position until someone comes to relieve him. He's going to be mad as hell he missed the fun."

Tanzy didn't see anything fun about the situation. She just wanted to know Russ and the others were safe, but she couldn't see through the door or the single window.

When she had a house, she was going to have windows on all four sides. Tardy cracked the door and peered out.

"Can you see anything?" she asked.

"Naw. I expect they've got them tied up by now."

She wished she had as much faith in Russ's invincibility as Tardy, but she'd seen too many men die.

"Buck's at the corrals. Now he's riding off through the woods."

"Probably following the man who was hiding there."

Thoroughly disgusted with her inability to do anything useful, Tanzy put her rifle back on the rack. "Since everybody is determined I won't be allowed to help, I guess I'll clean up the glass."

"You'd better clean up yourself first," Tardy said. "Russ will have a heart attack if he sees you with blood all over your face."

Tanzy had forgotten about the tiny glass fragments. A look in the mirror revealed a few spots of blood on her cheek and chin. More on her neck and arms. A quick swipe with a damp cloth was sufficient to remove them. The tiny pinpricks were too small to notice. Fortunately, none of the glass slivers were embedded in her skin.

"Here comes Oren with one," Tardy called.

It was the man who'd tried to shoot Russ in the back. Tanzy was glad she'd shot him. She hoped he was in agony. A few minutes later Buck came back with the man who'd been hiding by the corrals.

"Welt's gone to help Russ catch the other one," Buck said.

It wasn't long before Russ came back with the last gunman, who looked like he'd run into a whole family of angry grizzlies. Apparently Russ had found a way to work out some of his anger.

"Welt is bringing their horses," he said. "I'll take them

into town. Tardy and Tanzy will come with me. The rest of you stay alert. This could be part of a plan to get us out of the valley so they can steal the herd."

"It doesn't look like the plan worked too well," Oren said, "not with two of them dead, two of them shot, and one looking like he lost an argument with a cougar."

Tanzy didn't care about the gunmen or the cattle. She only cared that Russ was safe and unhurt. When he looked at her and smiled, her heart turned over. It was in that moment she knew for certain she loved him.

The procession attracted attention even before it reached town. Tanzy rode ahead in the wagon with the two dead men, their horses tied behind. Next came the other three gunmen on their horses, their hands tied behind them, their feet tied under their horses' bellies. Russ and Tardy rode behind.

"What'd they do?" one man asked.

"Tried to kill me," Russ replied.

"One man against five? That don't sound fair."

"I don't think they were looking to be fair."

"Who are they?"

"I don't know. Never seen them before."

"Are they the rustlers?"

"They say they aren't."

"You can't believe a thing they say," one man said, "not when five of them gang up on one man."

"What catamount got him?" another man asked, pointing to the gunman who had both eyes swollen shut.

"Russ got him," Tardy said proudly. "Beat the snot out of him."

"Watch your language in front of a lady," Russ said.

"Sorry," Tardy said, apologizing to Tanzy. "I forgot."

Tanzy suppressed a grin. Tardy was so full of himself he

could hardly stand it. Russ had allowed him to wear a gun and carry a rifle. He was probably hoping one of the gunmen would try to escape so he could have a chance to use his weapon.

"Who are these men?" the sheriff asked Russ when they reached the jail. The news had already preceded them into town. The sheriff and two deputies were waiting for him.

"I have no idea," Russ replied. "I've never seen them before."

"Why were they trying to kill you?"

"They didn't say, but they surrounded my cabin and started shooting at me."

"I can't take your word for this," the sheriff said.

"Why not?" Tanzy demanded, stunned at the sheriff's response.

"Everybody knows he's a thief and a liar," the sheriff said.

"Have you ever known him to lie?"

"When he was a kid—"

"All kids lie at one time or another. I'm sure you did, too."

"He lied about the rustling."

"Can you prove he stole any cattle?"

The sheriff started to speak, then changed his mind.

"You have no proof that he's a thief, a liar, or a rustler. I was under the impression that an officer of the law was supposed to be above gossip and slander."

"I require proof that these men attacked him like he said."

"I saw them," Tardy said. "So did Oren and Buck."

"I'm not taking the word of some kid or any ex-cons," the sheriff said.

"How about mine?" Tanzy asked. "Or are you going to disqualify women as well?"

"I haven't heard what you have to say," the sheriff said, evading her question.

"I was in the cabin when they attacked. They tried to kill me as well as Russ. If you will look closely, you can see where pieces of flying glass punctured my skin in at least a dozen places. Now, unless you intend to call me a liar as well, you have all the proof you need to put these men in jail."

"You can go back to the ranch with me tomorrow and match all the spent bullet cases with their guns," Russ said. "If you or any of your deputies know how to track, you can follow the trail of their horses to see where and how they entered my valley. Or, if you want to save a lot of time, you can just ask them."

"We was paid to go in there and shoot up the place," one of the men volunteered. "We wasn't going to kill anybody, just scare them good."

"Is that why you shot at me through the window?" Tanzy asked. "Is that why one of the dead men tried to shoot us through the roof?"

"They were still shooting when I got there," Tardy said. "Why would they sneak in if they weren't up to no good? If they wanted to visit, all they had to do was come through the pass like anybody else."

The sheriff might fear Stocker, but Tardy was the nephew of the town's social arbiter and Tanzy was a woman. It was hard to discount what they said when their tale agreed in every detail with what Russ had said.

"I'll have to check your evidence," the sheriff said.

"Let me know when you're ready. I'd better go with you. The boys are a little jumpy right now."

"I'm the sheriff."

"I expect they know that. They just want to be sure you're on the side of the law."

"And where else would I be?"

"That's for you to decide," Russ said. His voice was quiet, his speech slow and measured, but there was no question about the challenge in his eyes.

"We probably ought to see about a hotel room," Tanzy said, anxious to keep Russ from getting into a fight with the sheriff. "I'm sure Tardy's hungry."

"Starved," the boy said.

"You can put up in the hotel with us if you like," Russ said to Tardy once they were outside on the boardwalk, "but I think you ought to see your aunt."

"She'll be after me to come back," he protested.

"Maybe," Tanzy said, "but she has taken care of you since your parents died. You owe her that much courtesy."

"I don't want to go back."

"Then try to explain and give her a chance to understand. I'm sure she loves you. Your leaving must have hurt."

Tardy looked like he wanted to argue, but he ducked his head and turned toward his home. Archie welcomed them into the Stocker Hotel with a covert smile.

"You'll be wanting two rooms," he said.

"As long as you're sure Stocker won't have me thrown out," Russ said.

Archie's smile vanished. "He's coming into town for the meeting tonight."

"What meeting?" Russ asked.

"The meeting to decide what to do about the rustling."

"You mean the meeting to decide what to do about *me* rustling."

"I can't say who they suspect is behind it," Archie said. "Do you plan to go and find out?"

Archie seemed to be trying to tell Russ something, but Tanzy couldn't figure out what it might be.

"I think I will," Russ said. "What time is it?"

"They're meeting in Stocker's saloon at seven-thirty."

"I'll be there. Now I'd better see about getting Miss Gallant something to eat before she faints from hunger."

Tanzy didn't like the look of the gathering the moment she stepped inside the saloon. The men appeared angry, impatient to find the man who was threatening their livelihood. The fact that Stocker was in the center of the most agitated part of the room added to her feeling of unease.

"I'm not sure coming here was a good idea," she said to Russ.

"I would prefer to know what they're saying about me."

"You *know* what they're saying. The question is, what are you going to do about it?"

"I don't know yet. Let's see what happens."

Tanzy didn't like the saloon. It combined the worst attributes of establishments of its kind. It was too small for the number of people inside, the smoke and liquor fumes were so thick she could hardly breathe, and the noise level was so high she could hardly hear Russ. The tables were too close together, nothing appeared to have been cleaned recently, and no one was required to leave guns at the door. She wished Russ had chosen a table closer to the entrance.

In a few minutes Stocker called for quiet. Some of the men chose to stand at the bar. Some sat down but continued to mutter with their neighbors.

"You all know why we're gathered here," Stocker said, "so let's get right to it."

"I'd like to *get right to* the thief who's stealing my cows," one man said. "If it doesn't stop soon, I'll be broke."

"How many have you lost?" Russ asked.

"I won't know for sure until roundup," the man said. "Maybe you can tell me."

Russ ignored his implication. "Anybody else know how many cows they've lost?"

Several ranchers said they wouldn't know until roundup, but they were sure they'd lost a lot.

"Nobody can say how many cows they've lost, so how do you know rustlers have been taking your cows?" Russ asked.

The room burst into shouts, with threats and accusations flying freely. No semblance of order returned until Stocker signaled for quiet.

"We don't have to know the precise number to know we've been losing cows," he said, addressing Russ. "We've seen the footprints leading away through gulches and canyons. We know they're being taken, and we know who's taking them."

"Do you know where they've gone?" Russ asked before Stocker could make the accusation that was on the tip of his tongue.

"No, but you do," one man shouted.

"I'll lay odds they're in your valley."

Accusations flew fast and furious, but Russ remained calm. Gradually, as the men exhausted their litany of complaints, they quieted down.

"There are no stolen cows in my valley," Russ said, his demeanor calm. "I've offered to let any delegation you choose come out so you can look for yourselves as long as you bring the colonel at the fort with you."

"You accusing us of lying?"

"Are you accusing me?"

"You're damned right!" several shouted.

"Where's your proof? You've been accusing me of stealing your cows for weeks, but not one of you has ever produced even a shred of proof to back up the accusation."

"We don't have to see the coyote that steals in the night to recognize it's a coyote," Stocker said.

"But you have to see him to know *which* coyote it is."

"Are you implying that one of us is doing the rustling?" one man asked.

"Any one of you would have as much to gain as I would."

"We're all honest men."

"Can you prove that?"

For a moment the room lay in shocked silence. Then everyone started shouting at once. Tanzy was afraid some of his accusers might attack Russ with their fists, but he remained calm in the face of their fury.

"You know why you can't prove it?" Russ asked when he could be heard. "You've been so certain I'm doing the rustling, you haven't looked at your neighbor. Have any of you followed the trails?"

"They disappear."

"You didn't bother to look hard because you were sure I was the guilty one. Yet when I offered to let you come check my herds, no one took me up on it."

"Don't let him confuse you," Stocker said. "He's trying to set us against each other, make us suspect the fine, upstanding men who're the backbone of this community. Who're you going to listen to, your neighbors or a lying thief who murdered my brother in cold blood?"

Stocker had worked the men up to a frenzy, but Tanzy saw a sudden change in the temper of the room when he accused Russ of having murdered his brother.

"You can sit here talking all you want," Stocker said, "going back and forth over ground that we've already covered, and you'll end up right where we are now, losing cows to Russ Tibbolt. How do you think an ex-con came in here without a cent to his name and was able to stock a ranch?"

"I'd have told you if you'd asked," Russ said. "I'd also have told you how to go about finding out who's stealing your cattle."

"How?" several men asked.

"First we need to establish as accurately as possible how many cows have been rustled. Then we have to study the trails to see where they go. If we can't follow them, then we should hire someone who can. If one person or gang is responsible for all the rustling, the trails will probably join at some point. Then you'll either find the cows or find where they've been taken. At the same time, we need to locate the most likely markets for stolen cattle. I think we should ask the colonel at Fort Lookout to help with this. He has many more trained men at his disposal than we do."

It seemed for a moment that the men were giving Russ's sensible suggestions serious consideration. Then Stocker spoke up.

"All that's a waste of time when we know you're doing the stealing," he said. "All we have to do is force our way into that valley of yours. We'll find the stolen cattle and more."

"There's never been a single cow in that valley that I didn't pay for. My men will testify to that."

"We've all had enough of your lies," Stocker shouted. "We don't believe anything you or your gang of ex-cons says. We're a fine, upstanding community of decent citizens. Even if you weren't stealing us blind, we wouldn't want the likes of you or those men anywhere near us to lead our young men astray, to degrade our women, to—"

Tanzy couldn't stand it any longer. She got to her feet and walked across the room to face Stocker. He was so shocked he stopped in mid-sentence.

"I have never heard such a lot of nonsense from a group of supposedly responsible, sensible, law-abiding men in my whole life. Russ has just given you a perfectly sensible way to go about trying to find the rustlers, but rather than do anything constructive, you prefer to sit around making accusations you can't prove."

"I don't think it's the best way," Stocker said.

"Then propose an alternative, but do something instead of just talking."

"I propose we raid his valley!" Stocker shouted.

Tanzy raised her voice so she could be heard over the murmurs of approval. "I don't see why you feel the need to *raid* his valley," she said. "I've twice heard him invite you to come look for yourselves. His only condition is that you bring the commander of Fort Lookout along with you."

"That sounds mighty suspicious to me," one man said.

"Would you want Russ and his men to be the only ones inspecting your herd to decide if you were doing the stealing?" Tanzy asked, turning to face the man before he could hide in the anonymity of the group.

"Hell, no. I wouldn't trust him on the place."

"Why?"

"Because he's a thief."

"Can you prove that?"

"I don't have to. I know it."

"I know you're a fool. Can you prove you're not?"

The man looked shocked. His shock turned to anger when he heard snickers around him.

"I was in the hotel when a group of you met to choose a delegation to go out to Russ's ranch," Tanzy said, "but you let Stocker talk you out of it."

"There's no point," Stocker said. "He'd have hidden the cows by the time we got there."

"There's no way to take cows out of that valley except through the pass," Russ said. "You can send someone right now to watch it, and we can go out tomorrow. That way I won't have time to warn my men to hide any stolen cows."

"You've probably hidden them already. You just used those men you brought in as an excuse to make us go out there on a wild-goose chase."

"I've often wondered why some of you are too cowardly to face what you know to be the truth, but I never thought you were stupid," Tanzy said, shocking the entire room into silence. "Setting aside the fact that such a proposal is idiotic beyond belief, how could Russ possibly convince five men to attack his ranch and agree to let two of their number be killed and two more wounded? Why would you suppose Tardy Benton and I would agree to it? I've got a dozen tiny wounds on my face and neck from splintered glass when a bullet came through the window. It could easily have been my eyes. Why would I take such a chance on being blinded?"

"Because you're in love with Russ Tibbolt."

Chapter Twenty-three

Tanzy spun around to see Ethel Peters standing just inside the doorway. Her complexion was pale, her face taut, her body rigidly erect, but her eyes flashed fury. She advanced into the room. "Deny that if you will."

It took Tanzy a moment to recover from the shock of such an accusation being flung at her in public. She'd never had any reason to believe Ethel disliked her, so Tanzy was unable to account for the sudden attack, the unexplained fury.

"Why would you say such a thing?" Tanzy asked.

"Because it's true."

"Even if it were, why do you say it like I'm guilty of some terrible crime? Why do you look as though you hate me?"

"You've made a fool of me," Ethel said, coming closer. "You led me to believe you were a woman of character, of honor, of decency."

"I made no such claim."

Ethel was thrown off stride for a moment. "It's only natural to assume a woman is honorable."

"And what did I do to lose this *assumed* reputation?"

"You took up domicile at his ranch," she said, pointing at Russ. "And you wouldn't leave when I came to rescue you."

"Do you have any evidence to prove I've done anything disreputable?"

"I don't need any."

"So you're like this man over here. You believe it, therefore it's true."

Ethel clearly didn't like the comparison. "Your behavior speaks for itself."

"What in my behavior makes you think I'm in love with Russ?"

"Because you're lying for him."

"So you also believe, like this man over here, that even though you have no proof and have not attempted to gather any, you are entitled to accuse Russ of being a thief?"

Ethel was cornered. She refused to answer.

"So by your standards I don't need to have any proof for the statement I'm about to make. I merely have to believe it's true and it will be."

"What are you talking about?"

"I'm saying you were in love with Russ Tibbolt. You tried to force him to marry you, and you've been furious at him ever since for having turned you down. But even though you don't love him now, you're determined he won't marry anybody else. You urged me to leave town the day I arrived. When you couldn't get me to leave Russ's ranch, you decided to force me to leave by accusing me of lying because I'm in love with him."

Ethel had turned ashen, her hands clamped rigidly at her sides. Tanzy didn't know whether she would faint or attack in a wild frenzy.

"That is a hideous lie," Ethel said. "You have no proof of anything you said."

"I have just as much proof as you do that I'm in love with Russ."

"I know you are! I can see it in your eyes."

"Only a woman who loved Russ could see love for him in another woman's eyes."

"You're a hussy. A strumpet."

"If loving Russ could make me that bad, you're worse. You're trying to destroy him for the sole reason that he didn't return your love."

"I don't love him. I never loved him."

"That's not what you wrote in your diary," a new voice announced.

Tanzy looked around Ethel to see that Tardy had entered the saloon, but Ethel didn't turn. Her eyes grew wider and she seemed about to dissolve.

"Richard Benton," she said from between pressed lips, "you're never to set foot in my house again."

"I didn't want to tell on you, Aunt Ethel, but I couldn't let you lie about Miss Gallant. She's the nicest person in the whole world. You know she's not doing anything wrong because I sleep on the couch just outside her door every night."

Ethel turned slowly. "As far as I'm concerned, you will sleep there for the rest of your life. And if you ever repeat a single word of what I may have written in my diary when I was a young and foolish girl, I will hunt you down and shoot you between the eyes."

"I don't know why you should be ashamed of having liked Russ," Tanzy said. "I think it shows remarkably good taste."

"Your opinion is not, and never will be, of interest to me." Ethel marched from the saloon.

For a moment you could have heard a pin drop. Then someone laughed. Then came the sound of someone trying to smother a laugh, which made it all the more difficult for everyone else to control their feelings. The room erupted into laughter and jokes that drove the hostility out into the night.

* * *

"Whatever possessed you to stand up for me?" Russ asked as they walked back to the hotel.

"I couldn't stand to see them accusing you just because Stocker's still angry after all this time."

Russ couldn't get over the way she had sprung to his defense, the way she'd stood up under attack, the way she'd turned the attack on the attackers. The townspeople had decided to ask Colonel McGregor for help in finding someone who could follow the trail of the missing cows. Stocker had been furious, shouting that they were wasting their time, but for the first time in Russ's memory, nobody listened to him.

"It also made me mad when they tried to ignore your suggestions on how to find the rustlers just because you've been in prison. There's nothing about being in prison that automatically makes you stupid."

"No, but it automatically makes you a liar and a thief."

"I don't know why they don't just come out to your ranch and find out for themselves, but every time they start to do that, Stocker stops them. It's almost like he doesn't want to find out who's stealing his cattle."

"Stocker doesn't want me proved innocent because he'd have to stop blaming me for everything. I think that's all he lives for these days."

"Well, I won't be a part of letting him persecute you."

Russ was having a hard time keeping his feelings for Tanzy a secret. He'd given up trying to pretend he didn't want to marry her, that he wouldn't do virtually anything he must to keep her close to him. He knew he had to wait for her to come to him, but he kept feeling she was already there, that all he had to do was reach out and take hold of what he wanted so desperately. But fear kept him silent.

What if she *didn't* love him? What if she tried and it just didn't work? He knew she liked him, but that wasn't enough for him anymore. He wanted her to love him as much as he loved her, to need him as much as he needed her. Strong, silent Russ Tibbolt, the man his cowhands depended on, the man five years of prison couldn't defeat, the man a whole town had tried to run off but couldn't, this Russ Tibbolt admitted he needed Tanzy Gallant. Without her, he would always be half a man.

He'd known for years he wanted a wife, children, friends, and a job he enjoyed. He had the friends and the job, but his distrust of women had barred him from the most important part of the future he dreamed about. He'd spent years accustoming himself to the reality of never finding a woman he could trust and love. Then Tanzy had gotten off that stage and everything changed. Possibilities abounded where none had existed before. Hope that could not be denied filled his heart, hope that was so strong it overcame his fears enough for him to open up a corner of himself to her.

Now, if she only knew or cared, all of him was open.

"I've developed a tough hide when it comes to Stocker's persecution," Russ said. "He's not going to change so I ignore him."

"I wouldn't care about that if the whole town didn't follow him like dumb sheep," Tanzy said. They had reached the hotel. "I don't want to go in. I'm still too wrought up to go to sleep."

"There's not much entertainment in Boulder Gap."

"We can walk."

"Where?"

"To the schoolhouse and back. I never tire of looking at the mountains."

They walked in companionable silence for a few minutes, Russ wanting to reach out and take her hand but fearing he would scare her away. She was too close, and winning her was too important, for any foolish mistake. It didn't make any difference that his hands ached to touch her, that he practically had to bite his lips to keep from kissing her. It was stupid. When he'd thought he had no chance of winning her, he had no trouble kissing her even when he was certain she didn't welcome his attention. But now that his hopes were so high, now that victory was almost his, he felt paralyzed with fear of doing something that would cause her to change her mind.

"The valley is surrounded by mountains," Russ said.

"That's one of the things I love about it."

"You love my valley?"

"It's too beautiful not to love."

Russ wanted to touch her, to kiss her, to wrap his arms around her and never let her go. Surely she wouldn't have defended him so vigorously if she didn't love him. Surely she wouldn't have faced Ethel without a moment's hesitation if she didn't love him. Surely she wouldn't object to his holding her hand even if someone might see them and spread gossip around town before morning. She couldn't possibly mind if—

"I've been looking for you everywhere. What are you doing out here at night?"

Tardy's voice coming unexpectedly from behind him was like a schoolteacher smacking his hand for misbehaving.

"I was restless," Tanzy said. "I didn't want to go to bed yet."

"Well, I do," Tardy said, "but I've got no place to go. Aunt Ethel meant it when she said I couldn't go back to her house. She wouldn't even let me inside to get my stuff. She just kept throwing everything through the front door and screaming I was a snake in her bosom, a sneak, and a pervert. What's a pervert?"

"Something you're not," Tanzy said.

"I tried to get a room at the hotel, but all the rooms are taken. What am I going to do? I was about to ask the man at the livery stable if I could sleep in his loft."

"You can share my room," Russ said.

"Thanks," Tardy said, breaking into a relieved smile. He looked as if Russ had just handed him his life's dream.

"Tell Archie to give you a key," Russ said.

Tardy grinned in that self-effacing way he had when he had done something he feared might get him in trouble. "I already asked him. I was sure you wouldn't mind my sleeping on the floor," Tardy hurried to assure Russ, "but Archie said he wasn't giving nobody a key to your room. He acted like I might try to do something to hurt you." Tardy's expression had changed from one of appeasement to indignation.

"Archie's always looking out for me," Russ said.

"We ought to be getting back," Tanzy said.

As much as Russ liked Tardy, he could strangle the boy for bringing his moonlight stroll with Tanzy to a premature end. Now he had to share a room with Tardy without letting him guess how much he wished he would disappear.

"I'm sorry your aunt threw you out," Tanzy said to Tardy, "but you shouldn't have told anybody what she wrote in her diary."

"I wouldn't have if she hadn't been trying to hurt you and Russ. You're the only people who never thought I was dumber than dirt and as useless as tumbleweed."

"Don't worry about it anymore. They'll all think differently very soon."

They walked back to the hotel, with Tanzy doing her best to convince Tardy he wasn't stupid and Russ repeating he was glad Tardy would be moving to the ranch permanently.

"I plan to work you so hard you'll earn your keep," Russ said, his tone tinged with irritation.

Tardy, poor innocent soul, grinned at the prospect. Russ didn't have the heart to stay mad at him. He knew what it was like to be unwanted. Nobody should have to feel that way, especially a kid, but couldn't the boy have chosen some other night to get thrown out onto the street? They reached the hotel much too soon.

"What are we going to do tomorrow?" Tardy asked.

"See if they want me to participate in the hunt for the rustlers," Russ said, "maybe buy a few supplies, and head back to the ranch. I expect a delegation will be out to search every inch of the valley before long."

"You never stole any cows," Tardy said.

"Let's hope they come to the same conclusion," Tanzy said.

Russ and Tanzy collected their keys and headed toward their rooms. Tardy tagged along. It was clear he wasn't going to leave them alone without a broad hint.

"Here's the key," Russ said, handing it to Tardy. "I'll be along in a moment."

"Don't try sneaking a kiss in the hallway," Tardy said, grinning. "I don't want you ruining Miss Gallant's reputation."

"I'll ruin your neck if you open your mouth one more time," Russ said.

Tardy merely grinned, tossed the key in the air, and headed toward their room.

"I may have to reconsider taking him on as a cowhand," Russ said. "He doesn't show the proper respect for his boss."

"That's because you're too kind to him," Tanzy said. "You're like the big brother he never had."

"Great! I'm acquiring family responsibilities without benefit of a wife."

"You've already got a family. The men at the ranch would never have made it without you." Tanzy slipped her hand around his neck and pulled his head lower until their lips were mere inches apart. "I hope you realize you're a very special person. Not many people could have survived what you've been through and not be bitter. Now you'd better go to your room before *I* ruin my reputation by standing in the hall kissing you."

She rose on her tiptoes and gave him a quick kiss. Then she turned, unlocked her door, and disappeared inside with what had to be the sweetest smile that ever curved a woman's lips.

For a moment Russ thought he would rip the door off its hinges to get at the woman who was driving him crazy. It took him several minutes to master the compulsion to pound on the door and demand that she let him in. It took him even longer to force his feet to carry him to his room. By the time he reached the door, he felt exhausted.

"I started to think you weren't coming," Tardy said.

"We were talking," Russ replied.

"I don't know what you've got left to talk about. You see each other every day."

Tardy had clearly never been in love or he'd know a lifetime and all the words in the world would never be enough. Some things were just so big, so all consuming, they defied time and words.

Russ looked at Tardy, *really* looked at him.

He saw a boy who was as tall as a man but inhabited the slender body of adolescence. He saw the smooth skin of a face that had yet to be marred by the roughness of a beard, eyes that telegraphed complete trust and unabashed admiration, a smile that could only be worn by a soul that had yet to fully comprehend the cruel unfairness of life. Somehow Tardy had reached the age of sixteen without becoming soured on his fellow man, disappointed but not despairing. He was still imbued with the certainty that everything would work out in the end.

Had Russ ever felt like that? Had he ever been that young?

He couldn't remember a time when he wasn't angry at the world and nearly everyone in it. He couldn't remember a time when he believed everything would work out in the end. He couldn't remember a time when he didn't despair of ever finding the happiness that had eluded him all his life. Until now.

"Do you mind if I take one of the blankets?" Tardy asked. "This carpet doesn't look very thick."

"You don't have to sleep on the floor. We can share the bed as long as you don't kick or snore."

"Tim does both," Tardy said, climbing in the bed with a cheeky grin. "If he ever gets married, his wife will have to sleep by herself."

Russ removed his hat and coat, but he couldn't settle down. He was too worked up to sleep. "I'm going for a walk."

"You've already been for a walk."

"I'm still not tired or sleepy."

"I don't know why not. You had a gunfight, dragged those men into town, then had a meeting about the rustlers. All I had was a fight with Aunt Ethel, and that wore me out."

"That's because you're still soft. When I get through toughening you up, you'll think a stampede is a morning's amusement."

Tardy snorted his skepticism.

"I don't know how long I'll be, so don't wait up," Russ said.

"Don't wake me when you get into bed."

"Don't hog the covers."

Russ paused outside the door, wondering what he could do. He didn't want to go to one of the saloons, but that was the only alternative to a solitary walk. Yet even though he didn't want company, he didn't want to be alone. As he walked the length of the hall, he told himself he was turning into a pathetic case. The outcast, the ex-con, the barely literate bastard son of a rich man's mistress thinking a respectable woman could love him, would want to marry him and bear his children.

"Can't sleep?" Archie said when Russ reached the lobby.

"Too much on my mind."

"I heard about the meeting. Do you think they'll come out to your ranch?"

"It won't matter. They won't find anything."

Archie looked around like he thought somebody might be listening. "I wouldn't be too sure if I was you. Who's to say some stray cows won't get over those mountains like those killers did?"

Russ's attention was riveted. "Have you heard something?"

Archie acted even more like a furtive, cornered creature, hunching down and lowering his voice still more. "Nothing definite, but there's something afoot. Could be somebody doesn't want you to get off the hook."

"Thanks, Archie. I'll keep that in mind."

"I'll tell you if I hear anything else."

"Don't get yourself in trouble."

Russ stepped outside the hotel, but he just stood there. Archie's warning faded away, to be replaced by the look in Tanzy's eyes when she kissed him, the caressing sound of her voice, the softness of her body as she pressed against him. He felt himself becoming aroused just thinking about it.

He tried without success to think of something else. He had memorized nearly every word she'd said to him during the last several days. He let them run through his head, examining each for hidden meaning, some sign of her feelings for him, some hint that she might be in love with him, but objective examination didn't show anything that couldn't be said with equal accuracy to a friend. Russ knew he couldn't settle for friendship. Only love would do.

He started toward the light coming from a nearby saloon but turned around before he'd taken a dozen steps. That wasn't where he wanted to go, and it wouldn't give him the answer to the question burning in his mind. He had to know. He couldn't stand this suspense any longer. He reentered the hotel and didn't stop until he'd knocked on Tanzy's door. It was a few moments before she opened it.

"Is something wrong?" she asked.

"No. I just have to ask you a question."

"What?"

"Ethel said you loved me. Is that true?"

Chapter Twenty-four

Tanzy was unprepared to have that question flung at her so unexpectedly. Being half dressed made it even more difficult.

"You'd better come in," she said as she pulled her robe more tightly around her.

"I don't have to."

"You do if you want an answer."

Her hotel room was basic without being bare. She had a bed covered with a flowered spread, a table with a pitcher and a basin, a ladder-back chair next to the window, and a badly scratched and gouged bureau. A thin carpet covered the wide-board floor. Cream-colored wallpaper with scenes of some European city covered the walls. A single oil lamp provided the only illumination.

"What prompted you to ask that question now?" she asked.

"What Ethel said."

"Sit down. This is not a short answer."

"It would be for me."

She started to say that men were less complicated than women but decided that wasn't true. She wanted a husband and a family, she wanted to be respected, and she wanted nothing to do with killing. Nothing complicated about that. She still hadn't unraveled Russ. She waited for him to be seated on the chair. She tied her robe securely and settled on the bed.

"I've been going over our situation for the last several days, trying to decide whether I could marry you. I believe you respect me and trust in my honesty."

"I always have."

"I believe you're not feuding with Stocker, that you want to put the past behind you and forget what can't be changed, but Stocker can't. I'm not sure I can face the specter of my husband or sons being killed."

"We could move away."

"I'd never ask you to do that. Besides, I'm not sure but I think I'd be ashamed of myself for running away. I'm not a coward."

"If I'd ever doubted that, I wouldn't have after today."

"People shouldn't be forced to run from bullies, but I'm not sure I can live with senseless killing. Do you understand what I'm saying?"

"Yes."

"Do you agree?"

"In principle, but that valley is mine and I'll fight to keep it."

"I always knew you would."

They sat silently staring at each other for a moment.

"You haven't answered my question," Russ said.

"I haven't because I wanted you to understand why my answer might not lead to the results you want."

"Does that mean . . ."

"I love you. There are times I think I've loved you from the very first."

Russ came out of the chair as though shot from a cannon. Before Tanzy had time to protest or open her arms in welcome, she was buried in a crushing embrace as he kissed her face in wild abandon. It was futile to attempt to remind Russ that she hadn't made up her mind about marrying him. Any word that escaped her mouth would have been swallowed by his. He had captured her mouth as though he intended never to let go. His kisses were hard, filled with the desperation of a man who'd waited a lifetime to hear those words, a man who believed he'd never hear them and had schooled himself to live without them, a man who saw her love as his only hope of redemption and meant to cling to it with every ounce of strength he could muster.

Knowing she hadn't yet committed herself to him, Tanzy tried to restrain her response. She failed. It was time she accepted that she loved Russ, that she wanted to marry him, that she wanted to be his wife and bear his children. Their problems would have to be faced some time in the future, but for the moment the future could be put aside. It *should* be put aside. They were in love. They should celebrate that love.

Tanzy had never guessed how wonderful it would feel to be in the arms of the man she loved, the man who loved her with such intensity. It was like being wrapped in a warmth that reached beyond the physical to embrace the spiritual, to heal her soul. Wrapped in love's embrace, all things were possible. Without it, much of life lost its meaning.

"I was afraid you'd never say those words," Russ said.

"Do you love me?" Tanzy asked.

"You know I do."

"Why haven't you told me?"

"I was afraid to do anything that might scare you away."

"A woman is never scared away by a man's saying he loves her."

"I didn't know what to do. Loving has never been good for me or my family."

"Not for me, either. And I'm not sure—"

"Don't talk. Let's just think about now. For once, let tomorrow wait until tomorrow."

He held her close, his arms meeting behind her back, her breasts pressed hard against his chest, his cheek resting on the top of her head. It seemed he was content just to stand there, to drink in the feeling of her in his arms, to let her nearness to his heart drench his parched soul with life-giving love.

"I've never held a woman like this," he murmured. "I never thought I'd want to." After a few moments he said, "I don't think I ever want to stop."

The power she had to make this man's life happy or to crush his soul terrified her. She wanted with all her heart to marry him, to make him as happy as possible, but she feared she might not be able to do that. Could she accept his love now, knowing she might have to reject it in the future?

Could she ignore *her* love? Could she ignore her happiness? Should she deny them both the comfort of accepting their love even if it could only be for a short while? Could she accept his plea to think only of tonight, to let tomorrow wait until tomorrow?

Yes. Life didn't offer many perfect moments. This might be the only one she'd get. Resolving to immerse herself in the here and now, she slipped her arms around Russ. Her fingers splayed across his strong back. She wasn't used to feeling small or weak, but his size and strength dwarfed her own. She felt engulfed in his embrace, surrounded by his strength, warmed by his heat.

"You can't leave me," Russ said, "not when it's taken me so long to find you."

"I don't want to leave you."

"Say you love me."

"I love you."

"Say it again."

"Is it so important?"

"It is when you've never heard it from the lips of someone you love."

"I love you," Tanzy said, letting her heart form the sounds and give emphasis to the words. "No matter what happens, I always will."

His arms tightened around her. His kissed her hair over and over again. She heard a sob of relief. It was faint and it was singular, but it was the sound of a dam giving way, the dam that had held back Russ's emotions for most of his life, the dam behind which he hid until drawn out against his will.

"Many people love you," Tanzy said. "Many more will in years to come. You'll never have to depend on the love of one person."

"I'd trade them all, now and forever, for you."

He lowered his mouth to hers. His kisses had turned gentle, caressing, soothing. The fear that she would somehow disappear, that he would lose what he wanted so desperately, seemed to have left him. She could almost hear him sigh with relief, feel the relaxation of the muscles that had held his body rigid and fearful.

She raised her hands to his face, relishing the roughness of his weathered skin, the strength of his jaw, the angular bones that formed the planes and curves of his face. She wanted her hands to memorize him, to absorb him, to know him as intimately as her eyes. She wanted to know all of him, bone and sinew, heart and soul. She wanted to claim him, possess him, chain him to her heart forever.

But most of all she wanted to free him from the prison he'd created for himself. She wanted him to believe he *was* loved, would always be loved, that he couldn't do anything that would stop her from loving him.

After the years he'd spent convincing himself otherwise, it wouldn't be easy.

"I should go," he said.

"Do you want to?"

"No."

"Then hold me. I need to know you love me as much as you want to know I love you."

After her mother's death, she'd felt as unloved and alone as he did. No one hated her or tried to drive her away, but no one understood the pain of her loss or cared what she felt. While people in St. Louis were kinder in some ways than those in Kentucky, they were more condemning. No one looked at her just as a person. She was always a woman whose employment had called her morals and character into question.

Love was almost as new to her as it was to him.

She loved the feel of his hands on her back, her shoulders, her arms. Their size filled her with a sense of his strength, his rough-hewn character, which didn't twist or break, which had weathered the storms of misfortune without losing the innate goodness so few people seemed able to see. She wondered what it was about the people of Boulder Gap that caused them to allow themselves to be driven to align themselves against a man whose nature and character caused the desperate and disenfranchised to bind themselves to him.

Maybe it was fear of his goodness as much as it was fear of Stocker's wickedness. Regardless of the reason, she made up her mind to protect him in the future. If she became his wife—and she couldn't imagine she wouldn't marry him—she would make the townspeople see what fools they'd been.

The feel of his lips on her bare shoulders sent shudders of pure pleasure arcing through Tanzy's body. His lips were warm, soft, and moist, and burned her skin with the heat that was radiating from his body. She felt herself lean closer to him, press herself more firmly against him. She couldn't touch him enough, get enough contact with his body. She wanted to touch him all over at once.

She untied the belt to her robe and allowed it to fall to the floor. She wanted to be closer to him. She rubbed her hands over his chest, gradually loosening the buttons on his shirt. His hand closed over hers.

"Are you sure?"

She answered by loosening the next button with her other hand.

"I love you," Russ said.

"I know."

"I don't want to do anything that would hurt you."

"I feel the same way."

He kissed her deeply, his tongue delving into her mouth, his hands cradling her throat. She slipped her hands inside his shirt to feel the soft hair that covered his chest. Her searching fingers encountered his nipple. She was surprised to find it hard and raised. She was even more surprised at his reaction to her touch. He started so abruptly, he broke their kiss. Delighted and curious at her discovery, she rubbed her fingers gently over his nipples, each passage drawing soft moans and tremors that shook his whole body. He took her hand in his grasp.

"You're driving me crazy," he moaned in her ear.

She smiled with the knowledge that she had such power over him. "Take off your shirt or I'll keep torturing you."

His smile was warm but filled with a hunger that was

almost brutal in its intensity. "I hope you don't think that's a threat."

She supposed a respectable woman shouldn't think such things, but his chest was magnificent. Soft brown hair covered his upper chest before narrowing into a trail that sank to his navel. Corded muscles rippled across his chest and created ridges of muscle down his firm abdomen. She let her hands wander over him, marveling at the combination of softness and strength, of heat and firm muscle. If Ethel had ever chanced to see him without his shirt, it didn't surprise Tanzy that she had fallen hopelessly in love with Russ.

Russ kissed the side of her neck, pushed the straps of her nightgown off her shoulders to allow him to place kisses in the hollow of her shoulder. He continued down her arm until his kisses had forced the straps off her body and her gown pooled at her feet. He laced his hands on her back and with gentle pressure brought her toward him until her bare breasts touched his heated skin.

A deep sigh escaped him. "You feel better than I ever imagined."

"You, too. I never realized my family was cursed with such puny men."

"That's because Mother Nature used up all her resources on the women."

"You have me at a disadvantage," she said.

"How?"

She lowered her hands down his side, over his belt, and down the sides of his thighs, then over his behind. "Too much of you is hidden from me." She reached around and began to unbuckle his belt. "I don't think that's fair."

He sucked in his breath when her hand brushed his arousal.

"You'd better let me do that," he said. He picked her up and carried her over to the bed, laid her down, and gazed at her in wonder. "I could spend the rest of my life just looking at you."

"Only if you allow me to look at you."

Russ sat down to remove his boots and socks. Then he stood to remove his pants. Tanzy had had too many brothers not to be acquainted with the male anatomy, but this was the first time she realized all men were *not* created equal. Mother Nature had been more than generous when she created Russ Tibbolt. He was almost frightening in his perfection. The mattress sagged under his weight when he lay down on the bed next to her. He slid his arm under her and drew her close.

"You don't know how often I've lain awake at night unable to sleep because I was imagining what it would be like to lie next to you," Russ said.

"I did that, too," Tanzy said. She put her hand in the middle of his chest and rubbed lightly. "You don't know how hard it is for a woman to be around you and not think of things she shouldn't."

"You have my permission to think anything you want."

"Do I have your permission to *do* anything I want?"

"You always did."

"Why did you jump when I did this?" Tanzy said as she gently rubbed his nipple. His body seemed to shudder.

"Because nearly every nerve in my body seemed to explode like lightning striking a pine tree, setting the resin afire." He reached over to cup her breast with his hand, gently massaging her nipple with his thumb. "Does this feel like that for you?"

"More like all my bones are melting," Tanzy said, her voice unsteady from the after shocks of his touch. "Your hand is so hot it's burning my skin."

He pulled away. She grabbed his hand and replaced it. "I didn't say I disliked it."

He leaned up on his elbow and cupped her other breast.

The sensations coming alive in her were causing her to feel giddy, as if she were no longer in control of her body, as if she were incapable of resisting what was happening to her. But she didn't want to resist. She wanted a lot more.

She reached up to pull his head down between her breasts. The feel of him nestled against her was wonderful. She couldn't get enough of it. She ran her fingers through his thick hair, holding him tightly against her, reveling in the seductive warmth flowing through her limbs and filling them with a delicious ache. That ache was intensified tenfold when she felt the warm, moist roughness of Russ's tongue on her nipple. She practically rose out of the bed, her back arched to force him against her harder, to make the feeling even more intense.

She got a reprieve when Russ's mouth deserted her nipples to plant kisses on her shoulders and along her arms, but the sensations came barreling back when he kissed her belly. The sensitive nerve endings telegraphed frantic messages of erotic delight to her brain and begged for still more.

Tanzy took Russ's face in her hands and pulled him up to where she could kiss him, to where she could give him some idea of the pleasure he was causing her. Her attention was almost immediately distracted because he lay atop her, his erection pressed hard against her abdomen. Her gasp caused him to break the kiss and roll off her.

"I didn't mean to crush you," he said.

"You didn't." She turned on her side and pulled him close. She slid her hand down his body until it came to a stop between his legs. "This took me by surprise."

"Surely you knew it would happen," he said, his voice husky with desire.

"It still surprised me."

He slid his hand along her side, down between her legs, and into her moist heat. "Your body wasn't surprised."

Tanzy sucked in her breath, felt unable to let it go. It felt like a huge balloon inside her was held captive by the tension caused by Russ's invasion of her most intimate place. She felt his hand moving and the balloon grew even bigger, until she thought she would burst. Then he touched a spot that sent lightning strikes sizzling through her body. The bottled-up air exploded from her body in one huge whoosh, leaving her shuddering with an ache so pleasurable she never wanted it to end.

"Don't be frightened. I won't hurt you," Russ said.

"I'm not frightened."

"Then please let go."

Startled, she realized she was gripping his arousal so hard it had to be painful. She released him and ran her fingers through his hair, felt his ribs and corded muscles through his warm skin. She couldn't concentrate because of what he was doing to her. He had turned on his side so he could take her mouth in hot, demanding kisses while he continued to probe inside her, seeking and finding the spot that reduced her to helplessness, rubbing and teasing until her body threatened to explode.

She tried to protest, but his kisses swallowed her breath, and he increased the tempo of his assault. Her body tried to escape his torture but couldn't get enough of it. The intensity of the feelings inside her continued to grow until her limbs grew rigid and her body rose off the bed. Then, just as suddenly, she felt moisture flow from her and she collapsed onto the bedspread, quivering with pleasure again.

She had barely recovered her breath when Russ rose above her and she felt him begin to enter her. For a moment she was certain she wouldn't be able to contain him, but he moved slowly, sinking a little deeper each time, allowing her to become accustomed to his size. She worried she might still fail until he gave a sigh and entered her fully.

He paused only a moment before he began to move within her. At first Tanzy was conscious only of being stretched to sheath him, but that feeling was quickly supplanted by the rebuilding of the fire that had only moments ago singed her mind and soul. She began to move with him, rising to meet him, falling away in preparation for meeting him once more. As the tension within her grew, she tried to force him deeper and deeper within her to quench the fires burning out of control. She threw her arms around his neck and kissed him with all the passion she could muster, but that only made her need more insistent. She never would have believed such delicious agony could exist, that she would pray for it to end and in the next breath pray it would never stop.

Russ's breathing became more rapid, his movements less smooth, which only served to increase Tanzy's torment. She clung to him, pushed hard against him, reaching for the relief she knew would come, that *must* come. Russ released a shuddering breath, drove deep into Tanzy, and froze. The pulsing deep inside as he released his seed set Tanzy hurtling over the edge into a world of brilliantly exploding lights.

* * *

Russ lay quietly, Tanzy sleeping wrapped in his arms, unable to believe what had happened. Tanzy Gallant loved him, was going to be his wife. A woman really, *really* loved him. She didn't care that he had spent time in prison, that nearly everybody he knew disliked him, or that he lived in a cabin in an isolated valley a long distance from town. She loved him and wanted to live with him. She'd said she never wanted to leave his side, that she would love him forever.

Even though she'd given herself to him twice within the last hour, Russ could hardly believe it was true. Not Tanzy, the one woman in his whole life who didn't allow compromise, who didn't allow herself to be swayed by the prejudices of others, the one woman who was willing to stand up to anybody when she felt someone was being wronged, the one woman who didn't wait for someone else to lead the way when something needed doing. She loved him. She was going to be his wife.

No matter how many times he said it, the reality wouldn't sink in. He couldn't make himself believe something wouldn't happen to change everything. It always had in his life.

His mother would have been fine after she'd married Bob Tibbolt if she hadn't fallen for Stocker's promises to give her things Bob couldn't afford. Adele would have been fine if she'd waited for him to return from Texas with the money to buy some cows instead of taking up with Stocker's no-good brother. He'd have been all right if Toley Pullet hadn't been so sure he could draw faster and shoot straighter than Russ.

But things started to go right for him after he went to prison. He met Tim, Buck, and Oren. After he got out, they helped him start his ranch. He bought cows that thrived on the rich grass of his valley, where they were protected from the harsh winters. His friends accepted Welt when he walked out on his family's business just as they accepted Tardy and Tanzy. Maybe his luck had changed. Maybe finding Tanzy was just the best in a string of fortunate happenings.

He looked down at her. Afraid of waking her, he caressed her hair rather than touch her cheeks, which looked pink and soft. He couldn't believe she was lying in his arms, looking like a sleeping angel. She trusted him to keep her safe. She trusted him with her future, with the future of her children. She trusted him with her heart.

The magnitude of that trust frightened him at the same time it filled him with hope and nearly indescribable happiness. He trembled with apprehension as well as anticipation. Everything he'd ever wanted was within his grasp. It was time for him to forget the past. Forever. The future looked too wonderful to do anything else.

He leaned down and placed a gentle kiss on Tanzy's forehead. She stirred in her sleep and snuggled a little closer to his heart. Slowly, gradually, a smile transformed her face. She truly did look like a sleeping angel.

His sleeping angel.

"I can't wait to get back to the ranch," Tardy said.

"Are you sure your aunt won't want you back once she gets over being angry at you?" Tanzy asked.

"She hasn't stopped being angry at Russ and that was more than ten years ago."

They were on their way home from Boulder Gap. Tardy rode his horse, alternately riding close to the wagon, then forging ahead or off to the side to check out something that interested him. Russ drove the wagon, his horse tied behind. Tanzy sat next to Russ, occasionally hooking her arm in his, continually looking up and being amazed this man loved her so completely.

Deciding to marry him had been a hard decision, but now she felt relieved and happy. Their life wouldn't be without its problems, but she was certain their love would withstand all tests. After a long journey, she'd found a home, a place where she could give her heart with the certainty it would be handled with loving care.

"Can't you make that horse go any faster?" Tardy said.

"You don't gallop a wagon over rough terrain," Russ said. "You'll shake it to bits. If you're so impatient, ride ahead."

Tardy didn't need a second invitation. He spurred his horse and quickly disappeared.

"Are you sure you don't mind letting him live with us?" Tanzy asked.

"He's good for us. I didn't realize we'd turned into such old men until Tardy arrived."

"He makes me feel tired, and I'm barely three years older than he is."

"He's just enjoying the freedom to be himself without being demoralized by withering criticism. I can sympathize with that."

Even dark memories had no power to dampen her mood today. They were in love. They'd stood up to the opposition in town, forcing people to question Stocker for the first time in years. They were on their way to a home as close to a private paradise as anyone was likely to find on earth. And the day was absolutely too splendid for words.

The sun shone with brilliant intensity, but the cool

drafts that flowed down from the mountains kept them deliciously cool. Overhead, the sky was a perfect deep blue without a single cloud to mar its perfection. A pair of golden eagles soared far above, riding the updrafts as they lazily circled in the sky, their huge wings stretched to the full extent of their nine-foot span.

Birds fluttered among the pine trees, searching for seeds and arguing with each other. Squirrels scampered over the ground and leapt from tree to tree, hanging precariously onto limbs Tanzy thought couldn't bear their weight. Grasses and flowers covered much of the land in luxuriant growth. Tanzy would have loved to stop and pick some if she hadn't been in a hurry to get home.

Home. It had a wonderful sound to it. She realized the cabin had felt like home almost from the beginning. Just like Tardy, she'd found her resting place without knowing it.

"Where do you want to have the wedding?" she asked Russ.

"We should have gotten married before we left town," Russ said.

"Why? Folks who think I've lost my reputation won't change their minds just because we get married. And those who trust me aren't likely to change their minds in the next few days. Where would you like to get married?"

"I don't know. Part of me wants to get married in Boulder Gap in the biggest wedding the town has ever seen. The more sensible part of me says it would be nice to get married at the fort."

"I don't know anybody there."

"We could invite anybody from town you want."

"I don't care. If you think—"

She broke off. Tardy was riding toward them at a gallop. Since Russ had drummed it into his head he was never to gallop a horse unless it was an emergency, Tanzy felt her stomach clench. Something was wrong. She felt Russ's body tense as he pulled the wagon to a stop.

"Oren said somebody's attacked the ranch," Tardy shouted as he drew close. "He said he can see smoke coming from that direction."

Russ handed the reins to Tanzy. "You ride back with Tanzy," Russ said to Tardy as he jumped from the wagon and began to untie his horse.

"I want to go with you. I can—"

"Any man who works for me learns to follow orders or he has to look for another job," Russ said. He vaulted into the saddle. "Your job is to keep Tanzy safe. Right now that's the most important job of all."

Russ galloped off.

"Don't just sit there like your brain has fallen out of your head," Tanzy said to Tardy. "Tie your horse behind and get in. I'm about to see if this horse knows how to gallop."

Chapter Twenty-five

"What did Oren say?" Tanzy asked Tardy as she whipped her horse into a fast trot. The trail toward the pass into the valley had been worn smooth by frequent travel and the wagon only nearly rattled the teeth out of her head.

"He didn't know what happened, but he saw smoke coming from the direction of the cabin and heard gun-shots."

"More men must have come over the mountains," Tanzy said, "but what could they want this time?"

"To burn Russ out," Tardy said.

"He wouldn't leave just because they burned a few buildings."

Tanzy could see a thin trail of smoke rising from the trees in the distance, but she heard no gunshots. She didn't know whether that was good or bad. She urged the horse into a canter.

"You'll jerk the wagon to pieces," Tardy said, his words broken into bits every time the wagon hit a rock or bounced over a tuft of grass.

"If I'd had a saddle horse, I wouldn't have been left behind."

She understood why Russ had ridden off without her, but it made her furious. This was going to be her home as much as it was his. She was equally determined to defend it.

The cows seemed unconcerned with what was happening. They continued to graze, placidly moving from one tuft of grass to another, calves frolicking like children with too much energy or sprawled out in the sun like they hadn't a care in the world. Tanzy suddenly resented their indifference. They were the reason Russ was in danger.

"I hope Welt shot whoever did this," Tardy said.

Tanzy wasn't sure she agreed. She didn't know how the sheriff would react if Russ pulled into town with more dead bodies.

"I'm more concerned with who did this and why."

"It had to be Mr. Pullet," Tardy said. "He was nearly crazy he was so mad last night."

"Mad enough to do something like this?"

"He wants to get rid of Russ and he doesn't care how he does it."

"How do you know?"

"He came to my aunt's house last night after she threw me out. I sneaked back in to get some of the stuff she hadn't tossed out after me, and he came in shouting he'd get rid of Russ if it was the last thing he did. Aunt Ethel said he was acting crazy, but Stocker said he didn't care what he had to do to get rid of Russ, that a scoundrel like Russ deserved what he got."

"What did your aunt say?"

Tardy blushed. "Something about you that I won't repeat."

They were close to the cabin now. She could have seen what was happening if it hadn't been for the screen of trees. As they pulled into the clearing they saw smoke coming from the bunkhouse. One wall of the cabin appeared to be blackened from flame, but the fire had been extinguished.

"What happened?" she asked. The men were carrying buckets of water from the stream to the bunkhouse. Tardy jumped down to help.

"Stocker's men came over the mountains," Welt said as he bent over to fill his bucket. "They tried to set fire to the cabin, but we were able to drive them off."

He filled his bucket and ran off. Tanzy jumped down from the wagon, tethered her horse to a tree, and looked for something to hold water.

"The fire's out," Russ said when he came out of the bunkhouse.

"Is there a lot of damage?" Tanzy asked.

"Not much to the structure, but the roof will need replacing as well as some equipment, a couple of mattresses, and the men's clothes."

"I couldn't get a good shot without coming out of the

cabin," Welt said. "If Tim and Buck hadn't gotten here as soon as they did, things would have been worse."

Tim came out of the cabin. "Oren is going to be mad as hell," he said. "It was his corner that got the worst of it."

"It was Stocker," Welt said.

"How do you know?" Tanzy asked.

"I recognized one of the men who's worked for him for a long time."

"Do you want me to go with you to report this to the sheriff?" Tanzy asked.

Everybody looked at her as if she'd lost her mind.

"You have to report it," she said. "Stocker has to be made to realize he can't bully people and get away with it."

"He's been bullying people for years and getting away with it," Welt said. "What makes you think things are going to change now?"

"There's law in Colorado now," Tanzy said. "People can't just set fire to someone's house and get away with it."

"They can and do," Welt said. "The sheriff won't believe us."

"You've got witnesses."

"Stocker's men all stand up for each other. How do you think they convicted Russ of killing Toley?"

Tanzy still clung to the belief that the law would control violent people. "If you don't trust the sheriff, you can talk to the commander of the fort."

"He has no authority over civilians," Russ said.

"What are you going to do?" Tim asked.

"Ride to Stocker's ranch and do to him what he tried to do to us," Russ replied.

"No!" Tanzy exclaimed. Everyone stared at her, but she looked only at Russ. "You can't just go burn Stocker's barn or bunkhouse. That will make you just as bad as he is."

"Do you have a better suggestion?" Welt asked.

"I just told you: talk to the sheriff or the commander of the fort."

"And Russ told you why neither will do any good."

"There must be something else you can do."

"What?"

"I don't know. You're the cowboys. You live out here."

"That's right," Russ said. "And we understand what it takes to survive. I have to make Stocker understand that he can't attack me without expecting something worse to happen to him."

"You can't do that," Tanzy said. "That's how feuds start."

Welt started to reply, but Russ signaled him to remain silent. "I understand why you have such a morbid fear of feuds, but I've got to show Stocker and everybody else I won't be bullied, that if they attack me they'll suffer. One day it will reach the point where Stocker isn't willing to pay the price of continuing. Then it will stop."

"Stocker hates you. He'll do anything he can to ruin you."

"He won't succeed. I want to ride out as soon as we can saddle up. Tardy, stay here to guard the house."

"I want to go with you." The boy was angry at being left out.

"I can't leave the ranch or the pass unprotected."

"Why can't Welt stay?"

"Because he's got more experience than you."

"I won't get experience being left behind."

"I know, but you have to stay behind today."

"I won't. You can't make me."

"You're right, I can't make you do anything against your will. Either you do as I say or you pack your belongings and go back to town."

"You know I have nowhere to stay."

"That's not my problem. The choice is yours."

Tardy turned and stalked off, but not before Tanzy noticed a suspicious wetness in his eyes.

Tanzy reached out to rest her hand on Russ's arm. "Thanks for forcing him to stay here."

Russ put his hand over hers. "I'm not cruel."

"I know that, which is why I don't understand why you have to retaliate."

"I've already explained."

"But I don't agree. Why can't you listen to me?"

"I did listen to you, but as you pointed out, I'm the one who lives out here and understands how things work."

"So my opinion doesn't mean anything to you?"

"It means a great deal, but it's wrong."

His words hit Tanzy like fists to her middle. That was almost what her father used to say. Russ wasn't any different from any other man.

Tanzy withdrew her hand and stepped back. "You're not going to do what I asked?"

"No."

"I see I was wrong."

"About what?"

"Your respecting my opinion."

Russ stepped forward and slipped his arms around her waist. "I do respect your opinion, but there will be times when we disagree. One of us will have to make the decision."

"Why can't it be me?"

Russ's eyes widened slightly. "I suppose there will be times when it will be you."

"But only about what to cook for dinner and how to decorate the cabin."

Russ pulled her closer. "You're a very strong-willed woman." He grinned and dropped a kiss on the end of her nose. "I expect I'll give in to a lot of things just to get some peace in the house."

Tanzy pushed against him, but he wouldn't release her. "So now I'm a harridan who uses bullying to get her way."

"You're nothing of the sort. You just like to get your way."

"Some things aren't a matter of one person making a decision and the other having to accept it. Some things are not negotiable."

She felt Russ stiffen.

"Are you trying to tell me this is one of them?"

Tanzy could see her happiness beginning to crumble right before her eyes. She wanted desperately to hang on to it, to do anything to keep it, but she couldn't if it meant she would end up losing another family to a feud. She couldn't go through that again. It would surely kill her.

Recollections of the previous night flooded her mind with such vividness she could almost feel she was living them over again. But hard on the heels came an equally vivid image of Russ's body being brought to her tied across his saddle. She knew she couldn't endure it. It would be better to have had nothing than to have everything and lose it.

"I don't know," she temporized, unable to bring an end to dreams that were still bright and new. "When I said I couldn't marry you, I said there were two reasons, the lack of respect for my opinion and the feud. This brings both back into question. I was serious when I told you I couldn't marry into a feud. Losing you now would be horrible, but having to bury you and maybe some of my children would kill me."

"Believe me when I say this isn't a feud. You just don't

understand how people do things out here." The boys returned with the horses saddled and ready to go. "Now I've got to go before Stocker thinks he can pull some other cowardly trick. I'll be back this evening. We can talk then."

"This isn't something that can be settled by talking, not when you and Stocker are determined to destroy each other."

"I don't want to destroy Stocker. I just want to be left alone, but I won't let him drive me out again." He kissed her hard. "I'll be back, I promise. I'm not going to die. I'm never going to leave you."

He quickly mounted up, and the four men rode out.

Tanzy stood watching, feeling her chances for happiness disappearing with the men as they rode out of sight. She turned and went into the house. She had a lot of thinking to do.

"Are they gone?" Tardy asked when she entered the cabin. He was standing at the window. He must have heard their conversation.

"They just rode out."

"Russ should have let me go. I'm not useless."

"Even if he did, I wouldn't have. You're too young."

"I thought you were my friend," Tardy said as he turned away from the window. "I'm not a baby."

"I know you're not, but—"

"You're all just as bad as Aunt Ethel. You treat me like I was six years old. I can ride and shoot. What more do I need to help burn a few buildings?"

"You need to learn that burning buildings doesn't solve anything. It just makes things worse."

"He has to do something."

"There are other options."

"He's got to do the same thing back. That way Stocker knows things are even and Russ won't back down."

It was exactly as Tanzy feared. Russ could call this battle anything he wanted, but it was still a feud.

"You can probably watch better from outside," she said to Tardy. "At least then you won't drive me crazy with your pacing."

"I'm not pacing."

"You will be soon. Go find some chores that need doing. The time will pass a lot faster if you're busy."

Tardy stomped out, but at that moment his disappointment was the least of her concerns. She had to make some decisions about her future, and she had to do it before Russ returned.

She was frustrated and hurt at what had happened to her. She'd worked hard to please everyone, yet everything she wanted had been taken from her. She was without a home, a family, friends, a lover, a future.

And she felt Stocker Pullet was at the root of her problems.

She'd spent hours and hours castigating herself for being so rigid, so fearful of what could happen. She'd told herself she couldn't let the past dictate her future. She'd spent even more hours cursing Russ's stubbornness and his inability to see what he was doing to himself. All this time she'd forgotten the true source of her unhappiness. She ought to be mad at Stocker, not Russ. He was the one who threatened to ruin her happiness.

Damn him. What right did he have to go around ruining people's lives with impunity? She was sure he had been grief-stricken at the death of his brother, but that was no excuse to send an innocent man to prison. Then there was Stocker's treatment of Russ's mother, making her his mistress, then publicly humiliating her when he tired of her. Stocker had been running roughshod over people for years. It was time somebody put a stop to it.

What about this business with the rustlers? Tanzy would have been the first to admit she didn't know much about rustling, but there was something suspicious about the way Stocker was acting. He was loud in his insistence that Russ was responsible for the rustling and that the ranchers ought to drive him out, but he thwarted every suggestion Russ put forth to prove his innocence. Consequently, Russ was still under suspicion.

Logic said if Stocker persisted in making accusations but continued to block all efforts to prove them, he was doing so because the accusations were false. There was no doubt rustling was going on. All the ranchers complained of it, even Stocker, but apparently it wasn't enough to get the ranchers so upset that they ignored Stocker and took things into their own hands. None of this made sense to Tanzy unless it was all a plan to drive Russ out. And if that was the case, Stocker was behind it.

Tanzy's thoughts hardened into a resolution. She knew what she wanted, but she wasn't going to get it without a struggle. It was time she stopped waiting for things to happen. She had to take a hand in molding her future. Russ Tibbolt was a fighter. He deserved a wife who was a fighter, not someone who sat back, folded her hands, and said *I won't* when things didn't go her way. He deserved a wife who could give him sons imbued with his same courage and determination, daughters who wouldn't compromise but would fight for what they wanted.

She had to *deserve* the future she wanted, and the only way she could do that was by taking a part in winning it.

That meant taking on Stocker Pullet. But what good would that do? No one would pay any attention to what she said unless she had some proof, but how could she get it? The easiest way was by getting close to him, but that would mean working in his saloon. She didn't like the idea, but she didn't have to worry about her reputation anymore. That was already gone.

She smiled to herself. It would shock Russ if she was able to resolve a situation he hadn't been able to remedy after years of trying. People were basically the same the world over. They did things for the same stupid reasons and selfish motives here as they had back in Kentucky or in St. Louis. If she was able to prove Stocker was somehow involved with the rustlers or had knowledge of what they were doing, Russ would never again be able to ignore her opinion. She was determined that their marriage would be one of equals.

"What are you doing?" Tardy asked when he found Tanzy hitching a horse to the buggy.

"Hitching a horse to the buggy."

"I can see that, but why are you doing it?"

"I'm going to town."

"What for?"

"I'm leaving."

It took Tardy a moment to realize she meant that her leaving wasn't temporary. "You can't do that. You belong here with us."

"I thought so, but I was wrong."

"Why? What's wrong?"

"I don't expect I'll be any more successful in explaining it to you than I was explaining it to Russ. Maybe he's right that I don't know how things are done out here, and maybe he is giving my opinions all the consideration they deserve, but I can't live in the middle of a feud ever again."

"This isn't a feud. It's just a fight to see who's stronger. That happens all the time."

"I thought I could accept that, but I can't."

"I can't let you go. Russ will kill me."

"Everybody in town thought you were wrong when you wanted to leave your aunt's home, but I supported you because I thought it was best for you. Now it's your turn."

"I don't want you to go." He sounded near tears.

"Do you think I want to leave the man I love, to walk away from what I thought was greater happiness than I'd ever imagined? I've argued with myself until I can't think straight, but the answer always comes out the same. I have to leave."

"After Russ kills me for letting you go, he'll come after you."

"Please convince him not to try."

"Of course he'll come after you. I wouldn't stay here another minute if he didn't."

Tanzy realized she'd have to accept that there were some things about the male mind she would never understand.

"Will you fetch my trunk?"

"No, ma'am. I don't mean to be rude, but I won't do nothing to help you leave here."

"Then you can tell Russ to bring it when he comes after me," Tanzy snapped. "That ought to salve both your consciences."

She drove out of the yard angry. When she noticed the horse's ears were laid back against its head, she realized she'd been taking her frustrations out on it. "Sorry," she said. "I'm not in a considerate mood right now."

She slowed down when she reached the pass. Oren wouldn't have stopped her, but she owed him an explanation. She didn't want Russ to blame him for letting her go.

"You shouldn't be leaving until Russ gets back," Oren said.

"I have something to do that can't wait. I don't know when I'll be back."

"What am I supposed to tell Russ?"

"Exactly what I told you."

"He won't like it."

"I'll be happier if he hates it."

Russ pushed his horse into a ground-eating canter. He hadn't been so angry since he'd discovered Toley Pullet had left his sister to die alone. What the hell did Tanzy think she was doing, leaving without waiting for him to come back? He wouldn't have left if he'd known she would do something like this. The boys could have taken care of setting fire to Stocker's barn and bunkhouse by themselves. They'd done a little more damage because Stocker's buildings were made of sawed boards, not logs, but Stocker had a big crew and they'd put out the fires before they did too much damage. That suited Russ. He didn't want to destroy anything, just let Stocker know he couldn't attack Russ with impunity. Anything he did was going to cost him as much or more.

He didn't know why Tanzy had left. The garbled story he got out of Tardy was so overladen with the boy's sense of ill usage by him and Tanzy that Russ wasn't able to make any sense of it. Interlarded with remarks about being treated like a baby were equally obscure references to his being a gentleman even though he'd refused to help Tanzy leave, feuds that weren't feuds, and a trunk that Russ had better not take to town even though Tanzy had asked that he did. He'd left Welt trying to soothe the boy's feelings. He couldn't think of anything except bringing Tanzy back.

He had thought anger would be his dominant emotion, maybe even confusion, but it was fear—fear that the future he'd believed was in his grasp had been snatched away again. He didn't even have time to hate Stocker for being the cause of it. All he could think about was convincing Tanzy that leaving would be the biggest mistake of her life. If he couldn't convince her to come back, he wouldn't stop until every one of Stocker's buildings had been reduced to ashes, until his every cow was scattered over the eastern third of the Territory. Stocker had tried to destroy his life twice. He would not go unpunished this time.

Memories of the night he and Tanzy had spent together kept bedeviling him. Everything had been so perfect. He'd never imaged it could be so wonderful to be loved. Maybe it seemed like a simple thing to others, but love had always eluded him before now. He'd felt it in Tanzy's touch, in her smile, in the warmth of her body as she yielded herself to him. He'd felt it even as she lay sleeping in his arms. The calm assurance that she was safe, protected, loved had rebounded on him, making him feel powerful, needed as well as loved. It was a heady sensation, one he could become drunk on more quickly than on whiskey. The thought kept going through his mind that his whole miserable life would have been worth it if he could end up with Tanzy.

He'd waited so long, become convinced it would

never happen to him, that his guard had been down. In the few brief hours allotted to him, he'd come to believe love would be his forever, had come to depend on it being there, and believed his struggle was over. Discovering none of this was true had been a painful wrench. A starving man who had food stolen from his outstretched hands will fight. Russ had tasted the food of love. He, too, would fight. He just didn't know how.

He rode into town, oblivious to the stares he earned. He was certain the news of the fires at Stocker's ranch had gotten around. He was also certain he was being blamed. He rode straight to the hotel, slid from the saddle, and strode inside.

"Where is she?" he asked Archie.

"She's got a room, but she's not here now," Archie said, his voice lowered to a whisper.

"When will she be back?"

"She didn't say."

"Where is she?"

"I don't know."

Archie was writing something on the back of an envelope. "You know it's the hotel policy not to disclose the whereabouts of guests without their permission."

"Policy be damned," Russ blurted out. "I want to know where she is."

Archie turned the envelope so Russ could read it. *Stocker's saloon.* "I'm sorry, but I couldn't tell you even if I knew."

"Damn you and damn your policy," Russ said as he turned and strode from the lobby.

What the hell was Tanzy doing at Stocker's saloon? One thing was for certain: In less than two minutes, he'd have his answer.

Chapter Twenty-six

Tanzy hadn't expected Russ to come after her so quickly. She'd barely had time to come to terms with Stocker about her employment. She didn't want a confrontation, but from the look on Russ's face, she was going to get one.

"What did you mean by running away when my back was turned?" Russ said, coming up to her without any preamble. "And what do you mean by being here?"

"I don't want to talk to you here." She was in a narrow hall that led to several rooms in back, one of them Stocker's office, but even this was too public for her.

"You're the one who chose the place."

"*You* chose the place by following me here."

"Did you think I'd let you leave and not follow?"

"You're not responsible for me. I can go anywhere I please."

"Not here. I won't let you."

Tanzy tried to walk past him, but Russ grabbed her wrist. She tried to pull loose, but he wouldn't release her.

"Why did you leave?"

"I told you from the beginning I would never have anything to do with a man who was involved in a feud."

"This is *not* a feud."

"Call it what you want; people have died, buildings have been burned, cattle have been stolen. That's more than enough for me."

"You don't understand. It's not the same out here."

"That's another thing," Tanzy said. "Every time I disagree with you, you say I don't understand, that people do things differently out here."

"They do."

"That's *your* opinion. Mine is that people are the same everywhere."

"Something as small as that and you'd walk out on everything we had?"

Tanzy pulled her wrist from his slackened grasp. The light was poor in the hall, but she could see his face. He looked hurt, angry . . . afraid. "What did we have, Russ?"

"Everything."

"We had a few brief hours when we *thought* we had everything. But morning came, as it always does, and daylight showed us nothing had changed. I was mistaken. You were mistaken."

"*We* weren't mistaken." He gripped her tightly by the shoulders. "Tell me what I have to do to get you back. I'll do anything."

Russ's look of entreaty nearly destroyed Tanzy's resolve to keep him from knowing what she was trying to do. She couldn't let Russ know because he'd do everything he could to stop her.

"I won't go back to the ranch. You and the boys will have to suffer with Welt's cooking."

"I don't give a damn about Welt's cooking. I don't care if you never cook again. I want you back. I love you. I want to marry you. I want—"

Tanzy had to force herself to say, "We both tried, but we failed."

"We didn't fail. We didn't even get a chance to try."

"Another instance when you don't respect my opinion."

"This is not about respecting opinions. You say you

love me one night and the next day you leave. It's like some child's game, now you see it, now you don't."

Tanzy had to get away from Russ. If she didn't, she was going to start crying. "I've said all I've got to say. I have to go."

He reached out for her wrist again. She turned to face him. "What are you going to do? You don't have a job. I know Ethel didn't give you back the teaching job."

"I asked Stocker for a job. I'll begin working in his saloon tonight."

She might as well have slapped him. It couldn't have shocked him more. "I won't let you work for that bastard."

"I can work for anyone I please."

"But this is a saloon."

"I know, but Ethel will tell you working in a saloon is no different from working in a gambling hall."

"I don't give a damn what Ethel thinks."

"Neither do I. It seems we do agree on one thing."

"What is going on?" Stocker's raised voice nearly drowned out Russ's words. "What are you doing in my saloon, you lying, thieving murderer? Get out before I have you thrown out."

"I don't want to be here any more than you want me here," Russ said, "but I'm not leaving without Tanzy."

"She's working for me now."

"I won't let her."

"You can't stop me from hiring her."

"I can stop you by breaking your lying, cheating neck."

"Both of you stop acting like little boys," Tanzy said, moving between the two men before they started slugging each other. "I don't need either of you to protect me. Stocker, if you're going to start a fight every time somebody wants to talk to me, I won't work for you."

"I'm not starting a fight. It's that—"

"And you," she said, turning on Russ and cutting Stocker off, "are not going to start fights with anybody who will give me a job. Now you," she said, turning back to Stocker, "have business to attend to, so go to your office and attend to it."

"I won't leave you here with that man."

"Russ is not staying. He has a ranch to run, and he can't do that from here."

The two men glared at each other across her.

"I'm not moving until you do," Tanzy said.

Still neither man moved.

"Stocker, I'm quitting this minute if you don't go to your office. Russ, I'll never speak to you again if you don't leave this building."

"If *you* don't leave this building, we'll have nothing to talk about."

"In that case, you have no reason to stay."

"You won't come back?"

"No."

"You're going to work in Stocker's saloon?"

"Yes."

"I would have gone anywhere for you, done anything."

She couldn't speak. Her throat was too tight. She waited, and gradually she could see the hope die in him. The words he'd expected to change her mind hadn't worked. Everything he'd dreamed had slipped beyond his grasp once more.

He turned and left without a word.

"Good. I hope that's the last we see of that son of a bitch."

Tanzy whirled on Stocker. "Let's get one thing straight right from the beginning: I don't know why you dislike Russ so much and I don't care, but if you ever say anything like that about him to me again, I'll walk out of here and never come back. Is that clear?"

*   *   *

"How the mighty have fallen."

Betty Hicks had confronted Tanzy on the boardwalk. It was impossible to avoid talking to her without crossing the street. "What are you talking about?"

"I'm talking about you, you lying bitch."

"Well, that's making your opinion very clear, but I'm still not sure where I've fallen to or where I've fallen from."

"Don't play games with me."

"I don't recall doing anything with you except being forced to speak to you."

"You can knock off the lady act. You're no better than I am."

"I never pretended I was. As you'll recall, I didn't believe working in a gambling hall made me a tramp."

"You'll find you're wrong, especially now you're nothing but a saloon girl."

Tanzy smiled. "So you've heard already."

"After the way Russ stormed through town, the place was buzzing..Everybody knows Russ threw you off his ranch and you came to Stocker begging for a job."

Tanzy struggled to fight down the urge to set Betty straight, but she realized she'd have a better chance of finding out what Stocker was doing if everybody believed Russ had thrown her out rather than that she had left.

"Stocker offered me the job before," Tanzy said.

"Well, now you'll have to set your sights on somebody other than Russ Tibbolt."

"So it seems. If you'll excuse me, I have to go."

"You can drop those hoity-toity manners. They won't be wanted in the saloon."

"I can assure you whatever I do will be wanted."

She just hoped she was wanted enough that she could get close to Stocker and find out what she needed to know.

"You can't let her work for Mr. Pullet," Tardy said. "You've got to bring her back."

"She doesn't want to come back," Russ said. "Now forget it."

"I can't," Tardy said. "She's the only one who really likes me. Besides, I think Welt's cooking will poison me."

"In that case I'll fix you something right now so we can have a little peace and quiet," Welt said.

"You'll have more peace and quiet than you can stand," Tim said. "This place will be dull without her."

Russ slammed his hand down on the table. "I've already told you, she doesn't want to come back so stop talking about it."

"Can't one of us go ask her?" Tardy asked. "Maybe you asked her wrong."

"Too late," Welt said, disgust in his voice. "He never did know how to handle a woman."

"Which is all the more reason for me not to get married," Russ said.

"But if you married her, maybe you could learn," Tardy said. "Being around these guys is nothing like being around a woman."

That came close to making Russ smile.

"I'm relieved to hear that," Welt said. "Have you any more words of wisdom or timeless advice before I throttle you?"

"Yes, I do," Tardy said, his mouth tightening stubbornly. "I don't know what went wrong, but you'll be real sorry if you don't fix it. You won't ever find a woman like Miss Gallant around here again, not if you live to be a hundred." With that he jumped up and stalked out of the cabin.

"Eat your supper," Russ said to the others. "I'll go after him. Maybe I can do better with a troubled youth. At least I know what that's like."

Tardy had run off to the corral in the trees behind the cabin. Russ found him leaning on the fence, a betraying moisture in his eyes. He put his hand on the boy's shoulder and squeezed. "We're all going to miss her."

"You've got each other. She was all I had."

"You've got us."

"It's not the same. You think of me as a kid. I suppose I am, but I didn't feel that way around Miss Gallant."

"She was like that with all of us. Somehow she made us all feel a little bit special."

"That's because she likes people. She always saw what she thought I could become, not the stupid dope I am. I always tried harder because I didn't want to let her down. Don't you love her? She loves you."

"How do you know that?"

"I may be a stupid boy, but I can see what's in front of my face. She was always happier when you were around. She did little things because she knew you liked them. And she kept all those things you wrote. She used to read them over every day."

Russ hadn't known that.

"You never took your eyes off her," Tardy continued. "Some evenings you'd sit in that big chair talking and acting like you were paying attention to what we were saying, but you'd be following her with your eyes."

"It was better than looking at you or Tim."

"You think I can't tell when a person's in love, but I

can. I know you love Miss Gallant and I know she loves you. I was hoping you'd get married so I could live here with you."

"You can still stay here."

"I was hoping you'd have babies. I never had any brothers or sisters. I always wanted somebody I could hold and love. Babies don't care if you're lazy or ugly. They'll love you anyway."

The air had turned cool with the sinking of the sun. The gloom of the gathering dusk reflected Russ's mood. He wondered how it could be that so many of the words coming out of Tardy's mouth were his own, so many of his feelings shared as well. He wanted a wife and lover, but he wanted children, too. Someone who would love him without any qualification, would look up to him in awe, who'd think he was godlike, that his every word was wisdom, his every rule unquestioned. It was probably a character defect that he wanted to be loved like that, but after being scorned and hated for so long, he longed for it.

But no childlike love could take the place of the love of a woman who knew your faults, could list your imperfections without stopping for breath, and loved you anyway. He'd thought he'd found that with Tanzy. Despite what she said, he still didn't understand what had gone wrong. He could have sworn she was willing to take a chance they could build a life free of the tension that had followed him for so long.

"I wanted just about the same thing," Russ told Tardy.

"Then why did you let her go?"

"Because she didn't want to come back. No matter how much you love a woman, how much you want her to be with you, you can't force her. It won't work. You'll end up hating each other."

"Do you hate Stocker?"

It surprised Russ to realize that in all the years Stocker had spent trying to ruin his life, he'd never asked himself that question. He'd thought he hated him, that he wanted him dead. He certainly thought he was a selfish, tyrannical man and wished Stocker would leave him alone, but that wasn't the same as hating him. "No. I think he's the worst man I know, but I don't hate him. I guess I feel sorry he's so miserable he has to be mean as a snake."

"I hate him. I wish he was dead."

Russ could sympathize. It would have been easy to hate Stocker, blame everything on him, but that wouldn't fix anything.

"Don't think about him. Think instead about yourself, about what you want to learn, what you want to do."

"Is that what you did?"

"Not at first. I spent several years in prison before I learned not to waste my time on anger and hate. The boys and I decided to put the past behind us, to concentrate on building something here. It wasn't easy, but we did it."

And now he was ready for the next stage, a family, but he knew he'd never have one without Tanzy. Her leaving hurt, but her betrayal, her working for Stocker, hurt even worse. He couldn't understand it. She wasn't a cruel person, but she couldn't have come up with anything that could have hurt him more. This was yet another time when a woman who was important to him had turned to a Pullet instead. What was wrong with him that made a man like Stocker Pullet preferable?

He was young and better looking, but Stocker was richer and more influential. He tried to do the right thing while Stocker forced people to do what he wanted. He couldn't understand why Tanzy couldn't see through

Stocker. He guessed it was just another case of him not being able to understand women. His record was truly dismal.

But even as he reached that conclusion he rejected it. He didn't understand what had gone wrong, but things had been different this time. They did understand each other. Something had happened to change her mind. She had been upset that he would burn Stocker's buildings in retaliation, but that didn't explain why she would go to work for Stocker, a man she disliked. There was something here he needed to figure out before his future slipped through his fingers.

"I don't know what I want to do," Tardy said. "Miss Gallant said I ought to get more schooling, maybe even college, but Aunt Ethel doesn't want me back."

"You stay here and do a good job and we'll see about some more schooling."

"I can't get ready for something like that without help. Miss Gallant is the only one who can help me."

"Talk to Oren. Maybe he can help," Russ suggested. "Right now I think we ought to go back and eat our supper."

"Welt isn't such a terrible cook, but he'll never take the place of Miss Gallant."

That was the problem. Nobody could take Tanzy's place.

The last week had been one of the most interesting in Tanzy's life. She'd taken up her position as hostess in Stocker's saloon. At first the men didn't know how to treat her. Some had tried to act like she was one of the girls who sold drinks and dances. Tanzy quickly set them straight on that. She didn't sell dances, she didn't sell drinks, and she would not be mauled. She started carrying a small fan to use to rap offending hands. Even when drunk, the men could feel the sharp discomfort across their knuckles.

Some avoided her, unsure of what to do. When that happened, she could go up to the man, start him talking, and soon beckon one of the other women to keep him company. Some attempted to treat her with such formality she had to exert herself to get them to relax and enjoy themselves. She quickly figured out Stocker didn't need her, that he'd only hired her because he liked doing anything he could to anger Russ, but she wanted to keep her position long enough to find out what was going on.

To that end she encouraged everyone to talk to her. A few beers, a few smiles, and a sympathetic ear and there wasn't much most men wouldn't tell her. She went to her bed every evening weary of it. She asked them about their lives, their families, their work. She asked them to tell her about the West, not neglecting any details. She asked about the rustlers because she'd been told they were lawless killers and that wasn't at all what she was used to. She learned a few things, none of it very useful. Cattle were being stolen from everyone, but not enough to threaten anybody's livelihood. There hadn't been any robberies since the attempt on the stage. The men who'd tried to kill Russ wouldn't say who hired them.

A stranger came to talk with Stocker one night just after she was supposed to have left. She had gone into the office where she kept her things and heard a voice she didn't recognize. That wouldn't have meant anything if she hadn't heard Stocker say Russ's name.

She froze, listening intently. She couldn't tell what the other man was saying, but apparently what he said made Stocker angry for he started shouting. She couldn't make out a lot of what he said because the other man was speaking, too, but it was clear he was talking about Russ and stealing cattle.

He had to be talking about stealing Russ's cattle.

Tanzy knew Stocker hated Russ and wanted to get rid of him, but she'd never considered the possibility that Stocker would hire someone to steal Russ's cattle. Or did she have it wrong? Had Stocker hired someone to rustle cattle from everybody so he could blame it on Russ? That possibility seemed even more farfetched until she considered the depth of Stocker's hatred for Russ. He'd said he wouldn't be happy until Russ was dead. Getting him convicted and hanged as a rustler and a killer was a way to do that.

Tanzy waited to hear more, but the man left. She hurried to leave the office but only saw his back. Stocker was still in his office. She stood there trying to think what to do next. It wouldn't do any good to face Stocker with her accusations or go to the sheriff with her suspicions. She needed some proof Stocker was behind the rustling, but she had no idea how to get it.

If she could search Stocker's office, maybe she could find something to take to the sheriff or even the commander at the fort, but Stocker kept his office and his desk locked. She didn't know what she would do, but she would think of something. She'd shoot Stocker herself before she allowed him to cause Russ to be hanged. Maybe that made her as bad as her father and brothers, but she didn't care. She was fighting for her future.

"Tardy, what are you doing here?"

"I came to ask if you'd teach me some more."

She hadn't been able to sleep after last night. Unable to stay cooped up in her room, she'd left the hotel early and walked down to the schoolhouse so she could be alone and have some time to think.

"You must have gotten up mighty early to be here at this hour."

"I stayed with Aunt Ethel last night."

"I thought she wouldn't let you back in the house."

"She didn't know. I snuck in after dark."

"Somebody's bound to tell her they've seen you."

"I don't care. Russ said he'd see about me getting some extra schooling, but I need somebody to teach me so I'll be ready. I came to ask if you could help me."

An idea occurred to Tanzy. "I'll help, but you've got to help me, too."

"How can I do that?"

Tanzy told him what she'd heard.

"You mean you still love Russ?" Tardy exclaimed, his face lighting up. "You're not leaving him?"

"Of course I'm not leaving him. I was angry at first, but—"

Tardy threw himself at her, knocking the breath and the rest of her sentence out of her. "I *told* Russ you loved him, that all he had to do was ask you to come back."

Tanzy laughed as she pried Tardy's arms from around her waist. "What did he say?"

Some of Tardy's excitement faded. "He said he had never understood women, not his mother, his sister, or you, so maybe it was best that he never got married. But he didn't mean it. He's been going around looking like he lost his best friend. He doesn't even complain about Welt's food. Tim swears at least once a day he's going to kidnap you and bring you back. If he knew that you—"

"You can't breathe a word to a soul."

"Why?"

"Because it would ruin everything. You've got to act

like you're still mad at me. People will tell me more if they think I don't like Russ. They know you do, so you have to pretend to be coming to me only because there's nobody else. Until we find out what's going on, you can't tell anybody what we're doing."

Tardy's eyes shone with eagerness. "What do you want me to do?"

"We've got to find out what Stocker's plans are so we can stop him. I've tried to get into his office, but it's always locked with a padlock. He's got a padlock on his desk, too, so there's no use thinking you can pry it open without splitting the wood."

"Can you steal the keys?"

"I don't know where he keeps the keys, but that's not what I want you to do. I need to know when that man comes to see him again. I want you to study every night in the room where I keep my things. When anybody goes into Stocker's office, come let me know. That means you'll have to be very quiet and stay awake."

"Where am I going to stay?"

"Do you think you could convince your aunt to let you move back in with her?"

"Why would you want me to do that?"

"It'll look better. Besides, she hates me, so no one will suspect you're helping me."

"She hates me, too."

"She was just angry at you for revealing she had wanted to marry Russ. I expect that hurt her pride. Did you bring any books?"

"No, but there's plenty in the schoolhouse."

"Then let's go in and get started."

Tanzy had to wait only two nights for the man to return, but she wouldn't have known it if she hadn't taken the precaution of checking on Tardy at least once an hour. She'd found him asleep on two occasions that evening. Clearly he was not one for late-night revels. She didn't see him beckon to her until one of the men asked when Stocker had started letting beardless boys in the saloon after midnight.

"I'm helping him with some studies," she explained. "Apparently he's got a problem."

"I've got a problem, too," one of the men said.

"You'll have a bigger one if you tell me what it is," Tanzy said as she got up and left the table.

"I told you to watch what you say," one of the men said in tones that were neither soft or dulcet. "That's a mighty particular lady. She don't put up with any rough stuff."

Tanzy smiled to herself. If she could convince this crowd she was a lady, Ethel wouldn't have a leg to stand on.

"There's some guy in there I've never seen before," Tardy said.

"You got a look at him?"

"I was taking a short walk to wake up when he came in. I don't think he saw me, but I caught a glimpse of his face when he opened the door."

"Okay. Be very quiet and let's see if we can hear anything."

Tanzy put her ear to the wall, but she couldn't make out anything they said. After several minutes of trying different spots in the wall with no success, she said, "You try listening at the wall. I'm going outside to see if I can hear anything through the keyhole."

"What if he catches you?"

"I'll be careful. Now be quiet and listen very hard."

Tanzy eased open the door and tiptoed into the hall. The noise from the saloon was louder out here. She reached Stocker's door and put her ear against it but couldn't make out more than an occasional word. She knelt down and put her ear against the keyhole.

"Have you got the herd together yet?"

"Yeah. Right now my boys are holding a couple of hundred cows, some from every rancher within a hundred miles."

"Good. Tomorrow I want them on the move so we can drive them into Russ's valley. I'll organize a posse from town to arrive before he can chase them out again."

"We'll have to kill the guard at the pass."

"Nobody will care. I'll see to that."

Stocker went on, "I'd love to be with you, to see Russ's face when those cows stampede into his valley, but I have to be in town to lead the posse."

"Get your sheriff to organize it. It'll look better if you're not involved."

"That's a good idea. I'll do that."

Tanzy started to stand, but her muscles had cramped from being crouched down for so long and she stumbled and fell against the door. The man wrenched it open before she could get her rebellious muscles to work.

"What the hell are you doing?" he demanded.

Chapter Twenty-seven

"I twisted my ankle and was coming to tell Stocker I'm going home," Tanzy said, scrambling madly to think of some excuse to explain her presence. "I must have stepped on an uneven board because it gave way right as I started to knock on his door."

The man gave her a hard look, but he reached out to take her arm and help her stand. She might have gotten away with it if Tardy hadn't burst out of the other room at that moment. "What are you doing to her?" he asked.

"What's he doing here?" Stocker demanded.

"He studies in the room you gave me," Tanzy said, hoping to stave off any ill-considered remark Tardy might be encouraged to make.

"Take your hands off her," Tardy said to the man. "If you hurt her, I'll tell Russ."

"Why would Russ care about her?" Stocker asked.

"Tardy thinks I ought to marry him," Tanzy said. "He won't believe me when I tell him I want nothing to do with Russ Tibbolt."

Tardy had finally recovered enough to shut his mouth, but it was too late. The look the man was giving her was definitely menacing. Before she had time to guess what he might do, he'd pushed her inside Stocker's office, grabbed Tardy, and shoved him in behind her. When Tardy tried to fight, he hit him so hard he knocked the boy out. He pulled his gun and aimed it at Tardy.

"What are you doing?" Stocker demanded.

"We can't let them go."

"Why not? They don't know anything."

"You can't be sure."

"You can't kill anybody in my saloon. You'd have everybody in here before you could get out the door."

"Tie them up and leave them here. Afterwards we can get rid of them."

"I forbid you to touch either one of them. If you don't let them go, I'll turn you in to the sheriff."

The rustler turned his gun on Stocker. "You may think I'm a fool, but I'm far from it. I've sold all the cows I've rustled before this last batch and none of the guys in jail know who hired them, so I'm clean. As soon as I get rid of that herd tomorrow, I'll be clean again. Now help me tie them up or you'll be the first one I shoot."

Tanzy screamed and fought, but it didn't do any good. She soon found herself tied and gagged, pushed into a corner opposite the still-unconscious Tardy, the door closed and locked. She lay there cursing her stupid mistake, racking her brains for a way to escape and warn Russ.

Ethel Peters marched into the hotel, planted herself in front of the desk, and demanded to see Tanzy immediately.

"She hasn't come down yet," Archie said. "She usually sleeps late."

"I don't care if she's had no sleep at all. My worthless nephew didn't come home last night and I'm sure she's responsible. I wish to speak to her immediately."

"I can't wake her," Archie protested.

"I can. What is her room number? I won't wait long," she said when Archie hesitated. "You'll tell me or you'll tell the sheriff."

"It's twelve," Archie said. "She won't like being waked."

"My poor, foolish nephew came home begging me to take him back, saying she'd bewitched him. He was fine for two days and now he's disappeared."

With that she marched off up the stairs, only to return moments later.

"She's not in her room and her bed hasn't been slept in."

"She's got to be here. She has nowhere else to go."

Archie hurried off but came back almost immediately. "Something's wrong. She didn't take anything. It's just like it was when I straightened up after she left for the saloon."

"The hussy. I expect she's run off with some man."

"She's no hussy," Archie said. "The men are all talking about how she makes them behave or she won't pay them no mind."

"I still say any woman who works in a saloon is a hussy. I'm going over there right now and demand that she tell me what she's done with my nephew."

"I'm going with you."

"I don't need help."

"Something's happened to Miss Gallant and I mean to find out what it is."

"You think she might be in trouble?"

"Miss Gallant wouldn't spend the night anywhere but in her own bed, and she wouldn't go off and leave all her belongings behind."

"We'll soon find out," Ethel declared.

Tanzy had given up on anybody finding her before Stocker returned. She couldn't call for help because the rustler had gagged her. She was worried about Tardy. He'd regained consciousness before the rustler had tied him up. The boy had attempted to drag the man off Tanzy and had been rewarded by a blow to his head. The trickle of blood down his face worried her. He had come around a couple of times, then faded off again. Why had she thought she could do everything by herself? Why hadn't she let Tardy tell Russ what she meant to do? Because he would have stopped her, and then they'd never know about Stocker's plans. Not that it would do any good with her locked up in this room.

She ought to be worrying about herself. Would Stocker let the rustler kill her to gain his revenge on Russ? What about Tardy? The boy was innocent. She was responsible for the threat that hung over his head. She tried once again to loosen the knots that held her hands behind her, but it was useless. She couldn't budge them.

She wondered what time it was. There was no window in the office. How long had she and Tardy been tied up? She'd tried to stay awake, but she'd slept off and on. Would they have time to stop Stocker if she got free right now? Why couldn't she think of something? She'd never felt so stupid in her whole life.

In the silence she detected a faint sound. It sounded like someone in the saloon was trying to open the door that led to the offices in the back. Apparently Stocker had locked that, too. It must be time to open the saloon; someone probably needed to get to the stock of liquor.

Her body sagged with defeat. It was too late. The sheriff and his posse would have stormed the valley by now. Russ might be dead. He might be on his way to jail, with Stocker and the sheriff having all the proof they needed that he had been rustling cattle. That meant she and Tardy were in even more danger.

Suddenly the voices were much louder. Somebody had unlocked the door, but it couldn't be one of the men who worked behind the bar. She heard a woman's voice. She heard Ethel Peters.

Frantically, Tanzy looked around for some way to make noise, any sound that would attract Ethel's attention. She tried to roll toward the door, only to discover the rustler had tied her to Stocker's desk. Furious, she jerked on the rope, but it wouldn't give. The desk was too large. Tardy was tied to the other side.

In frustration, she threw her head back. It hit the wall, sending a pain down her spine. She cursed herself mentally until she realized the voices had stopped.

"I heard something," she heard Ethel say.

Tanzy banged her head against the wall again. Despite

the pain, she kept hitting it until she was so dizzy she could hardly see straight. Someone banged on Stocker's office door.

"Is there anybody in there?" Ethel called.

Steeling herself against the pain, Tanzy hit her head against the wall again. When she didn't get an immediate response, she did it again. If Ethel didn't figure out someone was in this room soon, Tanzy was going to have addled brains for life.

"There's somebody in there," Ethel said.

"They can't be all right," Archie said, "or they'd be calling out and opening the door instead of banging on the wall."

"Somebody open this door," Ethel said.

"Stocker has the only key." Tanzy recognized the voice of the barman.

"Then break the door down. My nephew is missing. I'm sure he's in that room."

The barman continued to argue, but the only man who'd ever stood up to Ethel was Russ. A few minutes later, Tanzy heard wood splitting. They must be using a crowbar to pry the screws out of the door frame. She heard the welcome sound of metal against metal. The padlock was off. It took only a moment to force the regular lock. The door flew open and Ethel charged into the room.

"You!" she exclaimed when she saw Tanzy. "What are you doing here?"

"She can't tell you with that gag in her mouth, can she?" Archie said. He rushed over to remove the gag.

Meanwhile, Ethel had found Tardy. "Richard! Oh my God. He's bleeding. What have you done to him?" she demanded, turning on Tanzy.

"The rustler hit him when he tried to help me," Tanzy said, her mouth sore, her voice thick, and her words hard to understand.

"I don't believe you," Ethel said. "Why would a rustler be in Stocker's office?"

"Because Stocker hired him to steal cattle so he could blame it on Russ. I overheard him planning to drive them to Russ's valley so they can convict Russ of rustling and hang him. Tardy attacked the rustler when he started tying me up. He's planning to kill us when he gets back."

"I never heard a more ridiculous story in my life," Ethel declared. "You can't expect me to believe that Stocker—"

"She's telling the truth," Tardy said, sitting up and holding his head.

"He's got it all planned," Tanzy said. "Stocker didn't want to kill us, but the rustler threatened to kill Stocker if he didn't help him tie us up. Then he made Stocker go along with him. They've left someone here who'll bring the sheriff and a posse to Russ's valley after they've driven the rustled cattle in. That way Russ can't deny he has rustled cattle on his property."

"I don't believe you," Ethel said. "Stocker has been accusing Russ from the beginning."

"And foiling every attempt Russ made to have the ranchers go to his valley and inspect it for themselves. Stocker knows there aren't any stolen cattle there. He knew if the men went, they'd see that, and his case against Russ would collapse."

"She's telling the truth," Archie said. "I was working the desk in the hotel when the ranchers met. They was getting together a group to go out and inspect Russ's herds. Stocker wanted them to go in shooting. When they wouldn't, he walked out, saying he'd have no part of it."

"He did the same thing at the meeting in the saloon," said the barman. "I was working that night. I heard him."

"You've got to talk to the sheriff," Tanzy said to Ethel. Archie had untied her and she was trying to stand on unsteady legs. "He won't believe me, but he'll have to believe you."

"You can't expect me to defend Russ Tibbolt."

"Do you still hate him so much you'd stand back and see him hanged? This town has already sent him to prison for one crime he didn't commit."

"He's not a rustler, Aunt Ethel," Tardy said. "I rode all over that valley with every one of his men. There wasn't nothing I didn't see, and there was no rustled cows anywhere."

"Yet twice he was attacked," Tanzy said, "once when I was there and the second time when we were in town. Someone is determined to destroy him. And if he can't do that by fair means, he'll do it by foul."

"I've heard Stocker in the hotel hundreds of times saying he wants Russ dead," Archie said. "He'll never forgive him for being a better shot then Toley. Toley was nothing but a Sunday cowboy. Russ learned how to be the real thing when he went to Texas. It hurt Stocker's pride that Russ seemed to always get the better of him in the end."

Tanzy could see the conflict raging inside Ethel. To believe what Tanzy said would mean admitting she'd been wrong all these years, and Ethel Peters made it a point never to be wrong.

"What do you mean, Russ was a better shot than Toley?" Ethel asked Archie. "Russ drew first."

"No, he didn't," Archie said. "I didn't see it myself, but I heard from more than one of the fellas who worked for Stocker that Toley drew first. They wouldn't say nothing

because Stocker paid them good to lie, but men will tell
you just about anything when they've had too much to
drink."

"I'm riding out to warn Russ," Tardy said, trying to
stand on legs even more unsteady than Tanzy's.

"You're going straight to the doctor," Ethel said.

"Somebody's got to warn Russ."

"What time is it?" Tanzy asked.

"It's just past eight o'clock," Ethel said. "I went in to
wake Richard for breakfast at seven and discovered his
bed hadn't been slept in."

"Then we still have time," Tanzy said. She no longer felt
tired. There was time to warn Russ, time to stop Stocker.
"Ethel, you've got to convince the sheriff what I've said is
true. You've got to convince him to gather a posse and
ride to Russ's valley. Russ has forgiven this town for what
it has done to him. He's tried to forget what Stocker and
his brother did to his family, but you kept manufacturing
hatred, remembering old grievances, inventing them
when there were none, and bullying people into treating
him like a pariah."

"I saw something else happening," Archie said. "People
nearly always know what's right and wrong even when
they don't do it, and they start feeling guilty. Because they
feel guilty about doing something that's not right, they do
it even more, like they're trying to convince themselves
they're doing the right thing."

"It's a vicious cycle," Tanzy said, finally able to stand
unaided. "Nothing can compensate Russ for all the lost
years, but you have a chance to end a great injustice. You
also have a chance to free this town from the yoke of
Stocker's tyranny. If you don't do it now, you'll continue
being his sheep for the rest of your life."

"I'm nobody's sheep," Ethel declared.

"Prove it," Tanzy challenged. "I'm leaving now. The rest is up to you."

"Do you really love him?" Ethel asked. For the first time in Tanzy's experience she didn't sound like the domineering town spinster.

"Yes, I do. I spent weeks telling myself why I shouldn't, but when I started teaching him to read, I saw a whole different man."

"He can't read?" Ethel exclaimed.

"He can now. He's the best student I ever had."

"Then he never knew what I—" Ethel caught herself before she finished her thought. "Never mind," she said, her customary commanding presence reasserting itself. "I will talk to the sheriff. If he won't raise a posse, I'll do it myself. Now, young man," she said, turning to Tardy, "I'm taking you to the doctor."

"Can you find me a horse?" Tanzy asked Archie.

"I'll get you a buggy," he said.

"I'm about to become a cowboy's wife. I want a horse."

Tanzy was relieved to see no sign of activity as she approached the pass into Russ's valley. She had ridden as fast as she dared, praying she would get there before Stocker and the rustlers.

"What are you doing back?"

It was Tim. He stood exposed on the rocks above with his rifle across his arms.

"I don't have time to explain," Tanzy said, "but I left to get proof Stocker was trying to pin this rustling on Russ. He's hired rustlers to steal cattle. They mean to force their way into the valley so when the sheriff and posse arrive, there will be proof Russ is doing the rustling."

"Nobody's getting by me," Tim said, beginning to unbend a little.

"Stocker means to kill you first. I've got to warn Russ."

Tim called out something, but she didn't hear. She was already galloping toward the man she loved, hoping he still loved her.

"I think you ought to go outside," Welt said. He'd entered the cabin in a hurry, tension showing in his eyes.

"Why?" Russ asked.

"Just go."

Russ turned and reached for a rifle.

"You won't need that," Welt said.

"What's going on?"

"You'll see."

Russ didn't understand, but he didn't much care. He hadn't cared very much about anything since Tanzy left. The cows that represented his success had become empty possessions that required much of him but gave nothing back. Even the friendships that had been so vital to him during prison and so essential to his success since had lost some of their meaning. Tanzy's departure had ripped the heart out of everything that was important to him.

"You've been acting mighty peculiar lately," Russ said as he headed toward the door.

"I'm surprised you noticed."

He'd been moody, morose, even hostile at times. He guessed that was why Tardy had left. Thinking about Stocker and how that man had poisoned everything in his life made him so angry he was seething. It wasn't fair to take his anger out on the kid, but now the damage was done.

He didn't see anything different when he stepped out of the cabin. The yard looked the same. A horse in the corral whinnied and some birds squabbled in the trees by the creek, but everything else was quiet. Then he heard an approaching horse. He rounded the corner of the cabin to see Tanzy riding a paint mare at a slow gallop. The mare was breathing as if she'd been ridden hard, long, or both.

His heart leapt at the sight of her. He'd forgotten how beautiful she was, how just looking at her made him feel good, how he'd come to count on seeing her every day. Or maybe he'd just tried to forget because he'd thought he'd never see her again. It didn't matter. His heart started beating so rapidly he felt dizzy. She was coming back. He didn't know why, but it didn't matter as long as she was here. Somehow he'd find a way to convince her to stay.

His second emotion, so strong it overcame the first, was anger, the feeling of betrayal, the loss of faith in himself and in her. He didn't want her coming back, stirring things up again. It was hard enough to get used to her leaving the first time. Seeing what he'd lost didn't make it any easier. He stood in the middle of the path, feet spread apart, arms across his chest

"If you've come for Tardy's things, they're already packed," he said when she pulled up her horse. "If you've come for anything else, you can turn around and go back to Stocker."

He didn't want to classify her expression. It looked too much like she was glad to be back, like she loved him but was afraid he would reject her. He had to look away. If he didn't, his will would fail and he'd be in the same trouble all over again.

"Do you hate me so much you can't look at me?"

His gaze flew to her face. "I don't hate you. I just don't want to look at the face that lied to me. Would you like to know if you haunt me still? You do. I see you wherever I look, whenever I think of something that reminds me of you. You took something important away from this valley when you left. I can't blame you if you can't love me, but I don't think I can forgive you either."

"I never left, not the way you mean, but I don't have time to explain now. Stocker hired some rustlers to steal cattle from all the ranchers, hoping he could blame it on you and hang you. When that didn't work, he came up with a new idea. He's planning to have the rustlers drive all the stolen cattle into your valley. He's arranged for the sheriff and a posse to arrive afterwards so they can find the stolen cattle here."

"They won't get past Tim."

"They plan to kill him. Stocker resisted killing Tardy and me, but he got a glassy-eyed look when he imagined what you'd look like when you saw the cows and knew you were going to hang. I think he's a little crazy."

"Where did you hear this fairy tale?" Russ asked. He didn't have any trouble believing Stocker would sink so low, but he didn't see how Tanzy could know something like this, or why she would tell him.

"When you left to burn Stocker's barn, I was ready to leave. It was a feud all over again. But I realized I loved you too much to leave you to face all this cruelty alone. I also realized that simply staying here wouldn't solve anything, so I made up my mind to find out what was happening. That's why I went to work for Stocker. I figured being around him every day would give me a chance to learn something. And it did. I learned a stranger sometimes visited him after midnight. I heard them say something about rustling and mention your name. When Tardy came to ask if I'd keep teaching him, I enlisted his help."

"He didn't run away because I got angry at him?"

"Far from it. He did his best to talk me into returning. When I explained what I wanted him to do, he couldn't wait to help."

"What did you do?" Russ wanted to believe her. God, how he wanted to believe her, but he didn't think he could stand being made a fool of again.

"I had Tardy study in the room next to Stocker's office. When he saw a stranger enter, he came and got me. I listened at the keyhole, but my legs cramped when I tried to stand and they caught me. They tied me up. They knocked Tardy out and tied him up, too."

She held out her arms for him to see the red marks on her wrists.

"How did you get out?"

"Tardy had convinced his aunt to let him come back home. When she found he wasn't in his bed, she blamed me. When she found I wasn't in my bed, she came after me. If she hadn't been so angry at me, I'd still be waiting for the rustler to come back and kill us."

"What makes you think I'm going to believe such a wild story?"

"Common sense. You may believe I don't love you and that I'm lying when I say I left to try to stop Stocker, but do you believe I would betray you to him?"

"No."

"Then you have to believe I want to help you. There's no other reason for me to be here."

"She's right, you know." He hadn't realized Welt had come up behind him.

"I know she's right about Stocker, dammit. It's just the rest that I'm having trouble with."

"The part about my still loving you?" Tanzy asked.

"Yes."

She slid off her horse. "Maybe this will help." She

walked up to him, wrapped her arms around his neck, and pulled his head down until their faces were only inches apart. "I've done everything I could to keep from wanting to marry you, but it didn't work. I love you enough to stand by you through a feud if necessary, but I also love you enough to take the risk of trying to stop it. This is my pledge that I'll always love you no matter what."

She rose on her tiptoes and kissed him.

Russ thought his legs would go out from under him. He tried to hold out against her, but the battle was brief and his surrender unconditional. If this was the way to Hell, then he would go willingly. He didn't want to fight his way to victory without her. She was the only person who could keep him from dying inside, who could rescue the part of him that had hidden behind a tough, rebellious, unemotional exterior all his life. The effort was suffocating him. She was his only way out.

"I hate to break up your reunion," Welt said, "but if Tanzy's right, I expect Stocker is on his way with those stolen cows."

Russ had to fight to pull himself out of Tanzy's embrace, but they could celebrate later. If they didn't stop Stocker, there wouldn't be any later.

"We need the wagon to block the pass," Russ said.

"I'll get it," Welt said, "but it won't be enough."

While Welt headed toward the corral at a run, Russ ran inside, got a rifle, returned, and fired it three times. "That'll bring Buck and Oren," he said to Tanzy. "When they get here, tell them what's happening. Have them bring poles we can use to loosen boulders and roll them into the pass. I want to make it impossible for Stocker to force those cows through."

"What can I do after I've given them the message?"

"Stay here."

"I can shoot," Tanzy said.

"I know you can, but this is too dangerous."

"It wasn't too dangerous for me to listen outside Stocker's door or spend the night tied up and gagged."

"I wouldn't have let you do that if I'd known about it. Promise you'll stay here. I won't be able to think straight if you don't."

"Now's as good a time as any, Russ Tibbolt, to make it clear I'll never lie to you. Consequently, I'm not going to make a promise I'm not sure I can keep."

"Are you always going to be this stubborn?"

"I'll probably get worse once I really know my way around."

Russ felt his heart fill with joy. "God, I love you, but I'm liable to beat you one of these days."

"You do and you'd better never go to sleep again."

Russ laughed. There was no time, there was no sane reason for it, and this wasn't the place, but he couldn't stop himself. Since the world insisted upon being crazy, it probably wouldn't mind if he went a little nuts now and then. Then again, maybe this was the most sane his life had ever been.

"Try to stay here. If you can't, don't let me know it. And no matter what you do, don't get hurt. If you do, I'll have to kill Stocker."

Chapter Twenty-eight

"A couple more ought to do it," Welt said.

"I think this is enough," Russ said. "We don't want to make it impossible to clear the passage afterwards."

"Do you think Stocker will show up with those stolen cows?" Buck asked.

"I believe he plans to be here today, but there's no assurance there won't be a hitch in his plans. Still, if he's got the sheriff and a posse scheduled to be here at a certain time, he's got to get the stolen cows here or he'll prove me innocent instead of guilty."

"Why don't I go along a ways and see what I can see?" Oren said.

"Okay, but be careful. Tanzy says they're prepared to kill anybody who gets in their way."

"Nice to know how important we are to him," Oren said.

But Oren didn't have to leave.

"They're coming," Tim called from his position up in the rocks. "He's running them. They'll be here in minutes."

"Keep down," Russ called. "As long as the passage is blocked, he can't get any cows inside. I don't want anybody taking any chances."

Just then they heard shots from the direction of the cabin. Not the three evenly spaced shots that was their signal for danger but irregular shots as would happen in a gunfight.

"Somebody's attacking the cabin," Russ said, racing for his horse. "Tanzy's there alone."

"I'm coming with you," Welt said. "Three men are enough to hold the pass."

Russ didn't wait for Welt to catch up. He spurred his horse into a hard gallop. He'd thought when he asked Tanzy to stay at the cabin he was keeping her safe. It had never occurred to him that he would be leaving her to fight off an attack alone. If anything happened to Tanzy, he'd go crazy.

The flurry of rifle shots that had started the fight ceased abruptly. Fear drove an icy stake into Russ's heart, fear that the fight had ended because Tanzy couldn't fight any longer. He was so glad to hear a resumption of gunfire that he nearly sobbed with relief.

"Stay alive until I get there," he shouted into the wind. "Please stay alive."

The ride across the valley had always been one of his greatest pleasures. Today he cursed the miles of rich grass and gently undulating land, the meandering stream with its willow- and cottonwood-shaded banks that forced him to take time-consuming detours, everything that kept him from arriving instantly at Tanzy's side. He cursed the mountains that rose around him for allowing killers to penetrate into his valley.

Most of all he cursed Stocker Pullet.

Apparently the invaders had heard him coming because the rifle fire had ended when he raced into the trees behind the cabin. He grabbed his rifle, launched himself from the saddle before his horse stopped, and raced for cover behind the corner of the cabin closest to the mountains.

"They've pulled out," Tanzy said from inside. "There were two of them."

"Are you all right?"

"I'm fine. Just furious I didn't hit at least one of them."

Russ came around the front of the cabin as Welt raced into the yard. "They ran off through the trees," Russ said.

Welt headed off after them.

Tanzy came out of the house and Russ crushed her in his embrace. "When the shooting stopped for a moment, I was afraid you'd been hurt."

"I'm not about to get hurt until I've been married to you for at least a hundred years."

"Welt will tell you that much time in my company is liable to paralyze you."

"I think I'll see about finding something to interest Welt. Maybe something blond and pretty."

Russ laughed. "How can you make jokes at a time like this?"

"I can't think of a better time. Otherwise, I'd ride into Boulder Gap and kill Stocker myself."

"I forgot," Russ said. "Stocker's driving the herd toward the gap. I left the boys when I heard the rifle shots."

"Then we'd better go help them."

"We?"

"After standing off two men alone, you don't think I'm going to stay back and watch anymore, do you?"

"No, I don't. Can you ride bareback?"

"Just watch me."

They caught two horses in the corral, mounted up, and rode as fast as they could, each with a handful of horse's mane in one hand and a rifle in the other. The sound of rifle fire reached them when they were barely halfway back.

"Keep well under cover," Russ said when they reached the passage. "I don't think anybody will shoot at you, but you could be hurt by a ricocheting bullet."

"The men at the cabin didn't hesitate."

He felt certain they'd thought a man was inside, but that was unimportant now.

"What happened?" Russ asked when he reached the spot where Oren had taken cover behind the wagon.

"They tried to run the herd through at a gallop. Maybe they thought the cows would jump the wagon. When Buck and I started waving our hands and shooting in the air, the herd split into half and turned back on itself. They're all tangled up out there. The rustlers can't get close enough to get a good shot at us."

"It's not the rustlers I'm worried about," Russ said. "Keep your eye out for Stocker. Tanzy thinks he's crazy enough to kill me himself."

Russ saw Tanzy picking her way through the boulders. "Stay back," he said, but he didn't expect her to listen to him.

She didn't.

"What's going on?" she asked when she reached them.

"They've lost control of the herd. It's milling around in confusion."

"Where's Stocker?"

"I don't know."

"His hatred for you has driven him a little crazy. If he sees his plans falling apart, it might push him over the edge."

"I see another bunch of riders coming," Tim called from his high perch. "It looks like the sheriff and the posse."

"All we have to do is hold them off until the sheriff can arrest them," Russ said.

Stocker was out there somewhere. Russ wouldn't feel safe until he knew where.

It all ended rather quietly. The posse outnumbered the rustlers and was able to arrest them with ease. The rustler Tanzy had heard talking to Stocker couldn't wait to explain that he'd been paid to take the cows, that Stocker had been with them but had slipped away when he saw the pass had been blocked.

Meanwhile, Welt had shown up with the two men who'd attacked the cabin, one of them wounded. Once the rustlers had been secured and the herd turned, they all started toward town. They hadn't gone fifty yards before a burst of rifle fire sprayed the ground at Russ's feet. He grabbed Tanzy and dove under the wagon. Buck, Oren, and Welt scrambled behind the rocks.

"It's Stocker," Tim called out to Russ. "He got up on the other side of the pass. Keep down. He's trying to kill you."

Bullets smashed into the bed of the wagon, one of them penetrating and biting into the ground right next to Tanzy.

"Get under the front of the wagon," Russ said. "The bullets can't get through the seat and the wagon floor."

"There's not enough room for both of us," Tanzy said.

"I'm going to get out and see if I can get a shot at Stocker."

"Let someone else do it," Tanzy said. "If you kill him, the murder will follow you for the rest of your life."

"I can live with that. I can't live with knowing I let him hurt you."

The shooting stopped abruptly.

"You can come out now," Tim called. "The sheriff just killed Stocker."

"I guess that's all I need to know," the sheriff said to Russ and Tanzy. "I've got all the information I need for the trial.

Now that everybody knows you didn't draw first on Toley, it looks like you're going to be a hero in this town."

"I don't care about that," Russ said, "as long as people no longer believe I'm a liar, a thief, and a killer."

"Now that Stocker's hands have had their say, I don't think anybody's going to believe that anymore. They're liable to stumble over themselves trying to apologize. Me included."

"I don't want that either. I just want to go back to my valley and live the rest of my life in peace."

"That seems fair," the sheriff said.

Tardy was waiting for them when they left the sheriff's office.

"When are you starting back?" he asked. "I'm going with you."

"What does your aunt say?" Tanzy asked.

"She says you and Russ have been the first to get a decent day's work out of me, so she might as well let you finish the job."

"That's not exactly what I said, Richard Benton," his aunt said, coming up behind him, "but it's close enough. He's injured," she said to Russ. "You will give him time to recover, won't you?"

"It was just a knock on the head," Tardy said. "I've had worse."

"Nevertheless, you ought to take care of what brains you do have." She turned to Russ, and her expression changed. She looked embarrassed, but she also looked sad. "Tanzy told me she's been teaching you to read."

Russ figured if Ethel knew, there was no point in trying to keep the secret. Besides, he could read now. He nodded.

"Then you never read the letter I sent you."

He shook his head.

"You didn't get anyone to read it for you?"

"I was too ashamed to admit I couldn't read."

"What did you do with it?"

"I burned it."

"So you never knew what was in it?"

"No."

"So you didn't know."

"No."

"I offered to help you escape. When you didn't reply, I thought you'd rather hang than . . ." She looked as though her gaze had turned inward and she was staring into the past. A moment later she sighed and refocused. "I was very foolish to have wasted so many years. I should have made better use of my life."

"What are you talking about?" Tardy asked.

"None of your business, young man. You've already caused quite enough trouble as it is."

"Me! What have I done?"

"I think she means the diary," Tanzy said.

"Oh," Tardy said, his umbrage evaporating.

"Ethel, could I see you for a minute?" the sheriff asked.

"What for?"

"It's about Stocker's will."

"I don't know anything about it. You'll need to talk to his lawyer."

"I have. That's why I want to talk to you. Guess who he left his ranch to?"

"I have no earthly idea."

"He left it to his only relative who never asked him for money: you."

For the first time in her life, Ethel Peters fainted.

"I'm going to miss Tardy," Tanzy said. "It was fun having him around."

"He's not going to miss us," Russ said. "Now that his aunt owns the biggest ranch in Colorado, he'll have all he can do to learn enough to be able to handle that place in a few years. He's already trying to talk one of the boys into being his foreman."

They were headed back to the ranch in Ethel's buggy. She was still too dazed to protest when Tardy offered it to them.

"It was funny listening to him assure his aunt that she didn't have to worry, that he could tell her what to do," Tanzy said. "And she let him."

"Don't expect it to last long. Ethel Peters is one strong-minded woman."

"Did you know she was still in love with you?" Tanzy asked.

"I never had the slightest suspicion. She was always the one who criticized me the most."

"That should have been a dead giveaway," Tanzy said. "Women never bother with men they don't like."

"Is that why you've been pestering me ever since you got here?"

Tanzy punched him. "It was the other way around. You were the one who wouldn't leave me alone."

"If I had, you'd have left town with nowhere to go and nothing to do when you got there. You ought to be thankful I stopped you."

"I am, but I couldn't tell you. You'd hold it over me for the rest of my life."

"I'm only going to hold one thing over you."

"What's that?"

"Your promise to love me forever. You do that, and you can do anything else you like."

"If I do that, I can't do anything you won't like."

"That's what I like: an obedient wife."

Tanzy hit him again, but not very hard. Russ laughed, put his arm around her, and pulled her tight against him. The valley was beautiful, but it was still too damned big. It would take him forever to get to the cabin and have Tanzy to himself. He had a lot of years to make up for, and he was in a hurry to get started.

LEIGH GREENWOOD
The Independent Bride

Colorado Territory, 1868: It is about as rough and ready as the West can get, a place and time almost as dangerous as the men who left civilization behind, driven by a desire for land, gold . . . a new life.

Fort Lookout: It is a rugged outpost where soldiers, cattlemen and Indians live on the edge of open warfare, the last place any woman in her right mind would choose to settle.

Abby: She is everything a man should avoid—with a face of beauty and an expression of stubborn determination. Colonel Bryce McGregor knows there is no room for such a woman at his fort or in his heart. Yet as she receives proposal after proposal from his troops, Bryce realizes the only man he can allow her to marry is himself.

Dorchester Publishing Co., Inc.
P.O. Box 6640   _5235-0
Wayne, PA 19087-8640 $6.99 US/$8.99 CAN

Name: _____

Address: _____

City: _____ State: _____ Zip: _____

E-mail: _____

I have enclosed $_____ in payment for the checked book(s).

For more information on these books, check out our website at www.dorchesterpub.com.
_____ *Please send me a free catalog.*

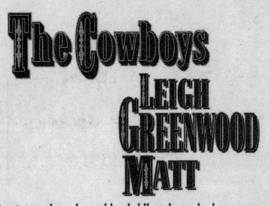

The Cowboys
LEIGH GREENWOOD
MATT

Matt's rough-and-tumble childhood taught him to size up a situation at a hundred paces. And to end his standoff with respectable society he knows he has to take a wife. Ellen agrees to act as a mother for the two boys he's sworn to protect, if he will be a father for the two children she brings to the union. It is a business arrangement. But nothing has prepared him for the desires the former saloon girl incites. She gentles him like a newborn colt, until he longs to be saddled with all the trappings of a real marriage. Until he understands he's found a woman to heal his orphaned heart.

___4877-9 $5.99 US/$6.99 CAN